# THE

# ABSENCE
# OF
# ANGELS

A NOVEL BY **W.S. PENN**

# THE ABSENCE OF ANGELS

by
W.S. PENN

AMERICAN INDIAN LITERATURE
and
CRITICAL STUDIES SERIES
GERALD VIZENOR and LOUIS OWENS, GENERAL EDITORS

University of Oklahoma Press
Norman and London

**Library of Congress Cataloging-in-Publication Data**

Penn, W. S., 1949–
   The absence of angels / by W.S. Penn
      p.   cm.—(American Indian literature and critical studies series; v.
   14; Gerald Vizenor and Louis Owens, general editors.)
      ISBN 0–8061–2714–7
      1. Man-woman   relationships—California—Los   Angeles—Fiction.
   2. College students—California—Los Angeles—Fiction.   3. Indians of
   North America—Mixed descent—Fiction.   4. Young men—California—
   Los Angeles—Fiction.   5. Los Angeles (Calif.)—Fiction.   6. Nez Percé
   Indians—Fiction.   I. Vizenor, Gerald Robert, 1934–   .   II. Owens,
   Louis.   III. Title.   IV. Series.
   PS3566.E476A63   1995
   813 .54—dc20                                                      94-34607
                                                                     CIP

*The Absence of Angels* is Volume 14 in the American Indian Literature and
Critical Studies Series.

The paper in this book meets the guidelines for permanence and durability
of the Committee on Production Guidelines for Book Longevity of the
Council on Library Resources, Inc. ∞

Oklahoma Paperbacks edition published 1995 by the University of Oklahoma Press, Norman, Publishing Division of the University, by special ar-
rangement with The Permanent Press, Noyac Road, Sag Harbor, New York
11963. Copyright © 1994 by William S. Penn. Manufactured in the U.S.A.
First printing of the University of Oklahoma Press edition, 1995.

         1   2   3   4   5   6   7   8   9   10

For Jennifer

Grateful acknowledgement is given to Patricia Hilden and Timothy Reiss for their endless encouragement, and to the Ludwig Vogelstein Foundation, the New York Foundation for the Arts, and the Michigan Council on the Arts for their generous support of the completion of this novel.

"All Indian time has a vertical dimension that cups past and future in a timeless present that forgets no injustices and anticipates all possible compensations."

Frank Waters, *The Book of the Hopi*

"He put in your heart certain wishes and plans, in my heart he put other and different desires. Each man is good in his sight. It is not necessary for eagles to be crows."

Sitting Bull

# CHAPTER ONE

## 1.

Death made Himself familiar to me at birth, travelling by wagon, dressed in Eastern cloth and a hardhat with a little light on the forehead.

"It's as if some people can't see where they're going," Grandfather laughed.

Death had made the journey to the City of Angels to guard the body of a newborn child in its crib. The baby was His, but Death couldn't get into the crib to take me. The crib was in an oxygen tent, and no one but the doctors who poked and prodded the baby and then stood with the elk's head necklaces hanging from their necks consulting each other's ignorance was allowed to reach into the tent. So Death waited patiently, and watched. At moments, He would go out into the waiting room and sit beside father, who seemed to be reading his hands like some ancient text; or He would slip into the maternity ward and stroke the belly of mother, who knew from the conspiracy of silence that her baby was not well. Death couldn't help but smile when the doctors told father that the child would not live.

As Death waited, Grandfather made the journey from Chosposi Mesa to the city. In his then new 1947 Plymouth, he made the fifteen-hour trip in eleven hours, never going above fifty miles per hour.

"It's not a matter of how fast you drive," he would say to explain how he did it. "It's a matter of concentration."

Without much imagination, I could picture him virtually motionless behind the steering wheel, his gray eyes focused on the horizon, concentrating on reaching the white space between the hills and the blue sky, the big wheels of the

Plymouth gobbling up an extra yard for every yard they rolled over.

No one believed him, yet all he said was, "When you drive as far as the eye can see, you have to see farther."

So Grandfather arrived at the hospital, the first time he had ever been in a hospital. Father says he said little. Only went to the isolated crib in its plastic tent and observed the form of the baby who was, as he said years later, green: "Blue from no oxygen. Yellow from jaundice." The baby's fists, which no one had seemed to notice, were clenched tight as though they grasped a key, and it was the fists that seemed to satisfy Grandfather.

"The baby will live," he told father, who was rapidly making extravagant promises to the God who tries to make all other gods unnecessary, and when he can't do that, enters a cosmic mitosis and calls himself the Trinity.

Then Grandfather took a disappointed Death by the wrist, put Him in the passenger seat of the 1947 Plymouth, concentrated on the grayness as far away as his eyes could see, and arrived at Chosposi eleven hours later.

To Laura P., the Hopi woman he had married, he said, "The boy has it and won't let go."

Laura P., who lived with Grandfather with a contention which could be mistaken for bitterness but was really a kind of boundless love, understood. She knew that Death had returned with Grandfather.

"The child of the mission is sickly," she said.

Grandfather simply nodded and, without taking off his cap, walked Death to the mission, where he left Him chained like a rabid dog beside the mission door.

Possibly, you could deduce that Grandfather had just invented entropy for himself. But I doubt that Grandfather thought it through. He understood that for every child Death misses He finds a replacement. Besides, he had seen the mission child's hands, and they were loose and flabby, the fingers like baby Gilas, wiggling and mean. And he didn't particularly wish to have Death hang around his own door. As he said, "Death is so boring." And he meant that, boring. Grandfather wasn't frightened of Death. Death was an uninteresting companion. So, rather than wait, rather than make up some strange moral complication, he walked Death to the mission and left Him. Five days later, the once childless missionary was childless again, and when Grandfather passed the building on his way to the trading post he retrieved the broken chain to take home and repair, in case he would need it again.

Every birthday, with religious devotion, father told me the rest. After Death was gone and the distant lament of the missionary's wife awakened me, I lay untouched by human hands staring out at the world through the translucent plastic of an oxygen tent. Other babies bubbled in their own tents with limp gloves welded into the sides like hands without bones. Some of them were so small that their little arms looked like flippers and fins; others had huge heads that, without hair, looked like relief maps with cliffs for foreheads; some of them looked just plain sickly. None of them were my hue of green and to father that made me special.

Small gaggles of medical men gathered about the tent, peering in with curious worried faces before they shrugged and left. Women in stark stiff white seemed to float among the tents on a cushion of air. Cassocked figures wearing surplices and silver crosses slipped in on neutered feet to stand over the sickliest-looking babies, waving their hands in the air above the tents as though trying to shoo the flies off food.

The weeks that passed were all the same and the only change seemed to be in the looks on the faces that peered down into my tipi like archangels. For the most part, I was content to sleep. When I did look up at the doctors wearing ponderous faces and elk's head necklaces, I wondered how it happened that they didn't know what Grandfather had known and I raised my little fists, shaking them to show that I had a good hold on *it* and that *it* was life. The doctors were too busy consulting one another's ignorance and wondering what to tell mother to pay attention.

When at last mother was strong enough to come in, I tried to wave at her to reassure her, but with my fists clenched, it must have seemed more like a threat than a promise. Mother, with her soft brown curls and hazel eyes distorted by the plastic of the tent, looked pretty funny and I laughed for the

9

first time in my life. I must have looked equally funny to her, except she didn't laugh. Rather, she stared down into my tipi as though I were a pet that she had taken for a long and arduous walk only to come home and have me misbehave in the house. Sliding her hand into one of the gloves in the side of the tent, she felt and poked me with fingers that felt like dry ice. Her voice sounded like tinsnips. Each time she came into the room, I hoped that she would take me out with her the way some of the other babies had been wheeled out, followed by the men in cassocks waving their hands and tossing fingers of water at the tents. But time after time she left me behind and I had to be content to rub the knuckles of my fists together or to box with the surgical hands hanging from the sides of the tent.

## 2.

Mother often claimed that I slept through anything. When I wasn't sleeping, she swaddled me in blankets, covering my face with a crocheted blanket so I could breathe through the holes.

"Hidden," Elanna told me.

"Disguised," Pamela said.

"You were," Elanna liked to say later, "one ugly baby," reminding me how, weighing 10.5 pounds at birth, I had grown large and thick with an aboriginal brow.

"It was one ugly world," Pamela insisted. "And oh did we love you."

"Yes," Elanna agreed. "We loved you."

Four and five years older respectively, Elanna and Pamela would run home from school and pull the blankets off my face and stare adoringly at me. Medium-sized with large bones like Laura P., Pamela's round face was open, her almond eyes expressionless. Elanna had the same high cheekbones Pamela had, but her face was thinner, her bones smaller. When I raised my fists up toward them and said everything I knew how to say, Elanna's adoring eyes narrowed and she smiled as though I were proof that she was smart. On weekends, they liked to wheel my carriage through Park

La Brea to the tar pits, where Elanna scared Pamela by telling her how the tar trapped dinosaurs. If nosy parkers peeked beneath my blankets, they defended me angrily and Elanna would embarrass them into calling me cute, her fierce little body shaking with as much rage as Pamela's shook with fear of strangers. I loved them both, adored the softness of Pamela and loved the sharpness of Elanna, and I never minded their calling me "Gargantua." They helped me understand that a few pounds at birth made a large differ- ence and that giving birth to a 10.5 pound bundle of green was not an experience any woman would look forward to with joy. The closest I could come to mother's experience was to imagine being constipated for nine months and then taking a humongous dump only to discover that it looked like a baby newt. The closest mother ever came to what I felt as that newt was about three feet. She certainly seemed joyless as she told us stories of Indians raping white women or as she performed her ritual of Sani-Flush to avoid getting pregnant again. With the same lack of joy, she finally gave up and stopped swaddling me in blankets. I must have been about four.

"Thank you, mother," I said, free at last.

"You're welcome," she replied.

### 3.

The salmon-colored stucco buildings of the school hunched across the street, our house one of the humble tract houses implanted around the huge asphalt playground. Out of these houses drifted words like spick and nigger and mackerel snapper, pinko and red. The high chain-link fence with galvanized barbs kept the words out of school on week- ends, but on weekdays some of them sneaked through the gates hidden like lice in the unwashed hair of the other children.

On their lips, too, my name, Albert Hummingbird, was transmuted into "Turdbird," "Birdturd," "Horseturd," and later to just plain "Shithead." I made treaty after treaty with them, only to learn that the secret nature of a treaty was to be broken.

"It happens, if it happens at all, that way," Grandfather said. "If you're a Negro or Mexican, an Indian, a Jew. If you're a proto-adult in the City of Angels and your Grandfather's name is Hummingbird."

Tommy A. (the parthenogen of Tom Frederic A. the Third, real estate broker, V.P. of the Los Angeles River Club, and a St. Luke's D.O.A. of a stroke on 5 November 1976) took to serenading me: "Hummingbird, Bummingbird."

"Cumbum," he hissed, as he strolled past, holding hands with Marily Avi.

I drew myself up as tall as possible. I sucked in my belly, hoping it would add to my height. I gave him a severe squinting look. "I wish you would leave me alone," I said.

Tommy grinned. "You wish," he spat. "You wish."

He spit at the ground and his saliva struck my sneaker. He pushed me on the shoulder as I stared at the spittle dribbling off my shoe. His saliva was thicker, more viscous than most boys'. In a spitting contest, he would surpass all the competition. Tommy A., it seemed to me, was born to win, and when he raised his fist and shook it, I walked away.

For the next few months, as we lined up in pairs after recess, Tommy spit on my shoes. I tried everything. I tried to ignore his spit. I tried asking him not to do that. I asked him why he wanted to do that. I warned him.

One afternoon, I had a brilliant idea. "An Indian," Grandfather said, "never kills rattlesnakes because he knows rattlesnakes want to meet up with him less than he wants to meet up with snakes. Given the chance, unless his mate is trapped behind the brave, the rattler will uncoil and slip away. All a human being has to do is remain very still and say, 'Let us not meet again this year.' Snakes understand that, and the human can go in peace." I came to that.

"Let us not meet again this year," I said to Tommy. I said it just the way Grandfather had said it.

"What?" Tommy sneered.

"Let us not meet again this year," I repeated, staring straight into his Scandinavian eyes, astonished at how blue they were.

It worked!

Well, not quite. When Tommy laughed, he didn't know he was laughing at Grandfather's words. He summoned a large lugey, hacking it up from the back of his throat. Against all of my training and all the instincts of my blood, I smashed my fist into his grinning, spitting face and then stood there stupidly, looking at the fist on the end of my arm, watching the blood begin to surface from the cut on my knuckle, wondering, in the midst of the commotion, where that fist had come from.

"On the other hand," Grandfather said. "White people are not rattlesnakes." That night, I had bad dreams in which Grandfather's oldest friend, Louis Applegate appeared, his face like a hatchet and his arm raised like a semaphore, pointing. The image stayed with me through the orange juice and carbon of one of mother's breakfasts.

The next day at school, the princi-*pal* gave me a lecture on problem solving in a socialized world. I failed to understand him. I felt as though he were drilling into the top of my skull and sifting sawdust into it. I kept myself to myself and concentrated on his adam's apple.

His bow-tie shimmered briefly, and then dissolved.

I concentrated harder.

By the time he decided on a "just" punishment for hitting Tommy, I'd made all but his voice disappear—the bow-tie, his swivel chair, the wall with its portrait of John Dewey behind him, the salmon stucco building of the school—and my eyes focused on the farthest gray line of the horizon.

At recess, I made a pact with Tommy. "When you want to spit," I said, "you tell me ahead of time and I will get out of the way."

After school, I served out my sentence, helping the janitor erase the blackboards and bang out the erasers, turning the yellow afternoon air white with dust. Marily Avi pursued me in her pert blue jumper and pink blouse.

"Ail-burt," she said, following me from room to room. "Oh, Ail-burt."

"Go away, Marily," I said.

"Oh, Ail-burt," she sighed. "You're so strong."

"Please?" I begged. The janitor's daughter, Margaret

Rocha and I could be matter-of-fact with each other, but Marily touched a nerve. I had to face up to it: When Margaret and I hid in closets with a flashlight and showed each other the essential difference between boys and girls, we felt scientific. But Margaret was not Marily, and Marily was not science. Still, when Marily cornered me in a cloakroom, I felt as though I was betraying Margaret.

It didn't stop me. I forgot everything, even Marily herself—except for her voice and the embarrassment I would always feel because she called it funny looking. I could think only of the white eraser dust floating away from my hands and dissolving into the heated air, until Marily pinched a little harder than she needed to.

"There are two kinds of liar," Grandfather warned that evening. "One forges all lies to fit the harness of the first lie. By the tenth lie, the pattern has all the appearance of fate. The other cares only that the lie is interesting or convincing (or both), and has done with it. He makes up new lies at will, as truth changes its chameleon colors or abandons its tail."

I had lied, but which kind of lie it was that I had made up about Marily Avi in the cloakroom, I didn't know. It had been meant to cover up the humiliation I'd felt for running away from Marily and, since it neither looked like fate nor convinced Grandfather, I quickly abandoned it.

On weekends, playing cowboys and Indians, I was assigned the role of Redskin. Even when for a change we played War the enemy was red and I was the enemy. I carried a peashooter while they used BB guns; Tommy's was a pump action and I knew that if he ever hit me, it would hurt. Like Trickster Coyote I stalked them, able to remain motionless for extraordinary periods of time, sneaking around and through the alleys and dried-up river beds called washes, placing my toes down before my heels so any object that might make noise and give me away could be avoided.

Tommy was the first to complain. "It's not fair," he said. "It's not even realistic," he added, feeling a historical necessity.

At first, I refused to wear the pigeon feathers Tommy tied together so I could be spotted the way hunters spot a deer's tail, but in the interests of peaceful play I finally conceded. The only time I wore those feathers, Tommy skipped a BB off my skull. For the rest of my life I'd have a white, bald scar just above the hairline to remind me.

Saddened by the ease with which Tommy had broken the peace between us, I took to riding my bike around alone, wondering what Bernie Schneider was up to. I missed him.

Bernie must have missed me, too.

One day, as I rode my bicycle down the alley behind his house, he leapt out from behind some galvanized cans, causing me to swerve and run my knuckles along the cement block wall that bordered his backyard. Bloody, the bones of two knuckles gleaming white through the blood that spread out over the back of my hand, I let him lead me inside to his mother, who washed and poured peroxide over the knuckles as Bernie watched, unapologetic, tense, wanting, I dare say, to be the object of revenge.

I didn't feel vengeful. Instead, I focused on the fish heads floating in the vat on the stove, feeling something I had only associated with Grandfather's house up to then, as the house and its smells seemed to close around me the way silence closes around the desert.

"There," Mrs. Schneider said. "Now sit and have some lemonade. Stay for dinner."

I couldn't stay for dinner. I didn't want to because of the fish heads staring up from the vat on the stove and because I knew that mother had gone to a lot of work preparing wienies. I did sit in the Schneider living room and drink some lemonade, wondering what to say to Bernie the ambusher.

On the mantel was a silver candlestick with nine candles, two of which were lit.

"What's that?" I asked.

Bernie explained that each candle on the menorah represented the days of creation. When I asked why there were nine candles and not seven, Bernie got a little angry and said because it took nine days.

Even though later I learned about the festival of lights, I decided at that moment that Jews had it all over Protestants because their God had taken 48 extra hours to create their

world. The difference in the myths was the difference between the people: Protestants are always tinkering with the
world, trying to finish off what their God didn't while they
envy Jews because their G-d took the time to put on the
finishing touches. Secretly, I preferred Grandfather's version
in which the creation of the Real People took only one mysterious and accidental day. I believed that my life was the result
of spontaneous generation from the blood of a monster.

"I've got to go," I said to Bernie.

"Say hi to Tommy," he said sarcastically.

"I'm going home," I said.

"Come back. Eat with us," Mrs. Schneider called as I left
by the back way, picked up my bike and pedaled home. I
punished my bike by riding down and up the square curbs
at each street I crossed.

## 4.

Grandfather had tried to prepare me for school, telling
me a tale about the creation of Nu-mi-pu, the Real People,
in which Coyote, hurt when people shunned him and angry
when they shot at him, met up with the monster Ilpswetsichs,
who was casually devouring the world. The first few times,
Coyote ran from Ilpswetsichs. He tried to warn the people
by howling in the distance when the moon was dim. They
ignored him. When the monster had eaten all the people
and half of the world, Coyote hid a knife between his legs
and let Ilpswetsichs catch him and eat him, too. Coming to
in the darkness, he began to cut his way out of Ilpswetsichs'
stomach. The monster ran east and west, north and south,
dripping blood and roaring with pain, begging Coyote to
make a deal with it. Coyote refused the deals the monster
offered, sawing the wound ever larger until at last Ilpswetsichs was dead and the hole was big enough for Coyote to
escape. From the blood that fell on the not-yet-eaten earth
sprang human beings; from the blood that fell where the
monster had taken out bites rose the seas and in them the
salmon which came once a year to spawn and be caught by
the Real People. When Grandfather was finished, all I could

say was, "I see," even though I didn't. For all the good it had done me, he may as well have been describing the distance to the trading post or the art of cursing, or attempting to explain the differences between love and death.

That summer, when my cousin and I went to Chosposi Mesa, I said to Grandfather, "This school thing's a real bitch."

"I know," he said. "I had only three years of it at Haskell from people who didn't want to teach us a thing. But I know." He said nothing for a long time. Finally he said, "You've got to learn, Alley. What, I don't know. But you've got to learn." Again he was quiet and I watched sad resignation steal across his big face like fog across a werewolf's moon. "Learning keeps you out of things," he said. "Like wars." I knew then he was thinking of his son the ex-pilot. My uncle.

Unlike father, who because of his education had been drafted into the petrochemical industry, uncle had enlisted in the Army Air Force, serving in World War II willingly with the hope that by serving, the stigma of his Indian blood could be purified. Uncle had found out otherwise. A pilot, he had been promoted to Squadron Commander because of his daring and skill.

The details after that are hazy, purposely hazy.

He received orders to send his men and their fighters on a mission from which he knew the precise Japanese would never allow them to return. There was no way. He was not to go along—as much as he would have liked to—and on a drizzly December morning, he stood, watching his six best friends arc up and away from the air base like the frogs his son would throw into the air, doomed to pass from one reality to another in one exploding mixture of flesh and metal. Now, he would say, "None of them was ever heard from again," phrasing it that way in order to create and maintain the possibility that one or more of them fell to earth and took root, living out his life as a tree, a rock, a frog.

Then, he said nothing. For two days he stood outside the aircraft hangars and watched the sky. He didn't speak. He didn't need to. His face and posture told everything to anyone who wanted to know. And he would have gone on standing there until he collapsed from hunger or exposure or, as

17

he probably expected, until his heart broke. But the military, while it can accept a vast range of erratic behavior, glossing over the occasional rape or murder, cannot tolerate for long the commander who stands breathlessly in the open air, his face sunburned and his eyes blinded by the sun he stares at, waiting for the voices he hears inside himself to return to base. Regretfully, the Air Force was forced to replace the commander. Two burly men in doctors' lab coats lifted him up like a fardel of two by fours, turned him so he was horizontal, laid him on a stretcher, and drove away as quietly as possible on the third day. Everyone pretended he had gone on leave. Instead, he was shipped home aboard a hospital ship. Each day, two different burly men came to his cabin, picked him up, and carried him to the deck, where he was propped against the ship's rail to stare at the sky. Each night, he was returned to his cabin and given an injection of vitamins; then the burly men sat around the poker table and tried to imagine what could possibly have happened to make a Commander into a carrot.

What those men could not understand was that in his absolute silence my uncle was waiting for what he believed to be there to be revealed to him. If he spoke, the men he had sent into the air that day would be dead. If he did not speak, then they remained suspended like sawdust in the container of his mind. It took a nurse who was used to working with vegetables to understand; or pretend to understand. With her practical diligence and the shock troops modern drugs, the carrot was slowly and painfully made to forget everything he had thought or felt on that day, to make the details hazy, and a month after he was released from the V.A. hospital in San Francisco with his vast collection of model fighter planes, he married his nurse. She even allowed him to hang the thirty-odd balsa wood models in his "study" in their new home. But she kept the room closed off from his family, because in each of the thirty fighters was a carved figure. Six different faces and ranks repeated five times: the same six men he had mailed into the guns of the Japanese. Even she found the expressions too ghostly to look at more than once.

Those model fighters would hang in that room, turning gently on the currents of air, until the Christmas my cousin was given a toy anti-aircraft gun with two rubber-tipped darts on either side of the rangefinder. My cousin and I slipped the lock on the study and practiced, unnoticed for hours, playing Japanese gunners, removing the rubber dart-tips first. Between the two of us, we got them all.

It was my first trip to Chosposi. I must have been seven. The age doesn't really matter, although it makes me curious how memories gather around certain ages like spirits to a vat of blood. My cousin had come with me well-supplied with firecrackers and cherry bombs and a bottle of his mother's toilet water, and we spent the first few mornings out in the nearby desert in search of tadpoles. He placed them in a jar of water before dropping perfume into it and watching the tadpoles swim up into the slowly dispersing poison and fall, swim up and fall, swim up—and then with a certain resolution, sink to the bottom and die. If we were able to catch adult frogs, he liked to stick firecrackers into their mouths, light the fuses, and throw the frogs in an arc across the stream, clapping his hands in literal joy when they exploded, showering us with entrails, eyeballs, and little shattered bones with snippets of flesh still clinging to them.

"Not high enough," he shouted, as I half-heartedly tossed a frog in the air toward some rocks. My scalp began to itch.

The frog came down splat on the wet rock and, taking a moment to reorganize its interior organs, leapt into a shallow pool. My cousin lit a cherry bomb and dropped it into the pool and waited for the explosion to make the frog float.

"I love to watch things pass away," he said.

I didn't.

To divert my cousin, the next morning, when Grandfather left for Johnny Three Feet's Trading Post, I made him watch as I picked the lock of the adobe hut stuck like a wart on the side of the house.

Careful not to damage the files Grandfather used to make brass wind chimes, I found a screwdriver and unscrewed the sides of his powersaw and pried it open. I was sure that inside it there had to be a baggy or a compartment that held the sawdust until it was sucked out by the spinning blade of the saw. We didn't find it.

Needless to say, when my cousin and I were done with the saw, it was ruined.

Grandfather understood. "It happens," he said, laughing.

Father, when he heard about it, didn't. He made me turn right around and come home, and when I got there, he made it plain that it would take the rest of the summer for me to earn enough to pay for the ruined saw.

My sisters only laughed, like Grandfather. "Gargantua strikes again," one of them—probably Elanna—said.

Mother put up with me, watching me drag about the house and yard doing chores, until she couldn't stand it any longer and she called me in alone beneath the antique ceramic rooster on the mantel. "Don't mope," she said. "Hard work builds character."

## 5.

Unless you count my cousin's frogs, I didn't see Death again until I was ten, and even then He was only a shadow of rumor hovering around the mention of mother's mother. I could have cared less. I felt no connection to the woman mother called mother and all I remembered of her was a featureless face and lace-up black shoes. Disapproving of miscegenation, she had visited us only when her being in town and one of father's business trips coincided. A trouble-shooter for petroleum refineries, father made numerous trips, but mother's mother lived some 500 miles away and I hadn't seen her since I was four. So when Death re-entered our house as a tone of voice, it took Elanna and Pamela to remind me of how mother's mother had always greeted them kindly, saying "I have a quarter for you," passing one to Pamela, who saved hers, and one to Elanna, who spent hers on edible seeds with the relish of a squirrel in a bull market. Then she would gingerly lift the edge of my blankets, smile and nod like a character out of *Dick Tracy*, and tell Pamela and Elanna they could take me away.

As mother boarded the Starlight passenger train to attend her mother's funeral, placing her hands lightly on each of her children's shoulders in turn, she tried to give us words to live by while she was gone. Squeezing me at arm's length, she said, "You're worth all the turkeys I've ever had to cook." I couldn't recall mother's ever having cooked anything resembling a turkey and when the conductor called out, "Aaaa-booard," what mother said next was lost.

When mother returned a week later, she looked dazed. She gathered the three of us together beneath the antique rooster on the mantle in the living room and gave each of us a book.

"This," she said solemnly, handing me a small leather-bound book, "is for you. My mother was saving it for you."

It was *Personal Investing*, a self-published volume of her mother's advice.

Turning to all of us, she said, "As you girls know, intellect is not given to each of you equally, though your conditions are the same. Albert, I fear, will have to use reason to control his passions. Above all, Albert, learn to speak plainly. Work hard, make up for what you are and you can make something of yourself. Or you can avoid hard work and ruin your future."

Pamela accepted mother at face value.

I had difficulty caring about my future and I didn't know what in hell mother was talking about.

Elanna, still knowing herself to be smarter than boys, especially brothers, gave mother a withering look.

"*We* got copies of Emily Post," she said later. Her green eyes were sharp, ready to cut me to pieces, but not without warmth. I was, after all, her baby brother.

"I'll trade you," I said. "Or you can just have mine."

These Rooster Talks, warning us about the ways of the world with the darkness and doom of a John Birch Society film, became a habit. Collecting us once again, mother said, "Now, *You Know What*." This was the talk she could launch like a Vanguard missile at any time and place, convinced as she was of the abundance of men and women who hung around schoolyards and drugstores waiting for little boys and girls, offering them candy or comics and taking them to out-of-the-way places to use for *You Know What*.

I didn't know what.

"Sex," Elanna whispered. Pamela said nothing and settled

for looking thoughtful. "Mother means when a man makes a woman have sex with him."

"What if he doesn't make her?" Pamela asked.

"Don't be silly, Pam. How else would it happen?"

"What if the woman makes the man?" I asked. Even though I remembered the lies I'd invented about Marily Avi and me in the cloakroom and felt as guilty as if I'd made her, I felt compelled to defend my sex.

"Fah!" Elanna laughed. "That's impossible. You'll see that, soon."

Curious about this thing called sex, I took to creeping around the house and spying on our parents. At night, listening to my father's voice through their bedroom door, I learned nothing about sex and a lot about begging. During the day, I popped up beside mother's stove like a tart from a toaster or hid out in father's garage. My ears grew large like an elephant's, recording each and every unspoken thought my parents might have.

On Saturday mornings, as father washed the car, I sneaked through the side door of the garage and hid, not making a sound. Without turning around or even slowing the rhythm of the circular strokes of the washrag on the car, father would surprise me by calmly asking, "What do you think you're doing there?"

Mother, on the other hand, never seemed to sense my presence and instead of calmly asking what I was doing there, she would scream "Aaahh!" when she came upon me in the broom closet.

Uncertain whether or not this was an essential difference between men and women, I tested it out on my sisters. Pamela never seemed to notice my creeping into her clothes closet. But then she was often there ahead of me and would surprise me as much as I tried to surprise her, finding her hunkered up beneath the coats and slacks with the sliding doors closed. Elanna kept company with Death. Down the street, near the dried-up river bed, was a small graveyard, large enough to bury the local Catholics but too small to bury Protestants or Jews alongside. There I would come upon her, leaning back against the cool of a gravestone, her small mouth moving slowly, almost, you might say, lovingly. Her eyes were closed and at first I was afraid she'd found religion and was praying.

"What are you doing here?" she asked without opening her eyes.

"What are *you* doing here?" I asked back.

"Talking to grandmother."

"Mother's mother is dead." I wondered why Elanna wanted to talk to mother's mother.

Elanna opened her eyes and smiled. She said nothing. The embarrassment of it was that I was so stupid as to go on and say, "She's not even buried here." She continued smiling as though to say, "Poor lad."

"So what *are* you doing here," she repeated.

I held my hand up to my ear and replied, "Phoning Grandfather." Grandfather didn't have a telephone. He thought they were unnatural and he didn't like the idea of his voice being lost in a crowd of voices bumping and pushing their way down wires above and below ground. "I don't want to sound like everyone else," he'd told me. "Neither should you. Besides, you and I don't need a telephone to talk."

"Grandfather doesn't have a telephone." Elanna said this with the arrogance of the several years she had over me before she realized what it was I had done and she blushed.

In the year following mother's mother's death, when the weather was nasty, I would visit Pamela in her closet. But on balmy afternoons, I'd creep off to the graveyard to be with Elanna. There I'd rest my head in her lap and she would scratch it, always careful not to interfere with the imaginary telephone I held to my ear. And so, for a time, Death became nothing more for me than a reason for having my head scratched.

# CHAPTER TWO

## 6.

The next summer, a thick, brown cloud settled over the City of Angels and people staggered under the weight of the air. At first, I didn't notice anything other than the glowing orange sunsets—which I treasured until mother told me that the orange was arsenic in the air, a poison a lot like the perfume my cousin had used to drop in jars of tadpoles— and an annoying tightness in my chest as I darted from hiding place to hiding place, playing War once again, now that Bernie Schneider had been included because of Tommy's frustration. Unable to find and kill me once I refused to wear pigeon feathers, he wanted another enemy and a Jew was as good as an Indian to Tommy.

When I noticed my pet hamster's loss of speed on his exercise wheel, I took the wheel off and oiled it, believing that hamsters only had one forward speed; still Custer slowed until, like a Ford motor car, he seemed to slip into reverse. One morning, I had to pry his little claws loose from the wire of the wheel, which had ceased to creak with his jogging. With intricate ceremony, I buried him in Wounded Knee, the dirt lot behind our garage that was set off from the rest of the yard by a chain-link fence.

Summers always had been a time to escape helping out around the house; but when I overheard Mrs. Schneider discussing summer camps with mother, I suspected that my life was going to change. I hid out in Wounded Knee munching dog biscuits with the obsequious puppy purchased to replace Custer and waited. When the old lady who lived behind us collapsed and died while collecting mulberry leaves for her silkworms, my parents packed my sisters off and all too soon I found myself being loaded onto a yellow bus headed for Lake Arrowhead with twenty-seven excited, brown-bagging campsters.

Mother had packed me a lunch of peanut butter and honey sandwiches, an apple left over from the drought of '56, and celery sticks—all of which I donated to the spirits of the road, hoping that those spirits, once they got a taste of one of mother's fabulous lunches, would turn the bus around. At least send it skidding into a ditch.

I did not want to go to camp.

Neither did Bernie Schneider want to be packed like a shrimp onto a bus and motored off to have healthy fun. Bernie wasn't into healthy fun.

"After all," Bernie told me, "Jews aren't into having healthy fun. We," he said proudly, "are into suffering and survival. Prunes, not vitamins."

I have to admit I was grateful for Bernie's sense of humor. Years later, after I had forgotten what Bernie looked like even as I stared at the pictures of him as a boy in denims with cuffs rolled halfway to his knees standing beside a sway-backed mare inside the camp's corral, I would remember his joke about the end of the world. It went: There are three religious leaders selected to announce over T.V. that a great flood will end the world in twenty-four hours. One at a time, they face the camera. The priest advises all good Catholics to confess their sins and say their penances. The Protestant minister speaks of hellfire and the day of judgment about to descend on mankind. The Rabbi, coming on the T.V. last, says, "Jews! You have twenty-four hours to learn to live underwater."

So it was, as the yellow bus sped towards the relocation camp on Lake Arrowhead, Bernie began to teach me how to live underwater. In the twelve hours between the first lesson and our first mustering out by the fit young man who was our cabin counselor, I only learned to hold my breath for long periods of time. Still, that was enough for the time I was to be in camp, and after I taught Bernie how to sneak through the woods downwind from the prey, it was sufficient to allow us to watch our cabin counselor with one of the girls who worked in the kitchens.

To describe her is virtually impossible. Bernie and I only

imagined talking to her, and most of that talking was merely of words on the way to something else, like pebbles on the path to the temple. She wore nylon shorts that covered three-quarters of her ass and a cotton T-shirt that somehow managed always to look wet. For two boys, those were enough for us to wish we knew her.

Our counselor didn't have to wish.

We watched from the brush in the woods one night as Rolf spread a sleeping bag on the ground and then slowly tied each of her arms to small trees. Even in the darkness, we could see the look in his eyes as he slipped those shorts down her legs that seemed, from our angle of vision, endless.

"Legs all the way up to her ass," Bernie whispered.

"Ssshh!" I said, trying not to choke on the air that burned my lungs. I'd been holding my breath.

Rolf slowly tied her ankles to stakes in the ground before he knelt and rolled her T-shirt up to reveal breasts that were iridescent in the moonlight. She lifted her head to watch him expose his very being, and her eyes! The look in her eyes was like some wild animal's.

Bernie tossed and turned in his bunk the whole night. Girls' names rolled off his lips like distant thunder. Even the next morning, he seemed to be shivering as he brushed his teeth. I had to row him out to the raft on the lake and dip him in the cold water every twenty minutes to keep his skin temperature even with the ice-cold of his guts.

I began to worry about Bernie's ability to survive, to live beneath the water of his dreams, but he insisted on going along to watch. He ate little, playing with his food like a sated cat; he ran miles in his restless sleep in pursuit of an illusion that he would pursue for the rest of his life. The only sign of health was that he settled on one name for this illusion, Tammy, and now the same thunderstorm broke over him night after night as though it were being blown back and forth over the landscape of his heart by alternating winds.

Before Bernie was shipped home, I tried in desperation to teach him how to make people dissolve. Night after night, we watched Rolf and Tammy pumping away at each other, trying to stare past them, past the desire we felt in ourselves. This at great risk to myself because I knew that if I succeeded in making the people dissolve, I might never get rid of the voices. Bernie failed. He failed because every time he reached the point of dissolution, Tammy bit her lip or ground her teeth loudly, or threw her head back and cried out, "Oh god! Rolf!" and Bernie clamped his eyes shut, breaking the magic of the spell.

We tried peeing in Rolf's Listerine. Tammy only cried out louder.

We put rubber cement in his hair cream. Tammy bit her lip so hard that night that a drop of blood congealed on her lip, glistening before it turned black.

Owls flew and foxes ran through the mid-night. Bernie's will seemed to fly off with them, speeding through space and time in pursuit of a dream he would never possess. Instead of dissolving the image of Rolf and Tammy, I stared past them at a vision of Bernie, ghostly and wasted, his gray worsted suit like prisoner's garb, trapped by the things he thought his Tammy wanted.

The sight of Bernie as alien frightened me so much that I broke and ran, spending the night on the high rocks overlooking the black and depthless lake. I sat there, staring inwards, dissolving myself, my logic, my will, until I was able to see beyond the perimeters of the lake and my age.

"Dreams," Grandfather said, maintaining a reserve because of my pain, "can get you."

Bernie became a haunt, hanging about the kitchens while the other children rode horses or swam. When he lifted his bow and aimed the arrow at the target fifty feet away, I could tell that he was aiming at something far away like love. In the evenings around the campfire, Bernie's singing was the low moan of a wounded animal. Years afterwards, I would hear the horn of a ship lost in the fog, and I would think of Bernie singing as he steered his life towards his vision of Tammy. Unlike a ship, even if Bernie found his port, he would never be able to unload his cargo.

After Bernie's mother had driven all the way out to Lake Arrowhead to collect him like a bundle of Third Class mail held at the post office, I looked around at my happy co-campers. To the unsuspecting eye, we all looked the same. I, however, saw them as future stockbrokers who would collect antique cars for fun. Boys who would attend the same colleges their fathers attended, receive identical marks, and after graduation marry their mothers, enduring the same lives. Girls who were learning to shop for boys and that soft toilet paper which is so important to women. Mixed in, because everything is mixed, were the sons and daughters of meter readers and liquor salesmen, a Jew (in absentia), an Indian, and some of the detritus that remains American.

One morning, by the row of outdoor pipes and faucets slung above metal troughs, I noticed a skinny runt of a lad putting toothpaste instead of Brylcream into his hair. Against his cocoa-colored skin, the foaming white looked either ridiculous or stylish, depending on your definition. His name was Buchanan Roy Leland.

"Buchanan?" I asked him, toweling his head dry after washing the toothpaste out of it.

"Named for my daddy's fav'rite president," he replied. "Ouch! You're hurting."

"Sorry. Buchanan? What did he do?"

"Nothing." Roy grinned. "That's why he was daddy's fav'rite."

Well, Buchanan Roy had been born in Oklahoma and he did everything. Anything. Like the lion with the thorn in his paw, he became my loyal comrade for the two days before I fled from camp. Roy stole two extra canteens from the kitchen. He procured a map and compass, and with the solemnity of a virgin on his wedding night, he gave me his Bowie knife, which Rolf had taken from him the first day and which he had recovered within minutes of the taking. And he did it all within forty-eight hours of Bernie's departure.

I treasured that knife the same way I'd treasured Bernie's friendship before he grew crazy with his visions of Tammy. After I dismounted from the mare I'd ridden out from camp and slapped her on her way back to the stables, I began to forget Roy as I focused on the horizon, stopping to check the compass every half hour until I reached the highway to Palm Springs. Roy no longer mattered once I was free, although as a parting reward I had shown him where to hide at night to observe the spectacle of Tammy's performances. I didn't worry that Roy would suffer Bernie's fate: Roy wasn't Jewish. Roy definitely lacked Bernie's imagination. For Roy, sex would always be poking the nearest girl. For Bernie, it would be the embellishments, the, so to speak, temporary lies or pretenses of corsets, cords, the soft cries and whimpers and moans. Bernie might masturbate; Roy would jack off.

As I stuck my thumb out, pointing east, I decided there were two kinds of friends at least. One who is trying to live beneath water, whom you are forced to leave behind if they drown. The other won't go near the water, and you simply leave him behind like a Burma Shave placard you pass on the road to who knows where.

### 7.

It will always seem strange that I remember Grandfather's large pores second only to his high forehead and white hair. Even now, when I close my eyes and speak with him, reaching out and touching him over the long distance of unreality, I remember his pores, especially on his nose.

I don't need the imaginary telephone anymore. Grandfather has been dead in white people's terms for over a decade, so the telephone receiver would be nothing more than a cheap trick to illustrate the way the horizons of death have shortened for me. All I do is concentrate, close my eyes, and listen to his voice coming out of the Absence of Angels. That concentration erases time and I can talk to him the way he was before he pedaled his way into the Absence of Angels, before he even owned the killer three-wheel bicycle.

Chosposi lay along the hills beside a small mesa that rose among gorges and dunes to a small flat plain, staring at the sky like the eye of a bird and lost among the other grander mesas in the desert. Behind the dwindling village rose the mesa wall. Before it was a long narrow canyon, leading out to the highway and eventually to the trading post which sat alongside the mission. The mission looked like a facsimile of the Alamo.

A Nez Perce, Grandfather had migrated and settled in Chosposi for reasons of his own. He had married Laura P., he told me, with the hope that the progeny of two half-breeds could inherit the right halves and be full-blooded again. His hope wasn't some snotty feeling of the superiority of blood. If anything, it was the desire to keep his children and their children from being susceptible to sunburn.

We sat side by side, gazing at the peach colors cast by the sun rising beyond the horizons of the known world. I kept quiet. Each time I turned to speak, all I could imagine saying was, "What large pores you have, Grandfather."

Behind us in the house I could hear Laura P. beginning her day. I knew her routine. She would stand before the Kachinas on her mantel convincing herself of the differences between people and animals. Then she would slip on an apron and softly complain her way to her potter's wheel or into the kitchen where she'd heat the vat of oil and begin frying donuts and the thinly rolled corn delicacies called Piki, which Grandfather would later take to Johnny Three Feet's Trading Post for sale.

Disturbed by the low tremors of Laura P.'s carping, a Patchnose snake slithered onto the rocks turned white by years of conflict with the sun, and coiled itself into the mood Grandfather generated. We—Grandfather, the snake, and I—could have spent the whole day like that, suffering ourselves to live in a silent time where nothing changed but the height of the sun and the heat of those rocks. But as I watched the snake with the respect I'd learned to give snakes, dangerous or otherwise, the rocks shimmered and then dissolved. The sun reached higher, turning yellow, and I envisioned father and mother, wondering what had become of me.

By now they should be aware of my disappearance from camp, and they would be worried. I felt inconsideration mixed with not a little fear: When father got hold of me, I would pay the bus fare for sure. Whatever halves of the blood father had received certainly did not include the pacific instincts of Grandfather. But then age does all sorts of things to a man. How was I to know that Grandfather, too, had been capable of violence when he was father's age just as I am, although less capable than father because Grandfather taught me to control my dreams, to wield my dreams like a grand eraser.

"If you remember too much," Grandfather said, "you expect more. Dreaming right, you can erase the memories that wear you down like dripping water."

In the midst of my worries (I was only beginning to understand what Laura P. liked to say, that it was a miracle I was still in two pieces), I decided to phone my sisters and have them tell our parents where I was. Using my imaginary telephone, I'd try Pamela's closet. If that didn't work, I'd wait until late afternoon and try to reach Elanna as she sat in the graveyard talking with mother's mother. At the very worst, I'd have to give in to realism and go down to the trading post and use the pay phone.

By the time Laura P. disturbed the sunning snake again, giving Grandfather and me the carefully packed goods to carry to the trading post, I couldn't stand the silence any longer. I had to say something.

"What large pores you have, Grandfather," I blurted.

Grandfather laughed.

It was miles to the trading post, but we didn't have a choice except to walk. After his children were finished bearing their own children, Grandfather had decided that the Plymouth deserved a rest and he had put it up on blocks in the garage behind the trading post, storing a case of oil and filters in the rear seat in case of emergencies. As the two of us hiked along beside the ribbon of highway, undisturbed except for the occasional Buick or Oldsmobile with louvered rear windows roaring past, I needed to speak. I began telling him about Bernie and Buchanan Roy.

"Jews are not white people," he said, when I'd finished. "Many of them are Real People like us. Though," he added, "some behave like snakes. There *are* useful snakes. Gopher snakes. This boy who gave you the Bowie knife. Be careful not to step on them."

I wanted to tell him about the other things that had happened on the way to Chosposi. Not to tell him was a kind of lying. As we trudged along the gravel edge of the highway the Saguaro Cactuses raised their arms to the blanching sun. Cactus owls peeped out and cried "rue" before beating a hasty retreat from me and the revelations of the sun. In the distance, the air shimmered with moisture and the asphalt turned deep black before it disappeared. How could I tell Grandfather about the days I'd left out, recounting my trip? Aren't Grandfathers asexual? It was even more difficult to imagine Grandfather copulating with Laura P. than it was to imagine father coupled with mother. All of a sudden, I skidded to a halt.

"What else is the matter?" Grandfather asked, looking at me with a slow inquisitiveness that bordered on indifference.

"Father has never had a . . . ," I said. I caught myself. I'd been about to say "a blow job." It was a terrifying revelation and it almost made me weep.

"Come along," Grandfather said.

Forcing my face to go blank, I caught up to him.

"Want to tell about it?"

I shook my head, no, mistrusting my voice. Grandfather was father's father, the same father who'd said that sex is not everything, even though he was lying when he'd said that. It was sex, the lack of it, that sometimes made my father crazy and taught me to diminish my presence around the house. Besides, where would I begin?

The car had skidded to the shoulder of the highway. A man had climbed out. The driver threw out a backpack as the man stood gesticulating, leaning into the convertible, bending like a rod that was not used to bending. Angry. Not wanting to find myself in the path of an angry man, I was about to high-tail it away from the road when the car skidded to a halt just past me and the door flew open. The man began to run towards the car.

"Hurry up," she said. "Get in."

I slipped the bandoliers of my canteens over my head and dropped the canteens into the rear seat. She put the car into gear and sped off. Without looking at the dash, she ran the tachometer up to 6500 and dropped the shift lever down to second, up to third, down to fourth, and then settled the

convertible into a comfortable 3000 rpm's, cruising along at
75 without fluctuating more than one or two miles per hour
in speed. I was impressed. I'd never seen a woman drive like
that. Till then, I'd ridden only with mother, who hunched
forward over the steering wheel, creeping down the highway
or braking through city traffic, periodically sucking air in
through her clenched teeth with a quickness that always
frightened me.

"Where you headed?" she asked.

"Grandfather's."

She laughed. "No sweat. Right on my way." I explained
where Grandfather lived. "I can take you there tomorrow,"
she said. "If you want to spend the night in Flagstaff."

"Sure," I said.

She reached behind the driver's seat and pulled out a bottle of Beefeater's. "Want some of this?" she asked. Holding
the bottle up, squinting at it, she said, "Brad was sucking on
this like it was his momma's titty."

Any boy would have lied about his age, faced with a woman
who talked like that, not to mention the way she was dressed
in a halter top and short shorts that were not made but
grown like new skin. She didn't care about my age any more
than she cared that I was a virgin, as she let her head fall
back over the edge of the bed that night and whispered a
litany of men's names.

Gerri was a drug runner. "I don't deal," she said. "I just
move the goods around from one place to another. Like
Bekins. Besides, everyone's got a right to lay back and get
away for a while, don't they?"

Even though I suspected that buying that answer was like
buying a used Ford with a flammable gas tank, that didn't
bother me too much.

What did bother me was her talking. Gerri popped bennies
and sucked on a new bottle of gin, chattering away like a
child up beyond her bedtime who hopes the heavy hand of
fate won't fall if she can keep the company distracted or like
a person who eats alone and develops a non-philosophical
dialogue with the self as a defense against solitude. The only
time she was silent was when she had the bottle in her mouth
or the one time she slid her lips around me, sucking on me

until I came. Her constant patter nearly made her dissolve, without any concentration from me.

When Brad found the motel and began banging down the door, I crawled out the bathroom window to sleep in the back seat of the car. Falling asleep, I dreamed I was a sea lion. I didn't like being in the water; I feared some animal or thing might touch me below the surface. Yet I didn't want to beach myself among the other mammals. Fear overcame desire and, as a ship looking a lot like the one in Bruegel's "Fall of Icarus" headed towards me, I slithered up beside a large lion who had the visage of Bernie Schneider. As the ship passed below, Bernie and I tied up white garbage bags and handed them to the crew of the ship.

I awoke with a pang to the sounds of Dempsy Dumpsters being lifted hydraulically and tipped into the back of a garbage truck.

I was smart enough, when Gerri and Brad found me in the car, not to let on that Gerri and I knew each other. When Brad tried to force Gerri to give him a blow job as the car cruised down the Arizona dawn, I kept my emotions disguised behind the veneer of impassive cheekbones, sensing the jealousy that had sprung up between us, like two crows strutting over the same carcass in the road.

Brad was dangerous, the fuse inside of him running just above peak load. Running drugs with Gerri put him in the company of nice people like Hell's Angels or Gypsy Jokers. Loving people who had godfathers instead of Grandfathers. Having to talk like them had dissolved the distinction between what Brad dreamed he was and what he believed they were. When they dumped me in Chosposi, I was relieved.

Walking along beside Grandfather on the way to Johnny Three Feet's Trading Post, I thought about Bernie's drowning, Tammy's impossibility, of Gerri. With the slow disgust of youth, I said, "There's not much to be said for experience, is there?"

Louis Applegate joined us, creeping tip-toed along the highway. Laura P. had the uncanny ability to hear soft sounds the farther away they were, and her fury would have been uncontained if she had heard Louis anywhere near her pots, his double thoughts modifying the symbols she had fired into the clay. Grandfather knew this, but he took a chance.

"Love is an acquired taste, Alley, like mayonnaise," Grandfather said. "There will be few women in your life you can sleep with and not catch cold."

Louis grinned noisily.

"Just you wait," Grandfather said.

Laura P. had been listening when Louis grinned, as I discovered when we got home. Once she'd overcome her anger, standing before her Kachinas and softly singing longer than usual, she added to what Grandfather had told me.

"My mother," she said, beginning to paint the endless mazes and spirals on her pots before firing, "was a beautiful woman. They say that even as a young girl everyone knew she would be the most beautiful of women, and before she was fourteen she already had several men who wished to marry her. When she was old enough for marriage, every boy who thought he wanted to marry her was given a chance to talk with her and convince her. She sat in a room of her parents' house each day grinding corn. The boys would come one by one to the window of the room and talk with her and try to make her laugh or cry or converse with them—anything to hold her interest and keep her from beginning to grind her corn again. When a boy failed, she would ask him not to return, until there was only one boy left and to his house she sent all the corn she had ground and she and my father were engaged to be married."

Finishing a large jar, she said, "I think you may be like my mother." Laura P. climbed onto a low stool and took down a small multicolored pot with the faded design of Water Coyote. "Here," she said, signing her name on the bottom with a paintbrush. "This one is yours. It can protect you from wasted conversations and keep you from dying of sleepiness."

"I don't understand," I said.

"You will, in time. Now leave me alone so I can finish these pots."

## 8.

I took to Nature. Rather, much like a hippie, I took to the idea of Nature, and in the mornings after I'd walked to the trading post with him, I'd leave Grandfather on the path back to the mesa and wander the canyons and ravines. I was astonished by the way a single flower would bloom at the top of a cactus. The way frogs buried themselves in the mud of streambeds, surfacing after a night of rain to lay eggs and die, seemed almost religious. Small owls moved into the tenement holes left by woodpeckers in the Saguaro Cacti, refurbishing them, habitating them, hooting from them—or at noon, peering out from their darkness at the chubby boy who watched them. The desert was miracle and the world was code. All I had to do was to decipher it and to that end, I wanted to know the names of things.

"Gila," the girl said. She was about my age. She refused to look directly at me.

"You fool," she said. She wore a rattlesnake skin vest over a white T-shirt with *ELVIS* stenciled across her breasts in red slashes. On the end of a pole she held up the live Gila I had been reaching towards. I knew that Gilas were deadly poisonous, but I had thought they were slow and had reached for its tail.

Rachel hunted Gilas, out of which she made coin purses to sell at the trading post. She'd nearly broken my wrist with her pole and then knocked me backwards.

"Watch this, you fool," she'd said, prodding the monster on its tail. Its neck and body had twisted with the speed of its hiss and its jaws had clamped onto the pole, not letting go even when she raised it off the ground. "They never let go. Even after they're dead you have to pry the jaws loose."

I imagined the bones of my hand crushed within those jaws while Rachel decapitated the Gila with a small machete, and watched the body cease its slow wriggling as she pried the jaws loose from her staff and then rolled a large stone over the head.

"It can still bite," she explained, "even after it's dead."

"I didn't know," I said. "Thanks." I felt slightly nauseated as I watched her insert a smaller knife in the belly of the Gila and skin it with the swift skill of a surgeon.

"You didn't know. Pah! White boys," she said.

"I'm not white," I protested.

"Oh, right," she said. "Nobody is anymore."

I felt injured. "My name is Hummingbird," I said. "Alley Hummingbird."

"Rachel," she said slowly, looking me over as though she was taking inventory of my blood. "Laura P.'s grandson?" she asked.

"The grandson of Billy Hummingbird."

"Almost the same thing," she said.

"Not exactly," I said. I couldn't explain how it wasn't the same. The how seemed to lurk in the telephones Elanna and I were in the habit of using. Were you to dismantle the phone through which Elanna spoke with mother's mother, you would find that it was not the same phone through which I spoke to Grandfather. This difference existed even in our names for things: Elanna called her "grandmother," and only she understood that I did not call her "mother's mother" out of some perverse or mysterious desire to be cute—that is who she was.

"Louis Applegate is my cousin's father," Rachel said.

"He's Grandfather's best friend. He's my friend, too," I said.

"Maybe that's why you're Billy's grandson and not Laura P.'s," she said, half-stating and half-asking it.

"You have to tell it the way you see it," I said, wondering if it took telling it for you to know how you'd been seeing it all along.

What I realized as Rachel and I explored the canyons together was that everyone has his sawdust even if not everyone is in search of it the way I was compelled to be. One afternoon, watching her stalk another Gila monster, I found myself gazing beyond Rachel, beyond the horizons of cactus into the shimmering glaze of desert air, and I could see that I was doomed to have at least one friend who wanted to be an Indian. He would know more about what Indians were, about their myths and the facts of their lives and histories, than I would ever care to know. Not being an Indian would eat at him until all that remained was a nut of wishful sorrow. He would end his life by marrying a little blond kitten from the midwest and live out that end by retelling stories about those years when he was like an Indian. He would know the what of being Indian while the how consumed him. The what of the power saw; the how of the sawdust.

"What are you staring at?" Rachel asked, hanging another Gila skin from her belt.

"Nothing," I said, startled out of looking into the lives of people I imagined around me.

"You look so sad."

"I'm not," I said, hearing the words echo across the canyon. I wasn't. I was more perplexed by why I liked this girl who had called me a fool. Her black eyes were set far enough apart to qualify her for membership in the insect kingdom. In fact, she looked a little like an ant on its hind legs. Her hips were large and low, her waist longer than an ant's but extremely narrow, and her head hinted of a child who'd been born with a weak chin. Her only hope, I thought, was to grow—and then she would resemble more a praying mantis than an ant. Yet I liked her. Even though she looked grace-less, her feet never missed a step as we walked down the canyon towards the mission.

I kept asking her questions about the flora and fauna until finally she asked, "Why all the questions?"

"I want to know about Nature," I said.

"Why?" she said, jumping from one rock to another as we crossed a stream.

"Because Nature is life, it's hope, it's . . ."

"Nature," she said, making a gesture that was more Italian than Indian. "Nature is Gila monsters and rattlesnakes." She spat, her spittle foaming on the parched ground before turn-ing into a black blotch. Spotting Johnny on the porch of the trading post, she added, "Nature is Johnny Three Feet."

Johnny Three Feet stumbled down the wooden steps of the trading post, waving an envelope at me. It was a telegram, and even before I opened it, I knew what the message was. Once I had phoned Elanna and father found out that I was in Chosposi and not the fresh air of Lake Arrowhead, I was doomed to be retrieved.

"Guess I have to go home," I said to Rachel.

"See ya," she said.

"You . . . you're welcome," Johnny spluttered, leering at Rachel.

38

"No thanks for this," I said, waving the telegram in his face before I walked away. I didn't like Johnny Three Feet. He had eyes that stared out at the world, defiant in their madness like photos of Charles Manson. It was not simply that he made me uncomfortable. After all, Laura P. had told me about the winter of '39 when Johnny's embryonic and slightly retarded self had been delivered from the womb of a woman frozen nearly to death and dying of frostbite. Laura P. had said that the main reason for letting Johnny live was to teach us tolerance. Fine. But I still resented the way Johnny used tolerance to force people to allow him to do things they wouldn't permit others to do. Such as put his arm around Rachel and sneak his hand up towards *ELVIS*, all the while drooling on her rattlesnake vest. It was a feeling I would never quite get over, even though I would eventually forge an uneasy peace with Johnny, fooling myself into believing that he was like a gopher snake, helpful at times, biting at others, but never poisonous and not worth stepping on.

Before I could hand Grandfather the telegram, he said, "You'd better get your things together. Your uncle is almost here."

## 9.

Sure enough, the rim of the horizon began to withdraw and all too soon revealed my uncle flying more or less towards Chosposi. The path of the plane resembled an FM radio wave as the plane climbed and dipped, climbed and dipped, trying to lock in on the antenna of hardpacked canyon that stretched past the foot of the mesa.

"Ho boy," Grandfather whistled as the two of us guided the plane down safely with our wishes. "Here." He revealed a plain round stone hollowed just off-center by erosion. In the center of the hollow was trapped a smaller nut of granite. He hung it around my neck on a leather thong, an amulet against my uncle's flying.

"*Ho* boy oh boy," Grandfather said, when he saw my uncle climb down from the cockpit.

It had been years since Grandfather had last had the shock

of seeing uncle, and it was a shock I had trouble getting over even after the plane had lumbered back down the canyon, strained aloft, and turned right for the San Francisco Peaks near Flagstaff. I knew that what I felt draining out of me as Chosposi was sucked back into unreality behind us was due to something besides my uncle and yet I couldn't, as uncle might have said, get past him. He had a flattop with the sides greased back in a ducktail. A studded biker's jacket, red socks and loafers with a penny on the strap, and a kilo of chains around his neck. "See ya later alligator," he'd said to Grandfather, and those words crowded together in my head with the lyrics of the songs he sang loudly.

Give me Laura P's singing, I thought.

"Take out those papers and the trash," uncle sang, "or you don't get no spending cash."

Give me Rachel's cynicism.

"Oh raa-inn drops, it looks like raa-inn drops."

Don't give me natural. Let me stay afloat above the desert where there are no landmarks. I tried to focus on the gray line of the horizon, but the line kept shifting so I kept my eyes on the felt dice swinging from the rear view car mirror he'd installed in the cockpit while I sent S.O.S. messages to Grandfather.

"Put your mitts on the wheel and hold her steady," my uncle said. "Pull back to go up, push forward to go down, turn right or left just like driving a car."

"I don't drive," I said, taking the wheel.

"Used to have automatic pilot," he said. "I disconnected it after the time I set it for Reno and I ended up in Bakersfield." He reached behind the seat. "You ever been in Bakersfield? Lot like Lodi. They are square, man, definitely ell-seven in Bakersfield."

Uncle pulled a six-pack of beer from behind the seat and opened one. "Time for suds that made Milwaukee famous," he said. He took a long pull from the can. "Ahh. A beer an hour keeps the heart from going sour."

"That's Coors," I said. Along with the fear I was beginning to feel, I was irritated by the way he was talking. This, I decided, is what comes from teaching school too long. I didn't know enough about uncle's future to blame anything else.

"So it is," he said, looking at the can without surprise. "You want one? Do you some good. You need to lighten up, take a load off your mind." He belched. "'Scuse me."

I thought I was managing to keep my face expressionless, but it made him laugh. "You know you're just like your daddy. I know what's going on upstairs with you. You're thinking, 'One of us should stay sober.' Hah. Listen, flying one of these things to me is like a baby crawling."

All of a sudden, he sat upright in his seat and stared out the window of the cockpit. The expression on his face reminded me of the other faces I would see in my life which suggested that what the person thought he was living for had changed, vanished, died.

I pushed the wheel forward a bit and watched the altimeter begin to unwind. Still, he stared straight ahead. I pushed the wheel more and the needle on the meter began to move faster. Then more. I began to panic, afraid that uncle would just go on staring until it was too late. The engines seemed to increase their rpm's and the wind began to hum across the ailerons and he still seemed not to care. At last, he pried my hands from the wheel, handed me his can of beer, and when he spoke, it sounded as though his voice came from a speaker, over a radio, as he took the controls and pulled the plane out of the dive I'd put it into.

"My son never crawled. You used to crawl all over the known universe, but when he wanted to get from point A to point B, he rolled. He could roll pretty well. But he never crawled."

As quick as a blink, his voice resumed its normal tenor and he laughed. "Can you imagine that? Your cousin rolling from room to room. Got himself dirty as a hedgehog in spring. Well," he said, taking his beer from me, "guess it doesn't matter as long as you get there."

"And back," I said, between gritted teeth. I was furiously frightened. I wanted to hurt him. Someday I'd pay him back for this flight.

Get there we did, nine in-flight cans of beer later. Despite the thick brown cloud that covered Los Angeles, extending as far west as Catalina Island and pressing down on its inhabitants like the heavy paw of a bear, its claws raking the lives of even the whales who had taken to the sea thousands of years ago to escape the invention of progress, I was amazed by the multitude of turquoise swimming pools. They were as numerous as the children of Abraham, winking at us like the Milky Way, reflecting the light of the full moon with the purple tint of the lights outlining the streets.

"Give a hi-dee-hi to my brother, will you?" uncle said, feathering back the engines and turning the plane so my side of the cabin faced the corrugated metal building that served as a terminal for light planes.

"I'll tell them hello from you," I said.

"Just my brother," my uncle said. "My brother's wife . . . well . . . oh, skip it, she's . . . your mother." Inside the door of the terminal, I could see the posture of a man I recognized as my father, waiting.

"Here," my uncle said. He removed one of the shiny pennies from his loafers and flipped it to me. I was tempted to toss it right back at him. Whether it was because my anger abated with the look on his face or because I was saving my strength for the figure inside the terminal, I don't know.

"Later, kiddo," my uncle said, slipping the headphones on, radioing in for clearance, the engines making dirt and leaves swirl as the plane turned and accelerated out to the runway.

I held on to the penny like a token with which to pay the busfare I expected father to exact. It wasn't that father was a cruel man; he was thorough. For example, if he sent me reeling backwards, heels over head, for spilling milk carelessly at the table, he would whack me a few extra times to be sure I got the point. Even if he was understanding, he would be so understanding that I'd begin to wish he'd beaten me instead. I could never tell where his sense of thoroughness would lead him. Someday, he would come home and find me in bed with a girl. Calmly, he'd send her home. Then he would sit down and explain to me the dangers of impregnating a girl at my age, and start to walk out. Some thought, some sense of incompletion would stop him, and he would come and knock the wind out of me.

In the terminal, father took hold of my left shoulder with his left hand. His hands were as big as Grandfather's and I watched the right one warily, staying in close to him so he wouldn't get full extension of his arm if he slugged me. When he put his right hand on my other shoulder, I expected to be lifted like a large Kachina and expelled through the nearest window.

"Hey," he said. "You must be tired."

I dropped the penny, let it jingle on the linoleum floor, left it like a hobo might paint "Kilroy was here" on a rock as a sign that I had been there. Like all signs we leave behind us in arriving and departing, the penny would probably be swept away by the broom of a janitor. Yet maybe, just maybe the penny found a corner where the broom didn't reach easily and it is still there defending the dust that has gathered around it over the years.

On the drive home, father said, "Listen." He was being quiet the way I have come to understand it is our nature to be quiet. There are so many things to say and so many ways to say them and have them heard that one seduces oneself into never beginning. If, by mistake, whether out of a sense of necessity or desire, one of us began, we ducked out of the sentence as quickly as possible.

"There's something I have to tell you," he said about five miles later. Even in the dark, in the reflection of the headlights, I could see the brown cast to the fog that was choking the angels of this city indiscriminately.

I waited. Except to lecture me, father had never spoken to me like this before. We had never just talked. I didn't know then that we never would, although I had begun to suspect it; what I didn't suspect was that father had noticed and would continue to notice that we never talked. Until he said, "After seventeen years, I still can't talk to you," I never imagined the possibilities of the pain it must have caused him.

Unlike father, mother was expansive. Bobby pins in her hair—she was trying to tighten the soft curls of her hair—she was standing like a sentinel on the back door steps waiting for me with her arms crossed. On the heels of her "you should not have run away from camp, you had us worried," she added with her usual logic, "Your dog took sick, you weren't here to care for him as you should have been and he got sick. We," she went on, pausing only long enough to suck air into the top of her lungs, "had to take him to the vet's and have him put to sleep."

I refused to believe her. At first.

When I realized that she was telling the truth, sleep sounded good to me, if only because it would allow me to redream this dream or dream a new one. All I could do was stare. Clyde was no Lassie, but then Lassie was a transvestite and Clyde had been mine. I didn't feel any of those feelings I was supposed to feel like pain or loss, only a tremendous absence as I remembered Clyde gamboling about over Custer's grave in the backyard. I was still staring, still hoping to sleep, when mother came into my room in her quilted bathrobe and sat on the edge of my bed, her hands clenched in her lap, and tried her best to comfort me. Poor mother.

"He *was* sick," Elanna said, scratching my head thoughtfully as I sat with her in the graveyard the next day. "It wasn't very fair of father not to tell you. Mother always has to do the dirty work. Someday, you'll understand."

I confess it was mother who put on her fuzziest sweater, unbuttoned the top button, and, wearing a basic string of pearls, served father meatloaf by candlelight and talked him into letting me accept the gift of another puppy from friends of theirs. I confess it because, though I was not very comforted by Elanna, I was discomforted by Pamela, who, not long after, blurted out in the darkness of her closet, "I hate her." An echo of what, unsurprisingly, she would say about pets. Pets, she'd decide, were things one should not become too attached to because, like mothers, they would one day have to be put to sleep.

"Though a living bitch is better than a dead lion," Grandfather said.

"Maybe. Maybe not," I thought as I re-enacted Custer's burial ceremony for Clyde and christened my new puppy Running Dog. Using the New Mathematics of plus and minus one, it seemed that I continually reached a sum of zero and even though zero was a cardinal number as well as an argument, it always came to nothing. So it wasn't that Grandfather might have been wrong about bitches and lions, only that he may not have been right.

## 10.

Robert Parnell O'Connor always insisted on using his full name because Parnell was somebody to someone, once, or so he'd heard. It was difficult for an Irishman to feel as important in deprivation and suffering as Jews or Mexican immigrants, and the Parnell gave Rob the right to feel a little superior to Tommy A., who was condemned—or so Bernie, Robert and I believed—by his boring WASP blood to insignificance. So when early in the school year Rob disappeared from school with the suddenness of a whisper, we weren't sure whether or not to be happy for him. Our teacher said he'd had a "tragic experience" with a voice that suggested the experience was his as well, and that made us even more curious about what it was.

Bernie Schneider and I wondered about it at recess and after school. Rather, I wondered aloud to Bernie, since he was unconcerned with events outside of himself. Well launched on his wanderings in search of Tammy, Bernie was interested in little else but keeping his head above water.

Tommy Anderson was the one who, with the hope of impressing Marily, brought the newspaper clipping to school the next day. The photograph showed the rubble of an apartment building, the tail section of a light plane sticking out from it as though the apartment had burst. Robert Parnell O'Connor Senior, newly remarried, had perished with his bride as the plane, under the cover of night, had crashed into their apartment.

The way the newspaper added it up, it was terrible and tragic. The way I added it up, using the New Math, was zero. Robert Parnell O'Connor had a father; he had lost that father. Zero. Robert had a new stepmother; she was dead. Zip, again. I tried a different formula: minus one father, Robert Parnell was plus one experience of suffering, and that still seemed to add up to nothing. True, Robert might put some distance between his sense of deprivation and Tommy's, and lessen the distance between himself and the Jews and Mexicans around us. But how real would be the gain against Bernie? Robert had suffered a loss, but one can get over loss. One never gets over a want like Bernie's which can't ever be satisfied. At best, Robert would be up less than one; and even that bit would be taken away when Thanksgiving rolled around and Tommy revealed a secret that no one knew he had.

Before I got on the horn to Grandfather, I checked with my parents. They proved to be unfamiliar with the formulae of the New Math.

"Married," mother said. "Serves him right for having his marriage annulled and marrying a doxy like her." Mother led you to believe that Robert Senior's death was the result of marriage. "That's what can happen," mother said.

Father said, "'God prepared a worm when the morning rose the next day, and it smote the gourd that it withered.'" Less penetrable than mother's answer, father's saying made me realize that father's gods had become the One God and thus, under the rules of the New Math, the sum of his experience was zero. Forsaking the old gods, he had bought a new one. Maybe mother's sum was zero, too, since she had something against marriage and yet was married herself. I fled, dialing Grandfather even before I reached the cemetery.

"Chicken Little," Grandfather said.

How right Grandfather was. I might have imagined the sky was falling, that year. It seemed that the brown sky was rejecting everything that ventured into it. Poor Robert Parnell O'Connor. Not long after he returned to school, prepared to consolidate the suffering he would tell us he had endured, a pilotless Navy fighter crash-landed on our playground.

Fortunately, most of the kids were in, or on their way in from recess, when I heard the incoming whistle. I looked behind me to see the fighter plane in the near distance, nosing out of the opacity of smog. I wasn't sure it was going to hit the playground as I watched Little Eric what's-his-name, alone on the playground. His job, given him in exchange for letting him play, was to bring out the equipment to recess and to collect it after the rest of us had run off to class, and he did it with fervor and pride. So there he was, struggling with the large duffel bag full of bats and balls, carrying it from base to base, setting it down and putting the base in it, and then hoisting it to his shoulder again to stagger on to the next base. At two hundred yards, he looked small as he spotted the incoming jet and fell back from it, ducking his head into the crook of his arm. "Exactly the way he'd field a hard-hit, one-hopper," I thought, as I dropped to my knees.

For years, we had been having daily air raid practice. Ever since the Russians had delivered Sputnik into the infinite and curving regions of the universe, we had been taught to drop below our desks on our knees, making ourselves look more like snails than human beings, covering the exposed skin of our necks with our hands to protect us from flying glass. Watching the films of atomic explosions, Bernie and I felt silly. We knew that flying glass was hardly the problem. The heat rolling out at the base of the explosion like the dust storms of the thirties would cook us like escargot.

At last all that practice paid off for me as I dropped to my knees and the jet lodged itself in the asphalt field of the playground, erasing Eric in a screeching, tearing explosion.

Poor Robert Parnell O'Connor wept tears, brown and gritty from the smog, frustrated tears that eroded the plump curves of his Irish face and left it lined and ancient with grief. Every foot he had gained on the ladder of suffering was lost because of some kid whose last name no one cared to remember. Even the photographs of Eric's wreckage in the newspapers were larger and placed more prominently than those of his father's death.

When the sky wasn't falling around us, we played Bombs Away in the wash, hauling stones up the railroad trestle and throwing them at the shack the hobos had built with the mission instinct of the Franciscan Friars. We switched to Bombs Away from Cowboys and Indians less because the game had become offensive to me, and more because Tommy A. was changing.

The rest of us had become somewhat obsessed with women (or, rather, obsessed with our own pudenda, we had begun to hope for and seek relief in the vision which hung like an island just beyond the powers of our swimming strokes). Tommy's worm was turning a different way. Maybe it was Bernie's wearing a breach cloth that caused Tommy's worm to turn. To me, Bernie looked slightly ridiculous. As for Bernie, I dare say he only wished to be prepared if his Tammy accidentally manifested on a sunny Saturday afternoon. But Tommy pursued Bernie. When he found him, Tommy refused to shoot at him. Tommy almost broke down into tears when Bernie refused to be his prisoner, insisting that in Cowboys and Indians, the Indian was either dead or not—never was he taken prisoner.

I had refused to acknowledge Tommy's strange behavior until one rainy afternoon when he and I were watching a Western on T.V. At one point, this large Indian buck bursts through the door of the settler's cabin, accompanied by the frightened screams of the white women trapped inside, grabs one of the women by the hair and drags her out to his horse.

"Oh," Tommy said, "I wish I could be like that."

"Me, too," I said, thinking it natural for all little boys to dream of being large and strong with caveman dreams of dragging women off to tents and caves and hotels on the coast of Mexico.

"She's so lucky," Tommy said. He put his hand on my wrist. "Don't you think?"

"He's the lucky one," I said, looking him straight in the eyes.

Bombs Away was my idea, primarily as a way to divert attention from the closet Tommy was slowly opening. On Saturday or Sunday afternoons we could be found in the dried-up river bed, trying to destroy the hobo shack. Bernie spotted for us, managing to escape his dreams enough to say "two degrees right" or "up six," the rest of the time indifferent to whether we hit the shack or not. Grown fat on white bread and peanut butter, I arced rocks at the tin roof glowing with the sun's heat, competing in the size of the rocks. Tommy, having selected delicate, round rocks, lofted them through the air, more concerned with the curve described by the rocks than with any effect on the shack.

All things come to an end.

"Vanity," father would say over and over. "All is vanity."

But it wasn't vanity or the awareness of it that stopped our game of Bombs Away. Possibly, it would have ended anyway, but one day there happened to be a hobo in the shack. The hobo also happened to be ten feet tall and black as mother's toast. As I ran from him, concentrating not on the gray line of the horizon but on the invisible demarcation of the Nevada State Line, he sounded like a freight train, gaining on me as I flung my fat round body along the tracks. At last I stopped, winded, unable to recall when the sound of his running had ceased, and was vain enough to think I had outrun him. It was that vanity that led me back to the trestle when I realized that Bernie had not run with the rest of us and that he was most likely still sitting there saying "Up six degrees," spotting for the artillery that had retreated without warning.

The hobo was hulking over Bernie, shaking his shoulders, saying, "Lissen. You tell your buddies they come 'round here again I'sell cut their little hands off." When he let go of Bernie and raised his fist, I thought he was going to strike him.

Picking up a rock the size of one of Tommy's, I threw it at him. "Let him alone you shiftless nigger," I shouted. As swift as a coiled snake, he was on me, holding me aloft with one huge fist and shaking me like a rattle.

"What'd you call me, boy?"

Fear bred a modicum of defiance. "A lazy Negro," I said.

He spat on the ground. "No, boy. Nah. You called me a shiftless nigger," he said. The strange thing was that he didn't seem angry. More amused. "Didn't you?"

I started to say I hadn't meant it.

"Didn't you?" He shook me hard, his black eyes staring straight through my skull the way Grandfather would have stared if I had used that word around him. "Didn't you, boy?"

"Yes," I said.

He dropped me on my feet and I turned to run, but he grabbed my shoulder and my will to run vanished in the largeness of his grip. "Now lissen," he said. "I want you boys to call some things to mind next time we run into each other. One is," he looked at Bernie, "you were foreminded 'bout hanging around here. You tell your mates that, hear? T'other is that nigger ain't a color but a state of mind. Plenty niggers all colors in this world an' next time we meet you call to mind that I ain't one." He released my shoulder. "Now git."

"Come on Bernie," I said, regaining part of my composure. To the hobo I said, "Let us not meet again this year."

He laughed a laugh full of teeth. I'd never seen so many teeth. "What'd you say?"

"Let us not meet . . ."

"I heard you." Laughing, he spat at the ground again.

He hit my shoe. He shouldn't have done that. That's what I told myself as I furiously cut a hole in the lid of a mayonnaise jar. A rag, a packet of cigarettes, the jar three quarters full of gasoline from the can father kept for the lawn mower. He should not have spit on Grandfather's words. Fed with that notion, I managed to keep my fury alive until the night. Spit on Grandfather, will you? I thought as I ran from the empty shack, the cigarette fuse smoldering, not waiting for the explosion but intent on reaching my street, my father's house, before the explosion and flames alarmed the fire department and the police. Spit on . . . , I thought, in bed again, my heart outracing the locomotive I could hear in the distance. Had I been able, I would have stopped the fuse. I would have made the night into a bad dream, even before I heard what Grandfather would have said.

"Gibbon," Grandfather would have scolded. "Bannock scouts."

It was the second time in my life I had done something I couldn't tell Grandfather. I would remember it always because it was the first time I heard and knew the words Grandfather would have said, if I had given him the pain of knowing what I had done. Never again would I want to hear the story of Gibbon's men sneaking up on the Nez Perce encampment and slaughtering women and babies in a surprise dawn raid. I lost twenty pounds of sleepless fat over the next few months, realizing that I was worse than Gibbon's Bannock scouts.

# CHAPTER THREE

## 11.

Without consulting us, father has decided to migrate north, climbing the map of California to escape the smog that hid Los Angeles from the light of the sun. Pamela and Elanna have been packed off to an event called Summer Round-Up, from whence they would return to our new home in Palo Alto. I have been assigned the role of companion, keeping mother company on the long drive north after the moving van has pulled away from the house.

Soon enough my brain feels as though it's sweating from the stifling heat in the car and I lean my head back against the hot vinyl seat covers, closing my eyes and trying to ignore mother's driving—her steering, rather. Mother doesn't drive. She hunches forward over the wheel, punching the buttons on the box set into the dashboard, making the automatic transmission shift without rhyme or reason, screaming in second or lugging along in high gear, as she negotiates the curves and grades called, as she's told me ten times if she's told me once, The Grapevine. Mother knows the names of things, but her names say little about the things themselves.

As soon as we were past The Grapevine, mother explains, steering over the carcass of some nocturnal creature and making the wheels go thump, thump, it will be clear sailing all the way to Palo Alto. I can only hope she's as right as the Franciscan Friars who stayed to the coast, their place names a day's journey apart, leaving the central valley to be named by the heresiarchs, madmen, and immigrants.

Mother talks to the car and the cars of other drivers who zip past us, a habit I will inherit and recognize years later as, heading east into the Holland Tunnel, I curse and kibitz drivers from New Jersey. Mother tells me that she doesn't want to move any more than I do because they had friends in the City of Angels. They were secure. In only two years, she says, father would have had full retirement from wherever it was he worked, and from then on, it would have been a matter merely of tending what they had acquired.

She says she's glad to have her young man along for company; who knows, she adds, maybe it will be better for all of us in northern California. And then she says, "It means The Tall Tree," and without a question or even a movement from me adds, "El Palo Alto. The Tall Tree . . . I wonder if there was only one tall tree? Or was it originally Los Palos Altos? Well . . . do you hear that noise, is that something wrong with the car?"

Acknowledging only the last question, I say, "No."

"How far do you think Bakersfield is?" she asks as we pass a sign that reads "Bakersfield—32 miles." "Do you think I should stop for gas in Bakersfield?"

I try to concentrate on the gray line of the horizon, drawing Palo Alto towards the car. Each time I focus in on the distance, the car begins to slew across the lines demarcating our lane.

"Mother," I say, drawing her attention to the fact.

Mother's vision is limited to the near distance. My concentrating on the far distance pulls the right side of the car ahead of the left. Were I to continue, despite what corrections she might make with the wheel, mother and I would begin travelling in a broad circle. From time to time, I am forced to look backward, focusing on what was behind me just to keep the car on the road.

Distance is doing what concentration might have done, making Marily and Tommy and Margaret into little more than symbols with voices. By the time mother and I reach Bakersfield, their voices will be too weak to penetrate the barrier of brown smog engulfing the city where men once spoke with the tongues of angels. My heart feels heavy, as though it's packed with sawdust.

"You shouldn't look backwards," mother says with the authority of a Harlequin Romance. She presses the power brakes of the '57 Rambler and skids slightly beside the gas pumps. Bakersfield.

"Can you fill the tank with regular?" mother asks. The gas jockey nods his head sideways at the driver's window, his eyes riveted on the distance as though he has heard for the first time in his life the fading tap-tap of his distant drummer.

"It should take about three dollars' worth, I guess. It's half empty, but I don't know how many gallons the tank holds, do you?" At $1.25 an hour, the attendant could care less. It takes him a month to save enough to buy more chrome for the chopped Harley leaning like an amputee on its kickstand in front of the station's office.

"I don't like to let the tank fall below halfway. My husband says it's bad for the engine and on long trips you never know what's going to happen. When you're not going to be able to find a gas station."

Her voice has a peculiar inflection, one which would better fit a small breed bitch in heat when confronted by a German shepherd. She always talks to supermarket clerks, A & W waitresses, gas station attendants, telling them whatever they might not know or care to know. In this case, there is a flirtatious and frightened edge to her voice. It is provoked by the size and gender and, more importantly, the race of this gas jockey. Mother has known Spanish men; this fellow isn't what she would call Spanish. He is indubitably Mexican. Mother has a fine sense of distinction. Possibly I am misjudging her. Some of the fear may have been caused by the fact that the gas gauge had dropped measurably below the halfway mark before she found this station east of San Luis Obispo. And running out of gas in a strange place rates among mother's top forty fears.

"You never know what might happen," she has said, over and over, hunched over the wheel and searching the horizon for the sign of a station. For mother, every mile takes the worry and concentration of two. She imagines rapists, pillagers, and plunderers lurking behind manzanita bushes beside the road, just waiting for an opportunity to take advantage of a helpless woman and "her young man." It was stupid.

It was never silly. Not then and not later. I was slow to see that all men were rapists to mother. It wasn't until Caryl Chessman, who used red lights to stop single women on the roads at night, had been put down in San Quentin's gas chamber, and mother had substituted her boss as the central character in her worried monologues, that I began to see what I had always suspected. Not until I was telling Sara Baites about mother did I begin to understand what I had seen. I was telling what had become my favorite anecdote about mother. "Mother," I said, "fucked my father three times in her life." It was either that or her three children were adopted. "And look what she got."

"Did it ever occur to you," Sara said, "that your mother married to avoid copulation?" If that was true, then father was the first rapist, not Caryl Chessman, and mother's coyness with gas jockeys and grocery store clerks was her enactment of the rituals of a fourteen-year-old girl.

I was always a little slow, I guess.

"Will you show me how to check the oil?" mother says to the attendant. Daintily, making sure her skirt covers her calves, she gets out of the car. "My husband showed me how to do it before we left, but I don't remember where the little stick thing is that tells you if you need to add oil."

The jockey considers mother for a moment. Decides. He'll check the oil because not checking it isn't worth the trouble of listening to her. I know the look on his face. I've seen it on my father. I've seen my sisters trying to disguise it. I've seen it in mirrors and in the stainless reflections of toasters. As he leans in and releases the car hood, I give him my version of the look. He grunts. I climb out to get a soda.

The gas station looks like the one Edward Hopper made famous. Two old, round-topped pumps with large tin numbers inside windows that seemed always smoky or misted with condensation. On the sides are yellow bulbs in which a metal fan turns as the gas bubbles through on its way to the nozzle. Inside the wooden shack that serves as shelter from the elements as well as a commentary on life in that county, there's a girl with skin the color of mesquite. In hip-hugger denims, cut-off T-shirt, and headband of silver conchas, she was a Mexican version of Gerri. She disdains looking at me. I put in coins, open the vertical door of the soda machine, and pull at the neck of a grape soda. The metal wedges that are supposed to release the bottle jam. I pull again, tearing the skin on my fingers on the bottle cap.

"Motherfucker," I curse quietly, giving the machine a kick in the chrome.

Concha moves on rollers like the chair; she slides back, swinging those golden legs to the floor and slipping over beside me, next to the machine. I can feel the way she walks even though I don't dare turn around because I've left off underpants in an effort to combat the heat of the long drive which mother is managing to make much, much longer.

"Chengado," she mutters. "Ésta máquina es una puta." Okay, I think. All right with me. Coolly, easily, she extends her hand towards me, palm up, and in a moment of perfect communication, I understand, reaching into my pocket and finding another dime. I drop the dime into her cupped palm like the dimes I used to drop in the church collection basket.

"What you want. Grep?"

I nod. Concha drops in my second dime, moves the coin return lever part-way down, saying, "Hold this." Slapping the side of the machine like an indifferent lover, she reaches in to the bottles and grabs a grape and a root beer simultaneously and deftly jerks them out. I don't mention the fact that I've paid for her root beer as I stand in the doorway of the shack sipping my grape soda and trying not to look at her.

Screwing up my courage, I say, "Qué hora es?" What am I supposed to say? What's a nice girl like you doing with a hog biker like that? She isn't a nice girl. The fat lazily rolling over the top of her jeans as she sits there seems to say that while she isn't nice, she's easy—at least for the proto-simian outside.

"Trés y media."

She isn't even pretty, eyes too far apart, her face flat, high cheekbones curving into points around her mouth like a teardrop or gourd. Even to look at her has already cost me something. Girls like that may be easy; they're never free. Still, that roll of fat speaks to me, hints to me that sleeping with this girl would be easier and more natural than with most of the girls you see walking around.

Three-thirty. We've been on the road since dawn and we're only halfway there. If mother pushes it, we might make Palo Alto by tomorrow.

Mother is following the attendant around the car as he washes the windows, including the side mirror, and then begins to check the tire pressure. It's odd the way mother can get someone like him to do everything but wash the car for her.

"I appreciate your doing all this," I hear her say. "We're going all the way to Palo Alto. El Palo Alto. Means the tall . . . but you know that, don't you." She giggles. "Moving. My husband has changed jobs. My children will go to new schools in the Fall."

The attendant drags the air hose to another tire and sinks over his haunches, unscrewing the cap on the valve and testing the pressure with the pencil gauge mother has purchased for the journey.

"They all skipped a grade." She is proud of this and oblivious to the blank look on the attendant's face.

He's wondering what's so special about skipping a grade since he's skipped several.

"Well. Half a grade, anyway. To tell the truth. The school years are different in Palo Alto. So they had to either skip half a grade or go back half a grade because they all started kindergarten early." As mother starts the car and presses the button for first gear (she likes to shift through the automatic gears; it gives her a sense of control), she tips the guy a quarter. The expression on his face echoes what Concha called mother as she watched out the office's window: "Cuños." I am not certain, but from the look on his face, I can guess what cuños means. I have a long time to decipher his expression because there is a truck about half a mile down the road, coming toward us as we wait to pull out, and I know mother will wait until that truck docks in San Luis before risking merging onto the road.

The gas jockey stares at the quarter in his hand. As he begins to recede into the distance slowly, as mother punches her way through the gears, he lifts his hand as though offering a host to heaven. The middle finger suddenly sticks out from the rest of the hand as he waves goodbye to mother and me. Oh, Concha, watch out, I think. You're in for it now.

## 12.

Mother has told the truth. I've been moved ahead half a grade in school. So had my sisters, once Pamela could be lured with Velveeta cheese out of her closet long enough to be tested, and once Elanna had gotten mother's mother's approval. With me, the problem hadn't been to get me to sit for the Stanford Binet Intelligent Quotient Test, it had been to get me to pass.

"He's a little slow," my teacher said to the principal. They had checked my first score out with Dr. Bene, a descendant of Alfred Binet, himself.

"You cannot score zero," Bene insisted, long-distance.

"He did," the principal said.

"Everyone is guaranteed 200 points," Bene said. "Even a master-sergeant in the U.S. Army can get two hundred points. Some of them score three hundred!"

Bene flew down from Stanford.

"He's slow," my teacher said, as Bene looked at the score sheets.

"Real slow," Bene answered. "Exceptionally slow." He sorted through the sheets. "The continental shelf will kiss Japan before this child learns to think," Bene said. My teacher laughed. The principal, his hand on my shoulder, tried not to laugh but I could feel his torso quaking with contained humor.

They gave me the test again. "His sisters passed. Very high scores," they said. His sisters. It seemed a little unfair to me to be compared to my sisters. They were older. And one of them had had all those years in the closets of the houses we lived in to polish her thinking while mine was still in the geological stage of being compressed by the weight of school.

"You can't score minus fifty," Bene said, again over the phone. He had returned to Stanford. He flew back again.

"I'll administer the test, personally," he said. He locked himself in a small room with me for three consecutive days. By the time we were finished, I knew how many punch holes there were in the acoustic tiling. And I knew how wonderful silence would be—if only Bene hadn't been there.

"This one's easy," Bene would begin. "You know this one." He'd ask a question.

"But that answer isn't one of the choices," he would tell me. Over and over he told me. I felt sorry for him. Each time he said that, his voice climbed like my uncle's light plane, and then, Bene regaining control, it dipped to the sonorous tones of the intellectual.

It was the middle of the second day. Asked a question, I gave my answer. "You've lost a coin purse on a baseball field," Bene said. He showed me a diagram of a baseball diamond.

"I don't have a coin purse."

"Okay. Keys. Keys, then. You lost your keys."

"To what?"

"To your house!" he shouted. "I don't know. Your house. Or . . . or . . ."

My house key, the only key I carried, was chained around my neck inside my shirt. I drew it out and showed him. "I never lose it. Father would . . ."

"Pretend. Okay? Pretend you've lost it in the ballpark. You have to find it. Okay?"

"Okay."

"You have to find it because your parents aren't home. Your sisters have gone away on a visit. If you don't find it, you'll be locked out of the house." (He ignored my asking whom my sisters were visiting.) "It's raining, and you'll be locked out of the house. Thunder and lightning. Heavy rain. Drenching rain. Lightning striking trees, telephone poles. Your parents won't get home until very late at night. You've got to find those keys!"

"Okay," I said. He was pretty worked up, so I went along with him. He sighed. Panted a moment, catching his breath.

"All right," I said. I closed my eyes. Grandfather smiled, sort of.

"The keys could be anywhere." He showed me the diagram again, zig-zagging his pencil around it randomly, without touching the paper. "Now how are you going to find it?"

"I'd . . ."

"Remember. Lightning," he said. "Rain. Where would you start? Just mark where you'd start."

"Here. Or here." I marked the edge of the field, then put an X in the center, too.

He stared at the X in the diamond's center longer than mother stares at the green lights in San Luis Obispo before driving on.

"How would you go, if you began here?" he said, pointing hopefully to the mark on the diamond's edge.

"I'd see if I could walk around the edge of the diamond, spiralling in to the center."

"What if you started here?" he asked. His voice seemed weak, tired.

"I'd try to spiral outward."

"Draw it for me, will you?" I drew a spiral for him.

I just happened to say, "That's how I'd do it, but . . . ," and he nearly leapt out of his chair.

"But what? What? Tell me."

I considered whether what I was going to say had anything to do with the silence in the room. "But mother," I said, "would start here and go back and forth across the field at intervals of two or three feet."

"Draw it! Draw it for me?" He quickly sketched out a diamond on a clean pad of paper and I drew it for him. "That's right!" he said. "That's the right way to do it. That way, you cover all of the field. Logically, you would find your key for certain that way. Right?" I shrugged. "Do you see why that's the right answer?" he said.

"You asked how I'd do it. Not how mother would do it."

"You mean you'd still try to make a spiral, even though I've told you the other way is the right way?"

I nodded. He looked defeated, as though a god had just determined his fate and that fate was bad.

"Mother's way isn't any fun," I said.

He was going to tell me that I wasn't there to have fun but there to find the damn key. He was going to remind me of the thunder and lightning and rain.

"Mother would be just as soaked as I would be," I said. "And what if I found the key right away, at the edge of the diamond?"

I didn't know what Dr. Bene did with his test after the third day. There were rumors, though, of a frazzled man haunting the ivied halls of Stanford. Eventually, I imagined, the frazzled Bene would change his name; or everyone would forget it, as he metamorphosed from a researcher into a character.

Mother, it turned out, had a very high I.Q. Mother was

very smart. I couldn't help but admire her for it. Even years later, before she partly recovered from her years in electro-shock therapy, when she would walk back and forth across the living room like someone trying to remember what it was she was looking for, despite her black and blue temples and the ghostly angularity of her face, mother had a gleam in her eyes that told me that she knew how the world worked. Even if she could not exactly tell me how that was.

## 13.

By the time mother noses the car down the grade north of San Luis, second gear has begun to go. Out on the highway, this doesn't matter much, as long as mother maintains cruising speed. Fortunately, the road has become flat and fairly straight, curving only as it swings past towns like King City. King City looks like a mirage in the sunset, and I convince mother that she can make it all the way to Gilroy before stopping for gas again.

"You're such a good little navigator," she says with the kind of naive affection that irritates me because it makes me realize the vast difference between me and mother's vision of me.

Only after the highway patrolman has ticketed mother for going too slow on the highway, and later, after she has stopped for gas in Gilroy, does the loss of second gear matter. The car gets up speed in first, and then the engine races as it tries to shift into second; races until it slams into third and lugs the Rambler up to speed. I have by then convinced mother not to shift through the gears using the buttons on the gear box, which takes some of the fun of driving out of the trip for her. I try to teach her to floor the accelerator pedal in first and run the car as high as it will go, then let the pedal up and pump it once quickly to make the car think it's time to shift to third, and then accelerate gently between 25 and 40 so as not to make the engine work too hard. That is too complex. I clamp my eyes shut and hope first and third gears will last to Palo Alto.

Truck headlights race towards us, growing brighter, larger, and then vanish as the car is buffeted in the after-air of the tractor-trailer rigs. Dusk has made mother quiet, but the on-set of night makes her want to talk as we pass fields, orchards, golf courses illuminated by streetlights, and a moon that seems pale compared to the lights. Along that road, the lamps are amber because of the heavy fogs that sneak in from the coast.

"What are you thinking about?" mother asks. She sounds like a lover who is worried that your silence means something like anger or despair.

"I know," she says. "You're worried. You're missing your little friends. You're wondering what Palo Alto will be like. I'll miss my friends, too. You'll make new friends, though. We'll start a new life. You'll see."

It is easier to say, "I know," than to tell mother the truth, that I am not missing my friends, little or otherwise.

"You'll like your new house," mother says. "It's got a nice yard."

"I know," I say, wondering how large the lawns were, how much of a Saturday morning will have to be spent mowing that nice yard.

"The driveway is large enough that we might hang a bas-ketball backboard over the garage and you'll have room to play."

"I know."

"You'll only have three blocks to your new school. Your new homeroom teacher is a very nice man, Mr. Mac. You're growing up. Soon, you'll be in high school like your sisters, and then you'll be off to college." Mother seems to be rush-ing things.

"Two doors down is a boy about your age," she adds. "I'm sure he's got lots of friends you can meet, and I'll meet the wives of the people your father works with. We'll get along okay."

"I know." I know, I know, I know.

I knew that Mr. Mac would be Chinese and his favorite story would be how he'd had to wear a large badge which said "I am Chinese" during World War Two, in order not to be beaten by any random all-American patriot on the street. Sometimes he would pause in mid-story and pull his citizenship papers from his desk to prove that he still carried them in case he was stopped and unduly questioned by official or self-appointed protectors of freedom for all. I could guess that the boy down the street would be named Pete Wright and would be a bully and that in order to ride my bicycle in peace around the neighborhood, I would have to be bullier. Or maybe Pete would live around the corner and two doors down would live a boy named Eric. It seemed that there always was an Eric in my life. The runt of the litter, he would follow me endlessly, in and out of school, like a retarded little brother, cheering me on each time I wrestled Pete Wright to the ground and sat on him, pinning him hopelessly with my advantageous weight, and threatening to pound him like cheap meat if he didn't cry "uncle." I knew that, despite my size of a beached baby whale and my Dreamer's hair waxed as stiff as toothpicks over my unusually high and pontifical forehead, a girl named Karen Karenovitch would chase me down like the hobo from Bombs Away. She would be taller than any girl or boy in school, and her deep voice would remind me more of the Russian shot-putter, Tamara Press, than of a girl with untampered chromosomes. "C'mere," Karen would boom and, locking her hand on my shoulder, she would drag me like a tackling dummy into a corner of the building and press her body and lips against mine. While it would be a somewhat terrifying experience, I wouldn't mind all that much. Karen would have breasts, huge in contrast to the apricots of normal girls. Her gingham peasant dresses would be two sizes too large as if handed down by sisters of a different race, and my hands would slide around beneath those dresses without inhibition. Disregarding the black hair on her hands and legs, pressed against the stucco wall, I would close my eyes and imagine her breasts were actually those of Sue Thurmond, Nikki Winters, or—in the secret recesses of my own obsession—Marilyn Riekse.

## 14.

How could I know all of that? Pamela wanted to know, once she'd settled into her new closet.

The same way I knew anything. By closing my eyes and recollecting, listening to Grandfather. My past spitting up the strained vegetables of future all over my adolescent bib. People were always the same: There had been an Eric, and there would always be an Eric. Even if his name changed, which I doubt, he will always be there to pick up the bats and bases, and to take it in the shorts because of a freak accident.

"No tabula rasa, then?"

"What?"

"Blank slates. We learned that our minds are blank slates at birth upon which are inscribed the designs of our developing characters."

"Characters don't develop," I replied.

"Ours haven't," Pamela said dejectedly.

"Like blank checks written in invisible ink, they only reveal their worthlessness. The amount remains always the same," I said, ignoring her. "Mr. Mac *was* Chinese. Mr. Mac did wear a badge. If I had paid close attention, I would have known that he would be arrested for molesting little boys before the year was out."

"Sometimes you . . . to play around with your dreams, . . . the world is . . . created in . . . way you . . . live with, if . . . going to . . . character who . . . survive the sleeplessness of now," Grandfather said.

"What?" I said. I could barely hear him because of the static interference in the ether between Chosposi and the stars we bounced the transmission off of, in the region I called the Absence of Angels.

I'd spent the first summer in Palo Alto crawling about on my belly beneath my father's new house, trying to discover a way to connect my imaginary phone lines to Ma Bell's. It was a silly and useless effort, but I was frightened by the distance between Grandfather and me. Palo Alto was the farthest I'd ever been from him, and because of the way my friends from the City of Angels had dissolved, I was worried that my connection with Grandfather wouldn't suffice.

All I succeeded in was establishing a working relationship with Black Widow spiders. Grown fat with the ease of northern California life, their cavernous sloth a contrast to my underground fear, they would drop down on their slender filaments and stare at me, blinking in the brightness of my flashlight beam. They scared me, not so much because their venom was so poisonous as because they seemed so matter-of-fact.

Giving up on my underground telephone lines, I took to sending messages to Grandfather by bouncing them off the moon at night or the stars during the day—the stars which we had learned in astronomy were always there, even though we couldn't see them with our naked eyes. Possibly it was the fact that the stars were moving away from me as the universe expanded daily; or it might have been the continent's inching its way toward Europe, or the interference caused by the paramilitary detritus the American and Russian space agencies dumped into the atmosphere. The end result was that sometimes when I spoke to Grandfather, the connection would shift and static would buzz through the Absence of Angels.

At night, as I lay there on my bed, pale and fat from all the days I had spent beneath the house, my feet growing towards the end of the bed, I worried.

"Grandfather," I said, "even the angels are dissolving," by which I meant Bernie Schneider.

Closest to me in spirit if not in dream, it took the concentration of a weightlifter to see even the outlines of Bernie anymore. It wasn't a case of time seeping into the cracks of memory and causing the images I had of Bernie to rust. He was dissolving. He would appear in my dreams with water cascading off him as though he had just emerged from the water on which he seemed to be walking.

"Alley," Bernie said, "help me. I'm going down for the third time."

I could see his feet dissolving where they touched the water—he was sinking, not beneath the water, but into it, as though the water were acid—and in the sad look on his face, I could foresee the hopelessness of rescuing him.

"I'm failing Hebrew," he told me. He couldn't refrain from translating every feminine name as Tammy.

"Adam and Tammy?" his Rabbi would say, laughing good-naturedly. But when he began coming to the Schneider home regularly for dinner, the Rabbi's laughter began to sound as hollow as Bernie's voice. As the Rabbi ate the gefilte fish, trying to pay attention and to imagine a way to rescue Bernie, if only to toss a life ring to him abandoned on his acidic sea, his laughter was the dry laugh of a Catholic. Even that good woman who wore long-sleeve shirts on the hottest days, that woman whose house had encircled me like the desert around Chosposi, seemed to weaken in the face of Bernie's intransigence, and instead of, "Stay. Eat with us," I heard her say, "Come next week, maybe. The week after." It was not for lack of love or kindness, but because everyone reminded her that she was losing her son, that all the Rabbis in the world couldn't put Bernie Schneider back together again.

Long before Bernie was sucked into the forces of dream and time, his voice was silenced and only his lips moved; I couldn't even be sure that he had tried to say, "Farewell, Alley." The last I saw of him, his arm stuck up from the water, his fist clenched as though trying to hold on to his dream. Then his fist opened, and a cloud of crows rose into the brown air, becoming dots on the horizon as they flapped away.

# CHAPTER FOUR

## 15.

Bernie dissolved long before mother took to waking her children for school by suffocation, pinching our nostrils and then clamping her hand over our mouths until our brains panicked and jettisoned us from our lumpy dreams. Sometimes I would awaken myself with laughter as I dreamt of Tommy A. guarding the gates of Los Angeles with a flaming BB gun, my family cast out by my father's ambition. Other times, I cried out in my sleep, unable to wake myself even though I would open the door to the dream and walk in and look at myself and command me to awaken. Thank god for mother, then; I had begun to fear what would happen if I got caught in one of those dreams, like a man in a room of endlessly reflecting mirrors.

At school, Parkinson's Law took hold, cloning vice-principals and deans of boys, to whom Mr. Mac sent me with the regularity of weather. Karen Karenovitch dragged me to and from recess, determined to win my acquiescence because I was the only boy anywhere near her height, except for William Barber, who insisted that I call him a black and not a Negro.

"If it happens," grandfather said, "it can happen that way, too, when the world looks dark and the knife you recollect from a summer of camp seems your only way out of clover leaves and cul-de-sacs."

William the Black became my best friend through basketball. Sports had not yet become more important than school itself, and our intermural contests were waged with the informality of inner city conflict. Instead of buses and coaches, we travelled to our away games on bikes, on foot, or in the cars of Spartan fathers who took the afternoons off from work to watch their boys defend the images they had always wanted to have of themselves. My own father seemed to lack the self-image other fathers had, and he never attended the games.

"He plays on a different court," my uncle would explain years later, when he came to watch me hold down the bench.

For me, being sent out onto the playing surface was like being sent wandering across the desert. The roar of the crowd was like the roar of the full moon in daylight. The tracks left behind as the other nine boys raced up and down the court were like the tracks of kangaroo mice. Each time I found the trail, the mice had gone, and I was left standing at the wrong end of the court. Nonetheless, I was a Renaissance athlete. Good enough to make all of the teams, but not good enough to start, I gained a familiarity with benches and a flat butt.

The week before our first basketball game against Mayfield, my school seemed filled with tension. The teachers seemed to be willing to let the athletes release tension any way they could, and Mr. Mac even allowed me to move from my desk at the back of the room to a desk right behind Marilyn Riekse. Even when Mr. Mac caught me staring down Marilyn's dress, he didn't send me to the dean.

"What's happening?" I said to William the Black one morning, as everyone stood around listlessly. Mayfield was an all-black school so William seemed the one to ask.

"What?" William said, distractedly.

"Why is everyone acting funny?"

"The game," William said. "This Friday. With Mayfield."

I failed to catch William's drift.

As I arrived at Mayfield's gym, a run-down quonset hut on the other side of town, across very real railroad tracks, Allen asked where my bike was. "I walked," I said, starting to suit up.

"You walked?" Allen said. "Alley walked," he said to the rest of the team in the locker room.

"Maybe he will, again," Stephen said. Nobody laughed, and we carried our street clothes into the gym in our travelling bags.

"Listen," William whispered to me as we warmed up. "After the game . . . ?" He looked around as though telling me a secret. "Stay close. Okay?"

Throughout the game, I thought about how, when Allen had said, 'He walked,' Walter and Stephen's heads had bobbed together like dashboard dolls with sprung necks. I began to suspect why when, with time left on the clock, I was left holding the ball. Literally. I began dribbling, wondering where my team had gone, grinning back at the black boys from Mayfield, who grinned in turn at me. When the buzzer sounded, I was surrounded.

"Congratulations," I said. They were grinning; they had won. It seemed the thing to say. Their center stepped up to me, crowding the private region in front of my nose.

"What's your name, boy?" he said. I sensed the danger in his voice.

"Alley."

"Alley," he said, taking a step backwards. "What kind a name is that?" I shrugged. It was a name, that was all, like William or Rachel.

"What's your last name?" one of the guards demanded.

"Hummingbird," I said, and it was as if the breath had been knocked out of the danger. They broke up laughing, bending in exaggerated laughter, grinning as wide as trucks at each other, until the largest boy caught his breath and said, "Come on, less go get the honkies," and they disappeared as quickly as my teammates had. Outside, the school had emptied like a Protestant church on the day of the Rose Bowl and I wandered home, repeating my name over and over, trying to discover what was in a name.

When Mayfield travelled across town to play on our court and even the fans joined in the after-game skirmishes, William the Black and I stood half-heartedly on the edges of no man's land, helpless. For me, it was less a matter of race and more that my name seemed to free me from that kind of hatred, a freedom I enjoyed and would later take advantage of.

It wasn't until ninth grade that I got my nickname, Two Point. Standing beside the basket while my teammates defended the opposing goal, William the Black spotted me on the fast break and selflessly passed the ball to me.

I caught it.

"Shoot," William yelled.

"Shoot it!" my uncle shouted from the sidelines. Without thinking, I put the ball up off the backboard and watched it slip down through the net.

"Two points!" William shouted, and it was in the reverberation of his voice that I became "Two Point Alley."

"Put in Two Point," the fans would shout.

"Where's Two Point?" the coach might ask, when I was late for the team bus. I became a team mascot, a good luck charm. When I managed to score two points, our team won the game. Coach Roach came to want me in the game early, have William feed me the ball and let me score, and then take me out before I got it into my head to try for four points. For the rest of the game, I'd sit beside Eric Engels, who'd made the team with persistence and tears, and watch the cheerleaders bounce and kick, their skirts swirling to reveal underpants untouched by human hands. Sometimes, I'd say something like, "I'd sure like to get between her bumpers. Wouldn't you?" and make Eric's arrested heart blush.

I didn't mind sitting on the bench. No more had I minded playing tackle on the football team. Unable to understand why the other boys wanted to play positions in which one could make all of the visible mistakes, I was content to submarine the opposing tackle and lie there on my belly, waiting for Walter's rubber cleats to run across my back as he dove for yardage. I simply did not understand that kind of competition, and on the way home from a surprising loss to a bunch of hicks from Livermore, I would sit at the back of the bus with William and the rest of the black athletes and pry a window loose from the bus, watching it flip silently into the darkness of night with more interest than I'd watched the game.

## 16.

Coming home from a Saturday's roaming with William the Black, I found my uncle's car out front. It was a warm afternoon. Father was wearing Bermuda shorts with dress shoes and dark socks. Uncle wore gym shorts and sneakers and padded around the yard after my father, talking to him about divorce. He asked my father if he had ever considered divorce, what with my mother. Father turned, his face rigid and blank with what my uncle took to be indifference and I could see was pain, and said to me, "Listen. I was thinking about you and me going on a fishing trip."

I said that I'd like that.

Since father rarely went to the hardware store to buy a new garden hose—an item he seemed to purchase more than any other due to the times I ran the hose over with the lawnmower—without a list, a pad of paper on which was written "hose," the conception of a fishing trip would take as long to shape up as the birth of an unwanted baby.

We planned. We shopped for fishing rods, settling on the cheapest fiberglass rod Sears and Roebuck sold. On a wild impulse, father bought a plain billed cap, a webbed adjustable canvas belt, and a canteen. At moments I wondered why we hadn't purchased a tent, or backpacks, or powdered foodstuffs, but I decided to trust that father had taken care of that himself.

Locking Running Dog in the house, I practiced daily casting into the center of an old tire I dragged home, concentrating on ignoring mother as she sneaked in and out of the house, cleaning. When the trip shrank before the onslaught of business into a day trip, I was forced to give up my Hemingway dreams of packing through the Tetons. Nonetheless, I remained undaunted. There were plenty of places father and I could drive to—the Yosemite Valley wasn't more than four hours away, and if we started early, we'd get in several hours of fishing before darkness pushed us out of the state park.

When the day to leave came and we were packing the car with the bag lunches I had made to prevent mother from making them for us, father commented on how much fun this was going to be, just him and me, the boys, on a trip together.

On the way, father said, "I've never been here before. I hope it's good fishing," and though we were driving west into the Santa Cruz mountains, and not east towards Yosemite, I replied, "Whatever." Whatever was going to become a refrain for the day.

As I stood on the packed dirt ridging the pond and watched the dump truck back up to it and pour thousands of finger-sized trout into the water that bubbled with the confused darting of fish, I could only say to myself, "Whatever." It was, for all I could do to describe it, a psychedelic experience, focusing on the way I was out of place because of my size, my heart pounding with the strychnine of disproportionate feelings. Beside the cement pond, vaguely shaped to look like a teeny lake, the chatter of happy eight-year-old voices rose to my ears, surrounding my taller head like a mist.

Father stood beside me in his cap, arms akimbo, fists on his hips, and from time to time pointed to a spot in the pond which was saturated with the lines of children and said, "Try over there." When I reeled in a trout no bigger than a test tube, father stopped me from throwing it back, saying, "We'll want to get our money's worth."

All I could do was smile and say, "Whatever."

When father and I got home from our day at the pond, he flopped his cap onto my head and said, "Well, that was fun. We'll have to do it again, sometime," and I nodded vaguely, thinking that whatever happened, this wouldn't. Years later, I would look back and realize that the trip was doomed to failure because of the way in which it came about. The difference was that I would not regret its failure as I had at the time. I would see that the seductions of a fishing trip were the same as the seductions of love and sex and that what people called reality was actually unreality, involving a process of making plans which could never be realized. Besides, boys would always be seduced by promises from fathers which, when broken, make boys begin to see their dads as something more and something less than fathers.

Other weekends, when father wasn't travelling as a petrochemical consultant or changing jobs and trying to start up his own company again, when mother wasn't talking to any inanimate object that would listen, if the new Dodge wasn't in the shop, we packed ourselves together into the car and drove to my uncle's house. Two hours of togetherness on a journey which father demanded, mother hated, and my sisters and I feared. Mother spent the entire trip talking to the windshield, telling it the things she couldn't tell father, and her words rolled around the inside of the car like marbles seeking the limits of randomness. If we passed a car or truck in which the driver had forgotten to turn off his turn signals, mother rolled down the window and flapped her thumb and flat fingers together like a magician making a strange bird talk. The direction her hand pointed, she explained, told the driver which turn indicator was blinking, left or right. Despite the odd looks other drivers cast back at our passing car, I was convinced that mother understood a secret driver's code which only the best of drivers knew. After I was bar mitzvahed by the Department of Motor Vehicles, given my license as a sign of California adulthood, I was—and have always been—conscious of my turn indicators, never leaving them on accidentally, for fear that some woman will stick her arm out her window and blink her hands at me.

Often, on these trips, mother and father talked in low tones until father banged both hands on the dash and started yelling. My sisters cried, first one, then the other joining in, forcing me to break my vow of silence and expose myself to danger by whispering to them that "It" would be "all right." What surprised me most, having never thought of putting my arms around Bernie Schneider and telling him that everything would be all right, was that it worked. Before we arrived to the placid greeting of my uncle and the sometime appearance of his sharp wife whom I called the Vegomatic, both of my sisters would be laughing at the jokes I told them.

Oh, those jokes. I can remember them all in spirit and none of them in practice. For years, my sisters had liked to have friends over and then summon me into the living room and ask me to tell their friends one of my jokes.

"Alley tells the funniest jokes," Elanna would say.

"Tell the one about the man and his dog," Pamela would say. Their friends would grimace, trying to hold back their laughter, which would abort any joke I might tell. I would begin.

"Once," I'd say, trying to remember when I had told a joke about a man and his dog, "upon a time, there was a small

72

man with a small dog. It wasn't any ordinary dog, but then he wasn't any ordinary man." I would go on from there, adding, changing, modifying, forgetting the presence of those girls whose breasts jiggled inside the cups of their rocket bras when they laughed, concentrating only on finding an end to the joke.

"Tell us one about a beautiful girl," one of my sisters' friends might say, when she had ceased laughing hysterically at the joke about the man and the dog. Avoiding, instinctively, any story about princesses or frog princes and beginning with naturalistic detail like a true American boy, I began a joke about Tammy without revealing Bernie Schneider's secret obsession with this perfect woman. As instinctively, I selected one detail from each of my sisters' friends which I then presented as impossibly beautiful—the shape of one's breasts, the color and texture of one's hair, the fine but pronounced nose of another, and the legs of Minette, the only friend of my sisters whose name I can still remember. If nothing else, that instinct guaranteed a pause in the laughter as each friend agreed in turn on the beautiful features of my composite woman.

Always, the jokes seemed to have phenomenal success. The girls would be choking with laughter, their faces pumped red with blood by their happy hearts. Of course, I didn't know that they were laughing at me; laughing not at the joke but at the way I kept embellishing the joke, trying to find something funny in it as well as a way to end it.

In the car, with my arms around them, telling them it would be all right, I was fully aware that they were laughing not at the joke but at me, and still I told the jokes because it made them laugh and not cry, and because I had learned to take pleasure in those seemingly interminable stories. Besides, I couldn't think of anything else I could do to make them happy.

## 17.

"Many things begin in the back seats of automobiles," I say to Rachel the next summer, in Chosposi.

"In my case, I developed the need to make everything all right for every girl I'll ever come to know in my life. If I can't, I hate them."

Rachel stands there, holding a basketball in her palm like an offering.

"That, too, is like a knife," grandfather says. Like a boy who's been sent on to the prairie to dream the circumstances that will name him, I know what grandfather means.

"Mystical," Rachel says. She begins dribbling the basketball, punctuating the low complaints that come from inside the house where Laura P. is throwing pots. Over the years, she has chanted and rechanted her complaints into a metrical litany that functions like the music in a religious service.

"Heavy," Rachel says. "Old-man-speak-with-wise-tongue bullshit."

I am caught between Rachel and grandfather, listening to Laura P.'s litany like an agnostic who suspects there is something behind the surface of the universe, but who can't discern whether what's there is full or empty. Who won't discern it until the emptiness on the other side of life fills up with voices other than the dead pilot friends of my uncle.

"May all your days be fact," grandfather says.

Rachel's eyes are narrowed. Her body is as hard and thin as father's temper but she hasn't heard grandfather. "So," she says. "You wanna shoot some hoop?"

I glance at grandfather, amazed that he can talk to me alone, even in the presence of someone else.

"Go ahead," he says. "I don't need you dogging my heels all day long." Before he sinks like a sandbag shifting into his chair and closes his eyes and begins to snore, before my amazement recedes entirely, I see the sagging lines of father's life.

Rachel and I descend the mesa towards the mission school's gymnasium, passing the basketball back and forth. I feel grandfather's concentration relax, his love letting me go. "Lay off grandfather, will you?" I say. "Leave him alone."

It's a struggle for her. She was never one to hold back what she thought, and she'd become more blunt, direct, since my last flight to Chosposi. She mutters to the basketball, the inflection of her voice changing each time I toss the ball to her. Finally, she manages to say, "Sorry. It's not Laura P.'s husband."

"Grandfather," I say. "You mean."

She nods, running a fingernail along the fake seams of the rubber ball to the nipple where the seams met. "Phsst," she says, sucking in her breath and holding it. "It's that mysterious Oriental crap about 'it happens, if it happens at all, such and such a way.' As if you're just supposed to sit back and accept things the way they are. The way they're going to be."

"What else?"

"We may not be able to change things," she says. "But we sure as hell can try to prevent them from becoming in ways we don't like."

Could we? I wondered.

"We can, and we must," she says, turning on me with a prodigious coolness. "Do you know what that crap does for us? You have any idea what's happening to us because of that mystical stereotype? How much we've got to overcome? We're losing a way of life."

"What kind of life is it?"

"What?"

"Father says," I begin, slipping on the shale of my years, wondering why I'd said 'father says' instead of grandfather says. But father had said—hadn't he?—that the modern Indian had to learn to live in the world the way it was and not the way he wanted it to be. "It's not a red world," father liked to say, to which grandfather replied, without father ever seeming to hear, "No, it's pink. And black and blue. Mostly blue," grandfather would add in his sadder moments. Years later, after grandfather's ashes were scattered over his desert, he would whisper, "It never did me any good. Being red. If it can help you, make it."

I tell Rachel, "Father says that we have to live in the world the way it is and not the way we wish it were."

"Yeah?" Rachel snorts. "And what does your mother say?"

"Fudge happiness." I laugh. At quiet moments, when the pressures of the world were too much with her, mother was developing her soliloquies to the toaster, the bookshelves, and later to the lamp in the living room that snapped on with the martial regularity of the night's watch. Adages of her own making hung like ghosts about the house, cold spots that my sisters and I would touch, shiver from, and pass by.

"It's not funny," Rachel says harshly. I'm taken aback. I hadn't laughed because I thought it was funny. "Men can't possibly understand what it's like to be a woman."

Rachel and I play basketball in silence, except for her bossing me around the court, telling me to shoot hook shots her way and not mine. It seems that she has a chip riveted on her shoulder. No matter what I say, she's determined to interpret it wrongly, so I refrain from saying that if men couldn't possibly understand women, not at all, then there isn't much hope, even for Real People.

After an hour, Rachel quits. "I'm bored," she says. "You're worth shit as an opponent."

Needless to say, I'm feeling pretty low as I circle alone behind the trading post, on my way back up the mesa. Noticing that the door is open on the garage where grandfather stores the Plymouth, I look in and find grandfather leaning into the engine compartment. Feet that I recognize as Louis Applegate's jut out from beneath the car.

"How far was he?" grandfather asks Louis.

"East Texas," Louis replies. "He was on his knees, crawling, like he wasn't in any rush. But he might've spotted me and been faking it. If he gets to his feet, even catches a bus, he could arrive a lot faster. No telling."

"Best be prepared," grandfather says. "You got the drain plug back in tight?"

"Almost," Louis says. "Okay. You can put in the oil now and we'll start her up."

Even though I know how the unlikeliest things happen in real life, it still seems unlikely that I didn't wonder whom grandfather and Louis were talking about or why grandfather was tuning up the Plymouth as though preparing for a trip. That I didn't know that the shadow crawling on his knees across East Texas was my old familiar, Death.

## 18.

Except for Laura P.'s having to strain to touch me above the shoulders, I hadn't noticed that my size had begun to change, the fat stretching like canvas over the ribs of my skeleton, which grew thicker and higher with a will of its own. Pamela, grateful she'd stopped growing at five feet eight, liked to say, "It's a good thing you weren't born a girl." Elanna, an uncertain five feet four which she would always claim was five five and a half, would laugh and ask, "How's it going, Stretch?" when I came home from school.

Despite the nickname, I had no idea of how tall I was becoming, how imposing I was for people, male and female alike. To a tall person, everyone else is either the same relative height or short. Years later, I would say that tall people endured, if not suffered, just as much as short people. You can never find clothes to fit because your size is not one the Great Designer ever imagined. Stores hang merchadise from rafters at a height calculated to crease your temples; citizens and W.P.A. crews trim trees with the intent of putting out your eyes; chairs are too low, beds too short, doorways for the average, and automobiles designed for drivers without legs. In bars, little men will want to fight with you and Viking women will insist, even beg, that you dance with them. If you're tall and date a girl who isn't, you'll encounter the bitterness of tall girls and short boys who can't find dates. The only advantages to being tall are the ease of changing light bulbs and being able to reach an item off the top shelves for old ladies in supermarkets.

After he died, grandfather would tell me that size was a matter of spirit, the same way that distance was a matter of concentration. But then, as I drove mother to the store or took my sisters shopping, I didn't know that, and I acquired a girlfriend who was both short and small in spirit. Or rather, she acquired me. I don't know. With Allison DeForest, one never knew.

Allison invited me to a party at her house about the time mother's first toaster moved out and she spent the weekend in the hospital deciding on a new one. I went with William the Black and a supply of breath mints sufficient for everyone who drank the punch, to which I liberally added vodka. While Mrs. DeForest patrolled the hallway, following William from living room to back yard with intrigue or suspicion, Allison towed me into her bedroom, moving my paws around her body, whining like a well-oiled power saw and whispering,

"Yes," into my ear. When I moved away, briefly, and started to unbuckle my belt, she sat bolt upright and demanded, "What are you doing?"

"I thought. . . ." I saw myself, ridiculous, neither dressed nor undressed, caught like someone who has sneaked out a quiet fart that not only stinks but clings like plastic wrap.

"Well, you thought wrong," Allison said. "I'm saving my-self."

I stood there for what seemed all of my wonder years, giving her all of the silence I could muster, before I refas-tened my belt buckle and sneaked out of the room.

"Ask her if she gets interest," William said as we walked home side by side. I laughed. "If you ask me, it's the mother who's hot to trot. She was following me around all night."

I didn't tell William that Mrs. DeForest had followed him because he was black and she was certain he'd steal every ashtray and candlestick in the house. I was thinking about my uncle having said, "Nothing wrong with your mother that a little understanding can't fix," as I'd stared at mother who stared back blankly. It dawned on me that maybe Allison only needed a little understanding. Some patience. Maybe Allison's disease was the same as mother's.

"What the hell," I said to William, "maybe I was rushing things. We'll see."

Allison and I invented our own ball-less brand of Fast Break. One week, she'd be dragging me into bedrooms, alleys, parks by day or night, where she would get me panting like a dog about to expire from heat exhaustion. The next, she'd be pushing me away, saying "I'm not a whore" with all the trained moral force of her sex. At first, I protested that I didn't think of her as a whore.

Eventually, I replied, "You're telling me! With a whore, you get what you've paid for."

We would break up. She would wait a few days, and then call and I would succumb to the whine of her tear-filled voice. Again the tussle and tumble of young love would begin. Again the proclamations.

"All you want is my body," Allison would say accusingly, her sharp teeth clenched. I'd be stumped. It was, after all,

THE ABSENCE OF ANGELS

true, I did want her body. Though small, it was tight, and she flounted the tightness almost as well as her mother did, whether in jeans or in some silky blouse that became see-through at twenty watts. For a long time, I avoided telling her that all any man would want would be her body, that her mind was like generic imitation Parmesan cheese, pale and flavorless. My patience endured as my determination grew and my understanding shrank.

I came to be able only to say, "Fine," without remorse, when she'd tell me that we'd better stop seeing each other. When I walked away from her, she didn't recede beyond the horizons of my concentration, she simply vanished. Only when I saw her again could I recall what she looked like.

"You want my body" became a refrain for Allison and a challenge for me.

### 19.

About the time my uncle switched from singing "Let's Do the Twist" to "Moon River," Pamela emerged from the dark confines of her warm and protective closet to attend the local community college. She had evidently believed me on those trips to uncle's house when I'd told her repeatedly that "It would be all right," and the dreams she rode into the world were delicate, subtly marked by oranges, yellows, blacks. A spot of purple in the iris of each eye for contrast. She was beautiful, her flat face a cool facade capable of exploding into an intense and experimental sexuality.

In the secret hours of moonlit mornings, worn and tired from friendly bouts with the bottle or the local police, I would sneak past the metallic blue illumination of her boy-friend's car and into the house, strands of Johnny Mathis's lyrics of innocent, permanent love covering the sound of my footsteps as I tripped past father slumbering on the living room sofa. It was the nights of Johnny Mathis's silence that predicted what I knew four months later aboard my uncle's yacht: that Pamela would marry the boy who brashly hung his legs over the bow of the boat as uncle slewed across wavelets, spraying him, trying to shake him off like a cowboy off of a bull.

Elanna, on the other hand, unfooled by Johnny Mathis's or my promises, had taken her own view of the world astoundingly different from Pamela. Sometimes, those late and gin-drunk nights, I would pause at the insomniac door to her room and listen to the resistant strains of Baez or Peter, Paul, and Mary. Not so long after Pamela had begun fluttering off daily to the community college, Elanna took herself off to the university, where she joined the Free Speech Movement while learning how to fill out forms of enrollment properly. Then, as I leaned my forehead against the stony cold of her bedroom door, all that would seep out from inside was a mustiness, filling the hallway with the smell of disuse as though mother had vacuumed the house without a filter bag in the machine.

In my own room, I tuned the stereo to the local country and western station, and tried to think. My scalp itched and I was forced to cross my fingers to confuse my nervous system and scratch my own head, pretending that Elanna was there to comfort me.

Grandfather couldn't compete with Country and Western and all I could gather in were words like "sparkplug" and "filter." I got up and closed the drapes on my window, switched off the stereo, and lay back down, closing my eyes as tightly as I could, hoping with the dark silence to create a vacuum which would draw grandfather's words out of the darkness and into my ears.

At that moment, wearing a tie-dyed shirt of Elanna's, mother burst into my room, darted to the window, and threw open the drapes.

"Light!" mother exclaimed. "There must be more light. How is college?" she asked when the drapes were open.

"I'm not in college, mother."

She turned and looked at me, her gray eyes becoming greener as though the smoke in her mind had cleared temporarily. "You're not in college," she said.

"Not yet," I said. "Pamela and Elanna are."

"Excuses," mother said. "Well, it's your life. If you want to ruin it, go ahead."

"I haven't finished high school," I said.

Mother wagged her finger like the arm on a metronome. "Tcchh, tcchh," she said. Her eyes wiggled like jello and became grayer as the metronome slowed. "And why do you hate me?" she said.

"I don't hate you, mother."

"Why did you say you did?"

"I never did . . . ," I said. The frustrating thing about mother was that notions, like feelings, came and went from her mind like parolees reporting irregularly. While they were in her mind, they stayed until the stockpile was depleted, and we had no idea how large that stockpile might be. If, at one moment, she thought you ought to be in college, then you ought to be, regardless of your age and experience. Her trips to the electroshock therapist didn't really interrupt these notions but only dispersed them, making their focus general instead of specific. For example, if mother decided I hated her just before she went off to a brain cell barbecue, she would return believing that we all hated her, not just me. It was like an intermittent Korsakoff's syndrome, mother forgetting the lines that connected the points of her life. She was beginning to seem more than merely dotty.

"I heard you!" mother said. "You said, 'I hate you sometimes.'"

I could only look at her. She looked like a little girl who has been denied something promised. I was helpless.

"Well, young man, I'll tell you one thing. You're not worth a Christmas goose and I'm going to let your father deal with you."

Helpless. And weary. "I did not say I hated you."

"See if I put you in *my* will," mother said. "I won't leave you a wooden nickel."

What could I say?

"You'll be sorry," she said, "when I die. You'll see, you'll be sorry." She slammed out of the room.

"Fudge!" I said, beginning to laugh, but inside, not out, shaking with laughter at the absurdity of the conversation on the inside, with tears beginning to stream down the valley of my increasingly pronounced jowls.

## 20.

I couldn't help but laugh when mother said that about her will. The money in her family had been acquired by women, maintained and propagated by women, and yet, when her Christian Scientist mother died believing in Error and not in heart disease, it had come into the clutches of mother's father, a harsh man whose great love was the pursuit of cosmetic women. He had lost most of the money in successive alimony suits, and by the time mother's four-slice toaster electrocuted itself trying to swim Lake Tahoe on the way out of California, he was unwilling to contribute any of what was left to her medical expenses. His unwillingness was manifested by his refusal to make any mention of her illness, and the one time I drove mother the five hundred miles to visit him, holding my breath as we passed through the smog of Los Angeles, he spent the entire afternoon ignoring not only her but me. To him, I was the cause and effect of whatever seemed to be upsetting her. To me, he was a nastily illogical man who was capable of saying, "Only good Indian's a dead Indian." And did say it, mind you. I didn't want his money. It was his monster, his darkness, that that money represented, and my only escape was to disregard it.

I knew that I was supposed to say something to the effect that I didn't want mother to die, that I didn't expect her to die (yet), that she wasn't to talk that way, and that, in the end, I despised the quarters her mother had used to make her weak voice clink with the hint of substance. I hated the money, not mother, not mother's mother. As for her father, well . . . who would miss him? Come to think of it, who would actually miss mother? Would Pamela? She was becoming more and more ethereal and there were times I wondered if she would miss me. Elanna? Before Elanna had moved to Berkeley to sit around with men in Bob Dylan stubble and women with Joni Mitchell hair discussing politics and spiritual essences (both of which *my* friends would later reduce to Karma), she'd told me, "Mother has not had the best of lives."

"I know," I'd said. "Her toasters . . ."

"Listen, you mindless little shit. This isn't a laughing matter," Elanna had said. "Mother's life has been one of disap-

82

pointment. Cooking and cleaning and giving everything up for you and me and Pamela, having to pretend she liked those men who follow father home from an office which changes its address as often as you change clothes."

"I'll wear dirty clothes," I said.

"You know," Elanna said, her face beet red with anger, "you were supposed to have been a girl. You were going to be named Charne. But you came out a boy, a gargantuan baby weighing upwards of ten pounds. Another of mother's trials and disappointments."

I began to scratch my head furiously.

"Of course," she said, softening, "I was supposed to be a boy. Thank God it was you, not me, who was a boy. Can you imagine you as a girl, as big as you are?"

"What does it matter?" I asked, relieved that Elanna was no longer angry with me.

"It does," she replied. "I know it does. I just don't know how yet." But when mother entered the sanctuary of Elanna's bedroom and cleaned it out, throwing away every memento Elanna had of boyfriends and the small joys of adolescence, keeping only the copies of *Lady Chatterly's Lover* and *The Tropic of Cancer* to underline in indelible red at her leisure, it was Elanna's turn to hate mother and my turn to say, "Well, at least she's greatly simplified the job of reading Lawrence and Miller."

If no one missed mother, then no one would remember her. That seemed a fate worse than death, like never having lived at all. Sorrow overcame my sense of humor and I went out to find mother, convinced that I could reason with her and explain that I didn't hate her, that all I felt was a growing absence and that I couldn't hate someone who wasn't there.

Mother was nowhere to be found.

I found father in the garage, bent over the washing machine, his arms sunk into the tub up to the shoulders, making him look not a little ridiculous. I watched. Father cursed as best father could.

"Oh balls," he swore, as something inside the machine snapped.

I said nothing. Father was good at taking things apart—mechanically inclined, you might say—except that I couldn't remember a time when father had ever successfully gotten what he'd taken apart back together again. Machines, to father, were like Humpty Dumpty to all the King's men, a trait I didn't inherit but which father assiduously taught me by making me so nervous when I changed the oil on the car that I'd forget to replace the drain plug, only noticing the oversight when the fresh oil began running down the driveway past my shoes. When father was not around, though I had a bitter resentment for machines and their ability to turn on me, I was somewhat more skilled in dealing with them. And deal with them I did, disdaining the quarters vending machines asked for, tinkering with their works until everyone for blocks around could have a Coke compliments of the Coca Cola Distributors. How many times I would be arrested for theft, I didn't know, then; about as often, I suspect, as father was arrested by machines themselves.

I sat on the stoop of the door leading from the house to the garage smiling, watching father attack the washing machine with the fervor of a boy taking apart his grandfather's power saw, looking for the sawdust. I revelled in his cursing.

"Oh fudge!" father swore. I heard something clank inside the machine's carcass, and then fall to the cement floor of the garage, unreachable, unless one moved the machine. "Oh balls!" father muttered.

Father's arms emerged from the guts of the machine and his hands locked onto its corners as he wrestled with the washer like Antaeus with Hercules. Suddenly I saw him, years before my conception was even conceived, a boy struggling to discover the mysteries not of the universe but of the everyday. A shirtless boy, his body round but hard, crushing the horse's oats in his hands, trying to find the nourishment. I saw his frustration and his punishment; I saw his mother weeping because they couldn't afford to send him to college; most of all, I saw him standing before the minister, innocently believing that mother's "I do" was a beginning and not an end. I could have hugged father at that moment.

"Maybe you could get off your duff and give me a hand," father said, winded, beaten by the machine's specific gravity, his premonitory sense undamaged by the battle.

"What are you doing?" I said, rising, dusting off the seat of my jeans. "Trying to find where they keep the suds?"

I had meant it as a joke. Father had little patience for jokes at the moment. Letting go of the Kenmore, his left hand struck me across the eye, sending me tumbling back across the floor of the garage like a pink pelican. As I lay there, he crossed and stood above me, and I saw his body beginning to stoop, shrinking into the shape he had had as a child. Towering though he was from where I lay on the garage floor, I realized that he was no longer as tall as I was. That bodies are not Sanforized against time and emotion.

"You know," he said, leaning over me the way one would lean over a crib, "you're just like your mother." He stomped out of the garage.

Not much later, when I stood before the bench in Santa Cruz, arrested for assaulting a cigarette machine, my minor case undiverted by a McCarthyite judge from the social security set, I would recall how I had carefully removed every nut, every bolt, every belt from that Kenmore washing machine and then turned it on, running water into the tub and listening to its delicious and inevitable death as it came apart. I would be cited for contempt as I lapsed into silence before the judge, realizing that it was then, when I killed the washer, that the wonder years had begun to end, replaced by the dim digestion of the worried years.

# CHAPTER FIVE

## 21.

During those years, my reputation as a criminal was stamped by rumor like a grape into wine. My teachers began to look at me funny and on dark days they ignored me, not calling on me to answer questions, for fear my criminal nature would erupt. Only Marion McNamara, the quintessential Latin teacher in love with Julius Caesar, could stare into my darkness and see that whatever it was I had been arrested for did not make me either dangerous or romantic.

Walter and Allen, Stephen and Paul liked to hang around with me on the school's grounds. None of them wanted to take me home where the naturally suspicious eyes of their Anglo-Saxon parents would see the stains on my reputation. I was grateful, then, for William the Black, whose color seemed to make him impervious to the stain which could rub off by associating with me. The girls fluttered when I sat near them in class or outside, during lunch. Living up to my image or, rather, creating it and maintaining it, I disdained the Beatles and memorized the Stones while less openly I listened to Country and Western, to silky guitars sliding around booze, trucks, loneliness, replying, when Elanna mocked my taste, that Country music had "No lies in it." With the solitude of a Country singer, I drifted, at times teaming up with William in a duet of meanness, backed up by the five known hoods in the school. I wore a peace button with tiny engines on the wings of the symbol transforming it into a B-52 and with "Drop it" stenciled below that. Up close, I was the Midnight Rambler; at a distance, I was a liberal like most of my schoolmates.

Two Point Alley became Four Buck Alley as I began procuring liquor for anyone willing to pay me four dollars above cost. On Friday evenings William and I would borrow his father's Triumph Tiger, zip over to East Paly and meet Linc the Wino, and return by nine to the school parking lot, where we distributed the ordered liquor.

"The name Hummingbird protects me," I said to Allison.

She tried to sound dark and foreboding. "Next you'll be into drugs," she said. "You will ruin your life, Albert."

Fuck you, I thought, saying, "It's my life."

The first time I approached Linc, he was hanging out with a small group of men, young and old, on the corner, sharing a bottle of Ripple. "Hey," he said, as the rest of them looked dark and forbidding, "you lost?" I was a little frightened, but I told him no, I wanted to do some business. The look on his face made me add that I wasn't a cop.

"A cop? You hear that?" he said to the group. "*He* ain't a cop." They all laughed. "Shit, you're barely old enough to be a white boy. So what you doing round here?" He held his hand up to stop me from answering. "I'll tell you. You want some a this." He raised the bottle of Ripple.

I nodded, gaining courage. "My name's Hummingbird. Alley Hummingbird. I'm Indian."

He stepped closer to me and looked at my face. He made and remade a decision several times. "Nah," he said. Then, "Okay. So what? You expect that do you any good? Hummingbird. Hummingbird?" He paused, thinking. "Alley?" I nodded. It was up to him, now. There was no use giving him too many words to think about.

"Okay. So you're Indian. Name like that, you ain't Jewish. Still, you listen. I go in there," he gestured at the liquor store in the middle of the block, "buy you some of this and get caught, it's again' the law."

"Against the law, whether you get caught or not," I said.

"You ain't listenin'. What I'm telling you is you got to make it worth my while, and it make no difference what your name is, Alleybird."

"I'll make it worth your while," I said.

"Nah," he said, starting to leave me there, alone. "It ain't worth less'n two bucks a bottle. I got expenses, boy. Overhead." He held up the Ripple.

"Wait," I said. "I'll give you ten bucks for the trip in and out." He was interested. "I need eight bottles."

"Eight?"

"I've got people waiting for them."

"Minors?" I nodded. "That's ill-legal, boy." He shook his head from side to side slowly, as if his neck was stiff. "Money up front?" I agreed. "Okay."

I counted out the money. "You can take off with this, I know." He acted offended. "If you do, it's my ass with my customers. If you don't, you make ten bucks this week. Next week, maybe more."

Linc stood there in the dim light, squinting at me. "You know, Alleybird," he said, finally. "You're smart."

"I learn fast," I said.

I stood beside the unlocked trunk to William's car and watched him inside the store. I could tell from the hesitant way he moved, the way he wanted to look around to see if I was watching, that his every instinct made him want to run out the back door. Take a sure thing, and not a promise from some boy he called Alleybird. But greed functions as effectively with a wino as with a rich man, and even Linc could add up what two or three weeks of this would mean. Maybe not in dollars, but in bottles of Ripple, for sure—if, after a week or two, Linc hadn't moved up to something a little more palatable like muscatel or Thunderbird.

I came to like making those trips over into East Palo Alto on Friday and, as volume increased, Saturday nights. William began to worry more about getting caught; I began to look forward to the day I'd be old enough to get my own car.

"So we get caught," I said. "Worst they'll do is pour the booze out. Maybe take us down to the station and book us. They can't hold us. We're too young."

"We'll have a record," William said. "What'll our parents say?"

"Look," I said, slightly bored by William's fear, "the trick is not to get caught. If we do, records can be sealed."

"My father is a lawyer," William protested.

"We can keep it in the family," I said.

I should have known, as I heard William try to ask indirect questions of his father about sealing police records, or as I heard him stumble over the reasons he needed the car, that I'd be left holding the ball. But with the enjoyment I took in hanging out in East Paly, I ignored the future. Sometimes, I'd send William back with the liquor and hang out with Linc. I learned to shoot pool. I learned why a young man without a job and without the hope of an income might buy an expensive pool cue, and it was a reason similar to why a Chicano will spend thousands of dollars on chrome and fur for his car before he'll pay the rent. Money was fun to have and fun to spend, and more importantly, money could always be gotten: It was hope that was priceless, fear expensive, and despair that was free.

Linc never liked William the Black. "He's black as day," Linc said. "What color's his old lady?" When I pretended not to hear him, he added, "Betcha she's as light as scotch."

"What's wrong with that?" I replied, angrily. "What does it matter?"

Linc laughed. "Let me tell you, Alleybird, my friend. You can't be both in this here world. If you're black, you're black. If you're red, you're red. Try to be black and white or red and white, you come out lookin' like dirty laundry."

I knew he was right the night cops pulled into a parking space beside William's car. Without waiting, William started the car and drove legally away, and I was left holding the metaphorical ball.

"Ah, shit," Linc said as he set the case of liquor on the sidewalk. The cops were already out of their car, tucking their night sticks into their holders on their belts. "Sorry, Alleybird." He meant it.

"I am, too," I said, watching the taillights of William's car signal left and disappear.

"Why don't you take off. Lose 'em around the corner. Cut through the lot . . ."

"I'll stay."

"Hell, boy, don't worry about me. Not much they can do to me. You, t'other hand . . . ," but it was already too late.

Cops have a hard job. Full of questions like Dr. Bene, they rarely get the right answers.

"Come on, boy, what's your real name," the red-haired cop kept asking, with the suspicion of a nearsighted man used to dealing with delinquents. I watched him pace back and forth, clenching and unclenching his fists and fingering his night stick. "They should never have allowed your kind off the reservation," he said.

"We should've made stricter immigration laws," I replied, calling him Joe Friday because he was stiff and stubby, leaning slightly forward beneath the cause and effect of his simplified morality.

"My name's not Friday," he hissed. "Cut it."

"Does it matter?" I asked, allowing my face to relax and, with a narrowing of my eyes and lowering of my eyebrows, to suggest a grin.

"Leave the kid alone, Randy," Officer Lindel said.

Answering Lindel's questions, I tried to make Joe Friday dissolve. Whether it was the fluorescent interference from the buzzing lights encasing me and bleaching the room white, or the fact that I wanted to repay Lindel by paying attention, I couldn't.

Lindel telephoned my house and talked to mother, and I watched his face change from politeness to amusement to utter confusion. When he hung up, he looked at me with understanding and sympathy.

"What did she say?" I asked.

"Are you sure you gave me the right number?" I nodded. "Let me try again. That was 968–4123, right?" He dialed and again spoke to mother.

"So? What'd she say?" I asked again.

"She said 'Catsup. Ketchup.' The first time, she asked if I knew it could be spelled both ways, and pointed out that tests performed by an independent agency proved no preference for either spelling. The second time, it was like she knew she was speaking to me again. She said that it didn't matter because both have rat hair in them."

"That was mother," I said. "She's into market research, these days."

"Is she . . ."

"Crazy?" I knew he wouldn't say the word out of some notion of kindness or tact. "Not really. Confused, sometimes, but aren't we all, at times?" He shrugged. "She'll move on to something else as soon as she figures out *why* soft toilet paper is so important to women." He started to laugh. "No," I said, "it's not funny, really. You see, it's not that we all prefer soft toilet paper over newspaper; it's why the commercial claims it is important to women and not men."

"I'll take you home," he said.

On the way, he told me that the ball was in my court, that not much would come from this misdemeanor, and that I could have my record sealed. That way on job applications, I wouldn't have to say that I'd ever been arrested. As for Linc, he would spend a month in the city jail, drying out and putting on weight, which he liked to do every so often anyway.

When I said, "See you," he said, "I hope not soon." I had no idea how soon it would be.

Years later, as I stood before the judge with my lawyer, having my record sealed for the second time, having been arrested and booked an average of three times a year, I decided that I would never again allow someone else to have the kind of power over me that could leave me holding the ball. It was a decision that resembled Laura P.'s determination not to let Louis Applegate near her painted pots or kachinas; though until I'd made the decision, I'd believed that Laura P.'s determination involved a strange and unbelievable mysticism to which Buddhists, Indians, hippies, and Californians seemed prone.

## 22.

Conversations with Allison DeForest tended to repeat themselves, the only differences being time and detail and ending with whether we were or were not a couple. A boy can feign interest in these conversations only so many times and, regardless of how many that is, Allison had surpassed my limit long ago. Grandfather had taught me that Indian time was a timeless present that contained both past and future. Allison's time was an untimely present that discarded both past and future according to the needs of fashion. This time, fashion required us to uncouple and see other people, because I, as Mrs. DeForest so carefully explained to Allison, was a bad influence.

Over the past year, Allison had sometimes suggested that

perhaps she and I ought to see other people, while we continued our affair. I had finally come to realize that "seeing other people," like "I'm not a whore," was a phrase invented for the convenience of Allison and women like Allison. For Allison, love was power, and she enjoyed the power of making a man want her, instinctively recognizing that what he might want would be her body and not her mind. Some nights, William and I would hide in the bushes in front of Allison's house and eavesdrop on her tussling with her date in his parked car, listening to the strains of her stock phrases frustrate him as much as they had me. It made me feel better when Allison grew weary and asked, "Just what *do* you want?"

If Allison was a test of one's patience, as well as the challenge, then Mrs. DeForest was a proctor for all of the struggles of life. I came to see that Mrs. DeForest assumed Allison was a whore, and that it was her mother's disease that Allison had, a disease not uncommonly found in women like her. Mrs. DeForest would send Allison off for a snack of milk and cookies and sit me down on the patio for a "little chat," lugubrious affairs of questions and answers in which the questions didn't ask what they were meant to and the answers were assumed.

"What plans do you have," Mrs. D. would ask me, crossing her legs to reveal a calculated amount of thigh, "after college?" I had trouble seeing her eyes in the glare.

"What are your plans for the future," she'd say, without a question mark in the inquisition of her tone.

"Where is your colored friend today?" or "Where is William this afternoon?" she'd say, grinning slyly, as though I'd misplaced William like a coin purse.

Sometimes, her tone became sensuous and the chats were implicitly sexual, and through Mrs. DeForest, I began to learn the technique of the inquisitor who examines you as though you are already guilty, keeping you off base with shady eyes and the tonal implication that she knows much more about an affair than you would want her to know.

"Allison and I are very close, you know," Mrs. D. would begin. She'd pause, staring at me knowingly and allowing the suspense to build. "She's very young, you understand. At her age, it's not good to be tied down to just one person. I'm sure you'd agree that you're both too young to become, well, *very* serious."

Some nights, as I dropped Allison at home, stopping in for a Coke or coffee, Mrs. DeForest would send Allison to bed, offer me a baby beer, and time me as I drank it, asking if we'd had fun on our date. I went so far as to imagine that Allison and her mother were in league together, that they had arranged for Allison to warm me up and Mrs. D. to finish me off.

"I'm confused," I told William the Black. "I don't know if Mrs. DeForest wants to fuck me, or only to keep me from fucking Allison."

"I'll let you know," William said.

The inquisitory sessions dragged on and I began to fear, then hate them. I wondered vehemently why Allison was so cooperative about leaving me alone with her mother, and I began to experiment with answers to her questions.

"Rich man, poor man, beggar man, thief," I told Mrs. DeForest, admiring her thigh, "after college."

When she asked where William was, I discovered that saying "He's probably at the library" was not only sufficient but thoroughly acceptable.

"Really," Mrs. DeForest would say, her eyes shining with her own private dreams and visions.

"I'm very close with my whole family," I'd reply, staring back at her the way she stared at me. "Especially to my father. He agrees that Allison is too young." I would let this sink in and then add, "After all, she is only a year older than I am."

At times, I would simply say, "Yes," uncertain of what I was saying yes to, and eventually not caring.

What with the notoriety I'd acquired by procuring liquor for my schoolmates, not to mention the money I made and spent with abandon, Allison's friends were all too willing to go out with me. Their mothers and fathers were pushovers. Without waiting to be asked what I wanted to be, depending on their occupations, which were easily discerned from the literature on bookshelves and coffee tables, I'd tell them, "Doctor," or "Lawyer," or "Indian Chief."

Some days, I'd have two dates, taking one girl to the coral

cove near Half Moon Bay, where we'd roll around in the fog, and taking another to the movies or a dance that night. Always, as the frustrations that Allison so enjoyed creating were satisfied, the parents approved. I could hear them thinking aloud, "What a nice young man." Even though I was hardly what they would have called a nice young man, had they known, I'd fooled them. "Thank you Mrs. DeForest," I'd think. "Without you and your silly chats, when asked what I wanted out of life, I wouldn't have had an inkling of the answers. Not a farthing."

As for all of the times I listened to Allison say that she would rather we be friends, they were enough to teach me how to use the same phrase as an escape from a situation I'd become dissatisfied with, saying to a girl that "it might be better if we were friends" and not lovers. Women understood what I was about to say even before I finished. I found I could say, "It might be better if . . . ," and let them finish the sentence. Very few interesting variations occurred; always the variation was one I could say yes to.

"It might be better if . . . ," I'd say.

"We stopped seeing each other?" she'd say. "We were friends?" she'd say. "We saw other people?" "You cut your dick off?" she'd say.

Even to the last one, I've said yes, saying it with penitential regret, as if to underscore the seriousness with which I accepted responsibility for the mistake of indulging our physical passions. It was best, when that occurred, to underscore the underscoring by adding, "Listen, I . . . ," and then sink into pained speechlessness.

But all that came later. A knowledge gained only after I decided not to use it, not so much because it is cruel as because it is simply not fun. Still, for the beginnings of that knowledge, for teaching me that women know these tricks as well as men, for being the cause which allowed me to learn that satisfying my physical lusts was easy and therefore not as important as it might have seemed otherwise, for frustrating me until I dated most of her friends with a vengeance, respecting the ones who either refused to sleep with me or even to go out with me because they were *her* friends—perhaps, for these things, as well as the skill of experimenting with answers to authoritarian questions, I owe something to Allison DeForest (the little bitch). Perhaps I ought to say, 'Thank you, Allison.'

Maybe I will try.

## 23.

Father was unfooled by the answers I experimented with. At first, he picked on the way I dressed. "You'd think we were poor, the way you go around looking like a gypsy."

"It's an image," I'd say. "In a world of images." He was unmoved. "Besides, this jacket cost thirty bucks."

I knew I'd made a mistake when he stood up from washing the car and told me I had no business spending that on a jacket. Father wasn't cheap but he was frugal, having bought the notion that one earned money the hard way. It was a difference between father and me. Grandfather had said that the nature of gold was its color.

"So what's all the fuss about it?" I'd asked.

"Some people are colorblind," Grandfather had said. "They mistake gold's weight with its nature. They like to heft it around like mules." Grandfather had always tried to unload the gold, knowing that money was the easiest thing to obtain—much easier than love or a happy death.

"Where," father said, bending over the hood of the car and scrubbing the bird-doo from it, "did you get that much money to spend on a jacket?"

"Would you believe playing poker?" I asked, experimentally.

He stood again, and looked the way Mrs. DeForest might look at me, except father's eyes lacked the bleakness of her curiosity. He knew, and didn't know. Rather, he knew that I wasn't going to tell him the truth as well as that I'd gotten the money in a way he wouldn't approve of, and he was going to let me off the hook by not insisting.

"You've not spent much time around the house, lately," he said.

I shrugged as if to say that being busy in the day-to-day muck of life, I had no choice but to be out and around.

"I think you'd better start. And you can start with this."
He tossed me the washing sponge. "Earn a buck honestly."
Father was formidable. There was no arguing with him.
When I tried, he told me that after I finished that car, I
could do the other one. "And then," he added for effect,
"mow the lawn."

I did. I didn't mind too much, that day, because I was grateful for being let off the hook. Nonetheless, father tried to
make a habit of it. A sinlessly early riser, he banged on my
bedroom door at seven a.m. every Saturday and told me to
come on out and help wash the cars or mow the lawn or
spray malathion on the roses. Out of simple self-defense, I
took up residency in the one room in the house that had a
lock on the door, the bathroom. No matter how tired I was,
on Saturday mornings I would rise before father and sneak
into the bathroom and hide behind the locked door. As bath-
rooms are really very uninteresting places—unless they're
someone else's bathroom—I began to install a continuous
and rotating supply of reading material. Eventually, my habi-
tude of the bathroom would become so refined that there
were not only books and magazines spread conveniently
around the toilet, but blank books and pens as well, and
I'd deduct that portion of the rent which represented the
bathroom from my taxes.

About the time that father had told me that I'd better start
taking a part in the family, mother fell in love with the word
"boom." Evidently, mother had learned to appreciate the
power of Boom through her intricate preparations to torture
dinner on her gas range. She especially liked to light the
oven. She would crank the gas full on and stand holding a
lit match until we could all smell the corn odor of leaking
natural gas, then lean down and toss the match at the pilot
light hole in the oven.

"Boom!" she'd shout as the flames licked out of the oven's
seams and the gas ignited.

I'd come in from school, minding my own business, digging through the fridge for an apple that had few enough
rotten spots to make it worth cutting them out, and mother
would sneak into the kitchen as I was bent over the chiller

drawer sorting the apples from the other rotten fruit and shout, "Boom!"

I still have a shelf-like dent in the back of my head where I smashed upwards against another shelf the first twenty times mother did this. Mother was definitely falling over the side of her own mountain. We, children and husband, ignored it as best we could. We didn't know quite what to do except decide that madness was relative. We pretended that mother's saying "Boom" to father's business dinner guests was a private joke of the family's, and went on eating the food my sister and I had cooked without explaining to father why the food, though plain, was suddenly edible.

Mother noticed William the Black one afternoon when we came in from shooting baskets in the driveway. She was lighting the oven. Just as she said "Boom!" the temperature control knob blew off the oven and a jet of flame struck across the kitchen, singeing the cupboards. William grabbed a dishrag, wet it, and tried to cover the jet of flame. Fortunately, from my experience with mechanical objects, I knew valves, and while William's hand began to burn from the heat, I found a pair of pliers and shut off the valve behind the stove.

Mother was disappointed. Pulling herself together, she looked at me and inquired, "Who is your little brown friend? One of the Gold Dust Twins?"

"Your mother," William the Black said, "is definitely unique." We walked over the Stanford campus to look for girls. I wondered, how strange was mother? The few times I'd been invited into William's home, I had heard his mother say to his father, "The glass feels like it needs fluffing," meaning her gin glass, which she wanted refilled. True, it wasn't quite the same as mother's joyous exclamations to the oven or her quiet conversations with the new toaster. Nonetheless, William's mother did seem confused over the distinctions between real and human.

I know now that Boom, like her soliloquies or her hand signals to drivers with their blinkers on, was neither premonition nor madness but defense, her own Maginot Line against the loud and aggressive men father brought home from the offices he worked in. Mother could not tolerate the raising of voices. It made her shake uncontrollably. If anyone raised his voice—even in passionate defense of an idea and not in anger—she might lean over to the coffee table as she poured out for the guests and say, "There is no actual reason to shout, is there?"

Her speeches to the coffee table were always more formal than the plain speech she used chatting with the garbage dispose-all. We the children knew that. Father's guests didn't, and so they would stare at the painting over the sofa or out the glass door to the patio until their eyes watered. Whether these businessmen had wives of their own who talked to things, I never knew. However, I was fairly certain that beneath mother's monologues was the slightest hint of unhappiness. The merest frisson, the quietest rustling of the audience of her feelings during the drama of love and marriage.

"Love," Grandfather would say, sadly, "is like modern medicine. The treatments are for the disease, and not the individual."

## 24.

In his anguish after my cousin and I had shot down his six friends five times over, uncle turned to model trains, creating an entire world in his study.

He spent hours and years bending the copper track and hand-setting it with tiny little spikes. Only the spikes were not to scale. The railroad had yards on both ends with little cast iron engines that moved freight cars around, composing trains that would then be hooked up to the necessary number of engines and hauled realistically around the room, through papier-mâché mountains and across the high spider webs of trestles he had made from strips of balsa wood. On Thanksgivings and Christmases, he would lead any of the children, enlargements of their former selves, into the locked study and explain the workings of the Pillar to Post Railway Company.

It was a miracle of miniaturization. Little people did little things in little towns, driving an eclectic set of trucks and cars, or perched on Sears and Roebuck ladders, painting their frame houses with paint from teeny cans that said "Glidden." Lights went on and off in houses as day turned to night and back to day again. Trains stopped on sidings while the Daylight Express whizzed people to their destinations, and Negroes with white gloves could be glimpsed serving food or drinks in the sleeping cars. Uncle liked to point out the Negroes because Negroes, he said, had locked up the Pullman Car Porter's Union, a case of an oppressed people staking out a market of their own and protecting it with smiles. Uncle's eyes, which were usually a dull brown, glowed black and beady when he told us that. Privileged as I felt, privy to the workings of railroads which were slowly declining with the advent of turbo-prop planes and later jet engines, I almost could have liked uncle, were it not for the engineers of those trains. Each of them, leaning out of the cabs of their engines, looked awfully like the pilots who had once flown balsa wood planes.

I have often wondered if my cousin didn't bear some hidden grudge against those six men who had given him a carrot for a father. We had been young when we shot down those pilots and thus excusable for the pain uncle must have suffered when he saw the splinters of all those years. There seems no excuse for what my cousin at sixteen did to the people of Pillar to Post.

My cousin, however, had only his love of frogs and a revolutionary vision focused by the rock salt of the National Guard, tempered by his arrest and conviction for wearing a shirt made from the Stars and Stripes. Three years before he dropped out of college and went underground with the Weathermen, he practiced his skills on my uncle's railroad. It took time, and it must have taken a careful mind. Not only did the passenger train explode beside a fuel depot he had filled with alcohol, causing the entire little town of Pillar to incinerate, frying the little people as they tried to stop doing their little things and flee; at the same time, the biggest and most beautiful trestle blew, just as a freight train raced over it.

The only time my uncle's wife sailed down the San Francisco Bay to visit us, she laughed about the destruction of Pillar and said, "A real test." She laughed like tinfoil, her lips unpursing enough to let out a hiss that sounded like the nozzle of an air hose, as she sat on the deck of the yacht that uncle had bought to replace the Beechcraft he had crashed.

She was dressed in a white pant suit, starched until it was as noisy as her hatred for my uncle's family.

She must have felt, sitting among us aboard uncle's yacht, that the veterans' hospital where she'd met and married uncle was a Holiday Inn.

Father thumped his knee like a Bible and declaimed the ills of the world which were changing, the richer father became.

Mother could be heard below decks, whispering, "Fudge happiness!" at the short-wave radio.

Pamela sat on the bow, basking in the bravado of the boy I knew she would marry.

Elanna tried to converse with the athlete she had brought down from college for the weekend, a manchild who had to vacuum his hairy chest weekly and who, rather than talk to her, was given to slugging me on the shoulder in manly, locker room fashion, and saying, "Hey Alley. What's doin'?"

Every now and then my uncle's wife would slowly turn her head and fix her eyes on me where I sat apart, holding my arm, watching everyone else and watching her especially because I believed she could bite and that if she did, she would never let go.

It turned out that uncle's wife preferred not to bite people. What she bit were deeds—to the boat, the house, car, life insurance, pensions, anything that she could point to when uncle tried to leave her and say, "Go ahead." In uncle's one fling at happiness since the day he mailed his friends to their Japanese deaths, he would divorce her to live with a woman everyone in the family seemed to like, a Jewess named Karen who actually replied if you spoke to her.

Even before my cousin had demolished the tiny town of Pillar, leaving Post high and dry, disconnected from the railroad line, a city with a future made over into a city without a past, the peristaltic contractions and expansions of the world were causing me more than confusion and ulcers. The town of Post withered. The young people who had driven hotrods grew sedate and began driving Buicks or economy cars that whined noisily about Post, their windshield visors falling into the laps of their passengers, their mufflers rattling against gas tanks when they turned the corner. A boom town gone bust, able to survive only on the perpetual motion of its few remaining citizens buying from and selling to each other. At night, I dreamed of Post, cobwebbed and rotting, as my aunt hid the keys to the bolt locks she'd installed on the study. Sometimes I dreamed of myself living in Post all night long, undisturbed until the mornings when mother, dressed in slacks and rouged for the day, would sneak into my bedroom and cover my mouth with her hand and then pinch my nostrils shut, catapulting me into another wonderful day of school.

I loved the quiet solitude of the repeated trips to the principal's or dean's office. When the teachers tired of that punishment, I learned to love accepting their invitation to pick up my desk and carry it outside, where I would sit, watching the alternately blue and gray sky for private planes flown by pilots who sang, or looking forward to the next vacation when I could flee Palo Alto for Chosposi—where my slogging intellect didn't seem as slow as it did in contrast to my all-too-intelligent classmates. William the Black excelled, lettering in basketball, track, English, History, and Calculus. Imitating him, I did well in art and study hall. In art, I made delicate-looking pots that couldn't be knocked over by a high wind from Jamaica. In study hall, I planned ways to organize students, pencils, anything capable of being organized for any purpose, and I became so good at it that I managed to beat the captain of the football team in the election for class president simply by organizing to vote for me all of the girls who were too unpopular to date the captain, along with the hoods and wimps who made team coaches morally angry or thoughtlessly amused.

I didn't realize that I would always excel at organization. Now, aware of the way I cannot help but align cereal boxes on the breakfast table, or the compulsion I have to make all of the washed dishes fit neatly into the drainer, I wonder if that baby Grandfather saw clenching its fists in an oxygen tent wasn't born with a genetic need to reorder the way things happened in a way he could understand. When Grandfather had told Laura P., "The boy has it and won't let go," had he meant hope, love, life, or an ability to re-dream dreams to suit himself?

# CHAPTER SIX

## 25.

William the Black agreed to be my running mate for the class presidency. I figured he balanced the ticket. Allison began dating the captain of the football team, who ran against us. I didn't particularly want a girlfriend. If I was going to organize the less popular girls, I needed to be free to flirt with each and all, making William's and my ticket into a lottery in which any one of them could buy a touch of hope for a date to the next dance for the price of a vote. Nonetheless, a boy without a girl clamped to his coattails was suspect and so I decided to replace Allison with one of the less popular girls. I began dating Yvette.

Yvette was an iffy person. That is, the boys in the locker rooms liked to say, "Yvette would be fun, *if* she didn't take Vietnam so seriously." "Yvette wouldn't be bad-looking, *if* she were cured of smallpox." It was true: Yvette's complexion would have been described in contemporary cosmetological terms as a "problem" complexion. On the other hand, if she weren't talking about Vietnam, she was capable of being witty, and if we went to a party, she was capable of outdrinking me and most of the others, without her face twisting into that exaggerated loudness so many people adopt when they're drunk. She liked the way I grew quieter, the more I drank. Without throwing her body at me or making me enter an interminably boring wrestling match, she suggested we borrow one of the beds at the second party we attended—and she laughed unself-consciously at the clumsy way I sneaked the ruined satin sheets out of the house. She listened when I explained to her about Grandfather and my sisters, my uncle, or mother's terse, coded response to her world.

"Your sisters," Yvette said, "sound like women I might like."

"What about Grandfather?" I said.

"Of course I'd like him," Yvette said. "Would I have a choice?"

As for Allison, we agreed there, too, except that I found the tearful fluctuations in Allison's need to see or not see me bitter. Yvette found them amusing.

One night, double-dating at a drive-in, I had to wait for William in the bathroom. "I can't pee with all these Puerto Ricans around," William whispered.

Exiting into the lobby, I was about to say, "You know, Yvette would be great, if . . . ," when I ran headlong into Allison. We had a conversation. How pleasant the night was, the weather, next week's football game, how the campaign was going.

"I've got to go," I said. William smirked at me from the snack bar line.

"I've got to see you," Allison said. "Please?"

I had planned on seeing Allison without mentioning it to Yvette, but William the Black let the winds out of the bag.

"If," Yvette said, "I need to be jealous, then you are not who I think you are. Go ahead, see her. But do me the favor of telling me the results? *In* person," she added.

As I sat in the car parked in front of Allison's house, I realized that there were pleasures greater than a girl's complexion, such as being able to talk to her. When Allison tucked her head into my shoulder and hissed, "Put your hand in my pants," I heard my mother saying the same thing to father as far away as the City of Angels on a night that was as quiet as the twenty-five years of absence between then and now.

Horrified, saddened, pained, confused, and amused, I said, "No, thank you."

Allison pretended to weep.

I will always remember and always be glad that I drove that night to Yvette's house without waiting until the next day to say what I said, which was, "Thank you." Glad, because on the windy, hilly road home from Yvette's, I passed my old familiar, Death, going the other way in His white Corvair, a flag-draped coffin lashed over the splayed rear wheels.

"You might have run Him off the road," Grandfather said.

I doubted that it would have done any good, since Death had become little more than a delivery boy in those years, bringing home sons and brothers from an undeclared war that seemed to cut the insides out of everything from William the Black's projected income to Yvette's problematic smile.

"It was the wrong blood," Elanna said.

"The wrong ground," I replied.

"The wrong monster," Grandfather said.

For us, maybe. For Yvette, it was the only monster, and she threw herself into anti-war activities with the wounded fervor of someone who suddenly discovers her own existence drawn into question. Her brother had arrived home with a terminal case of the red, white, and blues. I threw out the button with the peace-symbol B-52 and the words "Drop It." After all, as Grandfather said, "Death is never funny."

Nonetheless, He can do funny things to people.

After Yvette had been back at school for a day or two, I found her sitting on the redwood platforms in the central quad. Groups of students seemed to expand and contract around her so that, though she was in the middle of a crowd, she looked as lonely as a cactus flower in December. No one knew what to say to her, and it was with this contagious hopelessness for saying the right thing to her that I sauntered over and sat beside her.

"Listen," I said. "Yvette?" Her head turned slowly towards me, as though it revolved on an axle of its own invention. She looked at my lapel.

"Where's the 'Drop It' button?" she demanded.

"I threw it out. I didn't think it was funny, anymore, considering . . ."

"Don't stop wearing it for my sake," she said.

"Listen. I'm sorry about . . ."

"I'll bet you are," she said.

"I am, Yvette. Truly sorry for your loss. For your brother's passing away." I felt awkward, stupid. It seemed that I might apologize honestly for not having run Death off the road that night as I left her house. But this. It came out flat and insincere.

"Words," she said. "Just words. Everyone says them, but no

one means them. Charlie didn't pass away. He was killed."
She laughed the way mother laughed at short-wave radios
and mirrors. "Do you want to know how he was killed?"

I didn't, but I said, "If you want to tell me."

Yvette stared at me. "He was assigned to an aircraft carrier.
I remember how happy we were because at least he wasn't a
pilot. He was relatively safe. Hah!" Her voice wasn't flat, it
was tempered. And cold. Her complexion's usual redness had
become blood red. "What fools we all are."

"How, then . . . ?"

"Bringing in a fighter, the plane slipped the sky hook, and
the cable whipped backward. Cut Charlie in half." She was
still staring at me, and I moved out of the line of the vision
she was seeing, sitting beside her. "Charlie," she whispered.
"That's what they call the enemy, Charlie. Tough to tell just
who the enemy really is, isn't it?"

Was it from panic, afraid that the way she was staring at
me would make me disappear, or was it from some inane
acceptance of the idea that people who have just lost their
brothers needed to be distracted, that I asked her if she
might want to go to the dance with me that coming Friday?
Maybe if I had sat there, silent, listening to her silence and
grief, she wouldn't have jumped away as though I'd struck
her and cried, "Leave me alone!" Perhaps I should not have
acquiesced so readily.

It seemed unfair. It was as though no matter what I said
or did, she would feel that it was the wrong thing. Her grief
made her need someone to feel it with her and her intelligence hinted that no one was able to feel it the way she did.
That's the trouble with old Mr. Grief: He comes knocking,
punches you out, and then closes a glass door between you
and everyone else; you can see them out there, a little mis-
shapen from the dirt and grime on the glass, and when they
speak to you all you hear are muffled sounds, inarticulate,
insensitive. Only someone who has had a similar grief can
press his nose up to the glass and speak loudly enough for
you to hear him—even to laugh, in your sadness, at the funny
way he looks with his concerned nose pressed against the
glass.

Yvette took to walking around school, alone, her hands

held out from her body, palms up as though in supplication, her lips moving in what could have been mistaken for talking to herself, the way mother did. Before long, I would understand, because of my own grief, how alone one feels, how one can resent someone's even trying to say he's sorry.

## 26.

I skipped that Friday night dance, and was up early Saturday morning. I washed both cars, enjoying myself as I hosed them down and then scrubbed them in sections which I rinsed before the soap could dry on the paint, the way father had taught me. It was mindless activity, and it felt good, made me happy partly for the activity itself, and partly because I knew how pleased father would be.

I was finishing buffing the wax off the second car when father came outside. "You've got a phone call," he said.

"All that needs doing is vacuuming them out," I said as I shook the dried wax from the towel. "Should I toss these towels in the washer?"

"No. Just hang them up," he said.

"Okay." I hung them from the open garage door, the way father liked. "Be back in a minute."

The phone call was from Allison, wanting to know why I hadn't been at the dance the night before. "I'd kind of hoped to see you there," she said.

"Well," I said, resisting the impulse to ask her what had gone wrong with the football captain. I knew what was going wrong between them. I was class president, and the football team had lost its last two games ignominiously.

"William was there," she said. I said I was glad he was there, as he'd planned the dance. "He came by here with some other people, afterwards."

"That's nice," I said. "Listen, Allison, it's nice talking to you, but I've got to go, okay?"

She laughed as though the two of us shared a secret. "Yvette showed up with some long-haired type. From *Stanford*. Boy was he creepy."

"I'm glad," I said as evenly as possible. "I'm happy that

Yvette decided to get out and around, and have some fun. She needs some good times. Is that what you called to tell me?"

"No," Allison said. "I assumed you *knew* that. No, I called because my father's out of town, and my mother's going out with some friends tonight. I wondered if you might want to come over and play some records. I've got some new ones. The Monkeys . . ."

"I hate the Monkeys."

"I bought the new Rolling Stones album."

"I don't think so," I said. "I'm sorry."

"What are you going to do, then?"

"I don't know. Go out with William."

"When was the last time you talked to him? He just called and asked me if you were over here. I think you're fibbing. You're making up excuses . . ."

"Maybe I am. So what?" It seemed odd that William the Black would have phoned Allison's house before he phoned mine.

"Please?" Allison said.

"Okay, I'll think about it. I'll call you this evening."

"Promise? Do you promise you won't just forget about calling me, like you did last time?"

"Okay, okay. I promise."

Perturbed, when I hung up I stalked past mother in the living room, where she stood beside the fireplace with her eyes closed, alternately singing and blowing into an attachment to the vacuum, as if she were clearing or testing a microphone. There was no sign of the vacuum itself. On the way to the bathroom to bathe my sweaty face, I spotted Pamela dashing from the bathroom in her bright orange underwear to her closet, where she would spend the day reviewing her butterfly collection by flashlight, as if in the collection were the answer to a question I, being male, could never understand. After rinsing my face and eyes, I returned to father. He was applying a coat of wax to the first car.

"What are you doing?" I asked.

"You missed some spots. See?" he said, kneeling to look across the surface of the paint. "Here." He put his finger on it to mark the spot, and then he applied more wax. "And here," he said.

"I meant to do a good job," I said.

"What?" father said.

"Nothing."

"Why don't you plug in the vacuum and vacuum out the insides of this car, while I check the other?" father said.

I picked up the end of the cord and plugged it into the socket.

Late that same afternoon, after I had mowed both lawns, front and back, trimmed them with the trimmer, and bagged the clippings, leaving them on the curb for the garbage collectors, I was shooting some baskets, concentrating on driving, twisting and turning along the baseline, laying the ball up softly on the reverse side of the hoop. When I grew tired, I paused to shoot free throws, a hundred at a time, trying to think only of what Coach Roach had said, "Free throws can mean the difference between winning and losing."

William the Black dropped by. "Forty-seven," he said. "Not bad. Not bad, at all." He waved at the head of the driveway. "I was counting."

Here," he said, stepping up to the line and holding his hands out. I passed him the ball. He bounced it ten times, slowly, concentrating, then raised it on the crane of his arms, and shot. It swished through the net. I caught it, and passed it back to him.

"What's wrong?" he asked, dribbling another ten times. I stared blankly out at the vacant horizons of suburbia.

William missed. I rebounded the ball and dribbled out past the head of the key, and then started back in towards him, circling, turning, and hooking the ball up with my left hand.

William batted the ball away, blocking the shot. "So," he said, dribbling out towards the end of the driveway. "Where were you, last night?"

"Home," I said, watching the houses beyond our split-rail fence shimmer and turn pink, and brown, and purple. They looked, for a moment, like little castles built on the quicksands of whim. I felt dizzy.

"Should of been there," William said. "I'll tell you, it was something. Place was packed out. Everyone was there. Allison brought along her little boyfriend." He made a jump shot from about fifteen feet out; I returned the ball.

"I heard Yvette showed up with a new guy," I said.

"If you could call him that, yeah. She was there. The guy was some dip from those socialist meetings she goes to. Man, I'll tell you, he's one fellow you don't have to worry about. He was so covered in buttons and pins, he looked liked he was wearing armor plate. Maybe he was a friend. A cousin, maybe, or somebody she just feels sorry for. You sure as hell don't have to worry."

"I wasn't worried," I said. "Who'd you go with?"

"Nobody," he said, shooting again. He stopped and grinned, and even against his light skin, his mouth was all pink and white. "Boy, am I glad I didn't take some girl." I let the comment pass. William didn't. "I got laid," he said.

"Never been a weapon invented that wasn't used," I said.

"Not exactly a new invention," William said. "But I'll tell you, it sure can feel new sometimes."

"And afterwards," I said, "it always feels old."

"Hey, Alley," William said. "What's eating you?"

"Nothing. Skip it."

"I won't skip it. Something's chewing you up. Listen, if it's that Yvette was at the dance with somebody else last night. . . ."

"It isn't. I don't know what's eating me. I just don't feel right, don't feel like I'm myself. Forget it, okay?"

"Okay," he said. We shot around some more, and then he stopped again and said, "Don't you want to know who it was? You want to hear some details?" I shrugged. "Guess," he said.

"Betty?" He had been dating a girl named Betty off and on during the year, having met her on one of our forages into Stanford University. She was a freshman, and only recently had found out that William was still in high school.

"Nah. Come on. You can do better than that. Who's the last woman you'd think of? The last *woman*, mind."

"Outside of Yvette and my sisters, I don't know any women." I pretended to think a minute. "I give up," I said.

He tossed me the ball. "Hang onto it," he said. "You ready?" I nodded, feeling more bored than dizzy. "DeForest!" he said. He grinned broadly, and his teeth looked to me like two files of little white Indians, all in rows.

"Allison?" I said.

"No," he said, still grinning. "Mrs. DeForest!"

"Allison's *mother*?"

"It was just there," he said. "Like Baskin-Robbins. Like Mount Everest. I dropped by Allison's house after the dance. And things just went from this to that; Allison went to bed after everyone else left, and Mrs. DeForest stopped me at the door while I was putting on my jacket and asked me if I didn't want another little drinky. That's what she said, 'drinky,' and I figured, what the hell, a drinky can't hurt." He looked up and down the street, from house to house as if he were issuing a challenge. "Think of it!" he said. "A white woman. I've got a little datey with her again tonight. Well," he said, finally, "what do you think of that?"

I stood there, the basketball round and heavy in my hands, running a backward search on my dreams. The dream I wanted to find, the dream I wished for, the one predicting a man the color of William who would tell me that nigger was not a color but a state of mind, that prediction slipping to little more than the memory of a memory, painful in the way it seemed neither to add nor subtract anything from the pressing weight of the basketball.

Not many years later, William the Black would be drafted by the middle class. Statistically, he would go to Stanford University, where he would play center for the basketball team and learn to say, "The poor keep themselves poor. Buying Cadillacs. Color televisions. Brand new babies. It's their own fault." The sentiment resembled one that mother expressed. I could forgive mother, since by then to have her say anything to me, regardless of its logic or truth, would be gratifying.

"It's a wonder any of us lived," William would say, peering backwards in time as he stood outside his all-white fraternity house at Stanford, squinting hard, as though the time between had been decades and not years, as though he needed a jeweler's loop to see the flaws in our friendship.

"Yes," I would say, thinking of the nights William and I

had raced about the streets and alleyways of Stanford in our dangerous game of lose and catch. The game was chasing or being chased by another car piloted by friends, headlights off, through unlit streets. The pursued car got fifteen minutes to lose the chase car before the game switched, and the chaser became the chased. I never lost. I would skid into alleyways at any speed, missing parked cars that loomed up like ducks in a shooting gallery, making William the Black whistle through the gaps in his clenched teeth, leaving a trail of transmission oil and gear filings.

"Yes. It is a wonder," I'd say, hurt a little but laughing, too, inside. I made William nervous, afraid that I would ask him to invite me inside of his all-white fraternity. William was not considered to be Black by his brothers. He was, after all, the star of the basketball team. Perhaps all that jumping up and down had jarred the color out of him. Perhaps it was his pale-skinned girlfriend, or some philosophical astuteness on his fraternity brothers' part, that made them see that in principle William was Black, but not in practice.

After graduation from Stanford, William would take an offer from a legal firm in San Francisco instead of huge, short-lived sums from professional basketball teams. "I hate basketball," he'd say. "Ten niggers jumping into the air every ten seconds." William would choose to play for a legal firm; and he would play very well until he injured his knee jumping for a partner at an office party.

I saw all this the day William stood at the end of father's driveway, issuing his silent challenge to the barons of lawn mowers and duchesses of vacuums ensconced in the private plywood and mortar castles that lined Emerson Street.

"Well," he said, "I've gotta run. Give me a call tomorrow, eh?"

"Sure," I said, hearing the far-off cry of crows laughing, their fragile black heads nodded together over the beginning of the end of William's and my friendship.

## 27.

Grandfather maintained that everything was connected like dandelions. Although it was a notion that I sometimes resisted in defense against Californians with sad vegetarian faces, there was a connection between Mrs. DeForest's porking William and mother's talking to toasters or coming all dressed in black into the garage to sing "In the Great By and By" a capella for her dying Kenmore.

"You're drunk," Allison said, when she opened the door.

I smiled as best I could with one eye swollen shut. "I know," I said. "I've just killed mother's Hoover." Removing the filter bag, I had taken it outside and vacuumed up gravel that father had strewn around bushes and trees. Allison lacked any philosophical grounds for or against war, but the idea of me killing anything attracted her like the glint of light off a policeman's shield.

"What happened to your eye?" she said, touched by the badge of my courage.

"It put up a fight. Hoovers don't take a fall easily," I said. "And this one's under warranty."

"You're nuts," she said. "Come in."

"Mumsy home?"

"I promised you she'd be out," she said. Her voice had a generic seductiveness.

"What can I get you?" Allison asked.

"Mulberry leaves," I muttered. I didn't want to be there. I'd had to get drunk even to come.

"What?" Allison said.

"Scotch," I said, "will be fine. Or gin or vodka or wine or beer."

"Choosy," Allison said. "Aren't we?" She went to her father's liquor cabinet and found the bottles that could be topped up with water so her father wouldn't notice.

"Evidently not," I said.

I accepted and drank the drink Allison concocted out of shots from every available liquor in the house. Then Allison dragged me down a plain corridor of words to her bedroom, where she sat in a half-slip and flimsy pullover shirt on the bed, inviting me with gestures learned from kiddie porn to violate premises formerly occupied by the captain of the football team.

"Why don't you come over here?" she said, petting the bed, stroking the coverlet with the palm of her hand while running her tongue around the inside of her lips, poking it out briefly like a snake or an old, sleeping dog.

I stayed where I was.

"Please?" she said. "I promise, it'll be worth your while." She slowly drew her shirt over her head and sank back on the bed with calculated abandon. She looked like she was doing a late night television commercial for adjustable beds. I went to her, kissed her, following my hands with my lips and tongue around her body. Gently, she pushed the top of my head down until my chin rested between her thighs.

"Put your tongue in me," she said and I did.

"Deeper," she said. Had my tongue not been fastened relatively firmly in the back of my throat, I might have lost it.

Allison was silent. As silent as a priest in winter. Not a moan or sigh came from her lips, only stage directions in a play that might be titled "Six Girls in Search of an Orgasm." It was then that I began to know—not understand—love without abandon. Over the years, there would be a kind of girl whose idea of lovemaking resembled a traffic cop's, more pleased with the orderly ebb and flow of the vehicles than with the sloppy disorder of gridlock.

"What are you doing?" Allison asked, when I began to unzip my pants. At the moment, I knew what I was doing and, angered and frustrated as I was, I was determined to bring the play to its logical conclusion, replacing my fingers with the painful need of release.

Something stopped me. Possibly, it was the thought of mother, or the sound of William the Black dribbling up the driveway outside the house delivering Mrs. DeForest to her door before heading home to call me and crow. Maybe it was the telephone, calling Allison to the kitchen. By the time Allison returned, if she did return, I was dressed and out the window.

I took a good look around my neighborhood, looking for Death skulking in the corners of darkness unlit by street-lamps or kneeling behind bushes in ambush. Then I stood there in the night wondering if I hadn't been the one who was unwilling to accept the fact that Allison and I were through, she as dead to me because of Yvette as Yvette was to me because of her brother. I wondered how many children are conceived out of psychological necrophilia—people, unwilling to accept the death of their loves or likings, sleeping with one another with all the impassioned joy of a memorial service.

Death was so harried, during that time, that his lips developed an uncontrollable twitch, making him look comically inept as he raced from pillar to post, collecting bodies. He was forced to hire bleak and wasted little helpers and the times I saw him weave past me in his splay-wheeled Corvair, bringing home a broken but living body to the families of friends, I could hear him grumbling about how hard it was, those days, to find good hired help. Walter's father was added to the body count and a former track star from our school hopped home to Palo Alto minus a leg.

Mother left to attend another serial in the funerals of the women in her family. The only vacations mother ever took nowadays from her appliances were to attend funerals and memorial services. While her own mother had died from a weak heart, these other women seemed to be dropping over the edge of sadness. Having mortgaged their hopes and dreams with alcohol, they bloated like balloons and burst, scattering on the winds like asbestos dust. The last one had consumed herself in the ashes of a late and drunken cigarette, and I imagined mother staring into her coffin and whispering "Fudge happiness," while confirming herself a teetotaller in the recesses of her own fragmented mind.

Coming home from a weekend with Elanna, during which her roommate's boyfriend had gotten me so drunk on gin that I had spent the night practicing my own personal mode of free speech in the bathroom, I once again overheard uncle and father talking about divorce.

The phone rang and I had to leave without finding out whose divorce they were talking about. Allison was on the other end, weeping into the mouthpiece, telling me that she was pregnant and asking what I was going to do about it.

"Nothing," I said. Allison seemed to be confused over the propagative qualities of fingers and tongues. It had nothing to do with me. I killed the connection and left the phone off the hook, and hurried back outside. When Mrs. DeForest rang me back later that night, filling the telephone lines with implication and accusation, I asked Mrs. D. what she'd been doing at the Ramada Inn on such and such a night, in the company of strangers like William the Black.

One reason I resisted the notion that all things were connected like dandelions holding together the soil of our dreams against the implacable disruption of earthworms and Death was that I couldn't figure out how all these things related to each other.

"Life," I told Grandfather, "is like an erector set. Every time I take it apart and try to put it back together again, it's different. Every construct seems fake."

"Like vegetables," Grandfather said, trying to help me see that father's working over the technology of *Sunset Magazine* was not dissimilar to uncle's careful construction of model railroads or his careful destruction of airplanes and yachts. Uncle was extreme; denying the death of his six friends left him living on the cliff edges of an untenable reality. Father, on the other hand, might ignore death, but he never denied it; that let him live in the middle ground of his own equally untenable reality. Somehow, this explained why uncle might leave his wife, the Vegomatic, while father in his mind had never left mother. Of course, mother was what you might call difficult to leave, since her ship had sailed over the edge of her own reality years ago. Her only connection to the world that was digesting me was electrical, the blips in her brain random and disorganized like bits of telegraphical information lost in the distances they had to travel over the wires of her cortex.

On his middle ground, father assumed Elanna was the adventurous one of my sisters and failed therefore to keep a watchful eye on Pamela. But Elanna was too much like mother must have been and was more interested in wider horizons which were, due to her intellectual nature, political. Pamela, in reaction against mother, was more stable in a commonplace way, and yet all too capable of succumbing to the incubus of the middle nights.

And me? I seemed to be somewhere in between: I had nearly raped Allison DeForest and yet had managed to slip that trap. On the other hand, I had been saved from intellectualism by a natural slowness, so well documented by Dr. Bene whom one heard of, from time to time, in Palo Alto, wandering the ivied halls of Stanford pulling a red wooden cart filled with papers behind him, or slipping out onto the football field during home games in an overcoat and watch cap, where he would feverishly collect the I.B.M. cards the fans used for confetti. I owed Dr. Bene a debt for making me find those keys after giving me a coin purse to lose on a field that didn't exist anywhere but in my memory. My ground was an imagined baseball diamond at the heart of America, and my purpose was plain and simple—to find those keys.

## 28.

Pamela had told me that adults try to return to the place of their happiest childhood memories, a fact she'd learned from the Buddhist monk who taught a course called "The Fear of Life" under the awning of the Psychology Department at the Community College she attended, and cross-listed in the catalogue with Lepidoptery 201, which Pamela managed to pass, having failed the course taught by the monk. So when mother met father and me at the door with "Preggers!" I went straight to Pamela's closet to look for her. By the time I returned to the living room, Pamela, her boyfriend, and his brother and sister-in-law were sitting on the edges of slip-covered sofas and ottomans in tense anticipation as father paced the room saying, "Oh balls!" It already had been agreed that Pamela and her boyfriend would marry.

Mother sat in a corner, wagging her hand like the arm of a metronome, counting the passage of time until she noticed me and turned to my father and asked, "Did you forget to shut the door?" To mother, I was becoming a stranger; the moments were rarer and rarer that she would look at me, the mists receding from the fog of her mind long enough to say, "You were a sleeper." She meant that as a baby I had been given to sleeping through anything and everything.

Even now I was tempted to curl around father's wrath like

an anemone. I didn't. Someone had to say something besides "Oh balls." I went over to Pamela and put my arms around her and told her that "It would be all right."

Pamela's gratitude, combined with the choric sigh of relief from my brother-in-law-to-be's odd relatives, made me over-look the rattle of the back door's knob, an ominous but frag-ile sound, as though someone was early for a party whose hosts he didn't know.

Possibly, not answering that rattling door was a mistake. I would think so, at times, as I sat in Pamela's closet trying to hold on to the sound of her voice, while begging her to for-give me for having lied. It was not all right. Several months later, I heard the same rattling at the door, alternating with a cat-like scratching on the wood as though the party-goer was tired of being left out in the cold, as Pamela miscarried, hemorrhaged, and died. At the door was a sneering, twisted little man, come in a Rent-a-Wreck van to make a pickup. Taking Pamela away, he made a point of letting me know that this time, Death had fooled Grandfather as well as me.

Mother closed the house into darkness, while father si-lently washed and rewashed both cars. Elanna came home from Berkeley, and she scratched my head absent-mindedly as together we retreated through whatever happy memories we had that had escaped the deluge of Pamela's bleeding to death. Casseroles appeared magically on the doorstep, left there by neighbors, and Running Dog grew fat on the food we couldn't eat and didn't have the heart to return.

Grandfather took it somewhat philosophically; but Laura Pamela could be heard cursing him and all the men in the family, exclaiming that now she knew why she had never used her middle name as the pots on her potter's wheel collapsed slowly into a pulpy mass of clay, over-wet from her tears.

Giving Laura P. time for her tears to soak into the hard red rock of Chosposi, Grandfather spent the next two weeks in his workshop, holed up in the artificial light of his own failure, making a pair of brass wind chimes which he bored and filed to perfection, until they gave off a hollow ethereal "bong," sadder than all the cathedrals in France. These he sent to me and I hung them above the plain and eloquent marker of Pamela's grave, spending hours in the graveyard listening to them until one night they were stolen.

For Elanna, Pamela's was a double death. Not only had she lost her companion from those childhood trips to uncle's house, but, when she discovered that mother had cleaned out her room, discarding everything that reminded her of what she had been, she felt as though she'd lost a good half of herself. I became doubly important to Elanna and she tried to smother me with caution, preventing me from buying a motorcycle and preparing me to resist the draft, while, at the same time, making me read. If I suffered one of the migraine headaches I began getting, Elanna would drive all the way home from Berkeley in the middle of the night to take me to the hospital for the codeine shots which allowed me to cease the painful vomiting. For her sake, I became a model student, reading through her assigned reading list so quickly that before I graduated from high school, I was already on the "esses"—Shakespeare and Sartre—reaching von Kleist by the time I was accepted to an expensive, private men's college for the next fall.

Elanna didn't approve of my choice of colleges but after Pamela's death, which seemed a betrayal, and after Allison DeForest had confused revenge with cowardice and sliced up her wrists twice, I wanted nothing more to do with women.

Not even mother could penetrate the furious indifference that I used to protect myself. But then mother changed, becoming thoroughly competent in an apparent attempt to make up for the lives that had miscarried around her. Where once her madness had been interesting, if not fun, after Pamela's death she became as methodically sane as father had been before. Closing the house in darkness for several weeks, she spent her days scrubbing the floors, polishing furniture, cleaning carpets. She changed the locks on the doors, surprising father when he came home late one night with his old set of keys. She installed timers on all of the lights in the house, so that after dusk you could be startled by a light blinking on, followed by one blinking off. She turned Pamela's room into a study, and registered for courses at the state university, throwing out her toaster and refusing after that to cook for what was left of the family.

No longer did the happy shouts of "boom" surprise me as I fished through the refrigerator. The few friends I had ceased to comment on how mother seemed strange, and instead treated her with the respect and lack of caring that they gave their own mothers. She would ask them the same questions their mothers asked, such as "How was your day?" and they would say, "Fine." When the washing machine broke down or the vacuum needed repairing, mother would roll up her sleeves and fix it with the tool kit she purchased after she enrolled in a shop class for women. The machine would work, when mother was done. When William the Black phoned angrily, now, to thank me once again for ruining a good thing with Mrs. DeForest, the messages mother took were more coherent than the writing I did late at night, having taken it up as a defense against the solitude I felt closing in on all sides. In postponed agreement with mother, I felt there had to be more light, and until I could get to the desert where the light was flat and plain, writing was the only way I could imagine to keep from being bored to death.

It was father who suffered most, perhaps. Thrown off guard by mother's changing the locks on the house, he became obsessed with debugging his roses with malathion. If I offered to help him wash and wax the cars, he simply stared at me as though I were an aphid or a Mediterranean fruit fly. He no longer brought men home from the office to have dinner and instead began eating out more and more often. The fact that mother no longer visited doctors and hospitals seemed to make him more generous and to get me out of his way, he would hand me a twenty-dollar bill and tell me to take a bus up to see Elanna for the weekend.

Two weeks after I graduated from high school, he took me out to lunch. Impatiently, I watched him from behind my wall of silence, as his face changed from confusion to decisiveness to pain. By the end of lunch, he managed to say, "You and I have never really talked to each other," to which I said nothing.

Before I left him there, he spit out the question I had known was coming all along. "What," he asked, "would you think if I told you I was thinking of divorcing your mother?"

I looked out the window, avoiding his face which I knew

would make me feel sorry for him, which would tell me better than any of his words that he was trying only to live in this world which he couldn't understand for better or for worse. I remembered the first time his brother had mentioned divorce and he had turned to me and asked if I wanted to go fishing, and I cracked open the memory of the time he had smacked me when I'd asked him if he was looking for suds in mother's Kenmore. Had I taken the time, put in just a little effort, maybe I would have seen that all father needed was someone he could put his arm around and promise that it would be all right. I heard Grandfather sigh as I looked straight at father, shrugged, and said, "Whatever."

What I couldn't say to father was that he was already divorced from mother, that in the flatulence of his neediness he had invented the intricate illusion that his wife and children needed him—an illusion held aloft and dry on the stilts of breadwinning over a swamp of resentment. I couldn't say that to father, not because it would have hurt him but because I didn't know it until the night when I sauntered into the no man's land of mother's living room and encountered her group raising its consciousness like a barn.

It was a small group and when I stumbled into its midst, sucking the salt out of a celery stick, I felt threatened and out of place. The one male participant in mother's group was pale, as though he'd not seen the light for years, and from the waist up he looked as though he had grown to his full height bound between boards. The women, in varying shapes and sizes, looked mean in their discontent, unsexed by disappointment and clothes.

"Anyone for Scrabble?" I asked, as they stared at me.

As I gathered together cans of food for Running Dog, who was cowering beneath my bed, and began packing my bags, the voices coming from the living room sounded like corn popping in a lidless pan. That night, I dreamed of a time when I would have been at camp as a boy, the face of my one friend resembling at one moment my father's face, alternating with my uncle's. When the nostalgic illusion of a girl named Tammy seemed, suddenly, to look like Pamela, I woke with a start and smiled, realizing that mother's encounter group was freeing me of a burden I'd never asked for, and having, had never wanted. Once again, with the vague feeling of a senseless repetition that was closing the gap in my life like the drip of a stalactite onto a stalagmite, I knew I was alone. Mother's newfound awareness of her own sanity would bubble and boil with trouble as it was heated by the bitterness of her divorce from father, and in the process I would be burned by its distillation, even as far away as Clearmont.

That wouldn't happen right away, though. In Chosposi, a month later, Rachel would discover a bundle of unopened letters from mother on the mantel of Grandfather's cement block house behind the mission.

"What are these?" Rachel would ask.

"Letters from mother."

"They're unopened."

"They all say the same thing," I would say. "Mother has taken up writing letters in an effort to re-examine her life, affixing blame like a postage stamp." I took the bundle from Rachel, separating the letters.

"If you read this one, you'd find out how much like my father I am." I pulled another one out of the bundle.

"This one says nothing about my father, but it asks if I am aware of how I kept her from living her own life. And this one disguises mother's hatred for men beneath the very cleverly deceptive question of when I am coming home for a visit."

"A mother can't hate her own child," Rachel would say. "Besides, how do you know, smart ass, if you've not even opened them?"

"Maybe you're right," I'd reply, handing the bundle back to her. "But if all things are connected, then to my mother I am my father. Besides," I'd say, grinning, "I've never been able to read my mother's script, which looks more like the marks left by the tails of gila monsters than handwriting."

"You are a fool," Rachel would say. "You know that? A real bastard."

Thinking, I don't need you either, I would reply as calmly as I could, "Anything's possible."

# CHAPTER SEVEN

### 29.

"It happens," Grandfather said, firing up a cigar, the blue-gray smoke obscuring his face. "Death huffs and puffs and blows sand in your eyes. Sometimes it may only *seem* as though it's happening and you reconstruct what *will* have happened out of the stems and stipes. Your heart clots with the fear of rejection and the happy frustration that comes from playing the game of love. You're overwhelmed by the immense and universal sadness of sunsets in the desert and you wonder if confusion isn't caused by celery having more salt than tuna."

A trail of smoke drifted toward the San Francisco Peaks, waiting in the distance. He looked at me, the lines around his mouth playing through love, anger, frustration, confusion. Pamela's death had aged him. His eyebrows had grown long and shadowed his gray eyes, giving them an unspeakably sad look as though he had seen things he did not want to see, things he could not or would not even hint at in the cloud of his confusion. His face looked heavy, reflecting less of what I'd once believed was quiet serenity and more the snuffling hidden rage and the inert balance of a Pit bulldog. The hinges on his jaws loosened as his brain began to rust.

More and more often I was having trouble understanding what Grandfather meant, let alone predicting what he would mean. He sat there, static but not still, and I was forced to close my eyes even as he spoke and try to listen to the distant whispers of what he would have said, a twofold process. On the one hand, I had to exclude everything he had already said. On the other, I had to exclude everything he never would have said. Only then could I author a reasonable semblance of what Grandfather might have said.

Not until long after Grandfather's death would I begin to suspect his apparent confusion had been calculated. He was forcing me to stop and close my eyes and look inward to know what he as well as I would have said—and, by extrapolation, what father, mother, Elanna, or the as-yet-unloved Sara Baites could possibly have said. I would begin to see that Grandfather had planted the seeds of fiction that summer which, when processed like tomato seeds, explain how I came to write with my eyes closed.

Rachel had come to love Grandfather and coming often to his and Laura P.'s house, she was saddened by what she imagined was Grandfather's senility. Yet Rachel only saw him while he was sitting still, and when he was still, looking out across the desert from his aerie on the side of the mesa, what Grandfather said, according to Rachel, seemed "all of a same."

It was. Everything that he had ever thought or felt or imagined was equal to everything else, each event an equally important subset to the one grand set that was Grandfather's life. The elf owls were as important to Grandfather as sunsets; he could slide from flint knives to skunks to cottonwood trees within the same sentence. Only Pamela's death stood out separate and unequal. On the other hand, when Grandfather was in motion, when he was riding the three-wheeled bicycle with the same even concentration that he drove the Plymouth, he became almost lucid.

"It's the natural process of aging. It's not senility," I explained to Rachel. "When Grandfather is sitting still and staring out at the gray line of the horizon, he's staring through time. The years are like fan-fold transparencies with the words of past and future written into them. On each transparency are the signs and symbols that predict and decipher his own life along with the lives of his children and his children's children."

"Pah!" she exclaimed. "Such clever images. You gift wrap reality with images."

"I don't mean to," I said. It seemed the problem wasn't one of images but of trust. Like someone who knows he's failed to live up to his own aspirations—like the self-appelled painter who keeps promising to take up painting again or the rich man who ignores the needle's eye—Rachel refused to trust me long enough to consider whether I might be right.

"Eighty-odd years folding back on each other," I said, "makes reading them difficult, if not impossible. You can hold them up to the light of the desert or the distant light of the stars, but when you try to read them aloud, you're going to sound confused."

"How do you know?" Rachel said.

I didn't. Nonetheless, I did know that when I hopped along beside Grandfather as he pedaled the killer bike to the trading post, he was lucid. As in driving the Plymouth, riding the bike he was staring out on a horizon of distance and not of time, and I could understand what he said. When he said, "There is a tale of a man who went up the mountain and looked over at the promised land," I could say, "Tell me," and what he would tell me each time would be consistent in its meaning if not told in the identical way. Each time, I would understand the tale of a man who looked over the mountain and saw not the promised land but the narrow barrel of an assassin's rifle and the inexorable darkness of Death—the only promise, as far as Grandfather was concerned, worth taking for granted. Without needing to close my eyes, I would know the man Grandfather meant was the same one Laura P. said had gone directly to the Multi-world.

"Directly," I would say to Grandfather. "Without passing Go."

"Without collecting two hundred dollars," Grandfather would laugh. "Let alone, needing them." He wasn't making fun of Laura P.'s beliefs but offering me a hope in the face and fact of death.

I was so willing to accept that offer that I failed to understand the hope. But the offer was a beginning. And months later, emerging from the dark closet of a near-coma—a nearness as immeasurable as the gray line of Grandfather's horizons when he parked at my newborn crib and inspected me with the beefy eyes of an inspector from the F.D.A.—I would recall what I'd seen and heard beneath the fog of sodium pentothal, and I'd understand. It was like a dream, but a dream in which I knew I was dreaming, outside of which neither the dream nor the dreamer existed.

The dream would begin with a butterfly, a brightly colored and delicately spotted monarch, flying in the monarch's usual curly-cued but ineluctable way toward an emptiness that waited on the other side of the sodium pentothal's peak. I wanted with all my heart to follow the butterfly into oblivion until a voice asked, "What are you doing here?" and the butterfly dissolved, disappeared. Whose voice, what voice, I didn't know; to the dreamer it seemed as though the voice came from outside of the dream. As suddenly as the monarch vanished, it was replaced in the dream by landscape, by canyons and streams, by cactus and hawks and caverns.

When I awoke, the fish-eye lens of my brain opening as if for the first time, I would find Elanna holding cherry-flavored gelatin toward my mouth on a spoon that seemed miraculously large. I would be fascinated by the way the Jell-o wiggled, and I would be able to do nothing but smile as Elanna, and behind her Grandfather, came into focus. Their eyes, his eyes, would tell me emphatically what he'd been trying to tell me all along—that I was condemned to live. Smiling, tears beginning to streak my cheeks, I would sit up and begin to eat that Jell-o.

## 30.

Ten months before that bite of Jell-o, in the aftershock of Pamela's death, my parents dueled over Elanna's and my affections, while they filed for divorce. Pamela's death had been an earthquake revealing huge faults which had existed since my birth but which had been bridged by the habit and duty of marriage. Now, when mother or father spoke to Elanna or me, they slipped easily into litanies of blame that began with the phrase, "Your mother . . . ," or "Your father . . . ," and balanced on the implication that love for one parent excluded love for the other.

Elanna stayed up in Berkeley for the summer and, left at home with mother, the inner workings of who was doing what evil thing to whom was as difficult for me to determine as the inner workings of her brand new heavy-duty washing machine. There seemed to be an abundance of bolts and screws in this machine, two for every one that should have been there, as though every extra bolt and screw would keep father from sneaking into the garage and tinkering with it.

"Your father," mother would say, "always did more damage fixing things than if he'd left well enough alone."

"So," father would say, having received a credit card bill, "your mother is on another spending spree, eh? There was nothing the matter with the old washing machine. She's going to bankrupt me if she keeps it up."

"Elanna?" I'd say, calling her late at night. "The latest is washers. Don't mention anything like dirty laundry," I cautioned. Both of us had developed Distant Early Warning lines against the surprises that mother and father invented in their battle for our sympathy. We became adept at modern diplomacy, able to talk about anything in general which was nothing in particular.

The washer was merely a beginning, a mechanical sign of things to come. Mother, with newly acquired self-confidence, bought a new wardrobe of brightly colored blouses, tailored slacks, and short, waist-gripping jackets, and then began adding new bolts and screws to herself, steeling herself with notions of security. You needed to know a verbal code just to be able to talk about anything with her and, seeing the way in which everything emotional was a sign of the physical and vice versa, I could imagine a time when to enter mother's house I would need an identification card to slip into a magnetic mechanism on the front door in order to release the lock. And mother changed the locks on her house as often as she changed her will—out of which I was being written because going away to college was a betrayal, leaving her alone to face my father.

Mother would be secure, no matter what. Taking a cue from the Vegomatic, mother took possession of nearly everything. "Except for the money your father embezzled from our mutual accounts," mother would say.

Whereas the Vegomatic remained in my imagination a secretive woman, quietly exulting in the power she held over my uncle and willing to take him back, mother openly swore she would make father pay for all the rigid years frozen in the icebox of their marriage. A careful editing job allowed mother to feel good about what she did to father. She ignored the years father had invested and the time he had served in the fluorescent isolation of the corporate world, and toted up the household chores she had done without any help from him. When I reminded mother of the repairs to the family car, the plumbing, the mowing of lawns, the paying of bills, balancing of checkbooks, and figuring of taxes that father had done, her face flared with anger and she went around the house slamming doors and cupboards, yelling about the bottom line. For decades, it was true, mother had been stuck with toasters and vacuums as her only companions—an undesirable fate—but father had been stuck with alarm clocks, hardhats, briefcases, and colleagues who were often less interesting than vacuums. So I was confused when mother called father's keeping a little money for himself embezzling.

Years later, Sara would laugh at me for behaving like a chipmunk with money, floating a hundred dollars here or there by subtracting it from the checkbook's balance while leaving it in the account. And when I heard Elanna talk about "her" money and not "their" money, I'd begin to realize how our parents' divorce had affected her as well. Marriage seemed to be a lottery played with a careful and suspicious system for winning, with definite limits set on the amounts gambled.

Partly to escape such conclusions, I went to Chosposi Mesa. Mother dropped me at the bus terminal, and then went home and telephoned the locksmith.

The desert was a relief. Its exposure to the immense sky and its shimmering silences seemed to enclose and comfort me. Around my neck on a leather thong I wore the stone amulet Grandfather had once given me, reveling in the way it bounced lightly against the flesh above my heart as I walked, or the way it pressed warm and damp against me when I was still.

I hadn't worn the stone for years, having taken it off when I made the high school basketball team and was allowed to sit on the bench and watch William the Black excel. But when

Pamela died, I had stopped to consider where not wearing the amulet had gotten me, wondering what might have been different with an ounce of magic. Hoping for my stars to be rearranged, I'd begun wearing it religiously.

As I stepped down from the bus in front of Johnny Three Feet's trading post, Rachel greeted me, fixing her eyes on the stone.

"What is that?" she demanded.

Rachel often derided the signs and symbols I wore around my neck to protect myself. I didn't care for rings or belts or bracelets. For me, the neck seemed the proper hanger. Possibly because accidents had always happened to my head and hands, I instinctively kept the hands unburdened for swiftness while weighting the neck to help the head duck and dodge the tree branches which reminded me I had grown beyond the length of any and all beds, my feet hanging exposed to the night spiders and insects that never bit.

"My stone. The one Grandfather gave me." I held it up to the desert light for her to see. Though it was plain, with little imagination you could see that it had a life of its own. It was that life that allowed it its stoniness, an inactivity that would seem to the unimaginative like death. "See?"

"See what?" she said, her black eyes squinting.

"Inertia. Tendency." To me, that was what Grandfather had achieved, the tendency when at rest to remain at rest and the tendency when in motion to remain in motion.

"Look at you. You keep hanging things around your neck you're going to be bent like a sapling before your time. Your mysticism is going to be the death of you."

"No. My life is going to be the death of me. That's why I need inertia."

"Pah!" she spat in the dust.

"It's good magic," Sanchez said. He had climbed down from the bus after me, and had stood aside, watching this exchange. He was expansive. "The spirit of the fathers. The knife of Coyote."

The way Rachel looked at Sanchez made me regret having told him the tale of Ilpswetsichs and Coyote. It had been a long and boring bus ride, filled with the breath of high-class bums, the compost smell of old people, and the ammonia of babies—all on their mutual way to London Bridge. Sanchez's lemony smell of fabric softener had been a relief when he'd sat in the seat beside me.

"I wasn't talking to you," Rachel said. Her eyes were as cold and hard as black diamonds.

"No problem," Sanchez smiled. He was a well-built, handsome guy, about six years older than I. "My name's Sanchez." He stuck out his hand. "I'm a friend of Bert's, here." Sanchez, learning that Alley was short for Albert, insisted on calling me Bert. At first it had irritated me; but I'd forgotten the irritation by the time we reached Chosposi because it seemed natural for him to call me that.

Rachel ignored his hand. Like a pendulum rises to its rest and falls, it hung there for a moment before dropping back to his side. She raised her eyebrows at me and then gave Sanchez a look that seemed to say, "I know who you are."

"So this is the Trading Post," Sanchez said. Cupping his chin in his hand in a mime of thoughtfulness, he squinted at the squat cinder block building. "First thing it needs is a wooden facade. Nobody in the world thinks of a trading post as being built out of blocks. A horse rail in front and some wooden benches in front. We could hire some of the old folks to sit on the benches and look mysterious, and charge tourists four bits to snap their pictures. Maybe an American flag over the door . . . no, that might be too too. Well," he said, "I'll catch up to you later. Business calls." He picked up his two carpetbags and disappeared into the darkness of Johnny Three Feet's.

"So," I said to Rachel, who was looking at Sanchez's back with acupuncture eyes. "It's good to see you. How have you been?" Rachel seemed harder and thinner than ever before. Her autodidacticism weighed like a block on her angular shoulders.

"Who is that?" she said.

"Sanchez. Have you seen Grandfather?"

"I don't like him," Rachel said. "He's shifty. What do you think he's doing here?"

I said I didn't know. I didn't, not really, although I had a pretty good idea. On the bus, Sanchez had told me that he was from Oklahoma. He worked for a company that invented time-saving products like the Vegomatic, one of those hand-driven devices which cut, chopped, and diced vegetables almost as well as a paring knife. In fact, Sanchez had been the inventor of the Vegomatic; and he had developed the way to market his device.

"It works a lot like televised religion," he said. "We offer them something to believe in. Something that works. For a while, anyway, until they figure out that switching the blades and cleaning the damn thing without dicing your fingers makes a knife a lot easier to use."

The company made a huge profit on the products themselves. But where they really got the people—a fact which seemed to give Sanchez real joy—was in the shipping and handling charges. When I questioned overcharging people for shipping, or charging them at all for automated handling, he said, "Hell, everybody does it. Order from one of those discount catalogues and you'll figure out that by time the merchandise arrives, it costs as much as it would in any store, if not more. You've just been allowed to wait several weeks longer in anticipation. The fact is, most people look at the price of the stuff without the shipping or handling and believe they're getting a real deal."

I had to admit he was right.

"It's the feeling that they're saving money, getting a deal, that mail order companies sell people. We add to the feeling, selling them faith by telling them that the Vegomatic is not sold in stores, implying that it's too good for stores. For the two months we delay before shipping out their new Vegomatic, until they open the carton, they get to believe."

When I asked, "Believe in what?" he burst out laughing. The bus driver watched us warily in his mirror.

"There is no what," he said. "Faith is faith. When those old ladies mail checks to Oral Roberts they don't get God in return. They simply get worked up into a frenzy of faith and express it the only way they know how. We do the same thing Oral does. We work them up into a frenzy. They send us money. You know, I bet you'd be surprised how many repeat customers we get after their first Vegomatic breaks, sometimes for another Vegomatic, sometimes for our Eterno-sharp Knife Set, which comes with a set of eight screwdrivers, a universal wrench, and a set of wooden kitchen utensils, all of which they get to keep even if they return the knives. You think Americans are just too lazy to return the knives, once they try to use them? No. They don't return the knives because to do that, they'd have to give up the faith we sold them. Cheap, I might add."

## 31.

Sanchez was a sort of enterprising Wovoka, a man who could use faith to make ice flow down the corridors of commerce in summertime. But of this, I said nothing to Rachel. Already Sanchez was no better than a Gila monster to her, and the turquoise jewelry he sported on his arms and around his neck and waist was cheap imitation and not the real thing. The turquoise was real enough, as was the hammered silver. But real to Rachel meant soldered together by someone with credentials that suited her. A piece of jewelry, regardless of its design, was more authentic the greater the number of Indians who had handled it. When I asked Grandfather whether that mattered, he chewed thoughtfully on the inside of his left jowl before he concluded, "De Toro of the Mad Eyes was played by Ron Stein," referring to "The Magnificent Seven Ride." A Jew could play a Mexican if his eyes were up to the role.

"So," I said to Rachel as we stood uncomfortably together outside the trading post.

"We don't need his kind here," she hissed, obsessed with Sanchez.

"I don't know . . . ," I began. Maybe it was the deleterious effects of experience, combined with the sometime loss of lucidity on Grandfather's part, but the older I became, the more Chosposi seemed an empty place, saddened by the immensity of its emptiness. Where once I had loved the slow, even pace of Grandfather's walk or the chirping complaints of Laura P. as she worked over her potter's wheel, lately I had begun to feel the hopelessness of the place. It was as though the process of birth had reversed itself and slowly, the blood was returning to Ilpswetsichs, the wound healing, and all that would be left was the Trickster Coyote himself, disgorged from the toothless mouth of the monster.

"You don't know shit," Rachel said. "Do you? You'd make a Gila monster into a pet. Or worse, let him make a pet out of you."

Rachel had refined her way of putting things, I could tell. Fighting back a desire to tweak her nose, I said, "Why don't you kill him, skin him, and sell him as an authentic artifact?"

"Maybe I will," she said, as Sanchez danced down the steps to the trading post, his limp carpetbags tucked beneath his arm. In his right hand, he held a wad of bills, two of which he peeled off before slipping the rest into a leather pouch that hung beneath the tail of his untucked shirt.

"Here," he said, thrusting the two bills at me. "Some of my magic. The only known cure for the common cold."

"What's this for?"

"Information."

Rachel scraped her moccasin in an arc through the parched earth.

"What information?" I asked.

Rachel gave me a narrow look, a look of hatred that could have been mistaken for love, if you stood on your head to make left right and right left.

"All right," Sanchez said. "Call it an advance."

"Against what?"

Sanchez pulled an amulet out of his shirt pocket, one of the ones made by Navahos which Johnny Three Feet sold to tourists who were willing to overlook the fact that the Navaho had few, if any, connections with the ancient Mexican civilizations, unlike the Hopi. This one was round. In the center was a cast relief of the face of Maya with bronze rays radiating outward from her crowned head. Sanchez flipped it to me like a quarter. "For figuring out an angle on this. A use for it."

"Use?"

"Yeah. You see, things like this sell for different reasons. A husband who just wants to live out his golden years in peace will let his old lady buy one, figuring if it keeps the old gal quiet it's worth twice the price. Or maybe a cheap-skate—you know, the fun kind of guy who wears those stretch denims that would be the color of puke if puke were blue because they're practical? He lets the little woman buy it be-cause he doesn't want to look cheap, and there's nothing a tightwad wants more than to look uncheap in front of other people."

"You lost me," I said.

"Never mind. The point is that its potential is not realized. Sure, some people will buy it for bric-a-brac to toss into a flagging conversation with guests they wish would go home. But I'll give you odds that two out of five husbands prevent their wives from buying it because it has no apparent *use.* That's what we need to come up with. If it were useful, Johnny would triple his sales." He thought for a moment. "Let me see that," he said. Turning it over in his hand he said, "Like a cookie cutter. Maybe that's it!"

"A cookie cutter?" I asked.

"Puts it into the wife's domain. Makes it impossible for your basic husband to deny that it has practical applications."

"What makes you think it's women who buy those things?" Rachel said with the thudding insistence of people with a cause.

"Those ain't your basic feminists in there, Gloria," Sanchez said. "Those are meat and potatoes run-of-the-mill human units."

To me, he said, "Imagine your basic husband asking his wife, 'What are we going to do with that, Betty?' and the little woman being able to say, 'Use your thick head, Nigel. It's a cookie cutter.' Nigel can't argue with that now, can he? And if Nigel complains about its cost, all Betty has to do is remind him about the barbecue tools he bought in Tucson, right?"

"You sexist," Rachel said. Like mother, Rachel had discovered feminism; where mother's had a mistaken odor like burned toast, Rachel's could cut you in two.

Sanchez seemed up to it.

"There are plenty of husbands dumb enough to buy those things," Rachel said.

"I think you're right," Sanchez said, containing his emotions with the fluid ease he had in handling tense situations. "Especially if they're cookie cutters. We'll get the cheap husband who wants to surprise his wife on Christmas with an exotic gift, the namby pambies who bake, and the little boys who want to buy a gift for mom.

"Tell you what," Sanchez said, reaching for his money again. "How about if I make you a consultant, too?"

Rachel held her hands up like a Jamaican traffic cop trying to halt a freight train. An odd expression crossed her narrow face as though her contention with Sanchez was, while hateful, also a pleasure.

"May as well," Sanchez said. He shoved some bills at her, making her bob and weave to avoid them. Deftly, he tucked them into the breast pocket of her work shirt.

I'd seen men do that with topless dancers or waitresses, leering the whole time with sexual insinuation. Never had I seen a man do this asexually. Sanchez—thank heavens—managed to, and even Rachel whose head swayed like a coiled rattlesnake seemed to understand this. She did not strike him. She did reach gingerly into her pocket with her finger and thumb, extract the bills and hold them dangling at arm's length over the ground shimmering from the heat and dust of tourists snapping pictures, and drop them with an exaggerated gesture of distaste. She turned and walked away.

Sanchez only grinned. He believed in the power of money, but that was divorced from any notions of power over people. "Money," he said, "is the key to the kingdom. It doesn't make you king. Though it can make you stupid," he added as he bent over and picked the bills out of the dirt and handed them to me.

"I think I'm in love," he said loudly. Whether Rachel heard him or not, her hips stiffened and her walk contracted with self-consciousness. He watched her recede into the sharpness of her own dignity.

"Some lady, that Rachel," he said. "The funny thing is that she'll give me her opinions for free as long as I make her angry."

It didn't take long to find out how true that was. Where I could predict the whats and hows, Sanchez instinctively knew the wherefores. Rachel pretended to despise him, and when she was around him she would make remarks aimed at provoking him, as though she felt a bitterness as ancient as her race. Caught between her and Sanchez, I felt like the victim in a silent movie, tied to the planks of my friendship with Sanchez as the planks slid into the sawmill of Rachel's cutting mind.

"Watch out for her," I told Sanchez.

"Wherefore?" Sanchez replied. "She's only dangerous if you bite, if you take the bait."

"Whereas," Grandfather would say when I asked him about that, "the bait may be the bite. There is a tale that tells it happened that way." How many hours and days I waited patiently for Grandfather to tell me that tale, to give me the clues that I could bundle together likes sheaves of truth. How many times did he remove his belt and lean back into the overstuffed driver's seat of the Plymouth and begin to snore, the pores of his nose expanding and contracting as he fell asleep. I began to despair of ever hearing it when Louis Applegate drifted through from the East.

"He can't tell you," Louis said.

"Why not?"

"It's not his tale to tell. It doesn't belong to him."

"Whose is it?" I asked.

Louis' face went through the entire rainbow of emotions before he managed to say, "It's Laura Pamela's. Your grandmother's. Only she can tell it. Only she knew ahead of time how it ended."

Wanting to hear the beginning, middle, or end of this tale, I spent extra time with Laura P. She accepted the novelty of my increased presence as though she was the center of things and everything naturally returned to her, as I sat waiting in silence for her to tell me the tale she wouldn't.

Pamela's death had not aged her the way it had Grandfather. She threw her pots, now, with a vengeance and the heat of her concentration seemed as though it could fire the clay while it was yet on the wheel. Sometimes in the middle of shaping a pot she would lurch to a halt and raise her head like a bird that hears the bell of the cat and chant "Pa-me-la," pounding the clay flat onto the wheel with every syllable. She'd work the clay anew and begin throwing a new pot, renewing the chirping soliloquies which she used like a metronome to keep a rhythm to her wheel.

After meeting Sanchez, she began to acquire a faraway look similar to the one Grandfather now wore like a papier-mâché mask. At first, she was content to claim that Sanchez had no shadow. Then she began to grind her potter's wheel to a halt and look up to sing to the wall, "Up, down, round

135

and range. Give progress up and *you're* surprised by change."
As her words seemed to bounce like bees off the adobe wall,
her face alternated between amusement and innocence, as
though she were seeing something that happened or something that will have had to have happened, and just watching
her facial expressions made me feel pluperfectly confused.

Each day, when she was finished painting the east or west
spirals on her pots, Laura P. inspected the palms of my
hands, patiently fingering the reddish spots which had appeared, grown larger, and begun to itch like a rash. One day,
tracing the path between the spots on my right hand, she
looked up and said, "Shit! Louis has replaced himself."

Letting my hands drop as though the spots were leprosy
and I was contagious, she sank onto the wooden seat of her
potter's wheel. Her body expressed defeat like a young boxer
staggering crablike to the mat after a blow, joint by joint
relinquishing to defeat so that his torso begins to topple even
before his knees begin to buckle. Defeat is like Death. We
think Death comes all at once when really He is running us
down from behind all along. The effects are slow and can
be ignored until with age the geometrical accumulation of
effects makes them unavoidable. We have moments in which
we see our own mortality which, fleet of foot, we sidestep; we
even have moments as adolescents when we thoughtlessly
wish we were dead. But all these are only warning signals as
the vessels of ourselves empty into shapeless puddles and
evaporate, drying us out, making our skin wither and crack
like parched earth.

Sometimes Laura would regain her composure enough to
ask me not to let Sanchez handle her pots, and I hadn't the
heart to tell her that Sanchez had become partners with
Johnny Three Feet. Before long, Laura P. began to walk
more and more sideways, glancing askance at the ceilings
of rooms or the empty skies, and demanding that someone
precede her through doorways. Pot after pot was ruined,
corn piki was burned and crumbled, and she became increasingly silent and distant. By mid-August, she was walking
backwards, her head tilted up and her eyes darting with
fright as though she feared ambush from above. The shad-
owless shadow of a fieldhawk (a hawk has a way of disguising

its shadow as nothing more than a faint and formless inter-ruption of light) would make her jump. One day she jumped literally out of her skin, and by the time I'd helped her up off the ground, she had regained her old composure. Taking my hands in hers and inspecting the palms, she'd said, "Dad had hands like yours when he was about the same age."

"She meant Grandfather," I said to Rachel, proud at least of that small knowledge.

"You idiot," Rachel said. "Don't you know? Since they were children, Louis Applegate was always going to marry Laura. They were engaged. Your Grandfather had agreed to be best man and he and Louis had already been to Phoenix to buy a ring which out of superstition your Grandfather was keeping until the wedding the next spring. That winter the snows were heavier than anyone hoped for. An anthropologist from the east showed up in Chosposi, and Louis took him in until the blizzard passed. Took him in. The blizzard lasted thirty days and thirty nights. It took another ten days for the roads to clear, and by the time the man could be packed off on his way to wherever, he had fallen in love with Louis' sister, courted her, and bought Louis' compliance with promises of a life free from sin and drudgery. When the man left, Louis' sister went with him. Louis had sold his own sister into the slavery of boredom."

"Did his sister love the man?"

"What would that have mattered?" Rachel said. "Boredom is worse than death. Nothing survives it. That's where Louis goes off to—the east coast, where his sister exists, staring out the penthouse window like a lost peregrine falcon at the skyline of manmade mesas where people never sleep. He goes out of regret and stays with her as long as he can stand it, before he has to return here for cardiac regenesis."

"So how did Laura P. come to marry Grandfather?"

"She couldn't live with Louis' regret. Your Grandfather had the ring. After a postponement or two of the wedding, your Grandfather stepped into his friend's shoes."

So that was how Louis Applegate came to be able to recog-nize Death crawling along on his knees in East Texas, I thought. Death on His knees looks an awful lot like regret in disguise.

# CHAPTER EIGHT

## 32.

Sanchez came and went that summer and it was not so much him but his approach to the desert that I clung to like climber's rope as the voices of past and present gusted through me. To Sanchez, everything in and of the Sonoran Desert was new and he was constantly amazed by even the smallest of things. Elf owls moving into the cactus holes drilled by woodpeckers; the tiny tracks of kangaroo mice that we would come upon in the silent hour of the false dawn, when the hunted had hidden and the hunters had closed their eyes against the white light of the desert sun; these were as large and exciting to Sanchez as the oceanic waves of clouds that would be highlighted by the sunset that preceded the nightly scurry of hunter and hunted like a secret signal to a jailbreak.

"This," Sanchez would say expansively, "this is paradise."

I could only laugh, tickled by his childlike feeling that everything was potential—unnamed, malleable, and waiting only for him to forge it into something different.

"Look at that," he would say, out on one of our walks through the desert, pointing at sandstone arched by erosion. "That's a souvenir stand if ever I've seen one. Could even sell a few burgers. Cokes."

My laughter lacked sarcasm and instead was gay and light-hearted.

Sanchez threw his arms wide and his body's frame would shake as his laughter rolled across the hard-packed desert, creating a shimmering mirage of sound. It was a laugh that would interfere with the thoughts of people nearby, causing people in movie theaters to "sshhh!" and the desert animals to dart for cover. Hawks and eagles would tilt their heads in question from their high perches when Sanchez passed below them laughing, seeming to take pleasure in his joy the way I did.

When he wasn't laughing, Sanchez wanted to know the names of things. When I told him, he would silently repeat what I'd say, licking around the edges of the words with his tongue. Coming to some irremediable conclusion about the nature of the flora or fauna, he would rename it. Most of the new names had apparent reasons. Collared Lizards were Roadrunners because of the way they evaded capture by running on their hind legs. Leopard Lizards were Lowriders because they were low and mean. And Hook-Nosed Snakes he called Jodies because he'd known a woman, once, who had a nose like that. "Her eyes twittered, vibrated back and forth when you talked to her, like she was overdosing on speed. Or like she saw danger, constantly, over your shoulder."

When I didn't know the names of things, Sanchez didn't mind. He simply made one up.

So it was that we emptied and refilled the desert with the detritus of civilization, and we could walk for hours talking in our own patois about Edsels and Isettas, Sonys and Hondas—and I will always laugh at Sanchez's saying that Gilas were like Hondas.

"They plod along," he'd say. "But when Honda bites into a market, they never let go." He said that with the same joyful admiration he had for Hawks, the X-15s of the desert: "It will be the Japanese who clean up the carrion of American industry. You watch," he'd say.

Sanchez's humor infected Rachel, but in a different way. When he built a magazine rack into the corner of the trading post, it was a matter of days before Rachel had a card table set up outside. Displaying covers from *Penthouse* and *Playboy* and pictures of bondage that looked like they were left over from the days of Cortez above a sign that exclaimed "Porn is Woman Hate," Rachel solicited signatures on a petition against some of the magazines sold inside.

Sanchez loved it. "You're great for business," he told her. "Do you know that in a week you've tripled our sales of *Penthouse*?"

Undeterred, Rachel bought a second card table and tried

to engage Sanchez in discussions of pornography. "Pornography is violence," she would say.

"Pornography is writing about prostitutes, and both writing and prostitution are time-honored professions, though the hourly wage is higher for prostitution," Sanchez would say. Seeing the scowl on Rachel's face, he would add that he didn't much care for violence and that if she could convince him that the magazines encouraged violence, he would remove them.

"But," he'd say, if her face became too hopeful, "I wonder if what you're calling porn is more self-hatred than woman hate."

"It's pure lust," Rachel would say.

"Lust, Rachel, is a force in the universe. Like it or not. Sometimes I wonder if it isn't the repression of simple lust that leads to violence."

"It's degrading," Rachel would say.

"I'll be fair, if you want, and sell *Playgirl*. On one condition, though."

"What's that?"

"That you tell me why men don't feel degraded by *Playgirl*."

Rachel didn't get many signatures. Her friends, mostly. The women who came to the trading post weren't the kind who would sign a petition against what they accepted as history. The one man who signed was a young priest.

"Listen," Sanchez said to her, seeing how angry and depressed she was becoming. "Why don't you give this up and help me do a calendar with photos of you as January and December?" Rachel started to swing at him. "Clothed!" he said. "With your clothes on. A calendar of Chosposi life."

"It would sell," I offered, meekly. Rachel gave me a look not unlike the First Look she'd given me as a boy when I'd reached for the Gila monster. It was as though I was a kaleidoscope and she was looking at something through me.

"Who would want pictures of people like me?" Rachel asked.

But already I could see in her what I had never seen before, vanity, that dreamy vision of self which is caused not by a willing suspension of disbelief but a suspension of will in order to believe. Sanchez had touched a nerve. Rachel was envisioning herself as a poster girl. It would take time and the vision of my own vanity to cease thinking of Rachel as weakening at that moment. That wouldn't happen until I realized that what Sanchez had touched in her was not peculiar to her but thoroughly human; despite our bitter arguments with mirrors and bathroom scales, we can all envision ourselves as poster boys and girls.

"I would," I said. "Even without your clothes on," I added, joking, ready to duck if Rachel wasn't up to laughing.

"As Bert says," Sanchez said, "it would sell."

"Anything sells," Rachel replied. Her voice was as crisp as the leather of the moccasin she pulled from under the table and tossed in my face. I picked at the glass beads on the toe. They were sewn into a red, white, and blue star with seven rays.

"That," Rachel told me, "is one of the items your friend here sold to Johnny Three Feet. Moccasins. Pah! And these." She bent and pulled something else out. "Cute little numbers, aren't they?" It was a cottonwood tomahawk, a stick drilled at the top with the heel of an axe-head pushed through the hole and laced into position with imitation leather thong. What looked to be canary feathers were stapled to the top of the handle.

"The tomahawks go for $2.50. The moccasins for nine bucks."

"So?" I shrugged. Inside the heel of the moccasin was a gold sticker that said "Genuine Handsewn Leather," and I couldn't help but choke back a laugh, recognizing Sanchez's careful implication that Indians had made the moccasins.

Rachel almost laughed herself when Sanchez presented her with the image of suburban men shuffling about their split-level homes in the moccasins, or their kids trying to hack the tails off salamanders with the tiny tomahawks.

She managed to contain her smile by giving me the bilious beady look of a snake about to strike. "'So,' he says. I should have known. You fool. I should have let you pick up that Gila monster. If I had, you wouldn't have brought that man here. He wouldn't have talked poor numbskulled Johnny into selling this shit as souvenirs. You haven't even considered the results, have you? It's going to be your fault, whatever happens."

"Now wait a minute," Sanchez interrupted. "Bert didn't bring me here. I happened to be on the same bus with him, that's all. You can't lay some guilt trip on him."

"He showed you around, didn't he?"

"Yeah, but . . . ," I said, discomfited by the way Rachel was looking at Sanchez.

"He made you feel welcome."

"True blue," Sanchez said. "But remember one thing. Bert made me feel welcome. You made me determined to stay."

"What does that mean?" Rachel said.

"You'll figure it out," Sanchez said. "Think about it. I'm sure you're smart enough to figure it out." He gave her a wicked smile and then said to me, "Listen, I'll be inside the post. See ya," he said to Rachel. "Soon."

"You *like* him?" she asked.

I confessed that I did.

"Why?"

"He makes me laugh. Really laugh. After all that's happened, I need laughter," I said.

"Your friend Sanchez laughs at anything," Rachel said.

"And everything. He can make even the audiences at a French film laugh." It was true. While the hero and heroine drove endlessly through the steady French rain, Sanchez would laugh and the rest of the audience would begin to wait for his laughter. Waiting created anticipation, anticipation possibility—and if your sister had bled to death in front of your eyes, you would think possibility was a laugh in itself.

"But everything is not funny," Rachel protested.

"Yeah, but once anything isn't even possibly funny, it's dead or boring. Besides, Sanchez doesn't laugh *at* things as much as *for* them." I could see she was thinking about that. "You might like him, too," I said. "If you would lighten your load long enough to get to know him."

"I don't want to know him," Rachel hissed, and stomped off toward the mission.

I stood there in the dust spit up by Rachel's leaving, feeling helpless and somewhat lonely, trying to remember a time I had seen her laugh and wondering what good laughter would do her. Maybe it wasn't laughter, alone, that I was talking about. Maybe it was joy, that willingness to enjoy that hung about Sanchez's laughter like branches on a spruce tree.

At the mission door, Rachel turned and shouted, "You know what your problem is? You're all means. You don't ever think about ends. That's where you and I part company."

"I hope not for good," I said to myself. In a way, she was right, or almost right. It wasn't that I never thought about ends. It was that there were only the illusions of ends. The only real end was death; means were what I enjoyed, the ways in which we go about moving toward the illusory ends. I couldn't prove that my way was the right way. Even thinking about it gave me a headache—and I'd been getting more and more of those recently. Little men with jackhammers started tearing up the inside of my head and I bought a Coke from the new machine on the porch of the trading post, removed the tin foil from an Empirin codeine tablet and took it, and waited silently for the calm of codeine the way the land waits, leaning toward the clouds which may or may not carry rain.

It had begun to seem that, given the way even Rachel was acting, every relationship with a woman got confused and entangled in the spidery webs of the unanticipated and unwanted. Perhaps it was the way these relationships began? If I hadn't acquired Allison DeForest (or her me—I still didn't know which), or if Rachel hadn't begun by calling me a fool, placing herself in a superior position and somehow extrapolating that one position to include all positions, would it have been different? If Rachel had been a man, would I have hit her the times she infuriated or hurt me? Probably not, I decided, as the first wash of codeine began to soften the marrow of my bones. Still, for an instant, I imagined slugging her just hard enough to knock the anger out of her and I could not help but grin. Not at the vision of Rachel suddenly domesticated like an animal, but at the realization that I was about as clever with women as Johnny Three Feet, named for his Neanderthal clumsiness, was graceful at basketball. Even Elanna, whose letters from Berkeley I tore open with the voracity of a nutcracker, had often said that she could forgive me only because she was my sister.

Sanchez came out and sat beside me. Johnny, who behaved these days like Sanchez's pet Malamute, followed him out and stood behind us. None of us said anything, until Rachel came back out of the mission to man her table for the afternoon buses.

"Well, hell," Sanchez said as he watched her organize her petitions, "I like her, even if she doesn't like me." Johnny gurgled with glee; he liked her, too.

"Don't worry about it," I said. "She's just angry."

"I won't," Sanchez said. "In fact," he added, leaning toward me so Johnny couldn't hear, "just between you and me, Kemo-sabe, I'm going to marry her someday." His burst of laughter made Johnny conscious of his size sixteen shoes. Even Rachel turned and almost smiled before she became aware of who was laughing.

"Marry Rachel?" I said.

"Here comes a bus," Sanchez said. "Let's go, John-boy."

I had a faint intuition of what bothered Rachel about Sanchez, then. He could refuse to talk about a topic that mattered to you, even about a topic he had brought up, teasing you with it, making you think about it more than was necessary. To Rachel, it was as though he functioned gaily on the surface of things, revealing only the tip of the mesa and rarely delving into the shadowy valleys below.

Had I thought about her saying that, I might have realized that she was, in part, wrong. Sanchez did think about many things, just not out loud in front of other people. And I might have been able to foresee that Sanchez was telling the truth—he would eventually marry Rachel—and that her initial protestations against him were not so much moral criticism as a sign of the attraction she, too, felt for his laughter.

"He irritates me," Rachel told me, trying to explain, "especially when you're around."

I should have wondered what he did when I wasn't around. At the time, I was most often stoned on codeine, and codeine had the power to temporarily erase past and future and leave me dangling in the happy present. I clung to that feeling; I needed it then because what I felt when Sanchez said he would someday marry Rachel was jealousy. I loved Rachel as I loved Elanna; I hated her, at times, because I knew she'd never quite forgive me for what I was. It was hatred which allowed me to see that Rachel never really wanted Sanchez to stop selling those magazines. His selling them gave her a reason to exist as much as she gave him a reason to become momentarily serious. But it would take a few more years and the death of Grandfather, whom I had engendered as the one, true ear, before I would see that.

## 33.

Sanchez paid me and paid me well to fly in and out of San Francisco, and on one of my trips I met the woman for whom my uncle had left the Vegomatic. It was the only time I would meet Karen Manowitz, in the San Francisco airport, where I had been trying to fly a stewardess named June—a hopeless exercise. June was due to take off for Denver, and I was carrying a shipment of softwood Kachinas, mass-made in Chinatown by unemployed garment workers, which Sanchez sold at outrageous prices at Johnny Three Feet's Trading Post. Yet June's little outfit pushed her breasts up into a pale, smooth heart that made me breathless with a subtle pain like pneumonia, and it was a way to pass the time. Besides, after hundreds of takeoffs and landings, I was curious about those yellow cups that drop down on plastic tubes, which Juney and her ilk demonstrated on each and every flight.

"Where," I asked her, "do they keep the oxygen?" June looked quizzical, then confused, and finally bored when I said, "After all, above the masks are coats and carry-on luggage. Not much oxygen, there."

"I take off in an hour," June said. "Let's see . . . I land in Denver at three o'clock and lay over for two hours before I turn around."

Sitting on a barstool, trying to work the conversation away from June's scheduled takeoffs and landings and trying to overcome the crashing boredom June obviously felt at my trying to fly her, I heard a familiar voice sing out, "Hey, Jude," and I turned in fatal recognition to spot uncle spotting me, on his arm a dark-haired woman whom I could describe only as compact. She wasn't short and she wasn't tall. Neither was she voluptuous. But her clothes and the skin that showed beneath or beyond the clothes were filled with comfortable economy, as though every inch of skin and clothing had been designed and engineered for maximum efficiency without excessive show or luxury. Rather than beautiful or sexy, she was well-made, and the comfortable, easy way in which she walked beside uncle made me relax so much that I nearly fell off the stool. Years later, when I thought about her, I would know what I'd come to mean by attractive, that seemingly empty and ineffectual word that I can't help using. Unlike uncle's wife who even in house slippers walked as though she were wearing spike heels, her body hard and sharp and her sex clinically hidden, this woman on uncle's arm was one you could hold without having to suit up in protective pads first.

"Hey, Alley," uncle called across the bar.

"Who is that?" June said. I did not appreciate the criticism implicit in her voice. The tone was that of a woman who plays Simon Says in bed, unable to relax and simply have an orgasm because her nerves cannot forget all of the close calls, the near misses of all the metered men she's had to endure in the backseats of taxis. "Oh, Juney," I said to myself, "Though we are about the same age, I am much too old for you."

"My uncle," I said. "On a jag. Excuse me." I left her sitting there.

"How you been, boy? Haven't seen you for . . . how long has it been? This is Karen Manowitz," uncle said. "Karen, my nephew, Alley."

"How do you do. Alley, is it?" I nodded. She smiled, and the temperature of the bar went up a few degrees, as though I were sitting by a window and the sun had emerged from behind the threatening clouds, warming me, making my bones stop hurting from the stiffness of June's ennui. I smiled back. Uncle sat us at an empty table, brought us drinks, gulped his while standing.

"Listen, Alley," he said, "you and Karen sit and get to know each other, while I go check on our flight. What do you say?" And off he went, singing, "Bee-bop-a-louie, she's my baby."

Karen watched him go and then we sat there smiling at each other some more. Just before my flight to Phoenix was announced, Karen said, "You're probably wondering what it is I'm doing here."

Long before I said it, I had known I would say it, if I could cease smiling long enough. "No," I said. "I know the how and why. The what," I added, "I don't much care about."

She nodded her head, tilting it to the right slightly. "Thank you, Alley," she said.

"You're welcome," I said. As I left the bar, I turned to look at Karen. "Listen," I said to her. I think now that I was intending to say something to her about sawdust or oxygen. Regardless, all I could do was wave and take up my incessant smiling.

I smiled all the way to Phoenix, watched closely by the stewardesses who suspected that behind that silly grin lurked a madman, even though I tried to explain to one of them that I couldn't help but smile because my uncle was, after years of carrothood, at long last happy.

When uncle divorced his wife, I heard the entire family sigh. Eventually, I would hear the intake of those sighs, a sound like a distant choir of children slurping soup in unison, when uncle remarried his boat and house, his pension.

"The rabbit fights for his life, the coyote eats lunch," Grandfather would say.

I suppose he was right. Uncle's remarrying the Vegomatic wouldn't matter much. His life was over long before and, by the time he eloped with his ex-first-wife, his horizons all distant except for the one brief trip he'd taken with Karen Manowitz. By then, my expatriated cousin had delayed a West German train for more than an hour—a crime the Germans could never tolerate, and for which they are pursuing him still. Sometimes, I wonder whether he is Rabbit or Coyote as my cousin tries to make up for his father in a world that is either too large to care or too small to bother.

## 34.

Sanchez was off foraging in other parts of the wilderness of civilization when I got back to Chosposi, and Rachel seemed to avoid me. She had given up her petitions and dismantled her card tables, and when finally I caught up to her, it was in one of the small canyons where she still caught the random Gila.

"I see you're back," was all she said.

"Johnny said you received a full scholarship to Arizona State."

"I did?" she said, confirming what I had suspected since Elanna's letters had begun arriving with the pages out of order, that Johnny steamed open and read the mail he was supposed to deliver. Most of it, anyway. He never touched the unpunctuated streams of mother's consciousness.

"Congratulations."

"Save it," she said, folding her hardened arms across her chest. "I'll turn it down."

"Rachel, why?"

"It's only white folks trying to buy off their own guilt." She looked meaningfully at me. "I won't be a statistic like some people I know." We both knew that Clearmont Men's College folded minorities into the batter of freshmen in order to allow rich white boys to encounter what they were not and thus begin the primal stages of self-definition. CMC already had a Jew and two Blacks, but I was an especially useful acquisition, as I was only part-Indian. Among the minorities, only I exemplified the mixture of bloods. My mixed-up beliefs would allow the white boys to see the results of miscegenation.

After giving up her protest of porn, Rachel began tinkering with helping the missionary's wife organize groups of Indians. What these groups—old and young, men and women, boys and girls, and any permutation of those—were supposed to do, no one seemed to know.

"Meet," the missionary's wife said.

"Find their own way to God," the missionary said.

"They already have a complex model of the universe. Gods like Taiowa and Spider Woman. Spirits and ceremonies," I said.

"That's all right, too," the missionary's wife said. "Unitarians do their own thing. As long as they meet."

The Indians who did attend the weekly dry-cleaning of their souls chose to sit on blankets on the floor, rather than perch on the wooden folding chairs left behind by a succession of other ministries. As long as the missionary told stories and told them well, they remained, trying not to laugh as the missionary explained to them that the ocean was a wet desert. None of them had the heart to hurt the missionary's feelings by telling him what they had known since the days of migration, and the missionary, interpreting their swaying silence as indifference, entered a repetitive search for stories worth the telling—and so it was that he himself came to believe that tides were caused by an angel stepping into or out of the waters of the earth.

Rachel, on the other hand, was less interested in telling stories and more interested in raising Indian consciousness.

"Of what?" I asked her, again and again.

"Of the world outside them."

"Why? Why do you want them to be conscious of the world outside?" I asked, trying to convince her that Laura P. knew more about how the world worked than if she'd made friends with a quark.

"Because they're getting taken," Rachel insisted.

"They may get taken, no matter what," Sanchez would say. "All we can do is try to help them control how they get taken."

Whereas Rachel was busily raising Indian consciousness, it was Sanchez's import/export business that taught them what it meant to be American. Sanchez did away with the person of the maker, turning Kachinas into a collector's item. It was a process not unlike numismatics or the collecting of art: The maker didn't matter; who mattered was the coin dealer and the gallery owner, and Sanchez taught the Indians to become dealers in artifacts. In short, Sanchez made them middlemen, and it was the money they made from dealing that gave them something to speak about when Rachel raised their consciousnesses to the level of speaking out.

Sanchez plugged himself into the world of Chosposi successfully. Authenticity for him was only a matter of re-entry. "What goes up must come down," he'd say, "and where I come down I figure I belong."

Nice. Some of the Indians even seemed willing to think of Sanchez as Pahana, the lost white brother whose coming was ordained. But for me, authenticity was becoming a problem as I ferried unpainted softwood Kachinas from San Francisco or trucked in tortilla presses cast with Indian designs from Nogales. The region I called the Absence of Angels was settling like swamp fog around me, and each time I went aloft in a plane I brought another Glad Bag of it down with me. Everything seemed to become long-distance and I was becoming obsessed with the need to reach out and touch someone. That, at least, will explain how I began to teach Johnny Three Feet to play a rudimentary basketball to the best of his physically challenged abilities. Whenever I became impatient with Johnny, I told myself that people like Johnny aren't around long and they deserve every break they can get.

"It happens that way sometimes," Grandfather said, muscles contracting involuntarily like someone suddenly sad or angry, skidding to a halt on his three-wheeler. "By accident."

Certainly, it was by accident that Grandfather had had enough liquid cash to purchase the three-wheeled Raleigh, the one I would come to call the "killer bike," from a purveyor of health who passed through Chosposi selling faith in vitamins, hope in exercise, and the charity of whole grains which, closing his drugged-out Californian eyes, he consecrated as "roughage."

Grandfather took to riding the bike to and from the trading post at a speed that forced me to hop every third step in order to keep up with him. At 88, he had, with his own obscure belief in ends and means, determined that he would live to ninety, and whatever he lacked in speed he made up for in heart.

"No sense rushing it," he would say. Reaching ninety was a lot like driving three miles per hour faster. It wasn't much of a change and either way you were going to get where you were going. "Point A to point B," he would add.

He would very nearly reach B, too, two years later. Ironically, it would be the bike which allowed his heart to remain strong, and it would be the bike which, in his stubbornness, he deliberately rode over a curb, putting him into the hospital. Even then, he would live on, falling short of his birthday by a matter of hours—a minor and forgivable failure of concentration, a miscalculation of the will and not of the heart.

That summer, uncle would fly into Chosposi in a borrowed plane and cease singing "We've Only Just Begun" long enough to comment on how Grandfather looked closer to eighty than ninety, and Grandfather would be unimpressed. Consumed with the novelty of joy over Karen Manowitz, having escaped from the Vegomatic by putting out of his mind the memories she had helped him slice, dice, and parboil, uncle exclaimed, "You're going to live forever!"

Grandfather merely looked sad. I was touched by that sadness and by my uncle's failure to understand that Death, when He came for Grandfather, would approach head-on like a slow but inevitable freight train. Grandfather would never want it otherwise.

The novelty of my uncle's joy, along with his denial of Death, caused his mistaken ebullience. Having known the Vegomatic, whose face looked hard and cold like the faces of women at Republican conventions, and having met Karen Manowitz, I was as unwilling to deny that temporary joy as I was to deny Johnny Three Feet's gurgling happiness when he made a layup, even though it made Grandfather look sad.

Like Grandfather, I felt pretty sad as I watched my uncle climb into the cockpit of his borrowed plane, the half-life of his joy revealed in the look on his face which was akin to the quick mnemonic look of the three-legged cat whose only thrill in life had been to hunt birds.

"See you later, alligator," uncle said.

"In a while, crocodile," I said, trying to grin.

He looked at me, holding the ends of his seat belt in either hand. "You know, Alley," he said. "We haven't known each other very well. But somehow I've always thought you understood, ever since you and . . . and my . . . son . . . ever since that Christmas when you and he tried to do what the Japanese couldn't manage." He looked as far away as Laura P. when he said, "They're still out there, somewhere. Aren't they?"

"Sure," I said. "Sure they are." He stopped staring up at the sky and fastened his belts. "Give Karen my love," I said.

"Consider it done," he said. "And you say howdy to my brother for me when you see him. He's been pretty uptight with me, lately."

"I will," I said, tempted to tell him that his brother's harsh attitude toward his taking up with Karen Manowitz was not moral disapproval but rather the mousse of feelings condensing around his own divorce from mother. I wanted to explain that, like the dicey numbers in a bingo game, father's feelings had been stirred up; that he was incapable of talking about them and to hear his brother talk about them only caused father unimaginable pain.

"Be well," I said, shutting the cockpit door and stepping back from the plane.

Uncle slid back the window and poked his head out. "Hey Alley," he said. "You still have that penny I gave you for luck?"

The expression on his happy face closed like the cockpit window when I said, "No."

I regretted that and it was this regret I would try to make up for later when my revolting cousin crawled through the window of my dormitory one night in the fall and demanded that I help him escape the country. I didn't know my cousin from Adam and with his red Afro and bleary eyes he looked like an implosion waiting to happen. His voice was clipped, reminding me of the voice of the Vegomatic; but for that, I might not have recognized him in the Clearmont darkness. His laughter was as old and bitter as one who had invested his life in the American Dream only to discover in his twilight years that social security isn't worth a sandbag against the flood of inflation. He did not re-engender things with imagination; he destroyed their old uses in favor of the new. He was filled with hatred, calling his father names like "Fascist" and popping pills to achieve what he called the cutting edge. His cloud of easy epithets made me furiously sad, and I defended my uncle with vehemence, reminding my cousin of his incineration of the people of Pillar to Post, of the little frogs he had liked blowing into the glorious afterlife as a child.

"Wow!" he said. "Whew! You aren't really that dumb, are you? The frogs were training, man. Practice. There's a difference, don't you see?"

Maybe it was the way his eyes became gelatinous, swimming beneath the shadows of his copper-colored Afro. Maybe it was the fact that he had called me dumb and I was weary of being called dumb in a dumb world. I thought at the time that it was an attempt to make it up to my uncle when, before he straggled off into the Mexican night, my cousin had demanded even more money and I handed him a penny and said, "Let us not meet again." This year or any other, I thought, feeling joy as I watched the candle of his hair recede, flicker, and disappear into the permanent realm of rumor.

Then, as I watched the plane wiggle around and taxi for takeoff, its tail wagging like a mechanical puppy on rundown batteries, I wished I could take back my answer. My uncle was only trying to find a place in the world where he could live without people thumping on his delicate dreams like tom-toms. As the plane's engine roared and strained, lifting into the air toward the San Francisco Peaks, the Absence of Angels turned the bruised color of regret. Within the year, the collective sighs of my family would signal uncle's leaving Karen Manowitz to return to the security of the Vegomatic and, for me, flying towards San Francisco would be like flying into the vacuum center of a storm, a vast cosmic sucking, pulling the jet over the Bay Bridge down towards the blue lights that lined the runway.

## 35.

Regret is the daughter of accident and the queer lover of Death, so it was no surprise to me that, with all the regrets in Chosposi, the little blighter Death decided to become my fellow traveler that summer, winding me into a cocoon of solitude like a silkworm. Each time I returned to Chosposi, Rachel seemed less happy to see me, giving me spurious looks of anxiety as though I knew something about her that could and would be used against her in a court of law. Sanchez, conversely, made great efforts to welcome me back, hailing me with a brashness that seemed extreme and insincere. Where his large laughter had once pleased me with the joy he took in the desert and had made me laugh with him, now his laughter sometimes seemed forced, needing booster rockets to escape the gravity of his heart. I felt chagrined when he laughed that way, and in public I wanted to dissociate myself from it.

More often, I was beginning to sink into the feeling that I didn't belong there. The more I struggled against it, the more I seemed to sink. I began to take long solitary walks, ostensibly looking for arrowheads on the grassy plains to the east of the mission, oftentimes spending hours developing a seminal skin cancer from the hot sun as I sat and watched Navaho work around their hogans from a distance. My skin turned the color of cut earth, and I could sit unnoticed, looking like a spot of ground lacerated by rain or time or tool.

One day, having overestimated my resistance to the sun and stayed out too long, I was staggering home along the westbound road into the mission, hoping to hitch a ride on any cart or car that might pass. Along the sides of the road were Saguaro cacti, regularly spaced enough for the placards Sanchez had hung from them like Burma Shave signs. *Unwise and Unfortunate*, they read, *the man who tries to pass / Nahochass / Navaho-Hopi Crafts and Historical Assoc. / Genuine Artifacts / The Standard for 99 Years.* I had almost reached the second set which read, *Cheer Up / Friend / You're nearly there*, when I noticed kangaroo mice hopping past, lizards and snakes slithering toward holes, birds abandoning the satin sky—a general movement of fauna as though something like an earthquake were coming. To the north was a stream of dust, rising from the earth like smoke. There was no road in that direction, so I assumed it had to be the smoke from a hogan drifting on the unfelt wind. I kept walking as a clanking, like rocks in a car's hubcaps, barely perceptible at first, grew louder. When finally I turned again, there was a modified van bearing down on me, a row of air horns above the cab blasting. I dove behind a mound of earth as the van swerved, screeched, and a tire blew, flipping it onto the passenger's side with a sound as unnerving as the metallic boring of a dentist's drill as it plowed to a halt in the dry depression beside the road.

The van was customized with metallic paint, flames stencilled on the front fenders, bubble windows, and a cityscape complete with brown, smoggy air fused into the rear window. The driver, a little man with pale skin flecked with black dust like a coal miner, was still belted rigidly into his seat, both hands riveted to the steering wheel as if he expected the van at any moment to struggle to its feet like a horse and off they'd go.

"You okay?" I asked, climbing onto the van and pulling the driver's door open.

His dark punk glasses were askew on his nose and his face seemed to refuse to move. It didn't twitch, grimace, laugh, cry, or show anger or despair. It simply and completely waited for the van to end this siestal interlude and get under way again.

"Hey," I said, shaking His shoulder. It was then I heard a sound that I have since come to associate with Death as if He were made from scrap metal—a rattling clinking sound like surgical tools falling into a sterilization pan or the jangle of a girl gilded by vanity.

"Hey," I yelled, "are you okay?"

His beady bilious eyes, like a Gila's with cataracts, blinked once and His oversized head turned very slowly up toward me. "Ho," He said. "It's you."

Dragging Him from the van, I stood Him on His feet and stepped back to take a look at Him. You could have strip-mined His person. He was encased in jewelry. Turquoise amulets hung from His neck; His arms, all the way up His loose plaid Sears and Roebuck flannel shirt, were mailed with tin and lapis lazuli; and on the heels of His Dingo boots were silver spurs. He staggered for a moment as the weight of the trinkets settled and His tiny feet took hold on the solid earth.

Extracting a screwdriver from one of the several pockets sewn to His khaki pants, He solemnly removed the winged figure of Mercury that ornamented the hood of His van. I watched Him, feeling as though I was watching a ritual the meaning of which had not existed until that moment and wondering why I neither feared nor hated Him—indeed, was almost glad for Him the way you're glad for an alarm clock even though you would rather be allowed to sleep. A small trickle of gasoline had begun to pool near His feet, and I was in the process of realizing the danger when He reached for the bulge of a cigarette pack in His breast pocket.

"Wait," I yelled. He raised His other hand flat against my caution as though He were stopping an exaltation of larks. Carefully pacing off ten paces from the puddle of gasoline, He lit a cigarette and puffed on it, musing on what to do with a lame van. When He couched the stub of the cigarette between His thumb and middle finger in a position ready to flick it at the van, I began to run, diving over a rise in the earth just before the explosion. Peering over the hillock, I saw His dwarfish figure emerge from the black billowing smoke and clink-clank off west-southwest, angling away from the road that would take Him straight to Nahochass.

For one reason or another, I started to run after Him as though He were a person I wanted to help, to tell Him that if He followed the road. . . . I stopped hurrying after Him when He turned, tossed the winged Mercury at my feet, and said, "Okay, already. I owe you one. You get to choose when and I'll pass over." Shaking His head, muttering, "You're going to be the end of me, yet," He resumed His slow, lugubrious clanking into the setting sun, sounding more like the movement of German tanks in a generic war film than Death on little cat's feet.

With Death around Chosposi, strange things began to happen. Death himself was strange. One thing I noticed was that most people failed to take notice of Him. Even when I pointed Him out to Rachel or Sanchez as He sat in His twenty-gallon hat on the porch of Nahochass, they refused to believe who it was.

"You fool," Rachel would say. "Death doesn't *exist* the way we do."

"Besides," Sanchez would add in agreement, "Death would be bigger, stronger, and smell a lot like a fish market on a hot day."

The more they ignored Death and pretended it wasn't He sitting outside Nahochass, the deadlier He seemed to become, and when I made the mistake of introducing Him to some gray-haired lady from Muncie, she fainted out of fear. To Grandfather Death wasn't frightening; rather, He looked only sad with a border of bitterness to His mouth resembling a retired stockbroker.

"It's a matter of expectation," Grandfather would say, spinning the dial on the Sony television Sanchez had bought for him in search of commercials. "He wants to take the series. But this is the only game in town."

Grandfather didn't care for the programs and, unless he could watch the 49ers, he spent a good deal of his time with the miniature t.v. plugged into the dash of the Plymouth, switching from channel to channel in search of commercials.

"Look how white people spell 'Relief,'" he would say, chuckling briefly before he added, "No wonder"—as though that commercial alone explained something profound. When he saw grown men dressed up like fruit in underwear commercials or like raisins in cereal commercials, he'd clap his hands and cry "Progress!" happily.

Laura P. became crablike again and her pots became what Sanchez called experimental and which were really failures of control, with spidery designs fired into them which had little or no meaning even to Laura. These pots were bought at crazy prices by a gallery owner from Phoenix, and she took to sleeping with her eyes wide open and throwing her pots with them closed, with the result that she sold even more pots and became richer. So rich, in fact, that she had to sneak away from the house at night and ritually bury the money in unmarked graves. Sanchez's idea of firing hundred dollar bills into the sides of random pots offered her momentary relief: She hoped that, by doing so, the people who bought her "art" would take it home and destroy it, looking to find the bills. These pots became, overnight, collector's items.

Even Johnny Three Feet fell under the spell of Death, giving up the gurgling pleasures of basketball in order to dribble around trying to look up little girls' dresses.

For me, Death was as boring as He had always been. He sat beside me when I wanted to be alone and began conversations bordering on monologues. Over and over, He slipped into telling me how this job was the hardest He'd ever had, and from there go on to tell me about His boss, a man who no longer participated in the company and yet reaped profits from it by remaining chairman of the board. And whenever

He had the chance, He'd remind me that He owed me one passover, but just one, asking if I wanted to redeem the debt now. After Johnny Three Feet molested a twelve-year-old girl, Death and I were observing the stiff and hateful behavior of the authorities who dragged Johnny weeping from Nahochass, and Death turned and smiled at me.

"He'll die in prison," He said.

I nodded. It was true: Johnny had an innocent stupidity that would make other felons hate him murderously.

"Now?" Death asked.

"No." Saving Johnny's life would require going all the way back to the snowstorm in which his mother had died and during which he had come into the world.

When Death sidled up to me after I had walked in on Sanchez and Rachel and surprised them in the act of dressing, He grinned salaciously and asked, "Now?"

I said, "No." I didn't mind Rachel sleeping with Sanchez. I rather welcomed it, hoping that Sanchez's innate irreverence would help Rachel put the flesh of humor on her sharp bones. Their sleeping together was only one of those all-too-explicable events that occurs between two people when one feels intensely about the other. In this case, Rachel had begun by hating Sanchez only to discover with each new instance of his generosity or humorous approach to the world that he wasn't so bad. As his so-called badness modified, the strength of her feelings hadn't, and gradually they transformed from hatred to love. If nothing else, it proved that what the feeling was called didn't matter as much as the feeling's intensity. When we really and honestly don't care about people, don't we settle for saying that they are "nice" or "kind"? It seemed normal enough to me that Rachel, hating Sanchez at the outset, would end by liking him; and so, even though their sleeping together made me feel excluded, I didn't mind, and I chose not to use up the one favor Death owed me.

Possibly, I might have changed that answer and taken Death up on his offer to passover and alter the way things happened if I had realized that hatred doesn't simply evaporate like dew after the deserted night. All that changes is hatred's object. Someone once said that hating Indians was only three letters away from hating Jews; we might add that hating men is only a hop, skip, and a gender away from hating women. In my own slow way, with the naive stupidity of a Johnny Three Feet, I imagined that Rachel's falling in love with Sanchez would allow her to be my friend again. After all, it was my liking of Sanchez that had made her withdraw from me. Why wouldn't her liking him allow her to like me again? We could all be friends.

Wrong. Maybe if Johnny Three Feet hadn't been arrested and dragged weeping from Chosposi, Rachel would have turned on him and not me. Maybes are of little use, though, in cases that are real and not properly imagined. From furtive looks and downcast eyes to questions suggestive in the dulcet tones of their inflection, Rachel began to attack me directly. It was not a slow process. "What do you *want*?" changed to "*What* do you want?," signalling her increasing frustration with me. When the same question became "What do *you* want?," I was forced into the corners of my own frustration and loneliness.

Sanchez seemed as embarrassed by all this as I was. One night in Phoenix we were shooting pool in a bar where the waitresses wore clothes instead of uniforms and I mentioned that maybe he'd like me to quit the import business for Nahochass. It had been a slow game, one in which each of us spent more time walking around the table and chalking up our cues than in talking the way we had been used to doing— airing the linen of our feelings. Sanchez kept watch on the door as though Death or Rachel might suddenly walk through it.

"Why would I want you to quit?" Sanchez said, lining up a shot.

"I don't know. I just get this feeling that things might be better for you if I did."

"No way, my friend. You were there at the beginning and you'll be there at the end."

"You're sure? You can be straight with me."

"Sure I'm sure."

"I figure that even after I go to Clearmont College in the fall I can come out most weekends. Holidays," I said. "You want another beer?" He nodded.

When I came back, Sanchez said, "It's your turn," took the

draft beer and moved to the far end of the table. After my first shot, he said, "Of course . . ."

"Of course what?" I said.

"Of course, I was wondering if it might not be better for you if you waited until next summer. I mean what with school and all, wouldn't it be better if you concentrated on your studies?"

"That's up to me, isn't it?" I was unwilling to let him off the hook he had baited.

"I guess," he said. "Then there's Rachel, too."

Now we were getting somewhere. "What about Rachel?"

"Well, she seems pretty uncomfortable with you. I don't know why. I don't even know if there is a reason. But every time you and I go out together, she gets pretty upset. When you're around, she fidgets a lot." He bent above his cue and then stood up before taking the shot. "I'm not saying you've done anything."

"I haven't."

"But maybe for her sake, it would be better if you stayed out of the business until next summer. I'm sure she'll calm down by then."

"If that's what you want, sure," I said, thinking, okay, I'll make it easy on you. Friend.

"It isn't what *I* want," he protested. "Not what I want at all. But you know women."

"Yeah," I said. "Women. We'd better get on back to the post, don't you think.?"

On the way back, we were silent. I wasn't angry at Sanchez or Rachel. I reminded Rachel of the way they had begun. No one wanted reminders like that around. Just as two alcoholics who love each other can't stay married after they've climbed on the wagon, so friends who remind us of our former enemies are unwelcome. No, my anger was for myself, the way I had this feeling of holding the ball once again, and of having to be left holding it.

## 36.

With Death, too, there had come mysterious strangers, men with crew cuts dressed in uniforms, enlisting Navaho boys as encoders of military messages. Their glossy brochures attracted me, especially because of what the Army recruiter said, that I could train while in school and after graduation be a part of something larger than myself. It was, after all, a thing I wanted; maybe the Army could provide it. That, at least, was the excuse I used for signing an agreement to enroll in R.O.T.C. when I started Clearmont Men's College, and even Grandfather seemed to approve, saying, "It's your country. You fertilize it, maybe it will fertilize you."

"Like a vegetable?" I said.

"Like red meat," Grandfather said.

It was this, my agreeing to join R.O.T.C., that served as an excuse for Rachel to excuse herself. Catching up with me from behind as I walked alone toward the reservation mission's gymnasium, Rachel knocked the basketball from my hand.

"Rotsy!" she said. "How could you?"

"Sanchez told you?" I said. "Could he tell you why?"

"Man," Rachel said, sneering. "I don't believe it. What happened to the peace symbols? What would your old friend Yvette say? Pah!" she spat, hitting the tip of my sneaker. "Sexism wasn't good enough for you? Now . . ."

"Shut up," I warned.

"You've gotta try fascism, too, now?"

"Shut your fucking mouth," I said. "You've got no right to judge people."

"Don't tell me to shut up, fool," she said.

"I just did. Shut up. See?"

Rachel reached up and slapped me hard across the face. For an instant, I was stunned not by the force of the blow but by the power of absurdity. What was expected? How was one to respond? Should I treat her the way I had been taught to treat women and turn the other cheek? I struck her with the back of my partially closed hand. I cupped my hand so the knuckles would hurt and hit her hard enough to hurt her a good deal. She never would have believed that I could have hit twice as hard. At least twice as hard. None of that bothered me. What upset me was the feeling of calculation. I'd done it coolly and without concern—a calculation alternating with rage and hatred. I was ready to strike anyone for any reason, good or not, before I would regret bruising Rachel's face.

"You shouldn't have done that," Sanchez said, the next time he saw me.

"Yeah?" I said. "Yeah? Give me half a chance and I'll do it again."

Sanchez walked away.

"There *is* an order to things," Grandfather said. "Even carrots are better than snakes."

I felt backed into a corner, wounded by the fact that Grandfather had no interest in my explanations. Still, I refused to regret hitting Rachel.

"You need to go," Louis Applegate said. "Like me, you don't belong here."

"Yet," Grandfather added. "Maybe you should go home until it's time to leave for college."

"Now?" Death said.

"Absolutely not," I replied.

Louis was right, and I knew it. Even as I boarded the bus out of Chosposi, confused as I was over ends and means, I envied Laura P. and Grandfather, Rachel and Sanchez their abilities to act on the basis of their individual visions of how the world ought to have been. My one action of that summer besides teaching Johnny Three Feet to pretend to shoot baskets had been to sock Rachel one. Although it was an end which I refused to have real regrets about, my refusal made me wonder if my imagination wasn't extremely limited.

Leaning my head back against the soiled doily of the seat's headrest, I wondered about ends and means. "Who," I said aloud, "is hurting who?," drawing frightened stares from Mrs. Joad, who sat across the aisle.

"Ain't no sense to get riled," she told her son. "We gone get there when we get there." True enough, I thought. True enough.

The potential of being challenged to explain to another person like Rachel how I came to enroll in R.O.T.C. bugged me as much as the persistent questions of Joad Junior about when they would get there, wherever that was, so I invented a story. At first, it was merely an idea: I had gotten into trouble, been arrested and tried, and released by the judge on the condition that I enroll in R.O.T.C. I fell asleep.

A high interior voice woke me. "Why," it asked, "would a judge release an Indian on that condition?"

"I wasn't guilty," I said.

"So? You don't have to be guilty, if he's seen enough John Wayne movies. A white judge might just throw the book at you."

"So the judge was Black. He knew. He understood."

"Fine and dandy, Randy," the voice said. "But if the Black judge found you not guilty . . ."

"Contempt of court. Even though I wasn't guilty, I was found in contempt of court."

It was only natural to add William the Black, Walter, Allen, Stephen, and Paul to the story. After all, I knew them, had been given to hanging out with them, and if anyone needed more details, I'd be able to describe each of them after his fashion.

"What was the charge for which the six of you were tried?" the voice asked.

Without hesitating I replied, "Assault." After all, that's what I'd done to Rachel, assaulted her in response to her assault on me. It was on my mind; it was also something I knew. In the same way I had mixed in my buddies, I added the catalyst of striking a girl with the back of the hand—not my hand, but Walter's hand—and by the time the bus rolled through Lost Hills, California, the story came out this way:

*On a drunken spree with William the Black, Walter, Allen, Stephen, and Paul, at Walter's new girlfriend's house. Her parents gone for the weekend, the six of us finished off most of the liquor in the father's cabinet while Walter and Cynthia ("Cyn-thee-ya," as she said it, with the slow imitation of the ascendant bourgeois) sprayed and spat at each other like two clawless cats in the upper regions of the split-level house. It was no accident that Walter slapped Cyn-thee-ya with the back of his open hand (it seemed to me more out of sorrow that the level of passion had declined to this cold farewell on the front stoop). It was accidental that Cyn-thee-ya happened to be the daughter of the county sheriff, a girl given to fabricating serious truths out of the flippant disorder of her unexciting life and what had merely been a quarrel produced for a small summer stock audience was transformed by the emptiness of the father's liquor bottles*

163

*into an assault charge for which we were arrested. Fortunately, recognizing the inherent dishonesty of the fiction, the Black judge dismissed the charges. Unfortunately, he felt obliged to cite me with silent contempt. It wasn't that I had refused to speak. My silence was the result of my tongue being drunk with too many words that turned and twisted inside my seething rage until they sorted themselves out at last, just long enough to say when the judge asked each of us if we had any regrets that my only regret was that Walter hadn't knocked the teeth down the lying bitch's throat. The words flew out of my mouth like crows, carrying off with them all the other words I might have said to the angry judge, and I had withdrawn into a silence more profound for its helplessness. The result was justice: With the logic of the power saw, the judge decided that the best corrective to my hate and rage was the U.S. Army. And so it was that I found myself imprisoned in the irony of a boy, trained by his sister to resist the draft, agreeing to enroll in the Reserve Officer Training Corps at the college of his choice.*

Telling and retelling this story to myself silenced the high voice questioning me inside my head. True enough, it was a lie. Yet it might be a convincing lie, especially since each of the functional characters was borrowed from what people called real life. Though William the Black's father was not a judge, he was a lawyer and thus close enough; Cyn-thee-ya looked comfortably like Allison DeForest and thus would give my voice feeling when I said "the lying bitch's throat"; strangely, the court-appointed attorney insisted on looking like my uncle; and even the D.A. had his natural model, with an appearance like Death in a motorized wheelchair.

Telling and retelling the lie as the bus rolled through Lost Hills and up the San Joaquin Valley didn't convince me of its truth. Yet in the darkness of my heart, the lie was the only knife I had. And at the end of the story *a* truth—not *the* truth—stood out: I had lost my sense of humor.

Only mother could restore that.

## 37.

Walking down my old home block late at night, mother's house was easy to spot. It was the one that looked like a

Christmas tree or an amusement park about to open, lights blinking on and off, inside and out, timed to discourage a burglar—at least to take two years off the finite number of his heart's beats as he sneaked through the house, deducting a month's worth each time a new light blinked on and a lit one went black.

The locks had been changed again. I spent two hours trying to find a way inside. Finally, I tapped a small hole out of the window glass on my bedroom, managed to lift the dowel rod blocking the runners, and slid the window back as quietly as possible. Crawling through the opened window, I fell into a web of cords strung with bells; the room's lights flashed on; and in the seconds it took for her not to Mace me with the can in her hand and scream "Ah!" I recognized mother. Changed, thinner but not skinny by any means, the flab on her right arm holding the Mace become hard with yardwork and the fixing of household machinery.

"What are *you* doing here?" she demanded.

I confess, hanging there half inverted in the tangle of bell cords, I didn't have what she would have called a good answer.

"Hi, mom," I said, trying to smile, staring at the nozzle on the Mace can that looked the size of a sixteen-penny nail. "I'm home," I tried to say, choking on the word, making it sound like "Imhm."

"You scared me," she said, unhooking the cords and watching me plop to the floor and then get up. "Look at yourself. You look like . . . you look like . . . ," she said, skipping like a badly scratched record.

I crossed to the wall mirror and looked at myself. I did look frightening. I hadn't considered it, but in the hot summery months I'd been in Arizona, my skin had become hard and dark, turning beneath the desert sun not red and not bronze but as near to burnt umber as humanly possible. I looked something like one of the young boys on the reservation I'd coached in basketball along with Johnny Three Feet; small, intense boys whose pleasure and understanding of basketball was not in obeying the rules like dribbling or not fouling but in charging down the court, throwing the ball at the hoop, and retreating—as though basketball were a form of counting coup with a ball and not a stick. I was taller, but I resembled them.

"You look like . . . ," mother said.

My god, I thought, like my father might have looked at my age. My high forehead revealed by the hair stuck back by the grease of bus travel through a hot climate; the high-cheek bones that didn't move, smiling or not; eyes that were deep and capable of being startled. Only my nose was different: it was mother's.

"At least I won't have large pores," I said.

"What? What did you say?" mother asked, folding the lapels of the terrycloth bathrobe over, nearly choking herself.

"Nothing."

"Let's get one thing straight, right now, young man," she said. "Your father spent the last twenty years muttering at me. Don't you start."

"I wasn't muttering at you, mother."

She sighed a sigh heavy with the struggle of rewriting her past, a sigh that told me to shut up. There was no sense in arguing with mother, no more sense than trying to convince an elderly woman who believes in God that there is no God. Besides being impossible, it seems, also, cruel. Why take away from mother the memories she needed to recreate in order to live?

"So," she said. "How long do you think you are staying?"

"I hadn't thought about it. Until school starts, I guess."

"Well," she said. "You can sleep on the couch. There are blankets in the hall closet. I would appreciate it if you would pick up after yourself every morning, put the blankets back in the closet, and not clutter up the living room. Feel free to have a friend over during the days I'm at work; but don't interfere with my meetings, and stay out of the study. I'm researching a book, in there."

"Thanks," I said, wondering whether the study was Pamela's old room or Elanna's.

Capping the can of Mace, mother smiled kindly. "There'll be toast and half a grapefruit for you in the kitchen, in the morning. Goodnight."

"Goodnight, mother," I said.

I stayed two weeks, eleven hours, and seventeen minutes. Some nights, I tried to read in the family room as mother typed away on her book or talked to the television set. At first, I thought she was talking to me, those times, but soon enough I recognized that what she was doing was rewriting the dialogue to simple programs like "Here Come the Brides" and "Gunsmoke." Miraculously, mother could type and talk at the same time. It was as though there was a silo of words, stored up over years of subsidy and regulation, that she opened each night, pouring out into the ears of Running Dog and myself.

Running Dog's ears rose and fell helplessly while she talked, as uncertain as I was whether he should be paying attention. During the ten weeks I'd been gone, he'd become independent in a funny way, jumping into my lap to be petted for about ten seconds and then hopping down in mid-pet, suddenly indifferent. Still, whenever I left the house, he went wild, barking, whining, and once even tearing the molding off the door's jamb. While I knew that father would tease him, pulling his ears when he was sleeping, I also knew that I had to talk father into taking Running Dog because father would take good care of him. I set out to find father and to do just that, before I left for college.

Running Dog, alias Tanya (as father called him), would live out his life with father, confused by his own sexuality, but nonetheless happy and content. The last time I would see Tanya, he'd be crippled with arthritis and age. Hearing my voice, my person nothing more than the shadow of cataracts and nostalgia, he would manage to lift himself onto his wobbling legs—it would take him several minutes—and come to me and lick my hand with a tongue the dryness of which told me that he knew this was important because it might be the last time. (I have always thought it stupid, weak, and sentimental that I cry more easily over Running Dog than any person's death—except, maybe, Pamela's—and I know that when father, deciding to take Tanya to the vet's to be put to sleep, said, "It was only a dumb dog," he was hiding behind the courage he derived from "dumb.")

Mother's house was suffering from inflation. The women whose voices sounded like popping corn had linked reasons to their anger and now they gave out with bubbly effluvia, lending the house an air or an aura, depending on which person said what. Joined by two Italian brothers with heavy beards stippling their faces in a way that made them seem shadowy, ephemeral, their gossamer shirts unbuttoned to the tender curls between their pectorals and their alto voices that competed with the women's, they made me feel not unwelcome but uncomfortable, rather like a sorry figure who had the misfortune to be male.

On Tuesday and Thursday evenings promptly at eight (heaven help the person who was late or absent when the Novallus brothers started in on them), these voices would be raised in a chorus of suffering and victimization and then would abate into a litany of emancipation. To me, who was consumed with the luck and love of just being alive, this was hard to understand. I liked one or two of these people when I had the chance to speak with them alone. But in a group, they seemed to me like any herd, butting up against the fences with which they'd surrounded themselves with the meticulosity of mother's lights and locks, moaning about the world beyond the fence. That world was controlled by men.

"Heterosexual men," Michael Novallus would add.

They read together, and they discussed what they read. With the surreptitious feeling I'd had sneaking *Lady Chatterly's Lover* off Elanna's shelves and reading it in search of an answer to the lack of fulfillment I'd felt with girls, I now sneaked Virginia Woolf's essays off mother's shelves and read them by flashlight when the house was dark and emptied of mother's friends. I'd felt cheated reading *Lady Chatterly.* I never understood how Mellors' constant use of the word "fuck" indicated anything other than a brain the size of a widow's mite; weaving bouquets of flowers into pubic hairs seemed an unbelievable waste of time. Now I felt cheated because Virginia Woolf's essays didn't seem to support the language that was tossed around in the living room as I sat in the kitchen listening. Running Dog cowered at my feet (he was never one for anger; I was able to think angry thoughts at him and he would behave). I felt cheated, too, because I was being classed in absentia with men like my father or William the Black.

Years later, as I cried over Running Dog's death by lethal injection, after William the Black's mother had replaced my mother as leader of this group grown large, parking her Mercedes in her reserved space at the community college where they now met, I would think of Mrs. Schneider. Her speechless suffering seemed all the greater in its speechlessness; her answer, represented in my memory by "Stay for dinner," all the more touching. She had gone on, and it was the inability of her son to go on that must have pained her most. But, by then, I had come to agree with Grandfather's Dandelion Theory of the world. Everything was connected; follow one shoot down beneath the ground and you merely pop up somewhere else; only the particular flower differed.

"It's a necessary first step," Elanna said when I phoned her. "Why don't you get out of there, come up and stay with me. Let mother do what she has to do."

"To your mother, you are your father," Mrs. Halkett said. She was one of mother's group. "Try to understand that."

I tried, during the final week, to convince mother that I was not father, even though I resembled him more than any son would have liked. Each morning, I quietly ate the half grapefruit and the toast I made in the counter-top oven which, having overthrown the tyranny of toasters, mother had purchased. Mother protested that she did not think I was like father, and to convince me of that, she often bought me expensive things I didn't want and then spent the next few days asking me if I really liked them, forcing me to thank her over and over until finally I couldn't contain the frustration of reiterated obligation and I would fight to control my voice, saying, "Yes, mother, I did thank you." It ended badly with my begging her not to buy me anything at all, and that Friday she went out and got me a new typewriter.

On Saturday, I had plugged the typewriter into an extension cord and was sitting out back, typing, filling the pages with phrases that said what I was not.

I am not my father, I typed.

I am not my mother's husband;

I am not white;

I am not a full-blood Indian;

I am not Rachel, nor am I William the Black;

I am not Tammy or Bernie Schneider (I don't even like Tammy);

I am not John Kennedy, Bobby Kennedy, or Martin Luther King;

I am not Running Dog;

I am not Custer;

I am not a power saw;

I am not a Kenmore washing machine;

I am not Allison or Mrs. DeForest;

I am not a Republican and I'm not a rich idiot;

I am not a kept woman or kept man;

I am not Laura P. or Louis Applegate;

I am not Johnny Three Feet (neither am I Sanchez);

I am not an elf owl or a Gila monster;

I am not Elanna, Pamela, or mother;

I am not very bright, but then I am not Dr. Bene, either;

I am not (I paused here long enough for the gardener to unload his lawnmower and roll it into the back yard) Grandfather.

I am not nothing.

"You see, mother," I said when she came outside with some iced tea. The gardener unloaded his lawnmower and rolled it into the back yard. "I really like my new typewriter. I really appreciate it."

"I'm glad," she said. "I did something right, at least." Mother invited the gardener over for iced tea before he began mowing the lawn. At first he demurred, but finally convinced by mother's coy statement that she'd made it just for him, and besides it was an awfully hot day and she wanted to talk over plans of what to plant next year in the garden, he came over to meet me. I guessed him to be about fifty, with gray hair and a wide, open face, the face of someone unconfused, with organic notions of life and compost.

"Tom," mother said, "This is my son." Tom smiled and reached out to shake my hand.

"Nice lookin' boy," he said. "Big and strong."

"He was big when he was born," mother said. "Ten pounds eight ounces. *Both* my children were big."

I fussed with the typewriter, trying to stay out of the conversation.

"That's good," Tom said. He seemed embarrassed, and at a loss for words. "Real good," he said. "My own boy was a good size too. You should see him, now. Big as a tree and twice as strong."

"Oh," mother said. "I didn't know you were married."

"Was," he said, running his index finger down the sweat on the glass of tea. "Widower, now, what they call a single parent."

Listening to mother play twenty questions with the gardener disturbed me. I had imagined that grown people overcame the tendencies of teeny-boppers to use indirect cross-examination, their voices twittering all the while. Mother's voice was like a sparrow's when a crow is around its nest. I was the crow.

"Maybe you could use a good home-cooked meal?" mother said.

"That would be fine," Tom said.

"What evening would be convenient?" mother asked, and when Tom said almost any evening, she said, "No, I mean for you," and looked straight at me.

"As with Tom, with me," I said. "I'm going to Elanna's for a visit. In fact," I said, closing up the typewriter, "if you'll excuse me, I'd better go call her."

In the kitchen, trying not to watch mother and the gardener slurp their tea on the patio, I called father to ask if I could drop off Running Dog. He wanted to speak with mother, and when I said she was busy, he wanted to know with what. "She'll call you back," I said.

"What's she doing?" father demanded. "Is there a man there? She entertaining one of those fag Italian friends of hers?"

"Dad, please," I said. "I'll have her call you back."

"I'm your father," he said. "I want to speak with your mother."

"I know that," I said, "but my mother is busy. She'll call you back." I was beginning to believe that I, along with Pamela and Elanna, had been products of rape, though I couldn't conceive of how a husband could rape a wife. With mom and dad, though, anything seemed possible.

"What's his name?" father said.

"Look, she's in the bathroom, okay?" I said. I hung up and went back outside.

"There's a note by the phone for you," I told mother. "I'm on my way. I'll head straight for Clearmont College from Elanna's. I'll give you a call, first, if you want."

"Try to do well in college," mother said.

"See you," I said. I wondered if maybe for appearances I ought to hug her goodbye or something. We weren't a family given to public displays of emotion. Even Elanna and I sidled up to each other and sort of hugged sideways when we saw each other. In airports or train stations, it usually sufficed for me to put my arm around her shoulders lightly, Elanna nodding her head towards my shoulder briefly. Years later— for the rest of my life—it would amuse me in a perplexed sort of way that I would know from the way Elanna's friends said, "So this is your little brother," that she felt the way towards me that I did towards her, and I would hope that she would derive a similar conclusion from the way the women I had in tow cringed slightly in front of the Elanna they'd heard so much about. In a way, I suppose, both of us had the cool surface that was the tip of mother's iceberg, beneath which lurked the molten frustration that was father's.

"Nice meeting you," Tom said. I nodded.

"Stay out of it," Elanna said. During my visit, she was busy getting ready to leave on a two-year archeological dig in Greece. I helped her sort through papers and records and books. Some would go to storage and others to the trash. "Don't get caught between mom and dad."

"I won't," I said.

"It's hard, I know," she said. "But you've got to recognize mother and father as independent, sexual beings. Each of them has had a hard life." She went on to tell me the hardness. In fact, in those days before college, I learned more about mother and father, about the world of men and women, than I'd ever known. I understood that mother's flirting with the gardener, as well as her biweekly encounter group, were necessary first steps. What I failed to understand was how mother could write a check to pay a man she was having over to dinner, and how a man who dropped by mother's house and ate her food could take that check. When I asked Elanna about it, she smiled and said, "That's why people get married."

"To get their lawns mowed?"

"To have their meals cooked," she said. "It's all a matter of your point of view."

"I'll miss you," I said.

"There," she said, snapping the latch on the steamer trunk. "Now we have to store the rest of this junk and we're done." To me, she looked like an Indian princess. "You'll be okay?" she asked.

I nodded. "As soon as I straighten out my point of view," I said. We laughed.

# CHAPTER NINE

### 38.

With Grandfather sinking into the singsong of commercial jingles, it was tough to get through to him from Clearmont. Only on days the dome of smog blew out from the City of Angels and amplified his voice did I hear him say things like, "Untested, as gold by fire."

"As soft as lead," I replied. Whether Grandfather was referring to me or to the boys doing boyish things around me, I didn't know.

Except for two token freshmen who kept to themselves like Siamese twins, there wasn't a Black person for miles around. The only Chicanos I had seen were Mexicans sneaking up the desiccated riverbed toward the outlying citrus groves, playing their game of hide and seek with the immigration authorities. Periodically, a green helicopter would hover above the groves, and men, women, and children would drop to the ground, scramble into unpicked trees, or run. Most would be caught, placed inside the green cars and vans waiting for them, and driven back across the border. Within the week, they'd be back to finish the harvest. No one took the game very seriously. The growers liked the cheap labor that no one could organize. The Mexicans needed the money. And the authorities had nothing better to do than drive Mexicans back across the border in their air-conditioned cars. It was as though the game had existed since time immemorial, the rules written by economic accident, and it never crossed anyone's mind to alter the way the game was played. Sooner alter the rules of Bingo that the old folks played every Friday night in the Clearmont Inn: the fury that that would generate was predicted in the hatred that the growers felt for Chavez's rocking their landlocked boat floating on subsidies of $250 per acre-foot of water—a fact my economics professor liked to point out, leaping onto the desk in the front of the room and shouting, trying to stir the minds and hearts of the boys who were either dozing or staring at the one girl in the classroom. She was always a daring girl who had crossed the street from either of the two women's colleges, and she would sit with the pretense of intellectual curiosity, enjoying the attention she received by default as the boys drooled like apes at feeding time. It was she that Proctor Tompson competed with, declaiming and pacing and hopping onto his desk—performing his Shakespearean comedy of economics in front of an audience that was too lazy to throw tuppence or tomatoes.

I liked Proctor Tompson, but I was not very good at economics. To me, the curves of supply and demand may as well have been bio-rhythms, and mine were always critical. Try as I might on exams, I rarely understood why there was any demand for the products supplied in the questions. It was in economics, however, that I finally began to see, to actually visualize Sanchez's genius in understanding how money spent itself.

Proctor Tompson liked me, too. I touched a nerve. I listened. He almost wept, the times he returned my papers and exams, and for half the semester, I thought his teary eyes were caused by the way my scores so lowered the mean score that nearly everyone got A's or B's. It wasn't until he handed me my second midterm and gently tapped my head, saying, "What's inside there, anyway, sawdust?" that I realized he cared about me personally. I was as mystifying to him as economics was to me.

Father had always grown angry when, as a child, I failed to explain properly the Specific Theory of Relativity (the General was easier because I could visualize the pilot in the plane and the stationary man on the ground gazing up as the plane flew over—both men embodied for me by my uncle in different times). Proctor Tompson was curious and slightly bemused, as though my inability to understand was less a problem with me and more a problem with economics, and for the first time I felt the faint stirrings of a desire to do well.

To Mrs. Tompson, whenever they invited the class to tea, I tried to explain Dr. Bene's experience of me—I didn't want the same thing to happen to the Proctor. Sitting in a corner of their living room, sipping the sherry she shared with me in her teacups, I got along famously with her, so well that one day as we were talking politics I felt free enough to summarize for her what I had learned in my Theory of Politics seminar.

"The world is all fucked up, as far as I can tell," I blurted.

"Isn't it, though," she said. Waving her cup at the boys gathered in bunches like grapes around the girls who had been included in the tea party, she would toast "the getters and spenders of the future," calling these lads the "have gots" and "will gets," categories from which she seemed to exclude me, whether out of kindness or her own innate ability to forecast the future on the basis of choices I had already made beneath my cloud of unknowing.

Delia Tompson wanted to know about me. I told her what I could in fragments and anecdotes, leaving out or skipping over events such as Pamela's impregnated death, trying to amuse her, not depress or sadden her. I told her about mother and her serial toasters, ending with mother's editing her life and final testament. I told her about uncle and his wife, the Vegomatic, about my cousin and his political tilt toward groups like the Weathermen. I tried to tell her about Grandfather, mentioning father and Laura P. in the process. I told her as much as I could, each time the subject came up. I made her laugh, and when I failed to make her laugh, I changed what I was telling her, modifying it until she did laugh. With each anecdote, making Delia Tompson laugh became more difficult and trying for me, not because of me but because the more she heard, the less she thought was funny.

One day, I commented, "You're not laughing anymore."

Mrs. Tompson looked at me, her face as blank as Grandfather's could be, and replied, "You know what your problem is?"

"No," I said. "But you're going to tell me, aren't you?"

She rose and went to the cupboard—we were sitting at the kitchen table—took out brandy snifters, filled them, and handed me one. "You're afraid."

"Of what am I afraid?"

THE ABSENCE OF ANGELS

"At first," she said, "I thought you were afraid of women. I mean the Vegomatic, your mother's toasters, that girlfriend you had in high school. But when you talk about your sister, or that girl Yvette, your voice changes. So I doubt it's that."

"I'm relieved," I said, sipping the brandy.

"Then I thought you were afraid of emotion, real emotion, the kind that makes people cry, you know? You didn't seem to feel close to anyone, man or woman, except for those people who could know what it was you were feeling, like your sister and Grandfather. You're critical of everyone; and yet you make fun of yourself as often as you make fun of anyone else. More often, even."

She thought for a moment, gazing down at her hands resting open on the table. In that moment, seeing the hazel color of her eyes and the way her features seemed to comply with the way her eyes looked, I saw that Mrs. Tompson was beautiful—had been and would always be beautiful, that to Proctor Tompson she was sexy because her body was so comfortable with who—or was it how?—she was. Because she was closer to my mother's age than my own, the possibility of someone being like her was overwhelming.

"I hope you don't mind," she said. "But I had the Proctor do some checking. Through your confidential files. How come you never said you had another sister?"

I shrugged.

"Are you afraid of pain?" she said.

"No," I said, seeing Proctor Tompson pull in the driveway and shut off the car. "Just afraid of being boring."

I was grateful for the Tompsons during that Fall. I had never felt my solitude more, although I was determined that wasn't going to bother me. I had Grandfather, even though as past and future closed in on the present like the walls of a claustrophobic nightmare, he was becoming more a memory and less a presence. I had Elanna. Her letters arrived from Crete in packets, being mailed whenever she had the chance. Whether all of mine got there or not, addressed care of the American Express office, I didn't know. It didn't really matter. I wrote to her every other night and the act of imagining her sitting in the pink dust of Iraklion and reading the words I wrote was sufficient. There was basketball, which gave me some company; yet I felt silly playing basketball with an all-white team. It just didn't seem right, and more than once I wondered how William the Black was faring at Stanford. It didn't seem unusual that it was at the Tompsons' that I felt least alone.

As for women, well, my college was flanked by two women's colleges. The problem wasn't quantity or availability. The problem was the women.

One college was a giggling sorority for girls who studied cocktail French and learned to string crepe paper across the rafters of dining halls, making them over into dance halls. Those girls caused names to creep out of my past the way the smog drifted out from Los Angeles to hover overhead and make you choke.

The other women's college was arty. The girls carried canvas bags stencilled with *Poetic License* or the portraits of Jane Austen and Virginia Woolf. Meticulously disheveled, they fired clay pots that leaned like the Tower of Pisa or that collapsed in on themselves which, because the pots could not be accused of having any function or use, the girls called "art." They went braless, their small fortunate breasts barely wrinkling their sleeveless, neckless sweatshirts. Afternoons, they could be found sitting beneath the shade of palm trees, bruising the prose of their own feelings as they wrenched it into iambic pentameter in the blank books they carried like passports. They, too, were there to change their names, but they would hyphenate theirs—Annie Smith becoming Annie Grover-Smith when she married Jay Grover, who would change his name to Jay Smith-Grover. Cute.

On weekend nights, I walked beneath the oak trees along the sandy riverbed, listening to the language of crickets punctuated by the chirps of courting. From behind one tree came, "C'est bon. N'est-ce pas?" From behind another, a disputation on the metaphysics of love, burdened by flashcard quotations from Heidegger and Sartre. It was there, most often, that I would find my roommate, Woody, searching for any woman left in the lurch by her date, willing to take up the baldric of her loneliness.

Woody was a case. A round-faced boy with hair so blond

that it seemed transparent in the moonlight. His qualifications for admission to the college seemed to be that his father was a judge in the state supreme court and a vulgar banality that made neurosis look like genius. He had quickly learned to be a transvestite, using the French his mother had used at the dinner table to get a free feel off the girls from one college and then easily changing his empirical clothes, using existential theories of pop art to obtain permission to run his hands over the chests of girls from the other college.

"I hate him," I said to Delia Tompson. "He makes me want to puke."

"It does seem ironic," she said, "that you came here to get away from women and you ended up in a boys school in which the only obsession is the knowledge of women."

I was not good at the languages of love, like French. I didn't want to be. My directness glared like a cold sore beneath the bright lights of the crepe-papered dances. Yet, unable to behave like a gamekeeper whose only complete sentence is "I want to fuck thee" (which the artier girls found charming), my reserve threw me into a peristaltic clumsiness on the lawns of *Poetic License*. I told myself that I was too old to patter once again down the path of the first steps of so-called love, trying to obtain the grail that those women knew I wanted. They were happy to be pursued, but unless I was willing to lie to them about marriage and family, they would not be caught. I was unwilling to lie—for that, I had only Elanna and the memory of Pamela to blame.

Some of the artier women were willing to put up with my advances as long as I was against the Vietnam War. And I was. But when they found out I was in R.O.T.C., I may as well have had cholera. The contradiction was too much for them, despite the story I'd invented to explain how I came to enroll in Rotsy. I made up other stories and still they shunned me without even hearing me out. It was, in a way, my first experience with formulaic rejections, and while it depressed me, it didn't make me bitter. I didn't have to approach these women, put the stories out there for rejection. Their rejections only served to make me more determined. While it seemed the world only wanted Mellorses or Maurices, I began to believe that one day I would meet a woman who would not need the false inventions and explanations in order to perceive the truth in the apparent contradiction. If I didn't, tough. I gave up inventing reasons for being in Rotsy, deciding only to tell the truth (I couldn't help but embellish it a little—out of exuberance, not need).

For the time being, if I wasn't at the Tompsons' house, I was content to follow the electric golf carts the elderly drove over to the Clearmont Inn and watch them play Bingo, or read, or try to figure out the inner workings of economics from the elementary texts that Proctor Tompson lent me, or take apart and clean my M-1. A month hadn't passed before I could break down and reassemble my rifle quickly and easily in the dark. That rifle was the first mechanical object that I understood and I eagerly believed that if I took care of it, it would take care of me.

## 39.

Elanna wrote, approving my decision to give up all but the embellished truth. "It's a good decision," she said. "Even if it means being a little lonely sometimes." Her letter arrived three days after I wrote to her about Sara Baites, telling her how funny it seemed that the moment I had found comfort in being alone, I'd made a new friend.

One cool afternoon in October, Sara had introduced herself to me after English class. We had just received compositions back from the professor. Mine had been on Nathaniel Hawthorne's *The Scarlet Letter*, comparing it to "My Kinsman, Major Molineaux" and suggesting that the novel was not a novel at all but a tale which had gotten out of control, the "Customs House" preface working with the rest of the book in the same way the first paragraph of "My Kinsman" worked with the rest of that tale.

After class, I was sitting at my desk searching and re-searching the comments on the paper for some indication of a grade, and then rereading the professor's final comments, trying to find a reasonable explanation for the fact that my paper was, as the comments indicated, "ungradable."

"Where you get your ideas is a mystery to any intelligent

reader," Professor Quinin had written, "and I dare say that while your writing is adequately college level, your thinking (or non-thinking) causes you to say things that are silly, unacceptable, and wrong."

"What did you get?" Woody asked, stopping by my desk. He had gotten a B + on his three-page essay on "Images of Darkness in Hawthorne," most of which he had plagiarized from an obscure monograph in the library, changing the vocabulary and shortening the sentences to statements with the rhythm of a tin drum.

"You learn as much putting someone else's ideas into your own words as you do putting your own ideas into someone else's words," Woody had said. "Besides, who's gonna catch me?" He had grinned, his forehead wrinkling beneath his pale mop of hair, shredding the pages of the book he had plagiarized into three separate trash containers.

When I showed him my paper he laughed. "I told you so," he said, gloating. "I told you not to write ten pages. All Quinin wanted was five." To Woody, delightful as he was, the problem was the length of my essay. He left to go celebrate.

"I hate him," a girl said. When I looked up, I felt for the first time in my life every joint in my body declare its independence from muscle and nerve in the onslaught of a smile that was neither flirtatious nor shy, on a makeup-less face that gave me joy to look at.

"No grade, huh?" she said. I shook my head. "Don't worry about it. Probably means it's an intelligent paper."

Marshaling my legs with the concentration it took Grandfather to drive from Chosposi to the City of Angels all those years ago, I stood up.

"Sara Baites," she said, introducing herself. "El Creepo is your roommate, isn't he?"

I nodded.

"May I see it?" she asked, holding her hand out for my paper. I handed it to her.

She flipped through it as we walked across the campus. "Looks interesting," she said, giving it back. "Don't worry about Mr. Quinin. He's only got a master's degree—still working on his doctorate—on Colonial American literature, of all the boring things. He's afraid of any new ideas, or old ones for that matter, because he's afraid he might have to change one of his ten thousand footnotes."

"He's an asshole," I said, finding my voice for the first time.

She laughed. "Not really. He can be really nice, if you get to know him. He's just boring, sometimes. That's what graduate school has done to him. But then that's what graduate school is all about, isn't it? Becoming obsessed with old ideas. Redressing them in laundered swaddling clothes, and then talking about them endlessly at cocktail parties the same way new parents talk endlessly about their baby. Believe me," she winked, "I know better than anyone how boring Quinin is."

I paused on the curb of the street that led to the Tompsons' house.

"I still gotta love him. Where're you headed?"

I was unable to think. Feeling like a pimple on the face of humanity walking beside her, I turned up the street towards the faculty housing, habit my only defense against panic.

"Proctor and Delia Tompson's."

"Mind if I tag along?"

My arms hung like elephants' trunks from my shoulders. I wondered if any male, heterosexual or otherwise, would have minded Sara's tagging along.

"Do people like you ever *tag* along?" I blurted.

"Am I being rude to ask?"

"No! No, sure, you can come along if you want. I mean, I'm just going to drop by and say hello. Chat for a while. It probably won't be very interesting. I don't know. I like talking with the Tompsons. They're sort of like the parents I wish I'd had, but for you . . . sure, come if you want."

"They're like the parents everyone wishes he'd had, don't you think? Because they're so damned happy. Disgustingly happy. Tell me," she said as we strolled beneath the shade of the mulberry trees lining the street, "do you always apologize ahead of time for being boring?"

"Yes," I said, regaining my wits. "It clears the air. Sets up the audience. Like a mediocre comedian who comes on stage and apologizes for his writers, no matter how bad he is the audience is going to want to laugh." We turned up the Tompsons' driveway. "Listen," I said. "I should warn you. I'm in R.O.T.C."

Sara frowned. "That's a strange thing to tell someone you've just met. Why?"

"Why tell you? Or why am I in R.O.T.C.?"

"Either."

"I don't know. I thought I wanted to be a part of something."

"So you picked Rotsy?"

"Something simple." I rang the doorbell.

"Is anything simple, these days?" Sara said.

"Duz detergent," I replied. "A free glass in every twenty-pound box."

Sara Baites became a part of my visits to the Tompsons. It turned out that she had known them for years, having grown up in Clearmont, where her father—Professor Quinin—had taught high school English for a decade before returning to college for his doctorate. Artless herself, Sara had enrolled in the artier of the two women's colleges. Her tuition was free.

"A little like you joining Rotsy," she said, grinning.

Sara had adopted her deceased mother's maiden name to avoid being stereotyped as a "P. K."

"He's a preacher too?" I asked.

"A Pontificator's Kid." Sara knew that using her mother's name, she would have to hear other students complain about her father.

"I do love him, after all. I can't say that I respect him, but I love him anyway. It's hard to respect a man who stops reading literature to read criticism and eventually reads only criticism of criticism. Daddy hasn't read a novel in years," she'd say, "though he can talk about any of them. He knows what to think. He's forgotten that he's forgotten how to think."

## 40.

Through Sara I met David Zarpin, ne Zarpinskic, a Polish Jew who had been accepted to the college either because his father had a great deal of money (he'd invented a process for photocopying that was more profitable to industry than the hula hoop or superball) or by mistake. It was, after all,

183

obvious that David was much too bright for a college for the children of the well-connected.

He rarely, if ever, studied. He could pass any multiple-guess examination; adept at patterns, he most always received the highest marks. Essays he tossed off with the ease of a man doffing his hat. To him, everything was a game and all that mattered was winning, which he could do and did do as easily as he could beat you at chess after spotting you his queen.

"Anything you want," David liked to say, "you can have. All you have to do is concentrate properly and it will come to you."

He sounded enough like Grandfather to be believable. Besides, he gave me proof, teaching me how to close my eyes and read the page of text needed to answer an examination question—something I'd forgotten how to do. He also taught me how to read a text I had never even looked at, let alone read, before a test. Illness was simply beyond consideration, if you focused the white blood cells properly ("Or in your case, pink blood cells," he'd laugh). I learned how to slow my heart rate even while on amphetamines, and for a while my headaches seemed to become fewer and less severe.

It was a carefree time.

When I tried to reach Grandfather through the Absence of Angels, I received the buzzing of a television's test pattern as though he had gone off the air for good. Father's long-distance complaints of loneliness and love I put out of my mind by dreaming up schemes to sue the telephone company for interfering with my right to life, liberty, and a dogged pursuit of happiness—schemes I would entertain Sara and David with until the time came that father could find another woman who had few, if any, conflicts with toasters and could make an honest woman of her. In the process, father would slowly change from a man who had defended a Chicano's right to buy a house on our block into someone who believed in bumper stickers and assumed all Negroes were on welfare. Like litmus paper revealing its true colors. He would actually tell me on the phone that when it came to voting, it was better to vote for the horse than the man, meaning, I guessed, that the incumbent was tractable and capable of being saddled.

"Next he'll tell me that when guns are outlawed only outlaws will have guns," I said to Sara, who was trying to console me. "That's the point, isn't it? Outlaw handguns and anyone who has one can be arrested before he can use it on someone?"

"Or she," Sara said. "Cruel and senseless violence is not a male prerogative. So what are you going to say? He is your father, after all. What can you do?"

"Hang up," I said.

Every fourth letter from mother I opened, sharing its contents with Sara and David as we crisscrossed southern California in David's G.T.O.—a fast, sky-blue car with a Hurst shifter and a six-pack that hummed with the vibration of our nerves as we raced around the back highways, our eyes glued to the road by speed.

"Hey," Sara would say, sitting between the bucket seats, "don't let it get you down. You don't have to understand. You don't even have to forgive her. She does love you. She's obsessed with loving you. That's why she keeps writing."

"She's got a funny way of showing it."

"Your problem is to find a way to avoid ending up with women like your mother."

"Fat chance," I said.

"More than a fat chance," David said, steering the car through a power slide. "Most boys marry their mothers, women like their mothers. If their mothers are like mine, that's not such a problem. With yours it is."

"And boys often respond to those women in the same patterns as their fathers," Sara added. "It is all we know, our parents."

"Or our grandparents," I said.

"Are they any different, really?" Sara said.

"Of course they are," I said with the authoritarian tones of the uncertain.

"I don't think so," Sara said. She reached up and began to scratch my head. "Let them go," she said. "Let them live their lives."

David's favorite trips were into Mexico. At first, we went only on weekends to Tijuana, where we'd sit drinking in the Blue Fox, a shabby little bar in which Mexican whores performed salacious acts on a roped-off section of the floor, cheered on by sailors and Marines on leave from San Diego. When the balance of liquor and amphetamines began to tip towards drowsiness, David would shout that the Navy sucked the balls of Marines, and we'd duck beneath the melee of swinging fists out into the Mexican night, find the car, and recross the border.

When we weren't carrying contraband, David let me drive. If we were transporting tequila or fireworks, he drove. Because of my youthful experiences with American police, I had an unfailing instinct for making customs agents suspicious. They'd ask me simple questions and I'd give them complex answers, and they'd pull us into the inspection station.

"You're great!" David laughed after we put the seats back in the car and drove away. "Man, I bet you talk to grocery clerks, telling them your problems or going on about nothing. Don't you know those guys are like dogs? They can smell fear. You gotta learn not to try to talk to them. Never give them more than they ask for. Remember, they're there to do a job, but they work for you not you for them, and they don't really want to have a conversation."

"In other words," Sara added, "you need to concentrate on not talking to the toaster."

David was a little like Sanchez. Like most rich kids or successful entrepreneurs, he seemed to see the world as his and living comfortably in it as his right. He played roles easily and well, telling me that roles were not a way of avoiding reality but a way of dealing with it. His roles were, as Sara said, something like my habit of making up stories.

"Games," she would say, "are not necessarily deceitful. They can be a way of living through a given situation. Is an actor lying when he plays a part? Or is he playing a game that allows the truth to slip out?"

I thought about that. I decided that Sanchez's roles lacked underpinnings. David had behind him or beneath him or inside him an orthodoxy that defined what he would become, regardless of the roles he might play along the way. (This underpinning was what William the Black had given up, consummating the loss by joining the all-white fraternity. I sometimes wondered if William's father, like mine, had been the one to give it up. Could William have gone back to Africa any more easily than I could go back to the reservation?) David's sense of tradition allowed him to face one of the jealous house-servants for the world's masters—a customs agent—and overcome his suspicions like this:

"Where are you coming from?"

Looking slightly bored, David would say, "Tijuana."

"Business or pleasure."

"Pleasure."

"Are you bringing any goods back with you?"

"No."

"Any fruits or vegetables?"

"No."

"Whose car is this?"

"Mine."

"Looks pretty fast."

"It is."

The customs agent would keep his eye on David as he filled out a slip of paper, watching to see if David became nervous or frightened. Finally he would lean out of his kiosk and say, "Okay, go on. Drive carefully."

David would smile and reply, "I will. Thanks."

How I envied him!

At the time, many of our so-called peers lamented the "fact" that people could never truly know each other fully, completely, and with real understanding. Dragging their butts into parties, they stood there talking to me and, if I happened to say something foolish like "I see" or "I understand," they said, "But you don't understand. Not *really*. You can't get inside my head."

Not that anyone would want to.

It dawned on me that only people, never spotted horses or dolphins, could invent this lament and I began to see that the lament could be reversed and become something to celebrate.

"It's a miracle that we can know anything at all of what another person is feeling or thinking," I said to Sara and

David. "As long as we aren't dead, we might not be able to feel exactly what the other person's feeling, but we can come mighty close. But these people," I'd tell them after parties, "seem born into an afterlife."

"Maybe some of them are only asleep," Sara liked to say. "And you can always hope to wake them up."

"That's a pretty big hope," I said.

"Worth a try," David tossed in.

How was the problem. "How, how, how," I often said, feeling odd in the way I sounded like Grandfather would have sounded without my inventing him. I began to fall asleep quickly most nights, dreaming of palm trees and writing, the vivid images of a Rapidograph pen filled with brick red ink poised above a blank book that rested open on my chest. The headaches that could make me writhe with pain until I vomited uncontrollably seemed to lessen and the codeine tablets were less necessary except as a defense against my roommate Woody when he brought Joanne over to our room to sleep with him.

Joanne, a fairly bright but unattractive girl whose voice whined in the dark, cloyed to Woody the way he cloyed to her, out of mutual default. I kept two codeine pills beneath my pillow for the times Woody would sneak in late at night and whisper, "He's asleep, come on," and I would roll over as if tossing in my sleep and swallow the pills, hoping to fall into the conch-like calm of the drug before they had finished undressing in the dark.

Sex had always seemed to me a private matter, and yet when I mentioned this to Woody, he gave me one of his patronizing blowfish smiles, accused me of being prudish, and told me not to listen, if it bothered me. I became adept at taking pills without water—a talent I've developed over the years to the point of being able to swallow whole handfuls of aspirin. More and more, I tried to stay away from the room, except when Joanne and Woody were having troubles. Then, Joanne would come by and want to talk to me, waiting for Woody, wanting to know where he was and what he might be doing. I knew that Woody was out chasing other women, becoming a typical American male. Joanne was a convenient fuck to him; but with the spirit of free enterprise, Woody was always trying to improve his lot. I felt sorry for her, and

I confess I didn't have the heart to tell her where I thought he was.

Strangely, because of Joanne, I passed German that term. She was good with languages, and having nothing better to do she drilled me for hours until I fell asleep dreaming endless dreams in which I wandered the paths of German sentences trying to find the verbs like Easter eggs. Joanne would doze off in Woody's bed, waiting all night for him, if need be, forgiving him quickly without even asking for an excusing lie when he failed to come home at all. I stumbled through my German tutorials until the night it dawned on me that Joanne was not to be pitied but admired. Why it hadn't occurred to me before that she loved Woody, I don't know. But the night she leaned over my bed in the darkness—I was halfway down the hall to sleep—and kissed me lightly on the forehead, saying, "Thank you," and then slipped quietly out of the room, I knew what Grandfather had meant by gold untested by fire. It wasn't that Woody hadn't tested Joanne. It was that the quality of Joanne's pure and absolute love for Woody couldn't be changed by it. And that night, when I finally fell back asleep, dreaming of writing, the Rapidograph fell out of my hand.

"Forget about her," David said. He looked like he hadn't shaved for a week. "She's a born victim. She likes being a martyr. It gives her life meaning, putting herself in situations that can only end with her being hurt. She'd manage to get mugged in Macy's at Christmas if she could. If you don't let her go, she'll drag you down with her."

"I can't," I replied. It seemed to me that if I let Joanne go, which meant not caring about her pain and suffering as ridiculous as it looked to people like David, I would be letting something of myself go with it. Maybe it was because her suffering, though small and apparently insignificant, was the true kind, the kind that came out of love and allowed her to feel pain as well as allowed Woody to get away with murder.

"Good for you," Sara whispered.

## 41.

Perhaps I ought to have listened more carefully to David's theory of victims, but I was too happy to have these friends whom Delia Tompson began to call her "little gyratory troupe." I began to love them all the same way Joanne loved Woody, without thinking, ignoring the moments no longer than the blink of a mouse in the presence of a cat. Their friendships and the times I spent with them were as addicting as amphetamines.

Amphetamines, I claimed, bought me time, let me waste less time sleeping.

"Like finding a coin purse on a baseball diamond," Sara said. "It makes you go in circles."

"Lay off," I told her. "Besides, I don't have a coin purse."

Sara laughed, not without affection, but with the same underlying worry that Pamela, Elanna, and I had had when mother had lectured toasters in front of father's business guests.

The truth was, the speed made the mouse feel invulnerable, ready to take on the cat and tear its claws out before gnawing out its intestines, and while it increased my energy for sex it reduced my drive with a rush. Combined with that invulnerability, the green and white dexamil spansules that I began carrying like an imaginary knife made me think like normal students did, even to the extent that eating two before an economics exam made the test seem a snap. My essays for English read like one of Woody's, simple, plain, straightforward, pale in thought—although old Quinin did complain once or twice that they were becoming voluminous. Late into the nights, I wrote in a blank book, stories quick and slight and funny, and I felt beyond the need to revise any of them. Everyone, after all, liked them—everyone except Sara, who could make me burn with a slow indignant rage by suggesting that they had, as she said, possibilities. Slow because I loved her and I was sure she suspected it, felt it, knew it; indignant because my all-too-obvious love neither prevented nor lessened her criticisms and I wondered what gave her the right; rage because she was right, at least in part, always, and I knew it.

"You leave everything out," she'd say. "Everything that might mean, that is."

"You just want plot. Naturalism," I said. "Nothing quick and lively. You want Dreiser and stop signs every other paragraph to tell you what the story means. Buildings leering Stephen Crane style, looming down on the characters fated to have their foreheads dented as the cornices of the buildings inevitably fall. Mere boys leaning over in the middle of a battle between North and South to pick up a shiny pebble, their bodies riddled with seventeen Gray bullets and shattered by the cannonballs of the Blues, and as if that wasn't enough, a lieutenant prying open the ragged corpse's hand to find the pebble saying 'Gee, a mere pebble, a mere boy,' repeating 'mere' nineteen times on one page just to be sure the reader gets the point."

Her father's course had done me a world of good. Sara raked her fingers through her hair and waited.

"You finished?" she asked. "You know that's not what I mean. Your wonder drug hasn't bought you time, it's made you lazy. You know that."

"How do you know what I know?"

"I just do," she said. She thought for a moment. "The same way you know what your Grandfather would say." She waited for that to sink in.

"Maybe you could be rich and famous," she said, giving me a supercilious smile. "You write well enough. Lord knows that the world seems to want writing that says as little as possible. The kind of thing people can read on buses and planes, or during their favorite soap operas. You're funny . . ."

"What's wrong with being funny?"

"Nothing. But ask yourself why people laugh at your stories. Are they laughing because you allow them to avoid the truth? If that's what you want, then you're making a jolly good show of it. You have to read more," she said.

Sara, for whatever reasons, began to complete the education Elanna had begun, lending or giving me books by authors I'd never heard of before—a collection of stories by George P. Elliott was the first. *Among the Dangs.*

"I want it back," Sara said. "And take care of it. It's out of print."

When I'd finished the collection my rage was subdued. "How'd you like them?" she asked.

"They were okay," I said. The truth was that they were

wonderful. Instead of instilling jealousy, they made me grateful that there were such books to be read. I had cried, secretly
embarrassed, over stories like "The N.R.A.C.P."

"Just okay?"

"Uh-huh."

Sara smiled knowingly—the same smile she would exhibit
with each new book as simultaneously she watched my stories
become heavier with intended meaning, stiffer, starker, and
far less entertaining. Giving me an Ernest Gaines novel one
day, she said, "You're ready for this. You've got to find something to write out of, like him."

It seemed only natural to turn to Indian myths, reading
up on them and then jamming them into my stories like
square pegs. When Sara saw these, she not only didn't smile,
she looked sad. "These aren't the way," she said. "You're writing in, not out of."

"What do you mean?"

"The problem is, even though you think like an Indian,
putting too much myth into your stories makes you sound
phony."

"I am Indian," I growled.

"And I'm a Moravian dwarf," she laughed. "Oh, Alley.
Partly, you are. Maybe that's what confuses you so much
about the world. I don't know. But partly, you aren't. Problem
is, when you try to pretend you are only an Indian and put
Indians into your stories, they come out stick figures because
you don't know them."

"What about my Grandfather?"

"What about him? You yourself said that every time you
try to tell someone about him that he comes out like a
wooden Indian in front of a cigar store. Remember when
you were thinking of going to Arizona this Christmas and I
asked if I could come along, you said no? Don't you see why
you said no?"

I was becoming furious. And hurt.

"You want to keep him to yourself. To keep what you imagine he is to yourself. You're afraid that if someone like me
went with you, I'd find out the truth."

"What's the truth, if you're so smart?"

"I don't know, do I? I can't, because you won't let anyone who cares about you know him, if you can help it. Maybe the truth is that he's just another old man who does old man things."

"My Grandfather is not just another old man," I said, clenching and unclenching my fists.

David knocked and leaned into the room. "Hey," he said. Feeling the tension pinging around the room, he fell silent.

"Hello David," Sara said. He nodded, glancing from me to her with raised eyebrows.

"What's up?" I said, grateful for the interruption.

"I was going to head into L.A. this afternoon. Wondered if anyone wanted to come along."

"I'll go," I said, looking straight at Sara. I went over to the small refrigerator Woody had installed in our room and took out a beer, opened it, and used it to swallow another pill.

"Sara?" David said.

"Aren't you taking a few too many of those pills?" Sara said. "You're going to fry your brain."

"One is too many," I said. "Anything else you'd like to correct? I mean are my pants zipped up, do my clothes match?"

"You are such a little boy, sometimes," Sara said. "I think I'll stay here. I've got some work to get done." She gathered up her things. "Besides, Alley here will have more fun if I'm not around to make him think about what he's doing."

I gave Sara the silent treatment.

Sara only laughed, shook her head, and walked out of the room without even slamming the door.

## 42.

"What was that all about?" David asked as he merged onto the San Bernadino freeway, having waited that long for me to calm down, for the edge to wear off the rush of amphetamine.

"Nothing," I said, leaning my head back on the seat, warmed by the sun striking through the tinted glass, as David dropped the Hurst down to fourth and the G.T.O. slid into the fast lane. I could feel the air outside slipping over the car's high-gloss finish faster and with less resistance than the air on the cars around us as David cut in and out of the fast lane, passing cars lugging along six miles per hour over the legal limit.

"So tell me nothing," he said. "Ah, shit!" David was looking into his rearview mirror. He downshifted and pulled the G.T.O. into the middle lane between two other cars doing the speed limit. "A cop. Now it'll take forever to get into the city."

I looked behind us at the highway patrol car pulling onto the freeway into the slow lane, where he lurked for a minute or two and then leapfrogged two cars and pulled back into the right lane, hiding from the inattentive drivers who were pulling away from us in the left lane. The metal grid bumpers made the black and white Dodge look low and mean as it stalked speeders, and drivers behind him slowed up to his pace. No one passed him, even though he was not doing the speed limit, and David slowed more, unwilling to let him get out of sight in the mirror. Traffic bunched up. Then the Dodge swung off an exit ramp.

"Okay," I said. "He's gone."

David kept his eye on the mirror as we passed beneath the overpass. Cars in the fast lane accelerated, picking up speed on cue.

"Look again," he said.

Sure enough, the patrolman had pulled off the exit and paused long enough crossing the overpass to let everyone believe he had given up the hunt. Here he came, back down the entry ramp, accelerating until he was right behind us, timing the cars that had passed us and then swinging out in pursuit of one of the unwary, swinging his red search light up and on.

"At least they play fair out here," David said, pressing down on the accelerator and beginning to leapfrog cars in the middle lane in order to stay out of the patrolman's mirror. A mile later, we passed an old clunker pulled over to the shoulder by the patrolman and David relaxed.

"So," he said. "Tell me that nothing."

I tried. "Once upon a time," I began, intending to tell David a funny story about a little Indian boy whose best friend's name was Bernie Schneider, and how that boy had taken apart his Grandfather's power saw. I stopped. There weren't any words. I struggled for them, fought for them, trying to earn my words the Smith Barney way. Giving that up, I closed my eyes, pressing thumb and forefinger into the lids of each of them. At first, nothing except the test pattern sound that Grandfather had abandoned me to. I was determined. I persisted the way even the worst of storytellers must. Finally, the words came through: "Oh Fab, We're glad, They put new Borax in you."

"Personification," I muttered. How the hell did Fab achieve that?

"What?" David said.

"Nothing. I can't tell you nothing."

David moved his hands on the leather-covered steering wheel. He glanced over at me, and then back at the highway. "Man, you're getting pretty weird, you know?"

I knew. "Sorry," I said, laughing halfheartedly and closing my eyes and feigning sleep. Who the hell was "They"? It'd been Grandfather's voice, I was certain, even though his voice sounded like someone with throat cancer drunk on whiskey. Was he merely succumbing like everyone else to the jingoism of television, losing himself, his hopes and disappointments in the rising tide of mediocrity or the undertow of senility? Was "They" some anonymous conspiratorial force in the world, the same force that mother in her man-hating letters delineated, seeing her superintendent of schools, her principal, as the They-incarnate, the people who, by putting new Borax into laundry detergent, could make us glad? Or was the "They" friends I was drifting away from like David, in front of whom I lacked words, knowing, as I did, that David's theory of victims extended beyond Joanne and her ilk to include Black people ("A people that can't pull itself together makes itself a victim"), Aztecs ("They helped Cortez destroy them"), and Indians ("Look at Joseph, thinking they would let him reach Canada; or the plains Indians counting coup against Henry rifles, dumb, man, dumb").

Who hasn't been victimized by "Them"? ("Jews.") Jews?

"I love you," I said, blurting it out, surprising David as he drove into Los Angeles.

"We're good friends. I love you, too," adding quickly, for safety's sake, "like I love Sara. I just wish you weren't so angry with her."

"Yes," I said. "So do I. So do I. I love you both, you know, but I still don't understand."

"What?"

"Nothing."

I didn't. I wasn't being funny, even though David chuckled. I didn't understand a fucking thing that had happened from the day that Death stood beside my crib to now. It wouldn't help when, not many years later, Sara heard that David, who had married a nice Jewish girl like his folks wanted him to do, had put his chin on a table, his tongue between his teeth, his hands clasped on the crown of his head, and bitten his tongue off, bleeding to death.

"On his birthday," Sara would cry. "His wife coming home from work with a cake for him. There he was. Can you imagine?"

"No," I lied, thinking 'So much for underpinnings.' "I can't." Though I could. All too easily. By then, though, I knew something. Maybe I didn't quite understand it yet, but I knew it.

I would call it the Big Bang Theory of Meaning. As the cosmos expanded, what people took to be meaningful shrank. Where, once upon a time, feeding your family was *Important*, or leaving something behind was *Meaningful*, everything was shrinking into the *Nut of Now*—Nikes now, a Mercedes now, a condo on the beach now, cocaine now. Just when the need for meaning was greatest, people were choosing to settle for the *Nut of Now*—a nut which disintegrated into nothing more than dust under the pressure of their own ignored mortality. Living for now, given my friend Death, was meaningless and the contemplation of suicide was only a winnowing fan that could sort out the wheat from the chaff and leave people in awe of being alive.

"Don't you ever think about doing that to me," Sara said, hysterical with the suddenness of David's death and the idea that if we hadn't drifted away from him, he might still be alive.

"I won't," I said, holding her, beginning to rock back and forth with the slow, even comfort of a low tide. Suicide, as an expensive callgirl of Death, might seem attractive at moments to other people. But the option of killing myself had been stolen from me when, after the doctors had decided I was not going to live, Grandfather took Death by the hand, drove Him away from my cribside, and chained Him outside the mission's door. Having heard over and over how I was never supposed to have lived, every moment was a gift, a luxury that I did not earn or deserve any more than the man who inherits his father's wealth. For me to complain about living was as silly and self-serving as the heiress complaining about taxes or poor people on welfare.

Besides, Death was *so* boring.

I had David drop me in North Hollywood. I'd get a bus back out to Clearmont. There were things I had to think about.

The school was still there, across the street from one of the many houses I had occupied as a child. The asphalt was cracked and grayed by the sneakered feet of children, but the stucco walls of the school's buildings were still salmon pink, as uninviting in color as the buildings were in their flat, prison-like design.

Walking down towards the wash, I came to the alley where Bernie Schneider had pushed me into the cement block wall, and I walked the alley, trying to find the back gate which had been Bernie's. Two Vietnamese children darted, one behind the other, from the gate that had led to the Schneider house. When one caught the other and began to hit him, I interfered. Whether they understood me or not, I didn't know. They stopped, backing away from my disproportionate size like mountain sheep before the monster Ilpswetsichs. Was I a "they" to them, or an "us"? Where did my impulse to explain to these strange children that I was an Indian come from? At the end of the alley I looked back to see the two children beginning once again to stalk each other, ready to lock into Greco-Roman combat, as if they sensed the endless repetition of history and their part in that repetition.

Sooner or later, those two boys, Americanized, will become uneasy allies seeking to understand the diplomacies of little girls and, failing to understand, they will seek to influence the world of girls covertly, finally to dominate it if they can. Their fragile alliance will look strong, at times. When they are playing softball and the one fails to charge the grounder coming at him at third base, hurries his throw, and slings the ball high and wide of the first baseman, the other will chant, "It's okay. Settle down. We'll get the next batter," as the girls twitter like a flock of starlings over his clumsiness. But when the teacher tells him to go to the blackboard and the one pleads that he can't, his little masculinity prodding at the pleats in his pants, the other boy will betray him and twitter right along with the girls who are covering their mouths but not their laughing eyes. The one will secretly hate the other for this and determine to pay the other back for the betrayal—and, if he is able, to make the girls pay, too. Even with this determination, which makes his eyes sparkle like a sniper's, he will live with the fear of being twittered at from that moment on.

Bemused, I headed down the boulevard along the wash I had played in as a boy, the dried-up riverbed fronted by houses. There was Tommy A., himself, polishing a pink Thunderbird pulled up on the Bermuda grass beside the house. There was no mistake: It was Tommy all right, with the same round, innocent, and hairless face attached to a body that had grown taller, into the shoulderless shape of a barber's pole. I stood, watching him buff off the Blue Coral, and when he looked up and smiled, I said, "Nice car."

"Thank you," he said. It was a '56 Thunderbird, a two-seater with porthole windows and a V-8 under the long low hood. Did he recognize me?

"A classic," I said. "Those were great cars."

"If you like, I'll give you a ride in it when I'm finished."

"Thanks," I said. "I don't have time."

"Maybe another time," he said. He was so upbeat, so filled with the potential of promise. "My name's Thomas." He wiped his hands on a cloth and circled the front of the car to shake my hand.

"Jack," I said, looking him square in the eyes. His face was so youthful. How had he managed to avoid aging? 'A mere boy,' I thought, wondering what Crane or Dreiser would have done with a character like Thomas. Crane would make it the

Courage of Queers; Dreiser, the Fate of Faggots. Neither would fit. A Pride of Lionesses? No, Tommy in his own way had always been a homosexual and he had never belonged to any of those subgroups. He was the sort of homosexual who could massage another man's back without that other man needing to feel threatened by attitudes, and if he belonged to a classifiable group then it was to a Humility of Homosexuals.

"Well anytime, Jack," Tommy said as I began to walk away. "You know where I live. You're welcome to tea. After six, though, it's happy hour."

I waved without turning around.

"Have a pleasant day," he called after me and, with something in my eye, I could hardly hear him.

"You, too," I said to myself. "You mere boy you." I dug a dexamil from my watch pocket. Through the teeth and over the gums, I thought, following the lumpish capsule as it worked its way down my esophagus, the gelatin dissolving slowly in the p.H. of saliva.

### 43.

Strangely, where amphetamines helped me to think properly for class work, they did the opposite when it came to the Army. I loved the Reserve Officers Training Corps, at first because anyone could belong, but eventually just because it was easy. The routine of polishing brass, spit shining shoes, pressing pants helped me forget. Any idiot could do well in Rotsy as long as he was willing to follow the rules and memorize a few children's rhymes about rifles. Rhymes and rules were what the Army's indoctrination was all about and it made perfect sense. After all, if you were going to kill another human being in the jungles of Vietnam, you had better imagine him as a human unit and in this case a Gook—not only alien but inhuman, stereotyped by catch phrases. The purpose of the bayonet was to kill; the purpose of a Gook was to be killed. If he was a friendly Gook, then he was called a Vietnamese and his leader a president. Unfriendly, he was a Gook and his leader was a commie dictator—a Manichean division that came readily and easily to Rotsy cadets and which I understood better than sawdust, although I wanted to know the distinguishing marks that would make you certain that one soldier was a Vietnamese and the other a Gook. I didn't, after all, want to make mistakes, even in the dark foliage of Vietnam.

"Don't worry about it. Shoot 'em first. Then ask questions," the officers told us.

Father had never let me play Little League baseball and the Boy Scouts had rejected me *a priori* with a premonition of my unpreparedness. But the Army welcomed me, and playing with the boys on the marching field, drilling through the manual of arms, was great fun. I laughed with heterosexual heartiness when another cadet slammed his thumb in the chamber of his M-1 during inspection, releasing the bolt from the heel of his hand and failing to clear his thumb in time. I loved the cold sweat of parade arms on hot days and disdained the cadets who locked their knees back on purpose until they fainted and were dragged to the shade of the armory. Willingly, I was consumed by something larger than myself, a something that seemed to hold the power over life and death.

If one had a knack for shouting orders from deep down in his chest without using his tongue to form consonants, he quickly became a squad leader, able to stand apart from the rest of the fodder and bask in the silvered gaze of inspecting officers on the parade review stand.

If one managed to steal the answers to the entire semester's examinations, he was issued a white glazed helmet and spats and placed in the Honor Platoon.

It was after one of the first Rotsy lectures. Sergeant Potter had talked at us for ten or fifteen minutes before switching off the lights and showing us training films. Made by the same propagandist who directed Driver Training films for high school students, the films emphasized slogans that Potter introduced to us. Action-packed and full of special effects, each of the short clips was direct and easily understood: "You take care of your rifle, it will take care of you." After the films, I had the same secure sense that I'd had as a child when I was being toilet-trained. There was a right way (and time and place) and a wrong way (and place and time), and in case you could have missed the point, the director had added a heavy twist to the endings.

The one about keeping your rifle clean, for example, focused on Christopher and Sammy. Christopher (who insists on using his full and not a nick name) always cares for his equipment, breaking down his rifle every night, cleaning and oiling it, lifting it high above his head when fording streams or rivers, falling on his face in the muck and ooze rather than let his rifle be sullied. His buddy Sammy thinks he's silly, preferring to relax and catch some shut-eye rather than continually clean his equipment. Sammy is lazy, cleaning his rifle only when an officer makes him. Where Christopher looks—even on patrol—like he's just been returned from a Chinese laundry, Sammy is wrinkled and untucked, his brass embarrassing. Yet the pair love each other like brothers (we are told this since there is little time in a short film to convince us of it). Sammy's admiration for Christopher causes him to make an effort at cleanliness; he wants to be like Christopher, but his wanting is frustrated by his inherent tomorrow attitude.

"What's the use of polishing my brass?" Sammy asks. "It will only be tarnished tomorrow." (This elicits grunts of agreement from the cadets watching the film—it is true, after all—and out of the corner of my eyes, I see Potter grin in the light from the projector; Potter knows his cadets have been sucked in, set up for the higher truth to come; Potter has the film memorized, having shown it with the regularity of communion.)

The brass, Christopher kindly explains, is U.S. Government Issue and the government's property. It must be taken care of. Sammy and he are representatives of their country, their government, and more, the United States Army, and as such they ought to look their most presentable (Sammy's protests that this is war are cleared up by Christopher's telling him that in war or peace, it's the same). Finally, Christopher wows the film audience with a powerful syllogism: All soldiers who care for their equipment are good soldiers, he cares for his equipment, therefore he is a good soldier. Even Sammy is rocked back on his heels by the obviousness of this, though he still has trouble changing his habits (therefore, Sammy is not a good soldier).

Sammy and Christopher get caught in a fire fight. Like the good soldier he wants to be, Sammy charges the enemy emplacement. His rifle jams and he is pinned down by semi-automatic fire. Christopher, trying to save him, exposes himself needlessly and is cut into human confetti; using Christopher's rifle, Sammy manages to save himself. The end of the film is a shot of Sammy weeping over the body of his buddy, who has forgiven him his slovenliness with his final breath as Sammy swears he will change.

When the room lights clicked on, Potter was front and center, obviously moved by the film. "That, gentlemen," he said, "is why you will polish your brass every day. In one week, you will be issued M-1's. In two weeks, you will be able to break your rifle down, oil it, and reassemble it in less than ten minutes, blindfolded." He smirked. "It can get real dark in the jungles of Vietnam." Potter did a left face, snapped his heels, and out he marched, slamming the door like an exclamation mark.

Most of the cadets were shaken, leaving the hall quietly like Baptists after a sermon on hellfire and damnation. I loved the simplicity of the film's message and the way the director had accomplished his task almost without my fellow cadets knowing it. Still, there was a vague feeling of dis-ease which I couldn't place until Woody sneaked up behind me and slugged me in manly fashion on the shoulder.

"Don't worry about it," Woody said, beaming like Ken at Barbie. "Most of us are gonna get desk jobs and ride out the war on swivel chairs. Only niggers and beaners get put on the front lines."

And Indians, I thought. "Hey Woody?" I called as he left. "Yeah?"

"Fuck you."

Woody's smile hung in the room like a bad fart, and I gathered my notebooks and pencils together slowly.

On Potter's desk—one of those old office desks in which you can find pencil nubs, the odd paper clip, a scrap of paper with an unimportant note scribbled on it by an untrained hand, even crayons from the time the room was used for day care—was a manila folder. Finding nothing of interest in the desk, I opened the folder expecting to find Potter's cuneiform cues for his slogans.

Eureka. It took time—everything does—but no more than the 10 to the minus forty-third power it took to begin the universe for me to realize that here were the answer sheets to the entire semester's exams. It took a little more time— fifteen minutes or less (though my experience of the time was much longer)—for me to dash to the library and photocopy the set and return the folder to the desk.

As I descended the wide stairs outside the building, the sun was out and the sky seemed free of smog. I wore a smile as big as a banana, and I imagined I could hear my uncle in the distance singing what sounded like "Save the last dance for me."

"Fuck you, Woody," I thought, heading for the gym. "You ain't gonna leave me holding the ball."

I became the top cadet in my class, earning the spats, bandillero, and shiny helmet the way officers and top executives earn their rewards. With the care and assiduity of a scribe, I copied the answers of A through E onto a thin strip of paper, scrolling it into a dismantled Timex I bought on one of our trips to Mexico and telling Joanne, when she asked what I was doing, that I was looking for time. I found lots of it. The answers gave me confidence and the Honor Platoon gave me hope and when that failed, I crushed a dexamil spansule and dissolved it into lemonade, following that with another. I could ride with David into Ensenada and back, arriving just in time for an exam in political science for which I was ready, knowing that I would pass simply because of the length of my answers.

I became theoretical, and I could sit up all night with Sara and David and the Tompsons, talking, discussing ideas, rolling words around on my tongue like expensive lozenges. Delia Tompson would sometimes stop and look at me funny, as though she were wondering how I had changed from a goof into someone who believed everything he said. I didn't care. It didn't bother me at all when David began to ask me, "Aren't you doing a few too many of those?" each time I popped another pill. I'd laugh and explain with boyish delight that I had all plastic parts.

When father commented on the weight I'd lost at Thanksgiving, I told him it was basketball (which I had quit). Mother's way of taking notice of what was happening was to unlock the ladder of locks on her front door and stand there with her mouth open until she was able to say, "It's a ghost of himself." Mother had a way of making one look into mirrors, and this time instead of umber-colored skin I saw the color purple ringing eyes as beady as a Gila monster's.

"I'm now," I told the shadowy reflection. "I am in the world, among the dangs, enjoying my hour of last things."

"Death gives life meaning," I told Sara. "You've got to live on the cutting edge."

"Yeah, right," Sara said. "In the belly of the beast. At the heart of darkness. Downhill all the way," she said, matching me title for title.

When I told her how David had talked a prostitute into coming to our motel room for his amigo in Ensenada one night, Sara refused to laugh. I didn't tell her how I had known that I was past knowing when David managed, finally, to wake me up. Nor did I mention how I had felt that death would be a relief, at least the death of the tequila worms that seemed to have squatted in the abandoned corridors of my intestines. I couldn't remember what had been said beyond the whore's swearing at David for his little joke, and the picture of David laughing at my futile attempts to focus had made me break everything breakable in the room before he returned again, matching—with the infallible instinct of the drug addict—my sense of betrayal with the certainty of humiliation. Most of all, I didn't tell Sara that I had been scared, really scared, and only the notion that Death owed me one had kept me alive. Instead, I tried to make the story light-hearted, exaggerating details to make it funny for her.

She didn't laugh. "Alley. Oh, Alley," she said, shaking her head. "I wish . . ." She looked like a woman who doesn't believe in the life she witnesses and yet sees no alternative. "I don't know how this happened," she said, laughing sarcastically.

"What?"

She shook her head again and bit her lip. Her eyes were moist. "I can't," she said.

"Want one?" I offered her a dexamil, which she knocked from my hand.

While I was down on my hands and knees, trying to find the capsule which had rolled under my desk, she said, "Adam offers Eve the apple. It's almost funny."

"Found it," I said, standing up. "These little tigers cost money, you know."

"Oh, Alley. You've got to quit this. The next step is naturalism. The Stephen Crane Prize for speed freaks who have cooked their imaginations." She looked at me, reaching out to take hold of my hand. "What would Elanna say, if she knew?"

"Listen. Lay off, will you? I'll do what I want. The more you try to tell me how to behave, the more I'm going to want to do this just to show nobody tells me how to behave." I didn't like her bringing Elanna into this. "You're worse than the Vegomatic, you know that? Except we aren't married."

"Sometimes I think maybe we are," Sara said bitterly.

"What does that mean?" I demanded.

"Never mind." She sighed the way a parent will when faced with the persistent illogic of a child she gives in to out of love. "All right," she said. "Here. Give it to me." I handed the dexamil to her. "You have some water?" she asked.

"Beer," I said, going to Woody's dormitory-sized refrigerator and taking a can out and opening it. "Is that all right?"

"Why not?" Sara said. "Why the hell not."

# CHAPTER TEN

## 44.

I took so much speed that I began to lose all concentration. Everything became vague, shapeless, and I was fast going nowhere.

Sara took pills when I offered, figuring that every one she took was one I couldn't take. That made me unhappy. I'd bought the Cracker-Jacks mythology of the sixties, that you shared everything, even the surprise that came with every box. But it wasn't good for Sara.

The December rains came, making the sky turn dirty like the tiles in a bus station restroom. Due dates for term papers fluttered around like dying butterflies and with final exams approaching the campus took on all the pleasanter aspects of a city morgue. Woody's permanent smile wilted, and he seemed content to stay in with Joanne and study. Sara became bitchy, her adrenal glands overtaxed by worry and the occasional dexamil. David sank into reading potboilers like *Uhuru*, *Hawaii*, becoming solitary in his boredom while everyone else jogged to and from the library. Rachel, according to the postcard from Sanchez, became pregnant.

One good aspect to speed was the asymptote of its effects. I could increase the amounts to match the need until finally just the idea of taking more made me tired, and I found myself falling asleep, snoring like a dog in a field of ragweed. The time I bought chemically became instants of euphoria followed by miles of dullness. I became stubborn in my dullness, preferring, like Bartleby, Not To.

The smiles of senior cadets and officers in R.O.T.C. turned downward into frowns resembling an unhappy Kilroy painted beside the tracks of endless railroads. Almost daily, I forced the Army to remind me of its Commandments, and I began to collect more demerits than any cadet in the history of the college, if not the Corps. I refused to polish my brass if I had to walk through rain or fog to class. The rain was going to tarnish it anyway. Had I forgotten that first training film? No. But it seemed to me that Sammy had been right all along, at least about that.


One thing led to another, and soon enough I was wearing a peace symbol to parade and firing from the hip on the target range.

"I didn't think you were cut out to be a soldier," Proctor Tompson said over the dinner of baby beef tongue Delia had cooked for us.

I was amusing Sara, Delia, and him with a weak imitation of the humorless master sergeant who had thrown me off the target range. Permanently. He'd caught me shooting from the hip like Chuck Connors on "The Rifleman." Delia was being quiet, listening like a Texan to Country and Western, chewing a bite of beef tongue and looking at me in a way that made me wary.

"May as well shoot from the hip. Did you know that eighty percent of the grunts in Double U Double U Two never fired at anyone?" I said. "Some retired general went around and interviewed soldiers from both sides, and only twenty per cent admitted actually to aiming at another person. Do you know what that means?"

"It means," the Proctor said with his ability to tie everything up in bundles like Boy Scouts on a newspaper drive, "that the percentage of people who kill on the battlefield is the same as the percentage who make a killing in the stock market. Maybe they're the same people. Or their heirs, at least."

"It means," Sara said, laughing, "that you're as good a soldier as any one else. Shit, even you can hit a row of sandbags."

"As long as it holds still," I said. I took a bite of tongue. I could barely keep from gagging on the texture, but I managed to eat it for Mrs. Tompson.

"You know what your problem is?" Delia said.

She set her knife across the edge of the plate and took a sip of the wine the Proctor had brought up from his small but tasteful cellar. She jabbed the air in front of me with her fork.

"You level everything out. You treat everything as though it's equally important to everything else. The only time you take anything seriously," she said, giving Sara an apologetic look, "is when you're on drugs."

In the ensuing silence, my cousin could have delayed not one but two West German trains. Sara looked frightened. "Alley," she began.

"You're right," I admitted, hanging my head with the weight of the affection I had for all of them and staring at the veins and vessels in a slice of baby beef tongue. "A commander is as good as a carrot to me. With enough Vitamin A, you don't need carrots. The uniforms of the military are no more or less respectable than the Jesus jeans worn by Elanna's old Berkeley friends. One dandelion's head is the same as any other, a Gila is a Gila and you can tell one from the other only if you give them names like George."

Later, Sara came by my room to tell me she was sorry. I sat, knees pulled up on the bed, leaning against the cold stone wall of the room, reading and rereading the label of a fifth of J.D.

"Jack Daniels," I said, waving the bottle at her. "Son of Jim Beam and blood brother to Mr. Walker. Fire water that John Wayne trades Mexicans in westerns for their soul. Whee-ski. Bourbon in old Kin-tuck-ee. Want some?"

"Alley. I'm sorry," Sara said.

"Not half as sorry as I am, Mizz Custer."

"Oh. Wow. Listen, I told Delia about the speed because I care about you. I didn't want her to bring it up that way. Maybe she didn't know how else to bring it up. I know it seems like I betrayed you, but I didn't. You don't see that, do you?"

"Did you mention that you do a little yourself?" I asked, hating myself for smirking.

"She can figure that out for herself."

"Right."

"Have you ever thought about why I do it?"

"Because it's free."

Sara jumped like a hippie surprised by rednecks. Before

she slammed out of my room, she said, "I was trying to keep you from your loneliness."

"Solitude," I said, correcting her.

"Looks pretty lonely to me, fart face," she said. "See ya around."

By the time my roommate Woody staggered in pretending to be inebriated on cherry extract, I was staring into the empty bottle of J.D. as though the whiskey were love, trying to convince myself that there was more where that had come from.

David returned to college from holidays with his folks with the hint of sidelocks and wearing a little round cap.

"If you put feathers in it," I said, trying to cheer him up, "it'd keep your head warm."

David was changed, as though whatever his parents had told him weighed him down. He wasn't bitter about it but rather accepted it, except on Friday nights when he had to be in his room by sunset, and for a while I would drop by his room and keep him company. As he said, what was he to do on Friday nights, study? It was David who corrected my notions about the menorah and the Feast of Lights, and although I felt a certain loss, no longer able to envy Jews because their G-d had taken those extra days to create their world, I did envy him for belonging to something larger than himself. When he began to demand what had Indians contributed to Western Civilization, I managed to smile and joke about how a hamster named Custer had died for his sins.

"Indians are Eastern," I protested. "They live in space, more than in your kind of time." David's snickering when I said that wounded me more and more.

At the same time, I saw with the secret wisdom of spiders that I was being coughed up out of Rotsy like phlegm from an asthmatic. Counseled regularly by Captain R.J. Morrisey about the number of my demerits, I knew the Army was trying to tolerate me the way the Army Air Force had tolerated my uncle. After all, I still drilled with energetic precision and my exam scores did seem dishonestly high to Morrisey. When it came down to it, though, Captain Morrisey could not fathom how a boy opposed to war had come to enroll in R.O.T.C.

"It's easy," I said. I told him the story I'd made up about being charged with assault and battery, and his eyes seemed to clear like the desert air after a storm. "It isn't true," I added. "I could never hurt anyone intentionally."

The Captain looked depressed for a moment. Then he chuckled like Skinner designing a new maze. "What if your sister were attacked?" he asked. "What if some pimp tried to mug or rape your sister and you were there?"

"I'd stop him," I said. Morrisey smiled. Without even pausing to think, I said, "But I'd use force, not violence."

"What the hell is the difference?" Morrisey inquired.

Force, I explained, lacked the intent to do physical or permanent harm to another person. Prevention, not cure. "Like having your teeth cleaned," I said.

The strangest aspect of these tests of wit and wisdom was that I came to like Captain Morrisey. Genuinely. When Vietnam came up, he offered the defense of our country as a reason and instead of saying, "Whose country?" I rejoined with the tried but trite example of the Civil War and foreign interference. Neither of us won this endless game of dominoes. The second time Vietnam dragged its carcass into our conversation, Morrisey said that he had seen his best buddy blown away by a Claymore Mine. Having watched Pamela bleed to death, I understood what he meant well enough never to raise the gorgon of Southeast Asia again. Ultimately, Captain R.J. Morrisey decided that were I to go into the regular Army I'd serve out my tour in the brig being beaten and buggered by Marine guards. So he offered to do, and did, what seemed an act of courage beyond the call of duty: He wrote my draft board to explain that while I wasn't always conscientious, I was by nature not violent and recommended that when the time came I be given a I-O deferment. Meanwhile, he suggested that I consider withdrawing from Rotsy, although "that wouldn't mean we couldn't get together for a beer from time to time."

Before I could decide to withdraw, a dark little Major named Adjamien made the decision for me. Walking home alone from drill one day, I was trying to visualize a German sentence in the subjunctive. Finally, I gave that up and settled for conjugating the verb "fahren." Adjamien passed me going in the opposite direction, his figure tilted forward as if into a high wind, his uniform weighted with the merit badges of ribbon and metal that the Army hands out for everything from excellent typing to heroism on the drill field. Having just reached "fahrt" in my conjugatory detachment, I failed to salute him.

"Cadet!" he shouted, his voice high and thin and airy. I turned and walked back to him, tactfully maintaining enough distance between us not to bend his facsimile of a neck. He looked familiar, like he was cousin to someone I knew. He stepped in close, raising himself on his tiptoes, and demanded to know why I had failed to salute him. The way the nose hairs stuck out from his upturned nostrils told me he would not appreciate a joke about having overlooked him because of his height; I couldn't help grinning at the way height, in his case, meant absence and not presence.

"Just what do you think you're laughing at?" Major Adjamien said. He spoke each word clearly, spitting them out. Droplets of his saliva made me blink.

"I wasn't laughing," I said, rubbing my eyes with the back of my hand. "I was thinking."

Early in the semester, Max Rafferty had addressed a randy assembly of the college's boys and described the Big Man on Campus. "The sort," Max had said, "who has his thumb in every pie." Had I known that Adjamien was a Big Man on Campus, perhaps I would have refrained from explaining to him that I respected no one's clothes.

That evening, a ghastly-looking fellow in a senior cadet's uniform dropped by my room offering to fix things with the major, telling me in a lugubrious voice to call him "Sandy."

"It's the logic of muggers, Sandy," I told him. I knew who He was; I'd seen Him too many times in too many disguises not to recognize Him. What the hell, Sandy was as good a name as any for Him.

"Muggers," I said, "won't mug people in fur coats or silk suits. They respect fur coats and silk suits second only to Cadillacs."

"Now?" Sandy asked, knitting and unknitting his brows.

"No. Not now, either," I said.

"Okay," He said. "I still owe you one. But I have to warn you. Sooner or later you're going to have to take it. I'm not gonna ask too many more times."

"I know," I said. "But I'm going to take the best three out of two."

"Oh," He said, "I almost forgot. I promised to deliver this." Digging through his backpack of fears and dreams, He pulled out a package in a plain brown wrapper. Inside was a carefully carved jewelry box, inlaid on the top with silver and lapis lazuli. Inside it were a singular brass wind chime that went "dong" when you struck it and a top-of-the-line Swiss Army knife—the kind you can use for everything from whittling to root canals.

I didn't ask who had sent them. I didn't have to. "How'd you find me?"

"Smell," He said, grinning that grin of his.

"Smell?"

"Speed is like cheese," He said. "You can smell the person who uses it the same way you can smell fear." He punched me on the shoulder. "See ya around, Spike."

It turned out that Max Rafferty had been right. Major Adjamien had his thumb in every pie, all of them filled with blackbirds—trained blackbirds that flew one by one over my head and bombarded me with their inherited wisdoms. While I bobbed and ducked, they took away my spats, my shiny helmet, my M-1—and (the bastards) my sense of belonging to something larger than my self.

### 45.

"I feel like Duz."

Delia Tompson was making tea, and I sat at the kitchen table while the Proctor put the car in the garage. Delia swirled boiling water in the teapot to warm it before she added tea bags and fresh hot water. "Irish Breakfast all right?"

"Sure," I said, watching her, surprised once again at the

way Delia wasn't a woman who was once beautiful, not a woman people would say "held her age," but a woman who was still beautiful—more so the more you knew her. Unlike some people whose faces looked like a herd of Gilas had crawled across them, leaving them lined and saggy with disappointment, the lines on her face—the result of laughter alternating with thoughtful concentration—gave her character.

"You know I really appreciate this," I said as she set the cups on the table.

"You're welcome," she said. "Besides, you can help out around here. That will let the Proctor spend more time finishing up this series of articles."

After passing out from a headache bumping eight on the Richter scale, I'd spent the past four days being prodded like a frog in Biology Lab and injected with varying derivatives of codeine. The Tompsons had agreed to let me stay in their guest room while I made the studio over their garage livable. Together, we had convinced the resident surgeon, Hacksaw Satherwaite, that I would fare better in their house than in a college infirmary with V.D. cases, fakers of mono, and the random attempted suicide.

Delia composed a long letter asking, for fear of hurting mother's feelings, if my living with them was all right with her. Mother replied with a Xeroxed diagram of her house's floor plan. She'd labelled each bedroom of the house as her study, her bedroom, and the room the Stanford student was lodged in, drawing little blue-coated soldiers in each one to indicate occupied territory. Father lived in a one-bedroom apartment so he was less a problem of tact than a problem of tactics. He wanted me to have the tumor out in the college clinic; I insisted on the Stanford Medical Center.

"It's not that I distrust Hacksaw Satherwaite," I explained to Delia. "It's his loneliness. He looks like USC's place kicker in the last seconds of a tie game with UCLA. He looks at me, and his eyes swim with hesitant visions of glory."

"This is my head we're talking about," I'd tell the Tompsons over dinner. "I've got to have something there to protect my neck from falling objects, don't I?"

"The way I understand it," the Proctor said after my first visit to Dr. Joshua "you-can-call-me-Josh" Weinstein at Stanford, "is that this could be pretty serious."

"Like the red wheelbarrow," I said, trying to be upbeat. "It all depends."

I moved in above the Tompsons' garage. It was a slow time. At first it was slow because of the shock to my adrenal glands, after Delia flushed my entire supply of amphetamines down the toilet. After my brain recovered and I could remember a word longer than two syllables, the waiting passed pleasantly, and like an old dog who no longer has to guard the house, I began to put on weight.

"Nothing worse than a fat Indian," I said to Sara, who came by almost daily to visit.

"A fat and happy Pinko," she would reply. "It's good to see."

"You know," Delia said shyly one night over Cornish game hens, "if Sara would like to . . . I don't mean to butt in, so forgive me if I am . . . but if you would like to have Sara spend the night now and then . . ."

"What's the matter?" Proctor Tompson asked. "You look, to say the least, flabbergasted."

"No. I mean, yes, I am," I said, looking from him to Delia and trying not to blush. "I mean, Sara and I are just friends. Good friends."

"Through no fault of hers," Delia said.

"To be Sara's boyfriend . . . that would be like being invisible. Just being her friend reduces me to the outlines of a dork whenever we go into a bar together. You know, the comments the ridge-bellied roundheads make about what's a queen like her doing with a guy like me."

Delia laughed. She knew what I meant, if the Proctor didn't. "Do you think Sara wants to date ridge-bellied roundheads?"

I confessed I didn't.

"Sex gets in the way of friendship. You end up jealous and protective and worried, and the jealousy eats you up inside. And," I added, before either of them could say anything, "I am the jealous type. I've never been able to swallow that crap about jealousy being possessiveness. When Woody tells Joanne that she's being possessive, all he means is that he'd like to go out and screw around some. He uses the schmaltzy liberal line to excuse himself because Joanne doesn't and because he expects her to be there when he wants. Faithfulness saves a lot of time. Besides," I added, laughing, "keeping you from getting V.D."

"That's Woody, not you," the Proctor said, refilling my wine glass.

Delia said, "Jealousy is only a matter of bad faith. It doesn't have to eat you up inside if you don't let it. As your Grandfather might say, jealousy can eat you up inside only if there's nothing inside to begin with. As for sex . . ."

"What about sex?" the Proctor said, winking.

"Sex doesn't have to interfere with friendship. Does it?"

"Definitely not." Proctor Tompson raised his glass in a toast to his wife. "It's a matter of having the supply match the demand. You, Alley, are going to have trouble accomplishing that if you can't grasp the economic nature of life. From your final last term," he said gently, "I'd say you've always had a good deal of trouble just making change."

Living with the Tompsons, blushing my way through conversations (mother had always leaned toward the cabbage patch theory of sex and birth), I began to see possibilities. They seemed a long ways away. Never before had I seen a couple that didn't carp at each other. I'd always assumed that the happiness the Tompsons seemed to have together was partly show in front of company, but now I had the chance to overhear their voices behind the late night doors. Sure, they got angry and upset. But even when they argued, they didn't fight. When they did raise their voices, there seemed to be a basic assumption beneath them that said, 'even though I think you are absolutely wrong in this matter, there is nothing the matter with your being wrong.' It was as great a pleasure as realizing that Laura P.'s monologues about Grandfather were a kind of love.

The next time Sara dropped by, I was outside mowing the lawn with my shirt off. My first wish was that I could hide my clumsy, round body away from her. I could barely push the mower, my arms weak with a mental phlebitis.

"What's wrong?" Sara asked, finally, having noticed the way I redirected her attention away from my body toward any-thing—anything else.

"Nothing. Why do you ask?"

"Nothing," she said, mimicking me. Her tone seemed hurt. "Nothing. I come by to see if maybe you'd like to go for a walk or a drive and you act like I've got every communicable disease in the book."

"I have to finish the lawn," I said.

"I can wait. How long will it take?"

"I don't want you to wait. Listen, Sara." I felt an unreason-able loathing for the way her expression seemed to say that she was willing to overlook what I had just said. "I don't want a girlfriend." I meant to add that I didn't think I could en-dure the incongruity of being *her* boyfriend. It came out, "I don't want to be your boyfriend."

Sara looked stung, bitten by teeth that wouldn't let go. "No-body's begging, Spike." She wheeled and walked off down the street.

As I watched her, it seemed as if the trees parted in the breeze on purpose, letting the sunlight play across her proud shoulders, illuminating her figure with the lightness and color of a Mary Cassatt painting as she walked slowly away. In the same way that a Cassatt can speak to you, I thought I heard a voice—not Grandfather's, but a voice like out of the maple trees—telling me that for all the slowness I'd been hiding behind, this wasn't slowness but fear, that I had been afraid of something like this ever since the days in which I'd tried to teach Bernie Schneider to sneak up on the prey from downwind.

"Except," the voice whispered, "you have a choice Bernie didn't have. He drowned beneath the cargo of his hopes and desires; you are about to drown beneath the cargo of your unrealistic fears."

Without wondering where the voice had come from, I grabbed my shirt and stumbled down the sidewalk after her.

"Sara."

She turned with all the grace she had had on the day I'd met her, and for a moment I felt like the sailor whose radar has picked up a storm, deciding whether to run from it or to sail straight ahead into it.

"Listen, could we talk? Could we go for that drive?"

When she reached out her hand, I took it shyly, over-whelmed by the sensation that her hand—its size, softness, the length of her fingers—fit in mine.

### 46.

We drove in Professor Quinin's Impala to Lake Arrowhead. On the way, I tried to explain the only way I knew how, by talking about something else.

"Remember last semester when we were supposed to read *Billy Budd* for your father's class? Remember how I couldn't reread it and how angry you were because you thought that I thought it wasn't a good book?"

Sara reached over and slipped a Jerry Jeff Walker tape into the car's tape deck. "Do you mind?"

"Uh-uh. Anyway, it wasn't that I didn't like Billy Budd."

"I know," Sara said.

"What?"

"Go on. You were saying . . . ?"

"It's that every time Billy can't speak up to Captain Vere and tell him the truth, I get frustrated, angry. It was bad enough when we had to read the book in high school. When our teacher made us watch the movie I cut my palms with my fingernails I was squeezing them so hard. I couldn't stand someone who couldn't speak up, confronted as Billy was with injustice, so I pretended I was slow and refused to write a paper on it. Now, well, now I know why I can't reread *Budd*. It's because he can't speak. He's tongue-tied, speechless, be-cause things are so plain to him and he's confused by the fact that things aren't plain to Vere. I hate him for it because . . . in case you haven't noticed . . . I . . . I am just . . ."

"Like him," Sara said, steering the car through a set of curves as we climbed into the mountains. "I know that."

She parked the car just inside the ranger kiosk. "Want to walk?"

As we got out of the car, she looked at me across the roof of it.

"Except you're not as good as Billy was," she said. Coming around the car and taking my hand, she said, "But Billy always was something of the wimp. You know, too good. It's easier to deal with someone who's a little evil than with someone who's too good. We don't believe someone can be that good. And if we do begin to believe it, all we can do is kill him for being everything we're not."

We walked through the trees down towards the footbridge that cut across the tip of the arrow's head. "That's why you began writing stories."

"Why?"

"Because it's the only way you can say the things you can't say in person."

Sara crossed the bridge ahead of me, swinging down from the far end of the bridge towards a group of rocks that stuck up out of the water beside the shore. A solitary fisherman drifted in the center of the lake about a hundred yards away from us. He glanced at us once. In the distance, out where the lake was wider, a speedboat curled away from the fisherman.

"You know I used to think that one day you'd hand me a story and even if it wasn't good, even if it wasn't about love, I'd know it was written for me, to tell me things you couldn't say?"

"Are you kidding?" I said. I poked at the water with a stick. A crayfish scurried backwards beneath the shelter of the rocks. I felt like a young boy whose experience with girls had yet to begin. Awkward, scared, as though the driver in the speedboat might zip down the lake and whisk her away, both of them laughing at me. Like all fear, this one snowballed: If acquired the betrayal I'd felt when Pamela had died and its whiteness was muddied by the repeated and boring frustration of Allison DeForest. Sara was women, in other words.

But then, I thought, so is Elanna.

"So is your mother," Sara said. "Look. Alley. It's how you look at it. You know how David believes that nothing is accidental, that everything is foreordained but that it's possible we can't understand how or why?"

"Yeah. But I don't agree," I said, thinking of Coyote and

how it was his immediate cleverness, his ability to meet the accident of Ilpswetsichs and win out, that created Real People.

"It doesn't matter!" She sounded exasperated or tired. I wasn't sure which. "David looks at life one way. You look at it another."

She stopped and thought a moment. The fisherman reeled in what looked to be a lake bass, fighting it all the way.

"David sees the whole board. You see the board cut in two by a power saw. You worry about where the sawdust comes from. David believes he knows where the sawdust came from. But wherever it comes from, neither of you can put the sawdust back."

"I don't understand," I said. The fisherman reached toward the bass with his net.

"Neither do I," Sara said, laughing so loud that the fisherman turned his attention away from his catch just long enough to lose it. "Let me try putting it another way. Men and women have been at each other forever. Right?"

I shrugged.

"Since Adam and Eve. But consider. Maybe Eve got tired of competing with God for Adam's attention. You know, every time they went off to be together, here comes old Loud Voice, telling Adam to get out there and name some more names? Maybe Eve decided she'd give up Paradise to find out whether Adam loved her. Not out of weakness but out of desire, out of love. Maybe, even, she knew who the snake was—the same way you think you can recognize one of Death's disguises?"

"She must have been smart enough, I guess. Otherwise, she would've been a cheerleader for the Hittites."

"Exactly. So if you see it that way, then what Adam did was not give up Paradise but choose Eve. Out of love. Greater love for her than for old Loud Voice. Maybe Adam and Eve together chose to be human beings, to share not only that apple but their lives and deaths. You see? It can become a positive action and the reason for it is what you call sawdust.

"I wish I could convince you of the possibility, at least," she said. "The reason Adam ate that apple was the same one I had when I'd take speed with you. I wanted to be a part of what you were living, even if it was bad for me."

Was it possible? Sara Baites loved *me*?

"Yes, Alley. That's what I mean."


The sun was dropping toward the blanket of trees lining the ridge of mountains behind Lake Arrowhead as Sara Baites and I hiked in and out of the thickets of trees along the shore.

"All we need is a soft sunset filter on the camera lens and a dog," I said, starting to laugh and then feeling sad. It hadn't been very long since father had had Running Dog put to sleep and the mere thought of the trusting but questioning look Running Dog must have had on his face could make me cry. Sentiment had begun to do that to me: When I felt strongly about one thing, the memory of another could reduce me to sloppy and stupid sentimentalism, though I usually managed not to show it. In this case, shaken by the notion that Sara Baites might be in love with me, the thought of Running Dog made my heart cry.

"So?" Sara said. "What do you think?"

I shook my head and looked away for a moment, biting my lip. Taking her hand, I drew her away from the lake shore and through the trees toward the cabins and frame buildings of a summer camp I hoped was still there.

The main building, a Lincoln Log structure with a low peaked roof that hovered over a lodge hall with an open fireplace, a restaurant-sized kitchen and an open-sided eating deck with picnic benches, was occupied by thin balding men in orange saris.

"Hari, hari," one of them said, rounding a corner and nearly bumping into us.

"Hari," I said, trying not to laugh—not at him or his friends but at the way my hopes had never considered this reality. "Do you mind if we stroll around?" I asked. The fellow's face remained as inexpressive as Grandfather's had ever been.

"Au-buom," he said, smiling. He reached into a fold in his sari and pulled out a joss stick. His other hand procured a lighter which he used to light the stick. Then he handed it to Sara who took it.

"Thank you," Sara said. He held out his hand until I dug out fifty cents and dropped them into his palm and he disappeared as gently as he'd come.

"This used to be a summer camp," I said, steering Sara away from the main building towards the creek that divided the main building from the campers' cabins. Cabin number three, the one called "Eagle's Nest" by our counselor, which Bernie and I had changed to "Spotted Eagle's Nest," personalizing it the best we could, was still there. Though it was little more than a raised plank floor sided by worm-eaten split logs, with unscreened windows and a doorway that had never known a proper door, it was still there. Inside were the metal bunk beds with wire mesh springs on which Bernie had nightly tossed, waiting for Rolf to sneak his pants on and creep out of the cabin towards his rendezvous with Tammy.

Sara touched me on the shoulder, as if she knew that this former camp, this cabin meant something to me, even if I didn't know exactly what.

"There is a tale," I said, turning to her, my voice sounding like Grandfather's when he told me about the creation of the Nu-mi-pu. "About the creation of dreams."

I was beginning to realize that Bernie Schneider had not been the only one, all those years ago, to invent the image of Tammy and then to sink beneath the weight of her imagined perfection. I, too, a round little boy whose disguise was what Dr. Bene called slowness, had invented an image, had taken on a cargo of dreams. Mine had only lacked a name, lacked a name and a place and remained airy substance, the dream of a woman who was represented by all women.

Bernie's burden was Tammy. He had pursued it with an assiduity that only a Jew with his belief in law, obedience, and study could have. I, on the other hand, those nights he and I watched Rolf and Tammy pumping away at each other, had made them dissolve but had taken on the voices, the sounds of sex and love. I, with the patience of Job and the hopefulness of the little engine that could, had been spinning my wheels in slothful pursuit of those sounds.

So it was, after she said "Tell me" and I had told her as

best I could without boring her like Death, that Sara came to the same conclusion.

"It's the same cargo," she said as we sat on the rocks over-looking the lake. "The one difference is that Bernie gave his a name. Tammy. Not a name I'd pick, but I suppose I'm not Bernie. Yours, like interchangeable parts, probably had a succession of names. And," she said timidly, "forgive me for saying this. I know you hate psychologizing, but you also had Laura P., your mother, and even your uncle's now new wife, the Vegomatic. Maybe even Elanna and Pamela—a sort of combination for you, a composite that was positive, but fell apart on you when Pamela died."

"That raft," I said, pointing. "I had to take Bernie out to it every day and hang him over the edge in the cool water to stop him from shivering over his vision of Rolf and Tammy."

"Hey," Sara said, "let's swim out to it. You want?"

"I don't know," I said, looking at the shadows cast by the trees. "It's getting pretty late."

Sara didn't wait for me but began tearing off her clothes and heaping them on the beach. Feeling like I was miscast in a movie wet with romanticism, I followed her down to the water's edge.

"Come on," she said. "Hurry up." She stood knee-deep in the water, her temerity more frightening to me than her naked body as I began to slowly undress, neatly folding my shirt and beginning to unbutton my pants.

"Jesus," she said, running out of the water and pushing me to the sand. "Don't you do anything without thinking about it?"

She tugged at the cuffs of my pants, threw them into a heap, and then dashed backed to the water. Diving in, she surfaced and rolled on her back long enough to yell out the water was freezing. Then she began stroking out to the raft.

"It happens, if it happens at all, this way," I told myself as I sidestroked towards her, each scissor kick of my long legs making me gain a foot on her as she swam the crawl. By the time I had reached the raft, Sara was up on it, wringing her hair dry and beginning to braid it. My body had adjusted to the water's temperature but climbing onto the raft it was cold again, even though the sky was windless, and my penis shrank. I sat facing away from Sara, embarrassed and yet not embarrassed.

"You know you do have a funny body," Sara said. "But," she said before the sting of her words could swell, "I love it."

She pulled me farther up onto the raft and positioned herself beside me, beginning to kiss me all over. When she focused on my midsection, I tried to draw her up onto me, believing as always that I had a responsibility to give her her pleasure, that no one would take pleasure in doing that for me. Sara paused, briefly, and gently straight-armed me onto my back again.

"Relax," she whispered. "I want to do this. Just relax and enjoy it."

I did, as best I could. But when she slid up beside me, threw her arm across my chest and rested her head on my shoulder and said, "Ummm. That tasted good," all the embarrassment of years returned. "What's the matter?" Sara asked. "Didn't you enjoy it?"

"Yes," I said. "But . . ."

"So did I," she said.

"Really?"

"Really."

Staring up at the blue-black of the sky, I made a decision. "I believe you," I said, feeling that my words must have the ring of untruth and suspecting that Sara knew it. "I'll try to believe you."

"You can take my word for it," she said, standing up and preparing to dive back into the water.

Later, after we'd made love on the splintery floor of "Spotted Eagle's Nest," it was my turn to ask her if she'd enjoyed that.

"Yes," she said. Frowning, she asked, "Did you come?"

"Yes," I lied, smiling, knowing that it didn't matter, really, whether I had or not as well as knowing why. Of course, it would matter if it happened this way time after time. But once or twice, here or there, who cared? "Nothing gives me pleasure more than giving you pleasure," I said.

"That's your way of telling me you didn't come, isn't it? Come on. Want to try again?"

"No. It's okay, really. Maybe later, when we both feel like it? Now it would seem like work, all aimed at giving me some kind of physical satisfaction. I already have that," I added.

"I guess it's my turn to take your word for it, huh?"

"I guess it is."

On the drive home, Sara asked me what I was thinking and I told her. "I always thought I would marry an Indian," I said.

"That's strange. Why?"

"I don't know. I just did."

"Does that mean you're thinking about marrying someone who isn't an Indian?"

"Maybe," I said.

That night, which she spent at the Tompsons'—a fact that made the Tompsons happy (at least if Delia's saying "It's about time" meant anything)—I apologized for the way it sounded silly, for the way the phrase seemed to have so much sawdust in it and yet for the way it could sound empty and hollow if spoken even by the right person to a wrong one. "But," I said, "I love you."

"The only reason it sounds silly is that you don't have to say it. I know it. I've always known it. But . . . it's nice to hear," she added, drifting off toward sleep.

# CHAPTER ELEVEN

## 47.

Dr. "You-can-call-me-Josh" Weinstein scheduled *Operation Sawdust* for the first day of Sara's spring vacation, a date I asked for specifically, telling Dr. Weinstein that that way, if I died, she could save the plane fare. Weinstein raised his eyebrows less in surprise and more in an attempt not to grin. Recognizing with doctorly insight that I was one of those patients who'd be debilitated by false confidences and frightened by half-truths, he had been direct and honest with me. With a 50/50 chance, I had better odds than Harrah's, Lake Tahoe.

It wasn't the raw hardiness of 'Give it to me straight, Doc.' Rather, my attitude was formed by my old familiarity with Death. Having seen something of Death himself, Josh Weinstein understood my attitude. After explaining the possibilities in detail, he joked with me about the things he wouldn't know until I had journeyed halfway into the Absence of Angels.

I liked him. "You're the best, Josh," I'd say.

"That, I am," he'd reply. In an age when being good enough was an aspiration, it was refreshing to meet someone whose goal was to be the best at what he did, and I would grin a grin as big as a Bentley.

Sara didn't want to talk about it and she took my playful references to *Operation Sawdust* like vicious personal criticism.

"Death is strange," I'd say, and she'd look stung, distrustful and hurt as though I'd confessed to having an affair, as meaningless as it all might be, ultimately.

"I would appreciate not hearing about it," she'd say. "I do not want to talk about it."

But I needed to talk about it, not out of some morbid

225

desire to reap sympathy or tolerance, but out of a need to know and understand everything I could about how I felt, which I could get only by trying to describe it.

"When I was little, the first time I flew in a plane I was frightened by the way the wings moved up and down like a pterodactyl's. My uncle taught me about stress and flex and I learned that the time to be afraid was when the wings stopped flapping, not while they were."

I told her this in an attempt to explain how knowing made me unafraid; all I feared was the vague discomfort of not knowing.

"I was quite the fun child to fly with, after that. I'd make sure everyone *saw* how the wings were flapping. I thought that if they learned what I'd learned, they'd be unafraid, too. Mostly they ignored me, looked away from me, pretended they didn't hear me, lit cigarettes and ordered thirds on drinks."

"I would've, too," she said.

With the permission of the Tompsons, Sara moved into the apartment above the garage. When Delia worried about what her father might feel, Sara laughed and said that being a hard-line liberal was almost as hard as being an orthodox Jew.

"There are rules you have to follow consistently, whether you like them or not. Dad will work it out. Besides, his defense of his dissertation is coming up so I doubt he'll even notice that I'm not around."

In happy moments, when Sara and I were lying awake together in bed, I'd forget how upset she could become when I mentioned dying and I'd slip and say something like, "At least I've been in love once in my life. That's more often than . . ."

"Stop it, Albert," she would say. "If you don't, I'm going to move out. Stop seeing you, and move home. Seriously, Alley, I mean it. Promise."

"I promise."

It wasn't easy. It had begun to seem to me that it was not Death alone who was boring, but what people did with Death. To me, He seemed comical, like the fool in *Lear*; and like King Lear, I was almost grateful to have Him around. He touched everything. Even the aftermath of lovemaking was like a small death, and it was that which made making love with her so much fun. After each subsequent time, I felt like a virgin again, reborn, clean and fresh and unburdened by the worries so many men have about what to say in the harsh morning light to women they don't love. Oral sex still embarrassed me slightly, especially when it was Sara's oral and my sex. True, too, too much touching—hand-holding, hugging, squeezing, caressing—made me feel not embarrassed but slightly foreign. But I was learning to enjoy it; I even looked forward to the day I might be able to give Elanna a real brotherly hug. True to my nature and race, despite these small quirky feelings, I soon began to feel comfortable wearing only a T-shirt in the privacy of the apartment over the Tompsons' garage.

Sometimes, though, I'd look at my life, at the miracle of love, and think, "No young man deserves this happiness. *I* don't deserve such happiness, anyway," and I'd slip again and mention that Death had the viscosity of a bad fart in a vacuum chamber, telling Sara what disguises I'd seen Death wear, trying to make her laugh, to feel with me how laughable Death really was.

"I told you," she would say, sighing past her threat to leave me and move out if I mentioned it again. "You are *not* going to die."

"You're probably right," I'd say, feigning disappointment. "After all, Death still owes me one."

Sara would slam out of the room and go for long walks on which I would follow her at a distance, shouting apologies.

I was not trying to be cruel. Laura P. had once said it was a miracle that I was still in two pieces. Now, during those months, faced with the potential of Death, with an inward assurance the origins of which were as difficult to discover as the origins of sawdust, I felt as though the two pieces were becoming one.

At the beginning of spring term, I had attended classes with Sara, reading her assignments in history and art, and often studying with her late into the night. A few of the lectures were worth the walk to campus, but some of the teachers seemed to be unnerved by the presence of an audi-

tor who listened and thought about what they were saying
instead of taking down notes as though they were the words
of the prophets. Other teachers were just plain boring, pro-
ducing old ideas like magicians extracting planaria from a
top hat, seeming better suited to professions as keypunch
operators. Gradually, though I went on doing the homework
with Sara, I stopped attending the lectures, choosing to
spend my time the way people faced with the potential of
death do, getting things in order. Since I didn't have many
of my own things to order, I painted the Tompsons' porch,
mended window screens, replaced and puttied panes of glass,
mowed the lawns, or read. Whereas I had hated mowing
lawns as a boy, I now found that even a task as mundane and
sneezy as that gave me a certain pleasure and that pleasure
was increased when neither Delia nor the Proctor redid what
I had finished; they always appreciated what I'd done as
though it were really something important. Given those feelings, along with my increasingly cheerful mood, it was no
accident that when I repointed the bricks on the chimney, I
buried the top-of-the-line Swiss Army knife in a hollowed
brick like a time capsule.

"It belongs there," I told Sara, who surprised me in the act.

"The joy of daily tasks," she said.

"I feel like Wonder Bread," I said as I cleaned up. Sara
was already into her class work. "Vitamin enriched and
puffed full enough with air to float."

"Thanks a whole lot," Sara said, looking over the covers of
the book resting on her lap. "What's that make me, Skippy?"

This joy kept increasing, the nearer the operation came,
and when I wrote Elanna, downplaying the upcoming operation, telling her it wasn't much more serious than having a
mole removed, I said I was happy. In fact, I was, with an
elation and exuberance that made Death seem smaller than
ever before and that made unhappiness seem only a bad
dream. I began writing happy letters to nearly everyone I
could think of, letters that some readers might think mad
instead of happy because of the way everything related to
anything else—in other words, because of the endless meta-
phors. Saguaro Cactuses were billboards if you looked at
them without undue reverence; a hawk was an X-15.

Sanchez wrote back, happy for me and so infected by the exuberance of my long letter that his letter seemed entirely composed of verbs. But then Sanchez was happy, himself. Rachel's pregnancy was coming along without complications.

"Soon, there'll be one more red bogger interfacing with this patchwork world of ours."

The trading post had flourished since I'd left, which Sanchez attributed to Johnny Three Feet having been carted off and imprisoned. While Sanchez didn't dare to say that Johnny had kept the post from doing well, he did suspect that Johnny had been just weird enough to disrupt the consumption of goods by tourists, as though Johnny gave them indigestion. The post had expanded. There was a paved patio area in front and a parking area for cars and buses enclosed by a curb, and during the summer, they could count on a dozen or more tour buses a day stopping to dump money into the tills on their way to the Grand Canyon or London Bridge or Zion National Park. He ended by paying lip service to the disappointment of not having me return to work with him the next summer, yet, as he said, it was probably for the best.

"Given the torture of time, Rachel's feelings towards you may atrophy if not change, and then we can all visit happily together."

In a postscript he added that he knew he'd like Sara when he met her, and enclosed in the envelope were some Polaroids of the post—one with Grandfather perched on the seat of his Raleigh out front.

Elanna didn't write back. It wasn't because she didn't think of me; nor was it because she hadn't gotten my letters. Maybe she hadn't received all of them, but I'd heard the sounds of envelopes being torn open above the low-ratio growl of a jeep as it wound into the hills behind Iraklion and odds favored some of those envelopes being mine. One day, after I got a letter from father saying he had written Elanna, I realized what Elanna was doing, and when Sara got home from classes she found me trimming the Tompsons' hedge back to the size of an incipient bush in my distress.

"Shit," I told Sara. "Elanna's flying home for my operation."

"How do you know?"

"I phoned TWA. They said seat 17-A had been booked from Athens to San Francisco on a flight that arrives the day before *Operation Sawdust.*"

"So?" Sara said.

"I phoned Pan Am first. Row 17 is unbooked on their 747. Elanna always flies either Pan Am or TWA, and she always sits in 17-A when she flies west."

"She's got a right to be there," Sara said. "Don't you want her to come?"

"No. It's a waste of her time."

"Don't lie to me. You'll be glad to have her there. Besides, you can't keep her away any more than you can me."

"Huh," I said, not knowing what else to say. Sara was right. I was always glad to see Elanna.

Mother even responded to my increasing exuberance, writing me formal letters interspersed with dialogue from T.V. westerns. Not unsurprisingly, mother's favorite programs and movies were about cowboys and Indians, and sometimes she rewrote the scenes to make the culprit Indians allegories of evil. Mother never would forgive father for marrying her.

I worried most about father. He typed me letters, photocopied them, and mailed me the photocopies, sometimes forgetting to sign them.

"What's he doing, collecting an archive?" I asked Sara, showing her the letters.

They were long letters. Instead of delineating the mowing of lawns or washing of cars or installing of ceiling fans and solar hot-water heaters—the normal fatherly tales—they were about the Lord God (never God, always the Lord God), retirement, or the circumstances of my birth. Addressed to "Dear Son Albert," his letters were trying to tell me something in a very unfunny way, and it was then that I began to understand how my birth had skewed father's emotions and bruised his sense of humor. Remembering the time when my uncle had thought father was morally angry at him for shacking up with Karen Manowitz, it dawned on me that father preached at moments Grandfather would tease, not because he liked preaching but because his sense of humor had been stolen from him the day I was born.

"No wonder father's jokes were never funny," I said to Sara.

"What's wrong?" Delia asked that evening around the fireplace.

"Alley's just realized that his father loves him," Sara told her.

"Elanna used to tell me that father was a happy-go-lucky man, a boisterous man, before I was born," I said. "It seems strange that it's taken this long to connect the father I know with the one Elanna knew. I guess finding Death loitering about your son's crib like a sleazy dope dealer would murder your sense of humor."

Later, as Sara was falling asleep and I was lying with my hands clasped beneath my head staring into the monstrous dark, I said, "The world's a funny place, you know?"

"Not exactly funny," Sara said, yawning, her head sinking farther into the two pillows she slept on. "More a crazy place. Humor is just your way of describing it." She rolled over on her side and tucked her hands under her head.

"That," I whispered, "is a lot like what Grandfather might say."

"Ummm."


Sara and Delia and the Proctor fought valiantly against the glowering mood that descended upon each of them as *Operation Sawdust* approached. It was a contrast and contradiction to my own mood, which kept getting more amused. I understood and forgave, though even the Proctor heaved out sentimental statements about "finding one's true children"—by which he meant Sara and me. I tried to convince them—despite Sara's threats to wire my jaws shut—that while I could die, I wasn't going to. I tried to make them believe that the tumor was not malignant, but I was left feeling, most times, like a baby in an oxygen tent looking out, raising his fists to show mother that he had it. They were unconvinced, and by the time I was to leave for Palo Alto, I felt like I was freeze-dried, crystals of myself that needed tears to make me real.

The weekend before I left, Delia and Sara cooked me a

special dinner of my favorite food—green enchiladas, refritos, tostadas, chile rellenos.

"In case the plane needs help getting off the ground," Sara said, doing her best to joke.

"I may not even need a plane. Just a soft place to land when the rocket fuel is spent," I said.

Dinner was a quiet affair during which the scraping of forks and knives punctuated the erratic spatters of conversation. If I felt freeze-dried earlier, I began to feel as though I'd grown a large oozing pustule, Cyclops fashion, in the center of my forehead. I understood, at moments, that the silent heaving of conversation was for me as well as because of my leaving, and I forgave them. Other moments, I felt like a stranger on a subway, them looking at me only to look away when I looked back, pretending that I wasn't really there and I was disappointed, angered, wanting to make them realize their proximity emotionally if not geographically, and then less angry at them and more at myself for not being able to make everything all right for each of them. "People have disappeared on me all my life," I thought, pitying myself. "They are trying to make me not here."

By the time dinner was over and we'd moved to the living room for brandy, I felt like a black Mormon. Against that feeling, I excused myself and went to the apartment over the garage, and wrote a note to Grandfather. When I returned, I brought with me a pot thrown and signed by Laura P. and a kachina of Water Coyote. The pot, its spiral designs spinning east and west on opposite sides, I gave to the Tompsons; the kachina to Sara; and only then was I satisfied that they weren't disappearing on me but were only saddened by the possibility that I might disappear on them.

They understood the gifts without my having to explain, without me having to tell them that these were to be kept for me, not in remembrance of me, unless. . . . "But," I reminded myself, "Death does owe me one. So, if ever, then now." I said that as much to myself as to the luna moth beating against the window of the living room, as Proctor Tompson stirred the embers of the fire, refilled brandy snifters, and then stood, gazing meditatively into the middle distance.

People came by. Even though the Proctor was wise enough

to foresee Sara's wanting to spend most of the evening alone with me, he also knew that if we were to be alone too much she and I would only be sad, and I did not want sad. So he'd gone ahead and invited a few people by for drinks.

Doctor—"Professor, as yet," he reminded me—Quinin dropped by to give me a leather-bound copy of *The Scarlet Letter* and an up-to-date authoritative bibliography of Hawthorne scholarship.

"I'm touched," I said.

"It might benefit you to investigate some of the work on Hawthorne," he said, accenting the second syllable of Hawthorne's name in imitation of the way other scholars accented the first syllable of Thoreau's name. As if it mattered.

"I doubt I ever will," I whispered to Sara, who grinned courageously as I handed the books to her to set aside. "Still, I am touched."

Captain Morrisey, bringing a six-pack of Dos Equis, arrived while Joanne and Woody were hanging their jackets in the entry hall closet. Sara was cool to Woody; but even he looked good to me, and I was happy to see Joanne. She had shared the first faint beginnings of my love for Sara and, though she had not entirely found love, she was as happy for me as when I'd passed German with her help. If that meant having Woody's polyester smile sliding around the room like oil on the water, so be it.

"Hey," Captain Morrisey said.

"Captain," I said, giving him a salute less out of respect for his uniform and more out of friendship and gratitude for the evenings he and I had spent talking over pitchers of beer. The Captain had been the only one in town who understood how I felt as *Operation Sawdust* pulled me into it. He knew about facing Death, and he knew what it felt like to lose someone close to him to Death. Unlike my uncle, the Captain never imagined that his buddy, blown away by the Claymore, wasn't dead. But then, the Captain had seen his buddy die, and the effects of a Claymore don't leave much for the imagination to work with. I respected, more and more as the time had passed, the Captain's pain, his way of keeping his friend's memory alive. He could have been Indian, the way he could talk with his dead friend, know what his friend might have said—but for the fact that the Captain was Scotch Irish.

Morrisey was nervous, following me into the kitchen when I went for ice.

"Listen," he said. "I wanted you to have this." He handed me a box the size and shape of a jewelry box for a necklace.

"Before you open it, I want to explain. It may seem strange. But I looked around for something to give you to, well, wish you the best. Something to remember me by . . ."

"Besides my I-O from the draft board?"

He laughed. "Yeah. Besides that. Anyway, I did some shopping and nothing seemed to be the right thing. The other day I was sitting in my office after showing training films to some new cadets, thinking back on how we met, et cetera." Morrisey said, "et ke-TER-a." "The way you are, the way I am. What might mean something to you. I thought of Clarence and, well, I figured this might be something you would value."

I opened the box. Inside was a jagged sliver of metal, shrapnel, I guessed, from a Claymore Mine.

"It's . . . ," the Captain began.

"I know. Thanks. Thank you. I know what it means to you." I tried to grin. Reached out to shake his hand and spontaneously gave him half a hug.

"Best of luck, ex-Cadet Hummingbird," the Captain said.

"Ugh," Sara said, when I showed the shrapnel to her later, alone in our apartment. "Do you think that it's actually one of the pieces . . . ?"

"I think so," I said, laying the shrapnel beside the gifts my friends had given to me—the book from Sara's father, the sliver of metal shaped like the blade of a knife, the E.P. Curtis photograph of Wichita Walter Ross the Tompsons had given me. Looking at these odds and ends, I knew how truly funny Death was, for certain and for sure, in the way his presence made people try to tell you that they loved you, and I realized that I loved all of them, at least in part because of Sara. When you love one person as completely as I did her, you discover that love is the one feeling that is not only infinite but self-perpetuating and self-increasing. Loving her made me able to love the Tompsons, Captain Morrisey, Joanne, and it allowed me enough good will not to hate Woody but only find his actions at times hateful.

"What are you thinking about?" Sara said.

"Nothing."

"You sure? You looked so sad for a second. I thought maybe you were thinking about why David didn't bother to come by tonight. Have you talked to him lately?"

I shook my head, no. "Seriouser and seriouser," I said, smiling. David had grown more and more serious and not, in my opinion, in a good way. Heavy described it best. He and I had fought over beliefs: He maintained that my beliefs made me flip; I maintained that his ought to lift him up not sink him in the quicksand of depression like a dinosaur. I still loved him, missed him; loved him enough to let our former friendship become a thing held in the mind like a relic that could be dusted off from time to time, even invoked as exemplary, but alive only in memory. I assumed he missed me as well, equally, which was why he would not have come by tonight to say farewell.

"I wasn't thinking about David," I said.

"What, then?"

"About how funny . . . ," I began. The look on Sara's face made me stop and, my eye spotting the shrapnel which I would hang around my neck on a chain like the other talismen I bore with me, I said, "How funny it is that people keep giving me sharp objects, like knives."

Sara's foreboding expression became a smile. Relieved. "Come here," she said seductively, patting the bed. "Maybe I could have you in my mouth tonight?" she whispered, her eyes glittering with that special sprightliness she could have.

"No. Not tonight. If you don't mind. Tonight I'd like to be inside you."

Afterwards, as I lay awake staring up into the Absence of Angels through the roof of the garage, counting the stars like sheep, Sara turned to me, running her fingertips lightly over my chest.

"Promise me one thing, Alley?"

"Sure," I said, expecting it to have something to do with loving her forever.

"Don't ever give up laughing." Her fingertips slowed, becoming heavier as they caressed. Rubbing me always put her to sleep; were I to rub her, she'd stay awake all night, mostly because I rubbed her so rarely.

"I'm a lucky man," I said, unwilling to be seduced by satisfaction into sleep. I wanted to stay awake all night long, to talk, to hold.

"You're a wonderful man," Sara said, doing her best to stifle a yawn. She began to breathe heavily, a sure indication that she would soon be drifting towards the Absence of Angels.

"Sara?" No answer. Watching her even rhythmic breathing and the depression of the dimple she had on her right cheek when she smiled gently I thought, "I am I."

Drifting down from the Absence of Angels, Grandfather's voice said, "It happens. Especially at times like this."

### 48.

Father met me at the Pacific Southwest Airlines gate beside the metal detector where the security guards were hassling a dark man in a blue turban and gray beard, who was wearing a large button that read "Allah is Greater."

"Than what?" I said to father.

"Oh. Hi, son," father said, as though he hadn't seen me walk up to him.

He drove me straight to the Stanford Hospital. His pauciloquence made me wonder if I had a dog I didn't know about which had just died.

"So, how's tricks?" I said as we cruised the Bayshore freeway.

"Huh? Fine," he said. "I phoned the trading post. He's on his way. Alone. Your grandmother just isn't up to the trip."

"Besides, Laura P. hates Grandfather's driving. She says he doesn't see what's right in front of him."

"Hmm. Fine," father said.

"Did you know that the wings on planes actually flap up and down like a bird's?"

"Fine."

"Our pilot was stinko, though," I said. The blank look on

his face made him look, strangely, ageless, as though he might have been twenty-five as easily as he was forty-nine.

"Yes," he said. "Fine." He riveted the speedometer on fifty-five, obstinately staying in the middle lane despite the cars and trucks roaring past us on either side. Father had slowed down, some. "How was your flight?" he asked as we entered Palo Alto.

"Fine," I said, laughing.

Father checked me into the hospital while I put my street clothes and my getaway tennies in a thin locker in my five-man ward, and changed into the backless shift that would be my costume for the next few weeks. Then he came down and sat beside the window, next to my bed. His head hung above his hands, which he kept opening and closing like a book he didn't want to read but believed he should.

"Maybe you and I should go fishing, after this?" I said.

Father looked up from his hands. His lips were moving ever so slightly. "I'm not much of a fisherman," he said quietly. "As you know." He went back to lip-reading his hands.

I was almost grateful when the hard heels of mother's flats could be heard clicking down the linoleum corridor.

"I knew he'd do something like this!" she shouted at the nurses working the nurse's station. "He and his father. Just as I get everything back on track, they come up with something like this! Where is he?"

I could hear the tone of a nurse's voice trying to calm mother's hysteria, asking who *he* was, and then escorting her to the ward. The nurse gave me an oriental look and quickly disappeared.

"There you are," mother said. Seeing father, she added, "Did you help him plan this?" Father just stared at her; his lips ceased moving. "Let me tell the both of you right this minute, I'm not about to let either of you destroy my life anymore." Her head wavered back and forth like summer wheat.

"I'll wait in the dayroom at the end of the hall," father said, getting up and leaving without speaking to mother.

Mother clomped over beside the bed and opened her mouth. "Boom!" I shouted as loudly as I was able. She jumped. Boom did the trick, and her body relaxed like a tire punctured by a sixteen-penny nail.

"Hello, mother," I said quietly.

Her eyes were frightened, pink around the edges like a rabbit trapped by a predator it doesn't see clearly, and I realized that mother's hysteria was not a form but yet an expression of love, concern. For a woman whose baby son was not supposed to have lived in the first place and whose eldest daughter had died by pregnancy, handling the forms of love would be nearly impossible. Where one time I might have been embarrassed or angered by mother's behavior, I felt now very little but pity.

"Hey," I said. "You don't need to worry, mother. Everything will be all right. I promise."

"Promises!" she said, the hysteria beginning to resurface. "Promises, promises . . ."

"I swear to you, mother. Tell you what. Why don't you go on home and I'll give you a call when the operation's over. I'll even come by your house when I'm released. In the meantime, try not to worry?"

"Well," she said. She thought it over. Cautiously, as though avoiding dog-do on the floor, she tiptoed closer and touched my shoulder lightly with her fingers. "Well. Are you sure, Albert? You're sure you'll be all right?"

I reached up and patted her hand. "Yes. Now you go on. I'll call you."

"Okay," she said. She tiptoed away from the bed toward the open door of the ward, looking a lot like a child whose balloon has just separated from its string and flown away. In the doorway she turned. "By the way. I nearly forgot. How was college?"

"It was great, mom. I did very well."

After she left I was quiet, thinking about the things I might have said to her and wondering if any of them would have done any good. My ward mates tried to pretend as though they weren't in the room and hadn't heard the exchange between mother and father and me. The air hung humid with embarrassment. I didn't care. Sara had long ago convinced me that a person can only embarrass himself, not the other person. Or was it Grandfather who taught me that? It *was*

Sara who'd said once, after I'd misbehaved at a party and was apologizing for embarrassing her, "Don't apologize to me. Apologize to the others. Or to yourself. *I* still love you."

Father returned and sat on the empty bed across from me, silenced, I assumed, by memories which could never be anything but private. Watching him, his shoulders rounding over a body that was just beginning to slump with the first manifestations of age, noticing his high forehead rising above high but flat cheekbones, I was struck by the resemblance he was beginning to bear to Grandfather. "Father has large pores, too," I thought.

I was in the process of hoping that I, too, would look like Grandfather someday—which meant looking like father—when father raised his head with a willful determination and, keeping his face blank and unemotional, said, "Would you be quiet? You're always shooting your trap off," thus overcoming the barrier of silence mother had left behind her in the room.

The man in the bed to my right chuckled.

To his right, another man of about the same age dropped the magazine he had been holding up in front of his face and smiled, grateful that some one had said something. The dark-skinned boy across the room looked over without smiling, his eyes searching out everyone else's reaction to father's words as though he not only did not understand English but had failed to understand the attempt at teasing in father's tone.

Outside the window, beyond the screening wall, was a fountain in the center of a lawn.

"This is a great hotel," I said to father, pointing to the fountain. "Hotels always make me feel right at home. Even the decor's familiar."

"So," he said, getting up off the empty bed. "You've got books and magazines enough? Is there anything else you want before I take off?"

"I'll be fine, Pop," I said.

"I'll be here tomorrow. After work," he said, shrugging as though to apologize for the fact that he would wait until after work to come by when I was scheduled for early morning surgery.

"No rush," I said.

With the same deflated look mother had had, he approached the bed and took hold of my left foot beneath the sheets. I could tell he was going to be sentimental, if I let him. 'What the hell,' I thought, 'let him. Let's see what the old guy has got to say.'

"You know, I remember the day you were born. The doctor phoned me at work and even before he said it I knew he had bad news. He said he was sorry, but that you were not going to live. He said you wouldn't suffer any pain; that you were in an oxygen tent and that you would just slowly go to sleep. I remember going to the hospital and looking at you in that oxygen tent and all I could feel was grateful that you weren't going to suffer any pain. Strange," he said, "your Grandfather showed up, took one look at you, and told me and the doctors you would live. Son of a gun if you didn't do just that. Two weeks later, you were still in that oxygen tent, and starting to look like a human being and not a baby newt. A month later, you were out of the tent."

There was a look in father's eyes I'd never seen before, even though he had told me this same story, ending it at the same place. This time he added, "I've got to tell you."

"What?" I said, intrigued.

"You got any idea how long it took me to pay back your mother's family for all that oxygen?"

I began to laugh. "Be a real waste, wouldn't it, if I didn't make it through this? Not to worry, Pop, I'll do my best."

He nodded and squeezed my foot. "That's all I ask."

The fellow in the bed beside me was British and he was named Eric. He had had nine operations already on tumors that kept growing back on the bottom of his feet.

"Guess you won't be entering any 10K races," I said.

"For now," he said. One thing about the British is that their stiff upper lip attitude, while frustrating in the normal intercourse of daily life, is pleasant in abnormal or frightening circumstances, and I was grateful for Eric's good humor in the face of nine operations with local anesthesia—which meant spinal taps, one needle at a time until the body is deadened from the waist down.

"Sure it hurts," he said. "Each bloody needle hurts as they

work in closer to the spine. Hell, if it didn't, I'd think I wasn't obtaining my shilling's worth."

The man to Eric's right, beside the hallway wall, was named Duwayne, and from what Eric whispered to me when Duwayne was across the hall in the lavatory, he had a disease that didn't bode well.

The boy—he must have been about sixteen—across from Duwayne was "Malaysian or some such," Eric said. We didn't know his name; he didn't speak a word of English. He had a medical problem which was unique enough for the Stanford Medical Center not only to provide treatment free but also to pay for his flight into the United States. Both he and Duwayne would disappear between the time I went up to surgery and the day I awoke, but we didn't know that, and we spent the time between father's departure and dinner teaching the boy to speak English—at least teaching him to say our names, "hello," and making him laugh at the way we pronounced his name (which sounded like "Choyswan").

After dinner, Dr. Weinstein came in with my anesthetist to introduce him, and to check out blood pressure, et cetera, all ploys to let him talk to me and find out how I was doing.

"This is Dr. Green," Weinstein said. "He'll be the cowboy in the mask beside me tomorrow who puts you to sleep."

"So you're the druggist, huh?" I said. "You a good one?"

"Give you ten to one odds," he said, "that when I tell you to begin counting backwards from 100, you won't make ninety."

Dr. Green explained the procedure to me, beginning with a wake-up call at five a.m., when I'd be given an injection. At six, I'd be wheeled up to surgery on a gurney, and he figured that at about ten or so, I'd be wheeled down from the recovery room. "By tomorrow night, we might even be able to feed you some chicken broth and Jell-o."

"Galloping gourmet," I said. Neither Dr. Green nor I, nor Weinstein for that matter, had any idea that he was off by several days.

"So, Alley," Dr. Weinstein said when Dr. Green had left. "You seem in pretty good spirits."

"I am," I said as he loosened the velcro on the blood pressure band. "I've been trying to figure that out."

"What do you mean?" he said, beginning to push and measure the outside of the tumor.

241

"Well with everything that could happen tomorrow, I thought I'd be worried. I mean I could die, right?"

"There's a chance," he said. "The best we can hope for is a minor paralysis of the right side of your face. Make you look as though you're always half-laughing, though some people may mistake it for a sneer."

"So why do I feel so calm and cheerful? I mean, I don't want to die. I don't plan on dying. But it could happen and thinking about that makes me say, well, what the hell, the time I've had has been good and if I get more it'll be better."

"I'll tell you," he said. "I can't explain it, but I have noticed in a few of my patients a similar sort of . . . what? . . . elation, cheerfulness the night before an operation. They are always the ones to whom I've felt free to even use the word 'death' and not some euphemism; the ones I've been able to be honest with, like you. And I'll tell you something else. All, without one exception, have lived through some very serious operations."

"Statistics are on my side, huh?" I laughed. "I'll bet the control group was a downer. They must have been as much fun as the opening of *The Seventh Seal.*"

"There wasn't a control group, of course."

"You know what I mean."

"All the people who are so afraid of dying, they never live."

"Sort of," I said. "I think of them as the people whose death wouldn't affect the amount of laughter in the world one whit. Maybe that's just another way to put it."

"Maybe," he said. "Okay, I'm through with you for now. You can eat or drink up until midnight. At eleven, a nurse will come around with a sleeping pill for you, if you want it. Otherwise, I'll see you in the morning."

"Can I ask you something?"

"Sure."

"Are you a Jew?"

"With a name like Weinstein, you ask me that?"

"I mean practicing."

"Yes."

"I'm glad," I said. "Don't ask me why. I'm not sure. Maybe because it means you're Real People, at least in part. Anyway, I'm glad."

He gave me a quizzical look and then smiled kindly. "So am I, Alley. Oh," he said, looking back from the doorway. "I've arranged for you to be allowed visitors up until midnight, as long as you don't disturb the others in the ward."

"Thanks," I said. "I doubt I'll have too many."

"There are a couple here, now. I'll send them in."

Grandfather had arrived virtually at the same moment as Elanna. He'd driven the Plymouth in his usual tortoise fashion and, though he looked as ancient as his race, having aged greatly since I'd last seen him, I was glad he was there. Elanna had flown Trans World Airlines halfway around the world from Athens, and their coincident arrival seemed to reaffirm Grandfather's faith in concentration.

Elanna brought me an ancient scarab mounted on a simple silver backing that hid the lucky inscriptions on the beetle's belly, and hung it around my neck on its chain. Another charm against the sawdust of the world. It made me think of Rachel. I could hear her already criticizing my wearing it as I lay there on the starched sheets of unknowing.

Grandfather brought me a large bag of candied orange slices which I consumed with an almost sexual determination, slowly sucking off the sugar coating and then chewing the slices with my front teeth.

"You're going to be sick!" Eric kept telling me. "When you wake up from the operation tomorrow you're going to feel as sick as a toad in the hole."

"No," Grandfather told Eric.

"He's got a cast-iron stomach," Elanna said. Her voice was high and thin like a kitten up a tree looking about herself and wondering how in hell she had come to be there. She was frightened and a bit pallid; she felt helpless; and she was exerting every ounce of her energy trying not to show it.

"You all right?" I asked her. She nodded nervously. "You know you didn't have to come." Instantly, I felt as stupid as I had that day in the graveyard when she was talking to mother's mother and I had said that mother's mother wasn't buried in that particular cemetery.

"I couldn't not come," she said. "Could I?"

Grandfather settled into a chair on the other side of my

bed and began watching the television program Duwayne had turned on. Every now and then, the channels would change and Duwayne would say, "Hey, who . . . ?" and the channel would change back and Grandfather would grin.

"You know who I miss," I said to Elanna, "is Pamela." For a moment, Elanna seemed to share my feeling. It was as though both of us felt that Pamela was separated from us only by an argument, and a phone call and an apology could bring her back.

"Me, too," Elanna said. "I don't know what I'd do now, if . . ." She stopped herself and drew herself up. It wasn't her way. Nor was it mine.

"A closet isn't big enough for all of us, anyway," I said, and we both tried to laugh.

That was how we spent the time, trying to joke with each other, teasing each other about the past we held in common and yet envisioned with the difference of brother and sister, while Grandfather gazed at the television, speechless for the most part, yet lending a solidity to that corner of the ward. Eric chatted with us or read *Pogo* comic books, which he claimed were his favorite. I was glad not of the company but of this company.

By nine, I'd finished half of my orange slices, still to the dismay of Eric, when Sara entered.

"What are you doing here?" I demanded, outwardly angry but inwardly overjoyed.

"Visiting. What are you doing here?"

"I told you not to come."

"Don't be a fool," she said, introducing herself to Elanna and Grandfather. "Here, I brought some things." From her shoulder bag she took out three wrapped boxes.

"You're going to bury me with gifts," I said.

"This one's from me," she said. "Open it." It was a blank book of fine paper bound between upholstered covers.

"It's beautiful," Elanna said.

"This one's from the Tompsons." She handed me the second, which I opened to find a Montblanc fountain pen and a bottle of ink. "This last," she said, "isn't much. But I thought you might appreciate it."

"Ding-dongs!" I said, tearing off the wrapping paper to

find a baker's dozen of those Hostess cakes filled with cream and iced with chocolate.

"He's happier about them than the other two presents," Sara said to Elanna.

"Mother's cooking made all of us chipmunks," Elanna said, smiling.

"Oh, bloody heavens!" Eric said. "You Yanks refuse to accept good advice, don't you?" I began to eat the first of the Ding-dongs, offering the box around to Grandfather, Elanna, Sara, and him. "You are going to enjoy those things twice, once going down and once coming up."

"Have you ever seen me throw up?" I said to Sara. She shook her head. "You?" I asked Elanna.

"No."

"You'll see," Eric said.

"All plastic parts," I said to Eric, biting into another Ding-dong and patting my stomach. "They replaced everything with plastic when I was born. I don't get sick to my stomach."

"You'll see," Eric said again, having no idea what it was I would see when I didn't wake up the following day but sla-lomed through the gaps in the dotted line between coma and consciousness, stirring enough after five and a half hours under the knife to speak to the nurses in the recovery room (they tell me) before slipping down the backside of the mountain toward the valley of the shadow. Whatever I said could only be surmised from the looks the nurses gave me after I was finally awake. Even what I said after being moved from intensive care back to my original room in the brief moments of consciousness that began to occur more frequently had to be repeated to me later.

What I had seen in the 96 comatose hours of floating along the FM wave between the realities of life and death mystified me. Slugged by anesthesia and shock, I had followed an old man up canyons of red rock etched by Gilas and climbed an umber cliff, the ropes anchored by the pitons of Rachel's petulance, the carping of Laura P., and the carrot-like coaxing of Elanna and Sara Baites.

It struck me as odd that it was women's voices and not the symbolic commentary of Grandfather that pinned the ropes to the face of the rock. Even in my dream of a dreamer dreaming, Grandfather had receded to a shadow on top of distant mountains. But I knew he was there as well as I knew that Death was sniggling about in the shadows of the valley below.

Then, too, there were images of a butterfly and a rock with another pebble lodged in its middle. Those existed on a level similar to the image of the night nurse whose face was the first I remember seeing, and whose compassion was so warm that it wrapped me back into sleep. Gradually, I awoke, and spit out hatred and rage released by the sodium pentothal and aimed at people like Mrs. DeForest, shedding the weight of it and rising one foot closer to what Sanchez had felt in the desert, and one foot nearer Grandfather's shadow, which hovered, watched, and saw—and yet refused to speak, lacking the judgments that people like to call morality.

"But there was something *else*," I told Sara after I awoke and could recognize her. She sat on my bed haggard and worn from the worry and waiting of the past five days. Sara held cherry Jell-o in front of my mouth on a spoon. The machine I dubbed "Harry," which sucked fluids from the tube sewn into the side of my head, blipped out its purple light with the regularity of a lighthouse.

"Can you recall any of it?"

"Red rock," I said, "like the Sonoran desert. Canyons. An old man like Grandfather. The rest keeps swimming in my head. It's there and I feel it and know it, but I can't say it."

"Maybe it's not important?"

"Maybe. But it has to do with me. Me. And with life and death."

"Maybe it will come to you," she said. "Maybe one day it will all come to you. If you can't say it, then maybe you should try to write it down."

"Those are pretty big maybes," I said.

"This," she said, handling the blank book she'd given me, "is a pretty big book."

## 49.

The day came that Sara and Elanna had to check out of the motel room they were sharing and leave, Sara to return

246

to Clearmont and Elanna to return to finding and dusting and cataloguing the shards of ancient Greece. Elanna was scheduled to leave that evening; Sara was catching the Red Eye late that night. Though it meant spending several hours alone in the San Francisco airport, they'd decided to share a limo in time for Elanna's departure at nine. They liked each other, for which I was glad.

Off and on over the past few days there had been as many as eleven visitors in my room at a time, including Allison and Mrs. DeForest, who hung about uncomfortably in the immediate present, having deleted the past they shared in common with me. I abided them as well as Sara did, both of us grateful that cousins and family friends were in the room buffering what could have been either an awkward or hilarious situation. They left, and we were content to have only the four of us—Grandfather, Sara, Elanna, and me (father had come by before work)—when we were interrupted by the sudden appearance of my uncle, bringing along with him the ghost of my cousin and the Vegomatic.

Uncle's former exuberance, out of which came the singing of popular songs, had become a morbid sentimentalism in which his fleeting happiness with Karen Manowitz struggled against his discomfort with his present materialism.

"Maybe when you're out of here," uncle said, "you'll have time to take a ride on the river in my new Chris Craft." Having scuttled his sailboat, he had purchased—with the serene approval of the Vegomatic—a Chris Craft.

"Power boating is where it's at," he said. His voice sounded hollow like a confirmed bourbon drinker forced to turn to vodka or gin who tries to convince you of his pleasure in drinking those pale, tasteless liquids. It required a false belief in effect ("You can get from point A to point B without wind," he said) and a suspension of the memory of his pleasure in process ("Boating," he ought to have said, "is boring").

In the same way, when he told us about my cousin, he imagined that his militant son had entered the Soviet Union for no other reason than to learn a new language. "You know how good he is with languages," uncle said. "The son of a gun will be able to travel anywhere in the world, pretty soon."

If the Russians ever let him out, I—we all—thought.

Elanna's eyes had always been sharp, cutting. But in Greece they'd acquired a lightness as though bleached by the unyielding sun. The lightness turned dark and as sad as Sara's eyes, both as sad as Grandfather's, when uncle proclaimed that once again I had beaten Death. The four of us knew that no one beats Death. All one could do was try to score in the final minutes and force the game into overtime.

"Mighty white of you," I muttered.

"What?" uncle asked.

"Nothing."

Coming closer, he whispered in my ear, "Sara reminds me of a girl I once knew." He meant she reminded him of Karen Manowitz, and it was only the regret I'd once felt for telling him I had not kept the lucky penny he'd given me that prevented me from saying that we have to live with our choices. "Because you feel sorry for someone," I would say later to Sara, "doesn't mean you have to excuse him."

The Vegomatic, dressed in a blue-gray suit, her hair rigid with spray, sat crisply on the edge of the empty bed across from me. Every quarter hour, she rose and went down to the nurses' station and took several deep breaths, before returning to the room and taking root on the bed again.

Grandfather posed quietly beside my bed-head, where he had been for most of the last several days—except when Elanna or Sara were shoveling Jell-o and broth at me. He had left only to shower, and once to go out and buy white construction paper and magic markers which he used to entertain himself, making "For Sale" signs for the Plymouth. Every time I had tried to say that I would buy the Plymouth, he had interrupted me with a slow and convincing shake of his head.

I didn't resent uncle's intrusion into this last afternoon. I didn't even resent the wordless intrusion of the Vegomatic. But needless to say we were all relieved when, after her fifth trip to the nurses' station, the Vegomatic stood and adjusted the huge bowtie of her blouse and walked to the door, where she waited a few moments for uncle to notice that the visit was over. Finally, she uttered a syllable which sounded a lot like "Hilt" and, though reluctantly like a recalcitrant puppy, uncle left with her. Only after she left did I realize what had been making my head sting and my eyes dizzy. It was the invisible but palpable cloud of her perfume.

"Boy," Sara said. "Now I know why you always called her the Vegomatic. She could slice you up quicker than a carrot."

"She's about as much fun as a Treaty," I said to Sara.

"That's cruel," Elanna protested. "Her life with him hasn't been exactly what you would call easy."

"Maybe," I said, "But it's the plain and simple truth."

"There," Grandfather said, holding up the "For Sale" signs.

That evening, Louis Applegate came to fetch Grandfather, staying long enough to watch the fluid sucked from the side of my head by "Harry" drip into the tank on the machine. Elanna and Sara left with them. Eric was upstairs for the eleventh attempt at removing the growths on his feet; Duwayne and Choyswan had vanished; and I felt a profound emptiness invade the room. Yet I also felt profoundly contented. Maybe it was because the emptiness was only temporary—soon enough, I'd be able to rejoin the Tompsons and Sara, sooner than expected, according to Dr. Weinstein, who was pleased with the way my will to get out of the hospital had accelerated the rate of healing.

"Never," Weinstein had said more than once, "have I seen anyone who healed as quickly as you. Are you sure you're not a lizard?"

Maybe the contentment was due as well to the feeling that Elanna and Sara, like Grandfather, were still there with me and would always be there when I needed them whether they lived or died. I don't really care how it's put. Contentedness, unlike pain, doesn't need analysis because you don't need to get over it.

After Grandfather left to return to Chosposi, I sat propped up in my bed, my blank book and Montblanc in my hands, and wrote. I could not yet remember all I'd seen in the land of sodium pentothal, but I didn't worry. I simply enjoyed the feel of the pen's nib on the paper, the same way I enjoyed the colored lights that began to play on the fountain outside as the sky darkened, or the food when dinner was brought round, and even helping the nurses spoonfeed Eric when he was brought back to the ward.

Dr. Weinstein came early the next morning to check the amount and color of the fluid in "Harry's" tank.

"Feeling lonely?" he asked, wrapping the blood pressure gauge around my bicep and pumping it up.

"No."

"Fine," he said, releasing the pressure. "I think in another day or two we'll consider releasing you. I had honestly expected you to be here several weeks, but there's no real reason." He poked and adjusted the bandage that covered the right side of my head, into which the tube attached to "Harry" disappeared. "So what are your plans after you check out?"

"I thought I'd visit father for a day or two, drop by mother's, and then head on back to Clearmont. If that's okay?"

"Sure," he said. "Any doctor can change the bandages. You know a doctor in Clearmont?"

"Dr. Satherwaite at the college's clinic."

"Good. I'll have the nurses draw up a schedule for checking and changing the bandage. You can give a copy to Dr. Satherwaite." He stood up. "Guess I won't be seeing too much of you unless some problem crops up. You've been a good patient, Alley, and considering the fact that the tumor was the size and shape of a pear, you're coming along very well. We won't know how badly the nerves in the side of your face were damaged for at least five or six months. I'd like you to drop in for a quick check around next October, if you can. I like to see the results of my work."

"I'll make a point of it."

"Any Wednesday or Thursday afternoon, at my office. You don't need an appointment. I can fit you in for the time it will take." He rolled the curtain separating my bed from Eric's back. "I have to tell you, Alley, that I've rarely seen love and concern expressed so many different ways for one human being. Did anyone tell you that Sara was so frantic by the fifth hour of the operation that we had to sedate her and send her back to her motel with your sister? Partly our fault, I guess. We had no way of knowing it'd take that long."

"I didn't know," I said.

"And your aunt. The nurses tell me she used to be a nurse, herself?"

"Yeah, in a V.A. hospital."

"When she saw you yesterday, what with the pump and the bandages, she was so upset that she kept going into the restroom and throwing up." He laughed. "I tell you, you're a lucky man," he said, "in case you don't already know that."

"It can happen that way," I said.

"Well. See you."

"Take it easy," I said, feeling my former contentedness begin to expand to incorporate the novelty of the Vego . . . my aunt . . . caring so much about what happened to me.


### 50.

If I suffered pain during that time, it was only twice, and in retrospect even the pain felt good in its way. It let me know I was alive. The first time was when, after waking up, the nurse had breezily brought in a bedpan and the lingering effects of mother's toilet training made it impossible for me to pee into it while I was in bed. Like all institutions meant to serve people and not human beings, hospitals cannot tolerate a change of the rules. So the nurse gave me a shot that made the muscles around my bladder contract. Though the cramps hurt, I still couldn't pee. Three shots later, convulsed by cramps that could bend the fender of a car, I was writhing about, hoping for something fun to happen—like the nurse bringing in leeches to bleed me. Finally, while the nurse was out preparing a fourth shot, I unplugged "Harry" and wheeled him like a robot to the bathroom where I relived all the pleasures in the history of pissing.

The nurse was furious, chasing me down as I took "Harry" for a brief stroll down to the day room. Only after I loomed over her, threatening to wreak havoc on the hospital, did she agree to telephone Weinstein and obtain his permission for me to unplug "Harry" and wheel him around with me when necessity called. "Harry" and I stood beside the nurse's station as she phoned, and I could hear Dr. Weinstein laugh.

The second painful moment was the day the doctor re-

leased me. Early in the morning, as planned, he came to
sever the umbilical cord between me and my pal "Harry" by
pulling out the hard plastic syringe on the end of the rubber
tubing around which the flesh had begun to heal. First, Dr.
Weinstein raised and fixed the metal railings on either side
of the bed.

"What are those for?" I asked.

"I've been straight with you up to now, haven't I?" he said.
"There's only one way to remove the tube and that's to yank
it out. I'll tell you, it is going to hurt, probably like nothing
you have ever felt before. It won't hurt a long time, but you're
going to feel it since the tissue has grown attached to it."

"As long as you don't make me use a bedpan," I said.

Lacking his usual good humor which he had used with
me, he said, "I want you to roll over toward the window and
take hold of the bars with both hands and concentrate on
something pleasant."

I rolled over and put my hands on the bars and thought
of Sara.

"You ready?" he asked. Before I could answer, he had
taken a good grip on the end of the tube and yanked it out
and then grabbed my waist and held it down on the bed. He
waited as my knuckles turned pale and I tried to tear the
bars from the bed. A collage of yellows and reds and purples
pasted on the back of my eyeballs.

It seemed minutes before he said, "Well?" and I could answer, "You really know how to grab a guy's attention, don't
you?"

"Look at it this way," Dr. Weinstein said, "now you have an
absolute by which to measure all other pains."

"What," I asked, "is pain?"

It felt wonderful to be outside the hospital. Hospital air is
sterile and filtered, and for a boy raised in the City of Angels
where the air has tangible mass it's a little like trying to
breathe at 20,000 feet. So, as I climbed into father's car, the
air was heady and intoxicating and I felt as though I was
learning to breathe all over again.

I stayed on father's hide-a-bed for three days. During the
day when he was at work, I began to try to write down what

it was I had seen in the dark interiors of my semi-coma and, failing at that, took long walks with Sabina, the puppy he had purchased to replace Running Dog, whom I renamed Spotted Tail because of her markings of an Australian Shepherd. Palo Alto had changed in the short time I'd lived away. The Tall Tree, its landmark near the park, was little more than an upright trunk, its branches withered and its needles thinned by the exhaust from the cars that went to and fro on the main road nearby. On the second day, I answered the phone while father showered, and a woman's voice began to talk to me as though I were my father, asking how his son was. It was a pleasant voice, even though she was not a little embarrassed when I explained that I was the son.

"Nice of you to ask, though," I said. "I'll have him call you when he's out of the shower."

Father wanted to explain when I told him his lady friend had called, even though he needn't have. I was happy that he had someone. His inability to say whatever words he felt were needed brought him to the old recollection of how we'd never been able to talk to each other.

"It's all my fault," he said. "I was always too busy while you were growing up. And your mother . . ."

"Dad," I interrupted him. "I'll make a deal with you. Let's go fifty-fifty on the blame bit, okay?"

On the third day, I screwed up my humor and went by mother's house. Pressing the buzzer on the intercom speaker outside the door caused a set of spotlights to flash on, blinding me. I waited.

"Who goes there?" a voice said over the speaker. It wasn't mother or even a feminine voice. Neither was it convincingly masculine, but more generic like a monk's or priest's voice after years in the cloister, and I spoke to the speaker as I would have to a priest, with a certain formality.

"It is I," I said. "I've come to visit my mother." I could feel the cover on the peephole slide back and I knew I was being observed.

"Well, so it is," the voice said. "You."

Absurdly, the door's hinges imitated a low-grade horror film, squeaking slowly as the door was opened. Short, with tiny sandled feet, and pale to the point of translucence, He stood there in a brown robe tied at the waist by a cord.

"It's you," I said. "What are you doing here? Where's all your Indian jewelry? Where's your hardhat with the light on the front?"

His voice was higher than over the speaker but still without gender as He said, "I live here, now."

"You're mother's lodger?"

He nodded, grinning that toothy grin of his. "So what are you doing here? You don't belong here. We're even Steven. I don't owe you a thing, anymore."

"I told you, I came to visit my mother," I replied calmly, beginning to recall just the sketchiest details of what I'd seen in the womb of sodium pentothal.

"She's not home. And I don't know when she'll be back."

"Do you know where she is?" He nodded, but said nothing. "Well, where?"

"With her lawyer."

"Changing her will again, huh? May I leave her a message?"

"If you wish," He said. Behind Him in the hall I could make out the winged figure of Mercury that He had removed from the hood of His customized van.

"I see you still have Mercury," I said.

"Is that your message?"

"You know it isn't," I said. "Tell my mother that I am all right. Tell her I've gone back to Clearmont to the Tompsons' and if she wants, she can reach me there." I started to go and stopped. Whether I was jealous of Him or merely unwilling to concede to Him easily, I don't know. "What the hell," I said. "Why don't you just tell her I love her for me."

"Will do," He said, "if you're sure that's what you want."

"Enjoy her cooking," I said as maliciously as possible.

"I like it," He said.

"You would." I could feel the points of His beady little eyes on my back as I walked away down the driveway. When He called out, "Hey, Albert! See you soon!" I didn't even turn around. I didn't need to see His expression to know what He meant and to connect it with the "For Sale" signs Grandfather had so carefully made.

## 51.

Pamela used to say to me, "What you don't know can't hurt you," and even as a child I knew she was wrong. Not knowing worried me much more than knowing and ignorance had contained the constant threat of injury since the day I unscrewed Grandfather's power saw looking for the baggy containing the sawdust. Not knowing seemed to be a raw wound that only needed to be touched accidentally to hurt. What I didn't know as I returned to Clearmont was what I had seen in the five post-operative days of bobbing between life and death. It would take the death of Grandfather before I would be able to take proper stock of that.

At first, both the Tompsons and Sara were disturbed by the way I looked. With a large bandage covering my head from jaw to crown and cheek to nape and the paralysis which made me look as though I was sneering or that my face was asymmetrically lopsided, I was even a bit frightening to myself. The tumor had lodged below the focus of nerves entering that side of my face, and the nerves had been so damaged as to make my eyelid remain open while the eyeball rolled back and up whenever I tried to close my eyes—giving me a one-eyed stare of whiteness.

Nonetheless, they all became used to it. The Tompsons chuckled when I drooled like someone overdosed on novocaine. With a humor that I appreciated, Sara liked to have me "close" my eyes at parties, after people were inebriated enough fully to appreciate the effects of my stare. I obliged. Even after the bandages came off and my head simply looked as though it were listing to one side, the stare remained available for our mutual entertainment.

After several months, the nerves recouped enough to half-close the eyelid. In doing so, however, the nerves seemed to confuse themselves and with a playfulness of their own decided that the right side of my face should sweat profusely whenever I chewed food or gum. Sweat dripping from my chin was less amusing, and I gave up gum.

By that time, Sara and I had moved into a studio apartment in the married students' housing of the college (the power of the Proctor helped, as we weren't yet married) with the blessing of both the Tompsons and Professor Quinin. I had gotten a job setting type for the local paper. Actually, it was the third of three successive jobs. Each of the first two I lost because of my efforts to unionize non-union shops.

"Proof positive," Proctor Tompson said proudly, "that failure is often a better teacher than success. I wonder if you didn't learn more from me in that class than the rest of the students combined."

I had. But then unions to me were a lot like tribes and, though I lacked a specific tribe, the instinct for them was fierce in me.

The jobs supported us while Sara finished out the term. We enjoyed having the Tompsons to dinner and despite the lists of equal chores that some women made men read and sign like the Magna Carta, Sara became an excellent cook. I, preferring to stay behind the scenes, became a fair dishwasher, and I took pleasure in finding a new wine or cognac for the Tompsons to try when they came.

In June, we had a party for Doctor Quinin. He had successfully defended the footnotes of his dissertation and received the college's Good Housekeeping Seal of Approval, which meant there would never be anything at all offensive or thought-provoking in his lectures. It was at the party that I realized that Quinin had already set his sights on being a Dean and I told Sara that he would succeed because of his adroit way of mindlessly conforming.

"He only needs tassels on his loafers, argyle socks, and a pink shirt and he's there," I said.

That led to our first fight, during which I explained that to me it seemed odd how white people were promoted in direct inversion to their wisdom. Sara accused me of being white, which I ignored. She only said it to wound me.

"Have you ever seen an Indian Dean?" I asked her, laughing, and she said no, but she'd seen Indians be chiefs, and I said that was the point, that chiefs were such because the tribe respected their wisdom, which wasn't true anymore for Deans or Majors or Senators or Presidents.

She countered by trying to hurt me through Grandfather, asking why he hadn't been a chief, then. She was assuming that wisdom meant that one would want to be a chief, whereas wisdom does the opposite.

"I don't agree," she said, becoming adamant.

I tried to explain. "Wisdom means that if leadership is thrust upon you, you may accept it even though you don't want it; not wanting it means you will accept it with a sense of the responsibility and care thrust upon you. Whites seem to have become just the opposite. Every little boy dreams of becoming president, doesn't he?"

She still didn't buy it. I was beginning to wonder where her insistent refusal to entertain the idea came from.

"A chief must be wise," I said, "but not all wise men have to be chiefs."

"Well," Sara said petulantly, "maybe you should marry an Indian," and in the illogic of her petulance I saw what was bothering her.

"Oh, Sara," I said, trying not to laugh, "this has nothing to do with you. With us."

She wanted to know why not. "After all, I'm white, as well as the daughter of an unwise man."

"True," I said laying my hand on her shoulder. "But you have a good heart."

The way she looked at me out of the corners of her eyes as though suspicious of whether or not to take me at my word, wanting to believe that I believed that a good heart outweighed silly computations of blood, made me shake my head and laugh at her.

"My unfeathered friend," I said. "You are wise. Don't you see that that makes you Real People? Don't you know already that I'd rather be a Real People with you than anything else?" I tucked her into my arms and hugged her, feeling her suspicious body relax, disbelief draining away like untapped electricity. "Being human is hard enough," I said softly. "Besides, you can't help it if you're a honky."

"You . . . !" she cried, pushing me away—and then we laughed together for a long time before returning to her father's party.

The summer passed quietly. Sara and I kept pretty much to ourselves, content to work and save for the fall term when we'd return to school, spending our evenings with each other or the Tompsons for the most part, during which time everything became subject to humor.

Late at night I would often awaken as from a dream that was actually no dream but a memory, sneak out of bed without disturbing Sara, and write. I managed in this way to fill up the front sides of five hundred pages, and I turned the half-blank book over and began filling up the verso pages. I was increasingly obsessed by the need to write that dream-vision down, but each time I tried, conventions like naturalism got in my way, hanging around the edges of the manuscript like doodles. Worse, if I did write a good paragraph I was susceptible to tin-plated delusions of someone reading it and even taking it seriously. At first light, I would sneak back to bed, lying awake, concentrating on ways to hide my growing obsession from Sara.

Father married his lady friend, and I managed to meet her when I flew north to have the bandages removed for the last time by Dr. Weinstein.

Weinstein was pleased with his work and even more pleased that the nerves he had feared were irreparably damaged seemed to be regaining a good bit of function, and he took me to a quick lunch at the Stanford Student Union, where we sat and ate out on a broad circular deck. At one point a wild-looking man of about sixty in a tweed jacket with ragged suede patches on the elbows wandered past us on the asphalt path below. He carried a placard that read "REPENT!" and towed a small red wagon filled with pamphlets behind him on a leash. Students and faculty alike passed him by as though he were nothing more unusual than an unmowed lawn or covert action by the CIA.

"Is the world ending?" I asked Weinstein.

"I wish I could remember the joke my mother used to tell about the world coming to an end," he said, gazing pityingly at the man. "He used to administer intelligence tests. The story goes that he began to frazzle 15 or 20 years ago. He doesn't teach anymore, for obvious reasons. He went mad when they decided that his I.Q. test measured nothing more than the middle-class upbringing of white kids. The university gives him a stipend, ostensibly for research but really because the university hasn't figured out what to do with him yet. He's harmless enough."

"No shit, Sherlock," was all I could say.

After lunch I went by father's new house to meet his new wife. The way she treated me pleased me so much that when Sara asked me what she was like after I got home, I said, "She's as nice as her voice."

"Did you see your mother?"

"No," I said in such a way as to let her know I didn't want to talk about it. I had planned on stopping by, but I'd dropped by William the Black's fraternity house and had been so discouraged by the way he kept me outside on the stoop, the way in which he and I had moved down forking paths away from each other, that I'd driven straight to the airport and returned the rental car and then sat facing east-southeast watching planes land and take off.

About the time Sara and I were married with only the Tompsons and her father to witness, Sanchez mailed me a set of snapshots. I was amazed at the size of the Trading Post. It seemed to stand like an oasis of commerce beside an enlarged road. An entirely new building from what I could tell, it was simple and plain, flat stone and adobe with a broad wooden porch in front, the roof of which was supported by stripped logs. Gone were the American flag and the wooden Indian and instead there was a simple sign above the porch: "Ayawamat Trading Post."

"I'll be damned," I said.

"What does that mean?" Sara asked.

"I don't know," I said. Grandfather had taught me a little of his language; Laura P. none of hers. We had to resort to the library to find out it meant "Man who follows orders."

Another photo had Grandfather sitting astride his Raleigh outside the mission building, Laura P. at his side, both of them looking like doughy lumps on the landscape.

Then one of Rachel holding what looked to be a small litter—explained by the following picture of the baby inside. Sanchez's note with the photos told us that the baby was a girl and that they'd named her Rachel Laura, aged four months. She was beautiful. Despite the realities, looking at the small round brown face and the little clenched fists, I couldn't help but feel hope.

I wrote not Sanchez but Rachel, this time, daring to ignore all that had passed between us and simply tell her how beautiful Rachel Laura really was. A week later, I told Sara that Rachel had gotten my letter.

"How do you know?" she asked.

Not many weeks passed before Sara had proof that I had been right. Sanchez, Rachel, and the baby arrived for a visit. While I would have expected Sanchez to roll up in the tinted luxury of a Mercedes, they appeared one mid-morning in a battered Volkswagen van loaded with Pampers and jars of that vacuum-sealed strained mush people call baby food.

Rachel Laura was a high-tech kid, as Sanchez called her, and she proved it by regaling us with five variations on a theme during their two-day stay: She cried and ate, cried and was changed, cried and burped, gurgled happily, and then performed her pièce de resistance by sleeping soundly, bathed in the warm rain of Rachel's and Sara's motherly attentions.

Sanchez and I played manly roles during all of this, pretending that all their doting over the baby was silly—and then doted ourselves when Rachel and Sara were not around.

Both Sanchez and Rachel had changed. Rachel was shy and quieter; less aggressive as though some of her rage had become determination. Still angular and bony in body, her grace and calm seemed a contradiction, and it took some getting used to. When she spotted the scarab I wore hanging around my neck, she only smiled and said, "Laura P. told me you had acquired more weight."

"Elanna brought it to me," I said by way of explanation.

"Wear it well," she said.

Sanchez, though still with his former lightness of heart, revealed a seriousness of mind that I'd never have dreamed of. He still sold souvenirs and sodas, but now the souvenirs were authentic Kachinas and jewelry crafted by the Indians of the reservation. His mark-up was still four hundred percent and his profits were as huge as always. But where he had once derived pleasure from inventing gadgets that were useless and pocketing the profits, now the excess money went into the pockets of the reservation and his pleasure was in his dreams of scholarships, a clinic to be built behind the trading post, investments in shopping centers in Phoenix and Tucson.

"How did this happen?" I asked him. "What made you give up the Vegomatic and cookie cutters?"

"It just came to me," he said.

"Like a vision?"

"Like the stomach flu," he said.

"I wouldn't be surprised if he becomes a chairman," I said to Sara after they had replenished their store of Pampers and baby food and driven off.

"Are you jealous?" Sara asked.

"Not in the way you might think."

"No?"

"No."

# CHAPTER TWELVE

## 52.

The second week of December, Sara found me lying on the sofa, immobile as an Iguana at high noon, the tears in my eyes less from pain (I'd found an old codeine tablet and popped it) than from the feeling that something had happened, something important. It was there, like a word on the tip of my tongue, playing hide and seek across my cerebral cortex.

"What's wrong, Alley?" Sara said, setting her history education textbooks on the old maple dining table the Tompsons had donated to our housekeeping. The table tilted on its shorter leg.

"I don't know. Something has happened."

She sat on the edge of the sofa.

"Be careful of my hip," I said. "It hurts."

Sara frowned, worried. "Do you want me to call the . . . ?"

"Grandfather," I said. The word slipped out of my mouth and hovered briefly in the air.

"What about him?"

"Damn it. I should've known," I said, pushing her out of the way gently. "Where's my address book?"

"What?" Sara said. "What is it?"

I limped over to the roll-top desk we shared and began pawing through the cubbyholes, looking for my book with telephone numbers in it.

"He's dying," I said. The pain in my hip vanished as quickly as it had come. "I know it."

She didn't ask how I knew it, as I thumbed through the book, looking for the number at the Ayawamat Trading Post.

"Oh, Alley," she said. "I'm sorry."

"Don't be," I said, picking up the telephone, waiting for

the dial tone. There wasn't one. I pressed the buttons on the receiver's cradle and let them up again. "It's time," I said.

"Hello?" It was Rachel.

"Rachel? Huh. I was just calling you. I must have picked up the receiver before the phone had a chance to ring."

"Bert," Rachel said. "I have some bad news."

"Where is he?"

"You know, then?" Rachel asked. Her voice had relief in it, the relief of someone who's been steeling herself for an unpleasant task only to have the task supererogated.

"Yes. Where is he?"

"In Our Lady of St. Julian Hospital. In Phoenix. Sanchez took Laura P. down there, today."

"Good. So, what happened?"

As Rachel told me, I began to shake my head in suspended disbelief. Sara put her arms around my shoulders.

"Are you laughing or crying?" Sara asked, trying to decipher my face, after I hung up.

"The stubborn son of a bitch," I said. "He broke his hip."

"How?"

"Only he could be that stubborn. Willful. He rode the Killer Bike over the curb in front of the trading post. Instead of riding around to the ramp, he just up and decided to ride straight over the curb. The Raleigh tipped over and he broke his hip."

The image of Grandfather lying on his side, the left rear wheel of the bike revolving slowly, inexorably grinding to a halt, his hands still gripping the handlebars and him staring straight ahead with the same concentration he had had the day I was born, intrigued with his newfound perspective on the horizon, made me smile.

"He probably just lay there, not even wondering at the pain in his hip or how he had come to be there," I said to Sara, describing this image. I chuckled. Sara chuckled, tentatively at first, and then we began to laugh together, the chuckle blossoming like a cactus flower into one exquisite burst of laughter.

"Do me a favor?" I asked. "Phone Hughes Airwest and get me on the next flight to Phoenix, while I pack?"

"Two tickets, coming right up," Sara said, beginning to look through the Yellow Pages.

"You've got exams," I said.

"So do you."

"Yeah, but I need you to stay here and arrange for me to make them up."

"What if they won't let you?"

"They can fail me. You come out when you're finished."

"I want to go with you," Sara said.

"Uh-uh. Later, not now. I want some time alone with him," I said.

Sara phoned the airline while I threw some clothes into a suitcase and went into the bathroom to collect my shaving kit. The face reflected in the mirror over the sink was me and not me and for a few minutes I sat on the toilet lid and wept, briefly, my face in my hands—wept not out of sadness but because of that side of me which was incapable of feeling sad, out of a feeling that this was a change and an uncertainty of how great a change it would be.

"You're on a flight in two hours," Sara said, coming into the bathroom. "Oh, Alley, go ahead. You can cry in front of me. It must be hard . . ."

"It's not hard," I said, drying my eyes. "It's just . . . different." I began to smile, again. "Now everybody will think I'm nuts when I talk to Grandfather."

"I won't," Sara said. "As long as you don't mind if I talk to him, too."

Despite the effects of several in-flight drinks, I was annoyed at the way the brand-spanking-new nurse led me with her gum-shoed display of sorrow to Grandfather's room. He lay unconscious, a ridge of white sheets and pillows propping him up so that his eyes would have been staring straight at me if they'd been open. They were looking beyond my horizons to the place Grandfather wanted to go. Laura P. slumped in a chair in the darkest corner of the room, apparently asleep, her lips moving in fits and spurts as though she was praying for Grandfather's journey to be short. At her feet, chained to the metal leg of the bed, dozed my old familiar Death. He looked small and wizened. I felt sorry for Him.

"That's what can happen," I thought, "when people don't take you seriously."

"Mr. Hummingbird?" It was a doctor, clipboard in hand. He glanced about the room's interior before stepping in and introducing himself. "I'm Doctor Gaines. "You must be . . . let's see . . . ," he said, consulting his clipboard.

"Grandson. Alley."

"Alley . . . Alley . . . Alley . . . ," he said abstractedly, running his mechanical pencil down the sheet on his clipboard.

"Oxen-free," I said. The corners of his mustache twitched. "Albert," I said.

"Bert?"

"Yeah," I said. It must have been Sanchez who had filled out the list of family likely to show up.

"Right," he said, ticking the sheet on the clipboard. He crossed to the bed, took up Grandfather's wrist too quickly as though there were no resistance or weight, and checked his pulse, accidentally stepping on Death's fingers.

"Ouch! Watch where you put your flat feet you silly S.O.B.," Death whined, awakening and hunkering farther beneath the bed. He spotted me. "You!" He hissed, His eyes turning yellow with rage.

"Did you say something?" Dr. Gaines asked me.

"No," I said. I was intrigued by the way the doctor was able to overhear Death and yet not see Him. Death clamped His mouth shut and huddled down into His rage, shaking, waiting for the doctor to finish his cursory examination of Grandfather and explain to me that Grandfather needed an operation to repair his broken hip. They couldn't perform the operation because his heart was precariously weak.

"Until he's stronger," the doctor said, "all we can do is wait and see. I'll be back. Let the nurses know if you need anything."

As soon as he was gone, Death poked his head out from beneath the bed and began trying to get me to unlock the chain binding Him to Grandfather's bed. At first He was obsequious, using the oily, hand-wringing grin of a money-lender (Member F.D.I.C.). To me, He looked like Happy out of *Snow White*, and I told Him so. Becoming angry, He ran through His entire stock of disguises, growing large and threatening and then shrinking down to the size of a normal human with two heads, their faces staring at each other, one lovingly and the other hatefully. Then He changed into the figure of a martial angel who has flown into a high-voltage power line and frazzled His feathers. Finally, He resorted to seeming a hissing mean little thing whose scaly eyes burned with the determination of His bite.

"It's no use," I said. "I don't have the key."

"In your Grandfather's left hand," He said.

Sure enough, Grandfather's left hand was closed tight as though it was gripping something.

"When it's time," I said. "When his hand opens."

He sighed, transforming into a shape I'd never seen before, a stone-faced little man in a three-piece suit, clutching a briefcase like a life ring after a shipwreck.

"I can make you a rich man," He said. "Just get the key." He offered me tips on the commodities market to prove to me that He was honest and could be trusted. "Silver," He whispered. "Soybeans."

"No," I said. "Thanks anyway."


Even when Laura P. awoke and stood up, she didn't seem to see anyone but Grandfather as she circled crab-like in the corner of the room, her lips still moving constantly. As the hours passed, her shuffling movement seemed to become a loose spiral around her right hip and I could see that as her own hip stiffened the radius of her walk would close like a draughtsman's compass as though she were trying to drill her way into the underworld.

That night, I telephoned father to give him a status report, and then found myself a hospital's imitation of an armchair and dragged it into the corner of Grandfather's room by the curtained window, and slept.

The next day, Grandfather was conscious enough to let my uncle convince himself that his father was going to regain his strength and be able to have his hip repaired. Even the brand new nurse allowed her face to flirt with encouraging expressions when she came in to check Grandfather's vital signs.

"It will probably cause you some discomfort," uncle said to Grandfather. "But it's better than living the rest of your life in a wheel-chair."

My aunt, the woman I once had called the Vegomatic, knew as well as I did that Grandfather was not going to get better. Watching her face as we both listened to my uncle ramble hopefully on, it dawned on me what had made my uncle a bit mad. It had begun with those pilots, his six wartime friends. All uncle's adult life he had clung to the belief that people didn't die but only passed away and they not only could but would reappear as long as he refused to believe that they were simply and finally dead. He had it part right: They first have to die and journey through the Absence of Angels; then they could return. But uncle could do no other than believe that Grandfather was not dying. When I saw that, I saw in the eyes of my aunt that she had always known this, always understood this, and, in her own way, always forgiven it and found a way to live with it. She must have known, then, that for uncle to leave her and live with Karen Manowitz would have meant being fully alive, and in order to be alive, uncle would have had to recognize Death and admit to himself that his six friends had, on his orders, died. Observing the cool facade of her face, I was impressed by the immensity of what must have been her suffering. Especially when I considered how, raised on uncle's notions about passing away, her only son had been reduced to little more than an agent of Death and without any sense of belonging in his heart or his life had fled the country, forever.

That evening I had dinner with my aunt and uncle, showered and changed at their motel room, and had them drop me back at the hospital. As Laura P. mumbled her way through sleep, Death intermittently wheezed, snored, awoke with a start and looked to be sure Grandfather was still there, and then fell back into His own profound sleep. I was unable to sleep; somehow, it seemed that I ought to watch him die. Maybe I would learn something. I thought about my aunt and uncle, my mother and father, about everyone I had ever known—some of whom had passed out of the circle of my existence and knowledge but for many of whom I still had affection. I thought about Grandfather, little more than a semiconscious lump on a bed in a place he didn't want to be. When I thought about Death's offer to make me a rich man, the clumsiness of His attempt at bribery made me incapable of anything but laughter. Taking out the blank book Sara had given me in the hospital, I wrote "Grandfather is dying" over and over and over, until a page had been filled. I tore that page out and threw it in the wastecan, and began again. "Death is a funny thing, yet I am grateful for Him," I wrote, and, with the suddenness of an arrow, the vision I had had as I hovered on the treacherous but eloquent edge of life— like Grandfather at this very moment—came out as though not I but Grandfather was writing.

### 53.

Somewhere down the corridor a clock chimed as I stopped writing, finished, exhausted. "You were not the first and neither will you be the last," I said, as I went to telephone Sara. I felt like a constipated man who has discovered the gift of prunes.

"Alley?" Her voice was heavy with interrupted dreams. "What time is it?"

"Ooops." I saw that it was only five a.m. "Sorry, sweetheart. I didn't think about the time. I wanted to tell you." I felt stupid, waking her on the morning she was scheduled to fly out to Phoenix anyway.

"What is it?" she asked. "Has your Grandfather . . . ?"

"Not yet. He's close. But he's still breathing. No . . . I wanted to tell you I discovered a landscape, Sara, a place I can always go back to."

"Phoenix?"

I laughed. "No. No, it's inside, not outside. It's that other voice I've always heard, the other piece Laura P. meant when she said it was a miracle I was still *in* two pieces. Only now it's not confused. Even if it gets confused by what happens outside it won't have to fight against the inside . . ."

"I don't understand."

"That's all right. Never mind. I'll show you when you get here."

"I should arrive by dinner time," she said. "You want me to bring anything?"

"Just you," I said. "Hurry up and get here."

"I love you," she called, before hanging up.

"Me, too. You," I said. "I love you, too."

Day passed toward evening. The room's heavy olive curtains made the time seem to pass as though it were standing still. When I opened them a crack to peek out, the quality of the sun's light seemed always the same and only the angle had changed, as though the sun was vigilant over the events in the room. I sat, posed beside the head of Grandfather's bed, patiently watching his left hand, which was slowly losing its grip on the key.

In the hall, volunteers in pink candy stripes came and went, pushing gurneys piled with colorfully wrapped presents towards the children's wing, decorating waiting areas, preparing for Christmas Eve and the arrival of Santa Claus in the morning. Passing the open door to Grandfather's room, they seemed to hop a step, quickening their pace and keeping their eyes riveted straight down the hallway. It pleased me to see them as they passed.

Louis Applegate came in with Dr. Gaines.

"He says he's family," Dr. Gaines said.

I remembered the times I'd been visiting Grandfather and, looking out across the desert, we'd spotted Louis, little more than a speck of shadow in the summer's dust; walking up the mesa, his footsteps were uncertain—it had been too long since he'd been home—and he held his head and eyes up as though he were not approaching the place but the place was approaching and entering him. I recalled all the silent times he and Grandfather had sat, Louis gulping gallons of the orange soda he consumed daily and Grandfather smoking the cigars he had refused to give up.

"He is," I said to Dr. Gaines. Louis was a pleasant relief to the forced cheerfulness of the medical staff.

"His pulse is much stronger," the doctor said, looking at Laura P., then at Louis, and finally at me.

I nodded and smiled. "It has to be, if he's going to ascend into the Absence of Angels."

The doctor's mustache twittered. "If he wakes up, he'll probably be hungry. I'll tell you, if his heart keeps getting stronger, he'll be able to eat a horse."

"Half a horse, anyway," I said. Louis grinned. The doctor looked at me, wondering if he'd heard me correctly, and then chuckled indecisively.

"I'll have some food prepared for him. If he wakes up, press the call button and we'll have it sent right up."

When the doctor was gone, Louis surprised me by accusing Laura P. of chaining Death to Grandfather's bed, his voice overflowing with the regrets of all his life. Laura P. only stared at Louis as though she didn't recognize him. When she did stand, she walked over to Grandfather and laid her hand on his forehead, stroking the silver hair smooth over his temple, and even Louis could tell from her face that she loved Grandfather in a way that no longer existed in the world. Caught between this world and the next as she was, she didn't hear him.

"She'll follow him within the year," he whispered to me. He bent down and examined the lock of the chain and then asked me where the key was. I pointed to Grandfather's fist and Louis nodded, walked around the end of the bed, and gently opened the fingers and removed the key. He unlocked the lock and then poked Death in the ribs with his foot. Death awoke with a start and feeling Himself free began to bounce around the walls of the room like a cat stoned on catnip, and then vanished out the door.

"He'll be back soon enough," Louis said. "So. I'll say goodbye."

"Goodbye, Louis. Is there anything you want me to tell Grandfather if he wakes up?"

"What's to tell," he said. "See you." He stopped without turning toward me. "Remember," he said.

"I will. Take care, Louis."

Father and Sara arrived together, having met in the Phoenix airport. Sara had recognized him by his resemblance to me.

"You'll never be able to deny him," Sara said, giving me a hug.

Grandfather awoke, his eyes travelling from Laura P. to father at the foot of the bed, to me and Sara. His eyes flared briefly when he looked at me. Father began to apologize for not coming sooner. Sara and I went for a walk to give them some time alone together. When we returned, we overheard Grandfather telling father that he would live until Christmas.

"That's . . . ," father began, realizing that his father must know that Christmas was tomorrow. "Father," he said. "Father . . ."

From the way he said it, I could tell he had many things he wanted to say. He was struggling not to become sentimental or maudlin, trying to find something funny in the situation to rescue all of us. While his heart felt the need for humor, his mind had been corroded by the uprootings of his corporate life, the price he had had to pay for it had been great—a price revealed in the struggle of this moment.

I tried to help him out. "Father," I said, imitating the way he had said "father." I figured we three could continue saying "father" over and over again until we tired of the litany.

Grandfather laughed, a breathy, weary laugh, what might be described a ghostly laugh. "Son," he said, and when father looked to me and repeated "son," the three of us were suspended in smiling. Then Grandfather closed his eyes and began to snore affectedly.

Sara and I remained behind as father decided to take Laura P. out of the room for a while and try to get her to eat something (I had not seen her eat since I'd arrived), using Laura P. as an excuse to go outside himself. It wasn't that he was frightened by death as much as he was nonplussed by it and, a normally articulate man when he wasn't trying to talk to me, being nonplussed frustrated him.

As soon as they left, Grandfather ceased snoring and his right eye opened and surveyed the room. Sara sat, trying to be unobtrusive, and he slowly rolled his head on the pillows and looked long at her. He nodded almost imperceptibly, and opened his other eye.

"What," he demanded, "are you doing here?"

I knew what he was asking. "Just visiting," I replied, and I knew that he knew that I meant I wasn't there to see him die. I was only there to watch over his departure from this life and make sure that no one interfered with his leaving.

Grandfather said something that sounded like "Oy-yo-hey," as though he were slapping his forehead and saying "What's to be done with you?" He went on looking me over, carefully, as though he were memorizing my face, and then he let his eyes close and he fell asleep again. This time he didn't snore; his breathing was calm though a little raspy. I took his wrist in my hand and laid my forehead in his open palm and closed my eyes. Sara went on reading while I felt Grandfather's pulse grow weaker and weaker and weaker.

The official time of Grandfather's death was 10:21 p.m. on Christmas Eve, his concentration having failed him by one hour and thirty-nine minutes. That wasn't bad, all in all.

"It happens," I remarked to Sara. "Anyone can make that mistake."

She and I left father and Laura P. at the hospital, and went to telegraph Elanna. Father wanted to take care of the details alone and that seemed to me his right, just as it would be my right when he died. There weren't many details to take care of, anyway. Grandfather was to be cremated, and Laura P., father, Sara, and I planned to scatter his ashes over a remote part of the Sonoran Desert.

Sara had rented a car at the airport and we drove first to Chosposi Mesa, where she watched as I picked the ancient lock on the shed beside Grandfather's house. Finding a brass wind-chime with a tone as near to the one he'd sent me when Pamela had died, I used a hacksaw to make a thin cut near the bottom. Then we walked out into the night beneath the bright light of the moon, hearing but not seeing the unnumbered creatures that move about at night when the sun is on the other side of the world. The cactus loomed up like bandits, and every now and then an elf owl hooted.

Sara was a little afraid of the night desert, but willfully trusting my sense of place. "It feels like myth out here," she said, finally, as we circled up a small box canyon formed by ridges from the mesa.

"It just is," I said.

At the foot of the canyon wall, Sara waited while I dug a

272

hole and buried the chime, and dragged a large flat rock over the disturbed earth.

"There," I said, brushing off my hands.

As we retraced our steps, I could tell that Sara was bothered by something, perhaps by my apparent lack of emotion, and her hand kept squeezing mine with the pulse of whatever it was. A breeze had come up, making the clean desert air feel crisp and cold. Finally, she asked, "Are you really grateful for death?"

"Yes," I said, feeling a chill run down her arm and into my hand.

"Why? Do you want to die?"

"Of course not," I said, smiling. "Without Death, though, love would not be a chance and chances wouldn't matter. Life wouldn't be interesting. Or mean anything. If we didn't know we were going to die eventually, why would we try to do anything at all? Living forever would be like living at two o'clock in the afternoon on a mild and windless day without any hope of change. There'd be no reason to enjoy anything, to laugh or cry or to feel or think."

She fell silent. A single cloud appeared in the sky and cut slowly across the bottom of the moon as we emerged from the canyon and hiked back towards the car. The rat-a-tat of a moonlighting woodpecker drifted down the wind and I imagined him, surprised by Mrs. Woodpecker having had triplets, hurrying to build a home to house them as soon as they could fly. I laughed.

"What?" Sara said. "What are you thinking?"

"How much fun being alive is."

Sara gave my hand a squeeze.

Thinking about tomorrow or the day after when we would scatter Grandfather's ashes across the desert, I stopped walking, looking around the outlines of my desert, barely visible in the moonlight. Beyond the moon, stars shone red and green and white, filling the Absence of Angels with expectant welcoming light.

"You know," I said. "When I die . . ."

"Stop," Sara said. "I don't want to think about that."

I grinned. "When I die, you can leave my body out for the

273

garbage collectors in a three-ply Hefty. You'll have to get someone to help drag it out to the curb, of course . . ."

"Stop it, Alley!" Sara cried. "I love you. I don't want to hear about when you die. I won't let you die."

"Don't be silly. You think our love will die just because I die? Do you think Grandfather won't always be with me? I'll remember him. That makes him immortal, in a way."

"Please?"

I couldn't help but laugh. "Okay," I said. She sighed. "But promise to have my heart cut out. Bury it and plant a Saguaro over it. That way, at least once a year, it will blossom."

Sara tried to cover my mouth with her hand. "Stop it, Alley. Stop, stop, stop!"

I was laughing harder. "I love you," I said, ducking away from her hand.

"Why?" she asked, wanting to hear reasons, to be assured by them that I wasn't planning to die very soon because I loved her.

"Because you make me laugh," I said.

The narrator-protagonist of this magical novel about urban mixed-blood Indian life is Albert (Alley) Hummingbird, a self-conscious, shy college student who masks his feelings with humor and who longs to reconcile the two cultures that have formed him. Alley is not supposed to live at birth, but his grandfather, a Nez Percé, rescues him from Death (who reappears throughout the novel as a petty, mean, pathetic, and ultimately funny character). The grandfather's teachings to Alley, which come from the afterlife region known as the "absence of angels," connect Alley to his Indian heritage when he most needs it. Otherwise his life is fragmented: a father who rejected his heritage, a mother who is slightly mad, and a friend, Sara, with whom Alley is in love.

"Full of a beautiful generosity of spirit. The depiction of the relationship between Alley and Sara Baites (one of the most lovingly detailed portraits of a woman in a recent novel I know by a man *or* a woman) I found particularly moving. This is a powerful first novel."—Arnold Krupat

"Skipping lyrically between his hero's childhood and young adulthood, Penn has produced a delightful work of magic realism reminiscent of John Nichols's *The Milagro Beanfield War*. . . . Himself of Native American and white ancestry, the author limns with insight the struggles of modern, urban, often mixed-blood Indians to forge a coherent identity."—*Publishers Weekly.*

*Volume 14 in the American Indian Literature and Critical Studies Series*

W. S. Penn, an urban mixblood, is a resident fiction writer and teacher of American Indian and Comparative Literature at Michigan State University. He is the winner of the 1993 North American Indian Prose Award.

On the front cover: *"Siblings"* by Anne-Marie Hamilton

# UNIVERSITY
# OF OKLAHOMA
# PRESS NORMAN AND LONDON

Cover design by Bill Cason

ISBN 0-8061-2714-7

9 780806 127149